DAUGHTER OF EXILE

DAUGHTER OF EXILE

TANA REBELLIS

Daughter of Exile

This book contains mature themes and subjects which may be Distressing for some readers. Please visit the author's website (www.TanaRebellis.com) to view content warnings.

Cover design by Kasey Morris | Little Piggy Publishing

ISBN: 979-8-9906356-2-3
ISBN (Hardcover): 979-8-9906356-3-0

For Mara, Madeline, Milli, and Dover.

"DUM SPIRO, SPERO."
"WHILE I BREATHE, I HOPE."

A Latin phrase of indeterminate origin.

(PARTIAL) JULIO-CLAUDIAN FAMILY TREE

**FOLLOWING THE EVENTS OF *THE LONGEST EXILE*
AND AS RELEVANT TO *DAUGHTER OF EXILE***

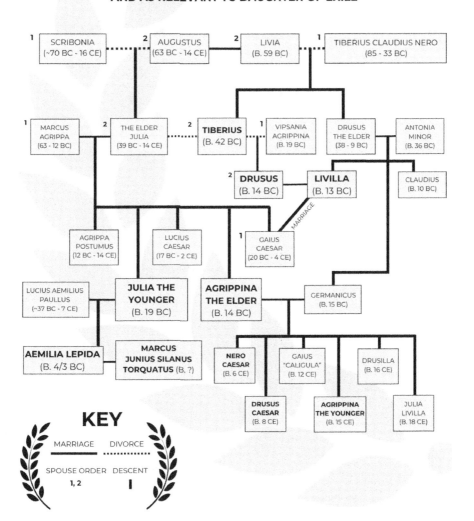

CHAPTER I

TITUS

Titus clenched his hands as he watched the island of Trimerus slowly fade farther and farther away, its rocky cliffs gradually disappearing with the passage of time until it was as if they were swallowed up by the seemingly endless blue water that now stretched as far as he could see. She—Julia—was gone.

Quintus, to his credit, did not disturb the soldier as he stood his silent watch, instead choosing to move quietly below deck. It was at least another hour before Titus joined him, his face stony and wind-chapped from his vigil. The faint trace of a scar—a wound acquired in the attack on the island the previous autumn—was still visible across his brow, a dull pink line that would fade with time but never entirely disappear.

"We'll be back in Rome before you know it," Quintus said, though his tone did not betray any particular emotion; the statement was merely factual. He did not elaborate, either, on what their return to Rome meant: that the two men would be parting ways.

Quintus would remain on leave in Rome as he awaited his next assignment—having made it clear that he wanted nothing more to do with Trimerus, the emperor's granddaughter, or the bastard child he himself had saved from its death sentence—while Titus would take advantage of the brief lull in duty to pursue the promise he had made to Julia: to find her infant son.

Titus only grunted in response to his commander, unwilling to engage in polite chatter as the ship bore them away from the woman he had come to love more than he had ever imagined possible. He had known when they began their affair that there could be no happy ending for them; even if she had not been a prisoner and he not her guard, the difference in their station was far too great to overcome. He had known from the start, and he had understood—but that did not mean he had been fully prepared for the wrenching pain that now seemed to course through him.

"You'll be alright," Quintus murmured, but Titus gave no sign that he heard the older man. He had already turned his back on his commander and closed his eyes, their usual brown warmth now turned to an icy blankness.

Titus and Quintus wound their way through Ostia, the port city of Rome, dodging the whores and merchants who hindered their progress in equal measure; the former attempted to lure them to their brothels with doe-eyed glances and gauzy dresses while the latter hawked pottery wares for all occasions and street foods that ranged from delectable to questionable. The permeating stench of human waste and fish guts was only alleviated in brief doses by sudden flares of the salty Mediterranean breeze that forced its way through the streets, as if it sought to lead the men to the harbor, where the promise of fresher air awaited.

Quintus breathed in deeply when they at last broke out of the cramped streets and found themselves suddenly surrounded by countless ships of varying size and purpose, with at least three quarters of the vessels in the process of being unloaded: boxes, barrels, amphorae, blocks of marble, and seemingly endless amounts of grain were being moved off the watercraft and then borne away into nearby storage facilities or to barges waiting on the Tiber, which would bring the goods directly to Rome.

"I forgot how disgusting the stink of a city could be," Quintus complained as he scratched at his nose. It was as close he had come to admitting that a small part of him missed their strangely idyllic form of life on Trimerus.

A small cat paused by Quintus's feet, examining the men to see if they had any scraps; when it saw that they did not, it quickly turned up its tail and trotted away, eyeing a sailor who looked to be in possession of a full fishing net. Quintus watched it go, a distant expression writ across his face.

Titus merely grunted in his new, usual manner as he scanned the ships in search of the one he had purchased passage on the day prior; it was a merchant vessel that would bring him to Messana, in Sicilia. From there, he would find another ship to Delos, and then yet another to Ephesus; next it was onwards to Kallipolis and beyond that to Byzantium, all perhaps with several stops—or more—in between, winding his way surely forward alongside merchants, sailors, slaves, and fellow passengers who had business across the empire. The final ship on his route, departing from Byzantium, would take Titus directly to Tomis and, he hoped, to Julia's infant son, who would now be nearly a year old.

Titus knew only that he needed to find old Lucius's grandson, the Moesian governor named Aulus Caecina Severus, into whose care the baby had been trusted without much explanation and certainly, he assumed, without explicit identification.

Titus carried no letter of introduction from Lucius to ease his way; the old man and Quintus had both been steadfastly opposed to seeking out the baby, insisting that it was best to let him live out the life he had now found himself in—whatever form that life might take. The soldier only hoped that Aulus had taken his duty seriously, faithfully protecting his charge, and that his own arrival would not be looked upon too closely or with much distrust—although he would deal with whatever he had to, when the time came. Titus had promised Julia he would find her child and take over the babe's care; he intended to do so, Aulus's presence notwithstanding.

"Over there," Titus announced as he at last caught sight of the ship that would take him to Messana. He gestured at a large merchant vessel with two masts and a deep V-shaped hull; a handful of men were carrying final supplies on board, and slaves were already in place at their oars. Departure was imminent.

Quintus cleared his throat, uncertain what to say next as he scratched at his gray stubble. He had accompanied Titus the short distance from Rome to Ostia, feeling some sense of obligation to the younger soldier despite his own unwillingness to pursue Julia's child, but he now stood awkwardly in his comfortable, civilian tunic, feeling naked without a sword at his hip; his hand hovered where its hilt should have been, as if he itched to act rather than to be left behind while his comrade departed for new shores.

Titus turned back towards his commander and gave a half-smile that recalled his old demeanor—one Quintus had not seen in weeks. "I'll be back in time for duty."

They both knew he wouldn't, but the words were ones they would pretend to believe. When Quintus was asked by his superiors to explain where one of his men had disappeared to, he could answer truthfully that Titus had *said* he intended to report in before his leave period expired; the commander had no idea if the younger soldier had deserted or had met an unfortunate end. Regardless, Titus would be unlikely to be welcome back in Rome, if he ever were to return.

"Be careful," Quintus said gruffly, and the two men clasped arms, a lingering touch that at once recalled their history together and imparted well-wishes for a future that now took them on separate paths.

Titus broke away first, adjusting his travel pack over his shoulder and shifting the short sword on his hip as he turned and headed towards the waiting ship. He did not look back.

CHAPTER
II

AEMILIA LEPIDA

I yawned and rubbed my eyes as my nurse coaxed me awake. "Go away, Amynta," I muttered sleepily, even though I knew it would do no good. In the end, Amynta always had me roused, dressed, and fed in time for whatever activity or lesson was planned for me that morning.

Amynta rubbed my back. "Come, *domincella*," she said softly. "Your aunt wants you to eat with her and little Nero Caesar this morning. Then your Greek tutor is coming in the afternoon."

I groaned and sat up, though I managed to bite my tongue to stop any more complaints from spilling out. I was thirteen now, near old enough to be married and to stop being a child, as Aunt Agrippina constantly reminded me, so best learn to behave as the proper Roman matron I would soon become.

In short order, dressed and mostly awake, I shuffled towards the *triclinium*, encouraged by the scent of my favorite wheat pancakes drifting from the room. My mouth moistened as I pictured the large spoonful of honey melting across my portion, but the dates typically served on the side—those I could happily do without.

Aunt Agrippina lay sprawled across a couch, her curls, as always, perfectly coiffed. That morning she had outfitted herself in swaths of green silk that set off her eyes, which were currently focused adoringly on the toddling child wreaking havoc in the room, despite the best efforts of a nurse who followed along behind him: my cousin, little Nero Caesar.

"Good morning, Aunt," I said quietly, my eyes seizing on the plate of pancakes already laid out for me. I moved towards them before my cousin could grab hold of them with his little, grasping hands, laying myself across the couch in imitation of my aunt before I began to eat, careful not to wolf down my food. Amynta hovered behind me.

We only took our breakfast in the *triclinium* because my aunt felt that it would do me good to practice dining formally—how to position myself appropriately on the couch; how to eat tidily, in small, dainty bites; how to motion for the slaves to serve me—delicately, as I was a lady, yet decisively, because of my rank. I would have preferred to dine alone, quietly, eating whatever my heart desired in however much a quantity my stomach demanded.

Aunt Agrippina smiled at me sweetly, my arrival drawing her attention from her eldest son. Her other child, Drusus Caesar, was as of yet too young to join us for meals, though a sudden wailing from down the hall reminded us of his presence. She was pregnant again already, too, quickly and easily fulfilling her duty as a Roman wife: she would soon have three children in the space of four years since her marriage.

"Hello, Aemilia," she greeted me. "I have good news this morning. Your uncle Germanicus has had yet another success in Dalmatia, and he expects to be back in Rome by year's end. Perhaps even as early as autumn, when his newest child will arrive." She rested a ringed hand on her belly as she spoke.

I smiled, as was expected, though I barely knew my uncle and so could hardly feel much genuine excitement at his promised return. Germanicus was constantly here and there on some campaign or another, only briefly popping back to Rome, but Aunt Agrippina was always telling me how she soon planned to start joining him on his tours, so that they might be together more often. I found it odd; my own parents' marriage had been nothing at all like that, and, in fact, I could barely remember ever seeing them together before my father's execution. When he had been killed, neither my mother nor I had even wept; it was as if a stranger had died, and our lives continued accordingly—until my mother was sent away.

Aunt Agrippina was still speaking. "I will be gone most of the afternoon, for Claudius's wedding to that Etruscan woman with the silly name, Plautia Urgulanilla, but of course the nurses will remain here with you children." Her narrowed eyes glanced at me, as if looking for a reaction, but I simply took another bite of pancake, careful not to let the honey drizzle down my chin. I slowly pushed an unwanted date to the side of my plate, hoping that my aunt would not insist I eat it.

Claudius, the younger brother of my uncle Germanicus, had been intended for me only a short year ago. But my mother's exile—on top of my father's treason—had changed all that; my great-grandfather Augustus no longer considered me a suitable match for the esteemed Germanicus's brother. Now that Augustus had adopted his wife's son, Tiberius, and in turn had ordered Tiberius to adopt Uncle Germanicus as his heir, Claudius had become the brother of a future emperor—and my aunt, the wife of one. Livilla, too—the middle sibling between Germanicus and Claudius—had been married off to Tiberius's own son Drusus, thus cementing a neatly organized familial alliance from which I was now to be wholly excluded.

In truth, I was happy not to marry Claudius. Whatever station it might have guaranteed me was not worth putting up with him; although he was only five years my elder, he had a terrible, annoying stutter and always carried himself in a hunching, awkward manner that I found entirely unappealing. His features, too, were ordinary at best, so did nothing to redeem his lack of other qualities. Still, I did not dare say as much to Aunt Agrippina—it wouldn't have been proper to comment upon such things, as she would be certain to remind me, and I was not in the mood to be lectured.

"Must I finish the dates, Aunt?" I asked instead, pushing another of them to the side of the plate, where it joined its rejected kin.

She sighed, once more turning her attention to her young son as she stroked her pregnant belly. "Your great-grandfather will find you someone else. Perhaps, if you're lucky, someone as handsome as your uncle Germanicus."

I assumed her lack of response regarding the dates meant that I did not have to finish them after all, and I pushed my plate away.

"Tell me more about what happened to my mother," I said suddenly. Aunt Agrippina whipped her head towards me, and I ducked my chin, my hand nervously seeking out and clutching the *lunula* hanging around my neck. The crescent-shaped amulet pressed reassuringly into my palm. "Please," I added quietly. There was a begging undertone to that single word.

"You already know," my aunt said, her words dismissive, though her eyes betrayed a hint of sadness.

"Only that she was a whore," I muttered, raising my chin again in quiet defiance. I had heard the word used plenty of times before, but it was the first time it had crossed my own lips. My aunt tensed, and suddenly shame filled my body. I was speaking about my own mother.

"Never say that about your mother again," Aunt Agrippina hissed at me, and I leaned away from her, tears welling in my eyes even before her reproach. My *lunula* bit more harshly into my hand, and I realized I was clenching it nearly hard enough to break the skin. "You cannot possibly understand."

"Then explain it to me!" I blurted out, my voice breaking as I let go of my amulet, my hands instead turning into small, balled fists at my sides. My mother had been there one day and gone the next; I still remembered Amynta waking me up in the darkness of night and moving me to my aunt's household, trunks of my belongings only arriving in the days afterwards.

My aunt had been the one tasked by Augustus with my care, and with explaining what had happened to my mother, but she had only ever told me that my mother had fallen in love with a man after her husband— my father—had been executed, and that it wasn't proper because they were unmarried. But I knew there was something more; I could tell from the way people whispered when they looked at me, and I stored away bits of information I overheard when people gossiped about my mother, thinking I was out of hearing distance.

Aunt Agrippina closed her eyes briefly, as if asking for patience from the gods. "Take Nero Caesar to play," she ordered his nurse, who quickly scooped up the tottering child and left the *triclinium*. My little cousin cried out in unheeded protestation as he was carried away.

My aunt adjusted herself on her couch, smoothing the fabric of her dress with pale, delicate hands. "Amynta, what has my niece heard about her mother?" She addressed my nurse, and the words had an edge to them.

I felt Amynta stiffen behind me in surprise and, no doubt, fear. She was responsible for overseeing my daily care; any mistake, however minor, would not bode well for her.

"I do not know, *domina*," Amynta answered, her voice quiet and subdued.

Aunt Agrippina pursed her lips in disapproval. "It is your task to know," she said coldly. My aunt then shifted her attention to me, and her tone became kinder. "Aemilia, I had planned to wait until you were a bit older to tell you—perhaps when you were married and could better understand—but I would rather you not piece events together based on whatever unkind whispers you are apparently overhearing. Your mother was not sent away to Trimerus only because of her... relationship... with a man who was not her husband."

I felt my heart racing as I waited for my aunt's next words; I was both terribly excited to finally learn more, but also frightened of what I was about to hear.

"This man's name was Decimus Junius Silanus, and he and your mother began their affair even while your father was still alive," she continued, her disapproval evident. "It continued after your father's execution, and, eventually, your mother became pregnant." Aunt Agrippina paused, letting the new information settle itself into my young mind.

"I have a sibling?" I asked, uncertain. When I was younger, I had hoped for a little brother or sister to play with, tired of spending so much time alone. Now, I was not so sure. I had grown accustomed to being a solitary creature—and any baby of my mother's would be too small to be of much fun now, anyway.

My aunt shook her head. "It would not have been allowed to be raised." She did not say what she really meant, but I understood quickly enough: my mother's other child had been killed once it was born.

I was able to comprehend, in a removed sort of way, why it was not proper for such a child to be raised in a respectable household, but I could not fully wrap my mind around the need to kill it. What harm could a blubbering baby cause merely by existing?

"Then why can't *Mater* return now?" I asked, my mind jumping back to my more immediate concern. If the problem had been my mother's pregnancy, it sounded as if that had already been dealt with. I felt little pity for the hindersome infant who had apparently kept my mother away from me.

Aunt Agrippina gave me a small, sad smile. "I wish she could come back, too," she said, the words hushed, as if we shared a secret, "but your great-grandfather is still very angry with her. I love her—she is my sister, not only your mother—but her behavior…"

I frowned, my mind racing. "What happened to the man she loved, Silanus? Is he not also at fault? Was he executed?"

She shook her head, and her face darkened. "He was sent away from Rome, into exile, like your mother—although I don't know where. I am not sure why Augustus spared his life. The proof of his involvement was beyond question." She scowled. "He should have known better."

I sighed, although my confusion still did not entirely lift despite the new information. Perhaps I would need some more time to process it.

Aunt Agrippina was speaking again, and this time her tone had shifted into the one she used when trying to impart some form of womanly wisdom to me. "Loyalty to one's husband, and to one's family, is beyond any sort of measure, especially when your family is that of Augustus. I hope, now that you know more about what happened to your mother, you can understand that."

Her eyes bored into mine, and I nodded in response, as was expected. Only then did Aunt Agrippina seem to relax, leaning back onto her couch once more.

"May I go, Aunt?" I asked. At her nod, I jumped off the couch and quickly left the *triclinium*, Amynta trailing quietly behind.

I did not dwell on the information I had just acquired. It all seemed too distant to affect me in any alarmingly direct manner, and I did not want to deal with my own emotions about my mother's exile: what she had done, where she now found herself, what her future might hold—and whether my own future might ever be linked with hers again, or if I would even want such a bond to resurface, given that her name was now almost an ill omen. I did not want to be looked upon as someone who was cursed because of her heritage.

I all but forgot my unnamed half-sibling, only vaguely linking him or her with distant, suppressed feelings of anger for being a driving factor in my mother's sudden departure from me over a year ago. With the passage of time, I began to think of my mother less, and Rome soon turned its attention to other scandals, mostly forgetting about the disgrace of Augustus's granddaughter. But while I did not dwell on it, I did not forget, not entirely. I never could.

CHAPTER

III

TITUS

An unusual number of storms, irregularly ferocious in both their intensity and duration, had hindered travel throughout the late spring and summer, and a journey that should have taken just over a month from Rome had now stretched on to an almost unbearable length of time. A crisp hint of autumn was beginning to tinge the air, and Titus found himself trapped in Byzantium, with ship after ship bound in any direction postponing its departure due to the uncertainty of the weather. No merchant wanted to risk losing his goods—or his life—to Neptune's domain: better to delay and arrive late than not at all.

The soldier wound his way to the port on a rare, particularly clear morning, determination etched across his face and reflected in each step. By now, he knew all the merchant ships that were planning to sail for Tomis at the soonest opportunity, and he hoped that at least one of them would be getting underway that very morning.

The first ship he reached had a pair of guards lazing on deck, protecting the goods within while the other crew were elsewhere in the city, perhaps acquiring supplies or, just as likely, whoring and gambling. One of the men nodded an acknowledgement at Titus. "Still here, I see," the guard called down as Titus came to a halt.

"Yes," Titus said simply. "Is your ship departing for Tomis today?" He didn't let his tone betray his hopefulness; if he appeared too eager, they would take the entirety of his remaining coins, knowing that they could easily drive up the price of passage. Unfortunately, given his frequent visits to inquire about their expected departure, they no doubt already knew that he was anxious to reach his destination. He was not in a good position to bargain, however removed he kept his tone.

The guard, though, shook his head. "Staying here at least another day, to see if the weather holds."

"Thank you," Titus called, quickly moving on.

The crew of the next vessel told him the same, and the one after that. Titus began to worry; there weren't many ships left in the port that were bound for Tomis, and his resources were nearly spent. Unplanned, prolonged stays at each of the cities along his route had rapidly used up what coins he had, and if he didn't book passage on a ship soon, he wouldn't be able to afford it. The life savings of a soldier—even a Praetorian—did not extend far.

"*Salve!*" a gangly, dark-skinned boy called to him in greeting from the deck of the next ship he approached, a small, one mast vessel that was meticulously well maintained despite its humble appearance. "You're the one who's wanting to go to Tomis?"

Titus nodded, fingering the hilt of his sword—an anxious habit that was newly acquired.

"We're pulling out within the next three hours or so," the boy told him. "It'll cost you, though."

Titus mentally calculated his remaining money. "How much?" he asked.

The boy grinned, and Titus realized he couldn't have seen more than thirteen summers. "How much have you got?"

Titus scowled. "I don't have time for your games, boy. I'll find another ship." He turned and began to walk away, but the boy's voice stopped him.

"We're the only ones headed that way today. If you want to get to Tomis soon as you can, to find whatever it is you're after, you don't have much choice."

Titus turned and shaded his eyes as he looked up again at the smirking youth. "Where's your master?"

"Father, not master," the boy corrected him proudly. "And he's busy. He knows you're looking for passage to Tomis and told me to tell you, if you came by—as he thought you would—that we're leaving soon." He nodded at Titus's coin purse. "By the size of that, I can see you've not got much left. I assume you've got mostly silver *denarii* in there, not just copper and bronze? We'll take the rest of it, if that's the case."

Titus rubbed the hilt of his sword with a single finger, thinking. He could travel by ox cart over land, but it would take more than twice as long to reach Tomis; alternatively, he could hire a string of horses, which would be agreeably faster than a cart, but he did not relish the idea of traveling alone on unknown roads where he had no doubt bandits and barbarians lurked. He also doubted he could afford it.

"Half," Titus countered.

The youth laughed at him, taking the time to adjust the belt on his tunic as he made Titus wait for his response. "My father'll kill me if I only take that. He was very direct in his orders. What will it be? Do you want to get to Tomis, or do you want to stay here?"

Titus and the boy stared at one another.

"Fine," Titus finally said, drawing the word out as he removed his coin purse and tossed it up into the boy's open, waiting hand. The youth's face lit up in a smile, his cheeks plumping as he peeked inside the purse to see the silver *denarii*. What the boy didn't know was that Titus had carefully tucked away a quarter of his remaining coins in his travel pack, and he was not about to enlighten anyone—after all, the deal had been only for what was inside his purse.

"Come on up, then," the boy called down, and Titus obeyed. When he reached the deck of the ship, the youth was waiting for him. "I'm Syphax, by the way."

"After the Numidian king?" Titus asked, and the boy smiled in response.

"Of course," Syphax said proudly. "I'm surprised you know. You don't look the type to care much about history."

Titus shrugged; he didn't have the energy or the interest to be insulted by the youth. He only cared that he was finally on a ship bound for Tomis—for Julia's son.

The first handful of days made for quiet and uneventful sailing, the sun shining in golden promise as calm waters lapped at the ship's hull. Titus took the time to mend a tear in his tunic and to sharpen his sword, though Syphax's near constant attention proved distracting.

"Are you a soldier, then?" the boy asked him, his keen eyes having quickly noted Titus's military footwear and weapon. "Why aren't you on campaign somewhere? Why are you going to Tomis, anyway?"

Titus studiously ignored him, checking his sword's tip with his thumb. A single drop of blood reassured him of its sharpness.

"Syphax!" the youth's father called. "Your help is needed here, not over there bothering our passenger."

Syphax sighed and obediently hurried over to his father, leaving Titus in peace as he sheathed his sword and focused his attention on his surroundings. They had left behind any glimpse of the shore long ago and were now in the deep waters of the sea, falsely reassuring with its rhythmical, lulling waves.

Titus closed his eyes as he remembered how Julia had come out onto the ship's deck as they neared Trimerus, over a year ago; he recalled the resolute determination on her face and in her voice as she made certain that he and the other guards would not forget who she was, despite her disgrace. He had already been mesmerized by her, even in all her arrogance. The memory was so crisp, so vivid; it was hard to believe that she was now so far away—that so much time had passed.

A breeze began to pick up, but Titus ignored it, turning his head away. He wanted—needed—to remember Julia. He had left her only months ago, but already it seemed an eternity. Each passing night, his dreams alternated between happy remembrances and horrifying possibilities: from the times they had made love, the conversations and laughter they had shared, to the threat of another corrupt guard infiltrating her island prison, the danger that she might be unwilling to wait, unable to hope, for his return, instead giving in to the reckless impulse to leave this realm on her own terms. It was an impulse that Titus knew she had experienced before, been dangerously drawn to. He had stopped her before, but now…

Only when the warm light of the sun on his eyelids began to wane did Titus fully return to the present, and the sight that greeted his opening eyes was a foreboding one: they were sailing directly into a dark, stormy mass of clouds, lightning sparking within as the waves, idyllic and peaceful only moments before, rapidly turned violent.

"You should go below," Syphax called to him as he trotted over. The youth spoke assuredly, but Titus could read the fear in his eyes. "Father says we'll try to skirt the storm, but it still won't be very pleasant."

Titus nodded. He was no sailor, but even he knew it was no small storm they were headed towards, and he wasn't entirely certain their small ship could outrun it—or survive it.

CHAPTER IV

AEMILIA LEPIDA

Aunt Agrippina was preoccupied with receiving visitors, all of them coming to congratulate her on the birth of Germanicus's newest son. The celebrations, however, seemed subdued. I could not tell whether that was due to the sickly nature of the baby, who had appeared quite pale and listless since his birth, or because all anyone seemed able to talk about—mostly in whispers—was a disastrous military defeat in Germania. Apparently, the commanding general, Varus, had lost three of our legions and then killed himself from the shame of it.

Varus's failure, my aunt told me, was why Germanicus was not present at the reception for his thirdborn son, despite having returned to Rome shortly after he received word of the disaster. She had primly and proudly proceeded to explain that Germanicus had gone to be of comfort to the emperor, who remained quite distraught about the loss of three legions.

Like any respectable Roman, I, too, felt my blood rise at the thought of half-naked, illiterate barbarians absconding with our legionary standards, but, in the immediate present, I was much more concerned with how terribly boring the reception for my newest cousin was proving to be.

I plucked at the slightly itchy dress Aunt Agrippina had instructed Amynta to dress me in, wishing I would instead be allowed to wear the flowing, colorful silks my aunt favored, just as my mother had done. Alas, I was told I was too young—that when I was married, I could wear them, as well as whatever jewelry and perfumes I fancied. So long as my husband would approve, of course.

Aunt Agrippina's voice carried across the room to me as I fidgeted, and I quickly stood to attention, straightening my back and schooling my face into the bland expression I had learned was the only acceptable one during events such as this. "Yes, that's my niece, Aemilia Lepida," she said. "Thirteen years now, and she grows prettier every day. Don't you agree, Decimus?"

My eyes flicked towards my aunt to see to whom she was speaking, but I could only see the man—Decimus—in profile. He was perhaps in his fifth decade of life, garbed in the purple-striped tunic and white toga of a senator, though the heavy folds of the fabric seemed to weigh his thin frame down. Large, brightly colored shoes peeked out from under the toga, a sharp contrast to the rather subtle mosaic on which the man stood.

Decimus suddenly turned his silvered head, and bright brown eyes appraised me from top to bottom. Startled, I quickly averted my own gaze, studying the floor's geometric designs with an excess of interest.

The senator's voice was surprising in its strength when he spoke, but I did not like the words I overheard. "Yes, she's quite lovely. Has a match been arranged for her yet, since young Claudius was paired with Plautia in her stead? I might…"

I quickly escaped down the hall towards the kitchen before he finished speaking, thinking that perhaps I would prefer to remain unmarried for a bit longer, even if it that meant I wouldn't yet be allowed to wear the silk I so admired. I hoped Aunt Agrippina would not scold me for my sudden disappearance, either.

My nose flared as I inhaled the scents escaping from behind the kitchen's closed door, and my stomach grumbled. Amynta had hinted to me before the reception—perhaps to improve my irritable temper—that one of my favorite dishes would be prepared that evening: white, flaky fish covered in a coriander crust, sprinkled with vinegar, served alongside lentils boiled with leek and mint. Quickly forgetting the elderly senator from only moments before, I pushed open the door to the kitchen.

The cook and his various assistants were busy moving about, chopping, mixing, and stewing all manner of foods and spices. I was spared a glance here and there—as I technically wasn't supposed to be in the kitchen—but they were all too preoccupied with their tasks to pay me much mind. I paused briefly as I closed the door behind me, closing my eyes as I breathed in all the wonderful smells.

When I opened my eyes, I looked to my nurse in the corner. Amynta had not yet caught sight of me, but the reason why was immediately obvious: she was perched on the lap of a red-haired man who looked much too large for the stool he sat on, and the pair were far more interested in one another than in anything else happening in the kitchen.

Amynta's companion was the first to become aware of my gaze, and the man's dark eyes fixed on me with a small, unexpected spark of recognition. When my nurse moved her hand across his cheek, seeking to reclaim his attention, he quickly clasped her fingers in his own and gestured towards me with a subtle lift of his chin.

Amynta's head turned, and as soon as she saw me she jumped up out of the man's lap. "Aemilia!" she cried out, her face flushing as she ran her hands over her dress, trying to smooth down the displaced fabric. Behind her, the red-haired man also stood, albeit more slowly, and stiffly adjusted a toga that looked out of place on his large, muscular body.

My nurse was already moving towards me. "*Domincella*, you're supposed to be at the reception with the guests. You don't want to hurt your aunt's feelings, do you? This is to honor your new cousin."

I was not so easily distracted. "Who is he, Amynta?" I kept my eyes locked on the red-haired man, although he now studiously ignored me as he continued to straighten his toga.

I sensed Amynta's hesitation as she considered her next words, but ultimately her girlish excitement about her suitor won out. I was reminded, then, that she was not so very much older than me, perhaps a decade or so at most. Had she not been a slave, she would already have been married, no doubt with several children of her own. Instead, she looked after me.

"His name is Rufus," she said, her voice hushed, though none of the kitchen staff paid us any mind, "and he's a Praetorian Guard." Her eyes flitted admiringly to the man, who now seemed to be standing at attention, passively observing the both of us as his large hand hovered searchingly over the hip where a sword ordinarily would have been affixed. Eventually, his hand clenched a fold of the toga's fabric in place of his missing weapon's hilt.

Now the reason for Rufus's apparent awkwardness with respect to his clothing was clear: the man was far more comfortable in a tunic and armor than in the toga he now found himself in. However, the emperor didn't like to cause a stir by parading the Praetorian Guards around in full military kit within the city, and so he ordered them to wear civilian clothing and to do their utmost to blend in. It was like asking a hairy, clumsy bear to mimic the exotic, lithe dancers from Egypt I had once glimpsed at one of my aunt's parties: the effort was amusing, but it did not fool anyone into mistaking the bear's true identity.

Amynta's next words were more forceful, although I detected an imploring undertone as her eyes sought out mine. "You mustn't say anything to anyone. Please, *domincella*."

"He seemed to recognize me," I said, my question implied. I did not yet promise to say nothing about her flirtations with the soldier.

Amynta smiled softly. "I've told him about you, of course. How could I not? I am sure he recognized you by my descriptions."

I frowned. "How long have you known him for? *Rufus*?" A small, sudden surge of jealousy coursed through me as I spoke his name, spitting it out as if it had a foul taste. Amynta was my nurse, but she was also, in some ways, my friend, especially after my mother's sudden and unexpected exile. I had always been accustomed to Amynta's complete and undivided attention—yet now I discovered she had been keeping something from me.

My nurse sighed, sensing my disapproval. "A few weeks or so. He returned to Rome not long before that, from some special duty he had been assigned to, on behalf of the emperor—though he can't tell me what it was." Amynta's face flushed. "Anyway, Rufus had a short period of leave, to do as he pleased, and we met by chance when I was out on an errand of my own."

"Why is he here now?"

Amynta narrowed her eyes at me, and I understood that her patience with my questions was beginning to wear thin—but there was little she could do. After all, my single word could ruin her: Aunt Agrippina did not like the female slaves of her household running amok, and so Amynta had no choice but to answer my questions and hope that I would keep her secret.

My nurse tucked a loose strand of black hair behind her ear before answering. "He is presently accompanying one of the senators who is here to congratulate your aunt on the birth of her newest son."

Rufus cleared his throat and finally spoke up. "Speaking of which, I should return to the reception and check in on him. I've been gone long enough as it is." He neared us, giving Amynta a roguish smile as he passed by; she rewarded him with a blush. I scowled when he turned his smile on me, determined not to feel intimidated by his height as I looked up into his dark eyes. "A pleasure to meet you, lady Aemilia."

My scowl still did not lift, and soon enough Rufus was headed out of the kitchen. His departure seemed to prompt Amynta to return to her senses, and she quickly began ushering me back towards the direction of the reception, scolding me for having left in the first place. The kitchen staff resolutely continued to ignore us as they carried out their tasks.

By the time I sullenly returned to the fringes of the reception, I saw Rufus whispering into the ear of the senator with whom my aunt had been speaking earlier—Decimus. The two men approached Aunt Agrippina again, Rufus lingering behind Decimus as the senator bade her farewell and once more passed along his congratulations, and then both men were moving towards the home's exit.

Rufus turned as the pair were almost out of sight; seeing that I was watching, he caught my eye and winked. It did not escape my notice that the gesture, certainly intended to be received as mischievous or playful, an indication of familiarity, was not matched by the rest of his stiff manner. Something about Rufus was off, something that lurked behind his unreadable, dark eyes, but I was perhaps too young, too naïve, to yet understand what it might be. I only knew that I didn't like him one bit.

I expressed my concerns to Amynta about her suitor that evening as she combed out my hair, but she only shook her head and laughed at me, dismissing my worries as the mere foolishness of a child who was not yet a woman.

"I don't see why you think he's attractive," I told her, my tone petulant. He looked little like the perfect-bodied gods depicted in artwork around the city, from exquisitely painted statues to painstakingly laid out mosaics—such was the image of male perfection that I held close to my heart, at the time. "His red hair is rather silly, too. I thought only barbarians had red hair."

Amynta sighed, and I could sense her amused frustration, although she was careful not to pull too harshly on my hair as she continued to comb through it, gently pulling apart little tangles that had accumulated throughout the day. "Rome extends far beyond this city, *domincella*. All sorts of people are Roman these days. Nobody *looks* Roman anymore."

I scoffed. "*My* family looks Roman," I said decisively, thinking of my mother, my uncle, my aunt and her children and the characteristics we all shared. "Anyway, *I* would never be perched on the lap of some man, in a kitchen of all places." My tone was haughty.

"You'll change your mind when you meet a young, handsome man yourself—gods willing, your husband. You won't know what's come over you," Amynta told me. "How they look is just a small part of it." She blushed then, but I didn't understand why; I simply scowled at her, denying that such a thing would happen to me. But Amynta did not pay me any heed, and I went to bed frustrated, worried, and feeling utterly powerless. I had seen what happened when a woman met a man she thought handsome, what happened when a woman lost control of her herself: my mother was the tattered, disgraced example of it, condemned to rot on some forsaken island. I vowed to never share her fate.

CHAPTER
V

RUFUS

Rufus wearily rubbed a hand across the back of his neck as he and Decimus left the home of Germanicus and Agrippina, the doors abruptly closing behind them and cutting off the faint sounds of merrymaking and celebration that trickled outwards from the reception. He breathed in the fresh air with near-desperate gulps, relieved to be away from the crush of too many bodies, the overwhelming din of their overlapping voices. He was not used to being around so many people.

The event had proven, for the most part, to be boring and predictable. Rome's elite fawned over the imperial house's newest, blubbering addition, who one day might form part of Augustus's planned line of succession. Rufus, though, had barely caught sight of the sickly infant; what he had glimpsed was wholly unimpressive. What, he wondered, was the curse upon the Augustan household? If the men did not die too young from some unexpected catastrophe—as the emperor's eldest grandsons had, his original heirs—they were instead ill and weak, as this new child appeared to be. Perhaps he took after his uncle Claudius, revealing a failing from his father's side in addition to his imperial mother's, who was herself both the daughter and the sister of exiled, troublesome whores. Yet it was upon these women that the emperor's line of succession was coming to depend; it was their imperial blood that remained the most undiluted, their marriages and progeny that mattered most.

There was another category, too, of men related to the emperor: that of the completely mad. Augustus's grandson Agrippa Postumus—once an heir to the empire—had found himself in this lattermost grouping, and although Rufus had initially doubted reports of the youth's nature, thinking that they were perhaps exaggerated rumors or politically motivated slanders, he was soon easily enough convinced of their truth. It had taken merely a few days with Agrippa on the island of Planasia to understand that his madness was not only very real, but worsening with alarming rapidity.

"Insufferable," Decimus was muttering to himself as he shifted his weight from foot to foot, brown eyes scanning the road impatiently even as his litter was hurriedly carried forward by waiting slaves. Rufus did not respond to his master.

The soldier could not remember exactly how, or even exactly when, Decimus had first wormed his way into his life, but it had happened, perhaps so slowly and gently that the younger Rufus had not realized into what sort of trouble he was headed. Now, too many of his secrets were held by the senator, and too much money had passed into his greedy, bloodied hands; he was tied to Decimus by a forced bond that hinged upon the ever-present threat of betrayal. And so, Rufus knew that there was little chance of evading whatever commands the senator thought to dole out, if he wished to continue living. He had become resigned.

"Rufus!" Decimus snapped at him. Gone was the earlier, false warmth of the senator's eyes, as was the lilting tone he had used throughout the reception.

Rufus straightened his posture, refocusing his attention. "Yes?"

"You've been wretchedly distracted ever since returning from that island. It makes me think that perhaps I chose the wrong man."

Rufus stared straight ahead, his lips pressed firmly together. He had done everything asked of him, had dutifully reported young Agrippa's every word, every action, that might lend itself to his master's cause. He had even bled for him. No, Rufus thought—Decimus had chosen the wrong man to back against the emperor. There was no hope of restoration for Agrippa, whatever his master thought. The youth would never become emperor.

Decimus adjusted his toga. The litter had arrived and was set gently down next to them. "Never mind that now. I suppose you did what I had asked." The words were begrudging, barely an acknowledgement of what Rufus had done—what he had risked. "Run along back to whatever it is you should be doing. Convey my thanks to your commander for… lending you to me."

"Yes," Rufus said flatly, his eyes fixed on the litter behind the man that stood before him. Decimus was friendly with his commander in the Praetorian Guard, yielding not-infrequent external assignments for Rufus as a flashy bodyguard for the senator. Improper, perhaps—but who would listen to his complaints?

Decimus hefted his toga as he stepped towards the litter, and Rufus turned to leave.

"Rufus!" Decimus called again, and the soldier stopped. He did not turn. "I expect to see more progress here. Continue seeing that slave girl. Get closer to her young mistress, Aemilia."

Rufus looked over his shoulder and lifted his chin ever so slightly, a silent, subtle acknowledgment of Decimus's orders. The litter was then lifted into the air and the slaves set off, bearing the senator unceremoniously away. Rufus breathed in deeply, one hand clenching the folds of his toga as he fought to calm himself.

He dreamed of Agrippa Postumus that night—an occurrence that seemed to haunt him with increasing regularity. In it, he remembered things as they had happened: the crazed youth setting fire to the island villa, nearly killing them all; Rufus, coming to him with a salve for his burns, applying it gently to his naked skin before he forced a finger into one of Agrippa's wounds, threatening him with urgent whispers and the promise of more pain if he did not cooperate.

After that, the dream always changed. In some versions, Agrippa spun around and killed him, ripping out Rufus's throat with his bare teeth, little more than a crazed animal; in others, it was Rufus who killed Agrippa, quietly choking the life out of him, trying to quell his madness, to drive it from him, but only succeeding in murdering him instead. The worst dreams, though, the ones that haunted Rufus for days afterwards, involved Decimus appearing on that cursed island, standing over the both of them, laughing as he beat them with a whip until their skin cracked open, shedding their blood until they lay in cascading pools of it—and still they bled more, the pain never subsiding, the beating never ending.

Rufus woke with a start, his body soaked in sweat, his hands trembling as he drew a shaky breath. His blanket was tangled around his legs, wrapped so tightly that one of his feet had begun to go numb. It was merely a dream, he told himself, a dream and nothing more. He had left the island, had left Agrippa Postumus, long ago. Yet still he thought, when the city was quiet at night, that he could hear the waves crashing against the rocks; the faint smell of salt-tinged air consistently seemed to linger on the breeze, inescapable. A quiet voice in his mind hinted to him darkly that he had not escaped the island, had not escaped the emperor's crazed grandson at all—but that he had become infected by them, and it would ruin him.

CHAPTER
VI

TITUS

Titus retched, his eyes streaming as he fought to open them against the harsh, blinding light of the sun. He felt insufferably damp and overwhelmingly hot all at once, and his throat ached as if he had screamed a battle cry for hours on end—against what enemy, he was not certain.

Faint memories began to tug at his mind as he fought to remember where he was, what was happening; grains of sand made his fingertips itch, and crusty salt rendered his clothes stiff and uncomfortable no matter what position he shifted his body into. The only immediate reassurances were the tangible weight of the short sword at his hip and the tug of the travel pack that, somehow, remained strapped across his back, though it now dug uncomfortably into his aching flesh.

The storm. He had gone below deck, at the urging of Syphax, but after spending an indeterminable length of time being tossed violently back and forth, with the occasional, worrying stream of cold saltwater finding its way towards him before pooling in the corner, Titus had decided he would prefer to take his chances up top, alongside the crew. After that, he remembered nothing, except the lingering shock of cold as he had somehow found himself in the water.

Finally, Titus's eyes adjusted to the sunlight, and he saw that he had washed up on a sandy shore that was punctuated by dark rocks of varying size and shape. Wreckage in the form of splintered wood and odd pieces of cargo, some of it surprisingly intact, was scattered along the stretch of sand in sad, unnatural clumps. It confirmed what he had quickly come to suspect since regaining consciousness: the ship he had booked passage on from Byzantium to Tomis was no more, torn apart by the violent storm that had caught them out on the open water, unprepared. The now gentle waves, lapping at his toes, were almost mocking, a reminder that Neptune could quell the seas as easily as he could stir them into a merciless rage.

Titus groaned as he pushed himself up, the muscles in his arms and legs silently screaming in protest as he worked his way to his feet, swaying unsteadily. His throat was dry and swollen, and his attempts to clear it only exacerbated its rawness. Mentally, he was dazed, trying to come to terms with what had happened—and where he was. His mind repeated two simple words, as if to remind him of his goal, and his promise: Tomis. Julia.

The soldier took a step and grunted in pain; his left leg had nearly given out with the movement. Looking down, Titus saw a sharp section of wood jutting out from his calf, dried blood surrounding the entry point. As if seeing the injury somehow made it more real, a fresh wave of pain washed over him, and he gritted his teeth. Closing his eyes, Titus reached a hand down and, grasping the wood with firm, unwavering fingers, he yanked it from his flesh.

When Titus opened his eyes, he once more found himself lying in the sand, blinking up at the too-bright sun. He had lost consciousness again, the burst of pain that accompanied the removal of the wood from his leg having overwhelmed him.

A vaguely familiar face entered his view, and Titus grunted in greeting before he was able to find his raspy voice. "Are you real, or are you here to take me to the Underworld?"

The face belonged to the ship's captain, and the man looked beyond terrible. He gave a sad smile as he looked down at the soldier. "You're not dead, though there are few others I can say that for." His voice caught on the last words.

Titus sat up, groaning again as he examined his leg. Fresh blood had anointed his skin, as well as the sand underneath him, but he knew that he would manage, so long as infection didn't set in; he would need to clean the wound sooner rather than later. He looked back up at the captain, and he could see the faint trace of tears. "Syphax?" Titus asked gently, inquiring after the man's son.

The captain shook his head and rubbed an arm across his face.

Titus unsteadily got back to his feet, adjusting his sword and travel pack as the captain composed himself. "Do you have any idea where we are? Where the closest settlement is?" His words were measured and even, though Titus was far less certain than he was pretending to be.

The captain nodded, his words short and clipped as he answered. "Apollonia Pontica should be nearby. We can't have been blown too far off course." He gestured in the direction he believed the city to be, then began to wander past Titus, his attention already shifting. "I need to check for others. Send some help, if you can…" He trailed off as his slow steps took him further down the shore, and he did not look back at the soldier as he examined the wreckage from his vessel—his entire livelihood, destroyed in mere minutes.

Titus clenched his teeth as he set off, each step on his wounded leg sending shooting bursts of pain through him. He paused only momentarily as he passed by Syphax's corpse; the small, bloated body barely resembled the smiling, mischievous boy he had known so briefly.

Just over two weeks after the ship's sinking, Titus had reached Tomis. The journey from Apollonia Pontica, a ride mostly by oxcart, had been anything but smooth, although the bumpy, achingly slow progress of the vehicle had proven less painful for Titus than walking on his still wounded leg—and it had the added benefit of allowing him some time to heal. A quick shock of pure vinegar seemed to have prevented the immediate onset of infection, though the soldier knew he would still limp for quite some time, if not forever.

Now, Titus hobbled through the streets of Tomis, the autumn air heavy with the Black Sea's coarse saltiness and the inevitable promise of harsher, colder weather still to come. He had quickly picked up from the local population—a combination of Greeks and Romans interspersed with Thracian and Dacian peoples, as well as more transient tradesmen from the empire's furthest reaches—that the governor, Aulus Caecina Severus, was not currently in the city, but instead was off helping to quash the long-running revolt in Illyricum that had now troubled Rome for a handful of years.

A particularly chatty youth who delivered fresh fish to the more well-to-do households of Tomis told Titus—after the soldier had purchased him a few drinks—that Aulus would no doubt be back soon. He had been spending a noticeable amount of time in their small city over the past year or so, paying frequent visits to Ovid, who was perhaps the most infamous resident of Tomis.

This piqued Titus's interest considerably; he had heard that the poet had been banished from Rome, but, until now, there had not been a particular reason for him to pay the exile much attention. His connection to Aulus—and thus, possibly, to Julia's infant son—changed matters.

"Why is the governor so interested in a poet?" Titus asked.

The youth shrugged and took another gulp of his drink. "S'pose he's a fan. Who knows? There was a rumor awhile 'go, though, that the governor stuck his bastard son there, letting 'im be raised with the slaves in Ovid's household." He hiccupped, thinking about his next words: it was clear that Latin was not his native tongue, but it was intelligible enough. "The big woman in the house, she had 'er own brat, too, so made sense and all, that she'd be the bastard's nursemaid. Nice'n tidy setup there, Aulus hidin' the boy, not letting his wife back in Rome catch on."

Titus frowned, thinking. "Where might I find Ovid?"

His companion yawned, fighting off his drink-inspired sleepiness. "Make a right out of here, then once you're straight through the forum you'll find a house with graffiti on it—a nice coitus scene. It's to the right of that... I think. Or the left." The youth scratched his head and let out a belch before returning his attention to his drink, and Titus knew he wouldn't get anything else of use out of him.

Titus clapped the young man on the shoulder as he stood, adjusting his sword and travel pack. The former had resulted in a few odd looks here and there; it was obviously a standard military weapon, but his current appearance—unshaven, his hair too long, and clothing that had undergone a great deal of wear—did not match the ideal for a soldier of Rome, who should always be well-groomed and tidy. Though he was not a vain man by any means, Titus still could not entirely suppress his longing for a lengthy, hot bath.

Sighing, Titus followed the youth's directions, passing through the streets of Tomis until he stood outside the house with the graffiti. Already a slave was hard at work trying to scrub the coitus scene off the residence's wall, with little evidence of success despite the sweat that trickled down his brow in thick droplets.

"*Salve*," Titus called to the man, announcing his presence.

The slave turned. "What do you want?" he asked abruptly, the impatience in his tone clear. "Can't you see I'm busy here?"

"My apologies," Titus said. "I'm looking for the home of Ovid, the exile. I was told he lived close to this residence."

The slave barked out a laugh, turning back to his work even as he began to speak. "Another of the governor's men, are you? He's been in such a frenzy lately, all over that little slave family that escaped. As if he can't afford to just replace them..."

Titus frowned. "What do you mean?"

The man spared him a glance over his shoulder, frowning as he examined Titus more closely. "Aren't you sent by the governor?" His tone had become suspicious, and his work had halted. Liquid dripped from the rag in his hands, and the smudged, partially erased face of the woman in the graffiti seemed to stare accusingly over the slave's shoulder at Titus.

Titus sighed, swinging his pack off his back and onto the ground. He fished through it for one of his few remaining coins, which, when he straightened back up, had caught the eager gaze of the slave.

"No matter, who you're sent by or not sent by," the man said hurriedly.

Titus nodded, his fingers toying with the coin now loosely clasped in his hand. "Good. Now tell me more about what's going on here, and what you know about that slave family."

10 CE

CHAPTER
VII

AEMILIA LEPIDA

My fourteenth birthday came and went, and still I wore the *lunula* of girlhood: unmarried, a child. Not that I minded; I had become wary of my near-inevitable future as a wife and mother after Aunt Agrippina's baby had died only a few weeks after his reception the previous autumn, passing quietly away in his sleep. Yet that had not stopped my aunt and uncle from conceiving again in surprisingly short order, and our household was once more to expect the arrival of a new infant, whose appearance, it was hoped, would chase away the lingering sadness of the most recent loss. Marriage, I surmised, seemed to be exhausting.

Amynta was chattering excitedly about the unborn child as she fixed most of my hair into a low bun, leaving loose chunks of it towards the front that would be gathered up into a smaller, rolled knob across the top of my head. My great-grandfather's wife, Livia, wore her hair so, and thus it had become the fashion for any woman of note. I felt that it made my forehead appear unflatteringly large—but, of course, no one cared what I thought. I sighed.

"Do you want children of your own?" I asked Amynta abruptly, interrupting her in the middle of her sentence—one to which I had not been paying particular attention.

Her hands paused momentarily, still holding strands of my hair. "If the gods will it, then yes." Her fingers returned to action, working themselves softly through my curls.

"You sound sad," I told Amynta, picking up a small, handheld mirror of polished bronze so that I could examine her behind me as she continued styling my hair. Many women—Aunt Agrippina included—had a special slave whose sole job was to care for and style their hair, but I had been told that such an extravagance wasn't suitable until I married and took over the management of my own household. Until then, Amynta was responsible for nearly all aspects of my upkeep.

Amynta's lips curved ever so slightly, but the resulting smile was forlorn. Her gaze remained focused on her work. "No matter, *domincella*," was all she said, but I was not put off.

"If you were not a slave, you would already be married, with children," I stated, my tone matter of fact. I had thought as much before, but I had never said so to Amynta. Now she winced, as if my statement struck her as a literal blow. I had not realized the harshness of my words, but I did not go back on them: they were true, after all.

"Yes," Amynta agreed quietly. Her hands continued to work my hair, but she was no longer keen to speak, either about her own future—or lack thereof—or about my aunt's current pregnancy.

I set the mirror down. "How is Rufus?" I asked instead, closing my eyes as I relaxed into Amynta's gentle hands. I still did not like the man, having glimpsed him periodically ever since the autumn, as he continued to pay occasional, secretive visits to Amynta, but I thought that a mention of her suitor might perk my nursemaid up.

I was not wrong. I sensed a renewed energy from Amynta as she worked on the finishing touches of my hair, her hands now moving more quickly and assuredly. "He is well," she said, the warmth in her voice making up for the short answer.

I sighed. "You should be careful," I announced primly. "My aunt has not yet realized what you're up to, but she isn't blind. And the other slaves do talk, you know."

Amynta laughed, and I knew my decision to bring up Rufus had been rewarded: her mood had lightened considerably. "One would think you were the nursemaid and I the charge, *domincella*."

I scowled as Amynta finished styling the last part of my hair.

I strolled through the rows of shopping stalls, Amynta nervously hovering just a step behind as she held an open parasol over me, shielding my face from the spring sun which, although weak, still bore the threat of tanning my pale skin. Several men from my aunt's household had been sent along, as usual, to process around me in loose formation on my shopping excursion—something which I was surprised my Aunt Agrippina still permitted, considering most reputable women instead had wares brought directly to their homes for private showings.

I supposed, though, that my aunt allowed it because the area was safe and respectable enough; it was one of the nicer markets, quite close to the large hill upon which our house stood. Homeless vagrants were kept far away, and only the better merchants in Rome were permitted to set up and run their stalls here. The emperor occasionally had his own men patrol the area, the promise of peace kept merely by their infrequent presence.

The merchants largely kept their eyes downcast, refraining from shouting out their special deals and shoving their supposedly rare pieces in front of me. In all likelihood, they did not know exactly who I was, but they could clearly see, based on my appearance and my companions, that I was from a noble household. They did not dare to harass me, but that did not stop them from quietly hoping that I would find something of interest in their stalls and instruct Amynta to open the not-insignificant coin purse she bore on my behalf.

My eyes passed listlessly over necklaces and bracelets in gold and silver, some decorated with beads and gems; I only briefly perused trinkets and boxes made of bone and horn and carved with all manner of elaborate designs, some Roman in style and others quite exotic—some, too, quite erotic in nature, although I had no business collecting such pieces. I had no interest, either, in the swaths of fabric that came in all colors and textures, nor the assortment of shoes that could, I was promised, be fit to any foot, no matter how large or small it might be. From further away, the scent of street foods reached my nose: sausages, hot meat pies, simmering stews.

I rounded the corner, stopping in my tracks as I nearly collided with an immense figure blocking my path. Amynta let out a small gasp, letting the parasol momentarily drop so that my face was suddenly flooded with bright sunlight, and I looked up, blinking, into Rufus's amused gaze.

"Careful," he said, flashing his typical wink at me. As usual, I responded to the gesture with a scowl, wholly distrusting its sincerity.

"Is this why you seemed so nervous and excitable today, Amynta?" I asked, rounding on my nursemaid. "You planned a little rendezvous without informing me?"

Amynta shook her head. "I promise, *domincella*, I had no such plans."

Rufus spoke up. "Please forgive your nurse, *domincella*," he said.

I felt my scowl deepen as Amynta's nickname for me crossed his slightly sun-chapped lips, carefree and teasing, as if he and I were friendly with one another. "Sometimes, I spend my free time near to your household, hoping that I might catch Amynta when she emerges for an errand. I followed you both here."

I sighed, a long-suffering noise that I did not even attempt to suppress. "Fine. I will be over there, continuing my shopping. Amynta, you only have a few moments."

I fought to keep my steps small, measured, and appropriately ladylike as I moved away from the pair, the men from the household tasked with my safety following meekly along. I was surprised, then, to feel a soft touch at my elbow.

I flinched as I spun around, finding myself uncomfortably close to the tall, older senator from last autumn's reception for my newborn cousin. He smiled reassuringly, his brown eyes appraising me. The household men kept their gazes averted; even they would not dare to cross a senator. It did not hurt that each man now also bore a small money bag affixed to his belt, little additions that were not there only a short time earlier.

"Aemilia, isn't it?" the senator asked, as if he did not already know who I was. "Aemilia Lepida?"

I nodded, swallowing. "And you are Decimus, the senator," I managed, lifting my chin ever so slightly. I would not be intimidated.

"It's true, what they say," he said next, smiling. I said nothing, waiting for him to continue. "You do resemble your mother."

I swallowed again, pressing my lips together. I had no response; people did not often mention my mother to me directly.

Yet it seemed that Decimus did not require an answer, as he continued on after only the slightest of pauses. "Do you write to her often?" he asked. I shook my head, but he was already speaking again. "And your uncle, young Agrippa Postumus? I remember that he seemed to get along well with you, when you were only a little girl. He taught you to swim, didn't he?"

I licked my lips, trying to keep up with the senator's words. How did he know all this? And why was he asking me now? No one had mentioned my uncle to me in a year or more. "He did," I managed to say, a small sting of sad remembrance making my voice forlorn.

Decimus nodded, still smiling, although he took a brief moment to glance around us, as if wanting to be certain that we were lost amongst the many others who milled about the shopping stalls. It was then that I began to suspect whatever conversation we were having, whatever it was that Decimus truly wanted to know, might not be wholly appropriate— or in my best interests. And yet instead of shying away, a small tendril of rebelliousness unfurled itself from deep within me, awakened from its slumber and called to action—to what end, I don't think I much cared.

"I don't write to my uncle," I volunteered with a sniff. "Aunt Agrippina wouldn't allow it."

Decimus gave me a sympathetic look. "It's not fair, is it? That your family has been discarded in such a manner? And you, too, poor girl—cast aside."

His quiet, sympathetic words further stirred the still-unfurling tendril of rebellion within me, and I felt righteously indignant in a way that had not before occurred to me. He was right. "Yes," I agreed. "I miss them. My mother, and Uncle Agrippa, too. They should be here." My words were more forceful than I intended, and I felt heat rising in my cheeks.

Decimus nodded. "I agree," he said quietly. "Perhaps, between the two of us, we can change things for the better."

"How?" I asked, intrigued. My heart was racing; no one had ever bothered to speak to me like this before, as if I were an adult rather than a child, a person of interest and potential rather than a little girl to be kept quiet, pushed to the side as a passive observer and nothing more. My earlier dislike of Decimus was rapidly receding, against my better senses—but I quashed them down.

The senator looked around us again, his brown eyes scanning the crowd. "It may take some time. I'll be in touch again. But, Aemilia," he lowered his voice even further and inclined his head towards me. "You must keep this a secret. You may trust Rufus—in fact, I encourage you to take him into your confidence—but don't mention our conversation to anyone else, even your nursemaid."

I frowned, and Decimus seemed to sense my sudden hesitation. "She would be obliged to tell your aunt," he explained.

"I understand," I said, nodding.

Decimus gave me a final smile and slipped away into the mass of shopping stalls. When I rejoined Amynta, Rufus was bidding her farewell. He met my eyes and, instead of his customary wink, he gave the slightest inclination of his head, as if knowing that we now shared a secret. Then he, too, was gone, no doubt following after his master.

Amynta, pleased by her brief flirtation with her suitor, did not have the capacity of mind to ask me what my conversation with Decimus had been about; in fact, I doubted she even noticed that I had been speaking with anyone at all. I did not feel obligated to enlighten her, even without Decimus's earlier warning freshly in my mind. It felt exciting—empowering, even—to have a secret of my own, one that might, if Decimus spoke the truth, change my family's fate. And I could help.

With a new lightness in my step, I resumed browsing the stalls, Amynta following along behind with my parasol, once more shading my face from the afternoon sun. I selected several pieces of jewelry that I knew Aunt Agrippina would probably not yet allow me to wear, at least in public, but I didn't mind. Suddenly, such matters seemed so trivial.

CHAPTER VIII

RUFUS

Rufus watched Amynta and her charge resume their meandering path through the market. The nurse still bore the faint trace of a blush across her cheeks, and her gaze remained distant, as if she were in a faraway place instead of mindlessly clutching her young mistress's parasol and shuffling along a half step behind her. As had been his master's plan, she had no idea what had just transpired between Decimus and Aemilia, merely a few feet away from her.

Rufus felt largely… unmoved by Amynta, if he had to put his feelings into words. She was not an unappealing young woman in shape or visage, even if she was particularly naïve—foolish even—not to suspect Rufus of any ill intent. But despite whatever positive qualities the slave girl possessed, he had never been much attracted to women, instead preferring his own sex.

Decimus, ignorant of Rufus's carnal inclinations and wholly uncaring even if he had known, had commanded the soldier to approach Amynta, to gain her confidence, and thus to get closer to the young Aemilia Lepida in the process—and so he had gritted his teeth and followed his orders, quashing down whatever faint emotions he still managed to feel.

It was not so much harder than anything else Rufus had done for the senator in the past: torture, murder, spying, threatening. Certainly it was easier than trying to keep an eye on that damned mad Agrippa Postumus, whose every move seemed to threaten his own life or that of those around him. He still doubted that Decimus's ultimate plan to restore Agrippa to Rome, and to secure the youth's place in the succession whilst grooming him as a puppet emperor, would come to fruition—but he was not about to share such doubts with the senator.

Now, Rufus turned away from the two young women, quickly moving after Decimus. The senator was already settling himself in his litter nearby, adjusting the cumbersome folds of his toga and picking at the heavy woolen fabric. He watched Rufus approach, motioning for his attendants to give them some space.

"Good work," Decimus said. It was rare praise, but he seemed especially pleased.

"Things went well with the young lady, then?" Rufus asked.

Ordinarily, Decimus would have scowled at him before uttering a reminder to remember his place, to leave the details to those who had the breeding and the experience to know better. But, this time, Decimus smiled at him, the expression genuine.

"Oh, quite well," the senator said. "Aemilia is eager to assist me, if she thinks it might help her disgraced family. She has a certain…" He trailed off, thinking about his next choice of words. "A certain anger, deep inside of her, I think. We must cultivate that, keep her agreeable—hungry for the retribution that she does not quite yet understand she even wants."

Rufus nodded, hesitating only slightly before asking his next question. "How will she help with your plans? She is but a child."

Decimus, instead of rebuking the soldier, smiled at him again. "A

48

child with Augustus's blood running through her veins. As of yet, an unmarried child. Perhaps, with certain suggestions, I might influence the candidates considered for her future match. Perhaps, when the time comes, her sons might be suitable candidates for Rome itself…"

Rufus kept his expression neutral as Decimus expounded upon the perceived possibilities of Aemilia's prospects. He was not particularly surprised by the senator's revelation. After all, it was obvious that the young Aemilia did not currently have the needed influence to help direct any events related to her mad, disgraced uncle—but her future, as of now, remained an open scroll, ready to be scrawled upon by Decimus's eager hand. It was a future that the senator wanted to keep amenable to his plans for power, part of his ongoing efforts to plant seeds across the empire in the hope that one—and he only needed one— might germinate, might grow without restriction. What better way to proceed down such a path than to ingratiate himself with a young, angry, impressionable girl of imperial blood?

Suddenly, Decimus's eyes narrowed, and he frowned at Rufus. "Haven't I told you, many times before, not to ask so many questions? You will do as you are told, and let me concern myself with the future. It is enough that you keep an eye on her, reminding her that she can wield more power than anyone wants her to know she even has."

Rufus simply nodded, his eyes shifting downwards to the cobbled street at the base of the litter. Decimus roughly tossed a small sack of coins to the ground in front of the soldier and then, without another word, waved for his attendants to return to their places; they quickly lifted the litter and carried the senator away. The resultant opening in the street was soon filled with passerby, laughing and arguing and bartering amongst themselves, none the wiser to the plots unfolding in their city.

Rufus stood still for a moment, looking at the coin-filled bag with an expression of distaste clearly writ across his face. Then, common sense quickly winning out over his rare moment of indignation, he stooped to grab the pouch, clenching the coins tightly in his fist as he stood back to his full height. It was, as Decimus said, not his place to question, to think. Only to obey. So long as he was paid, why did it matter to him who ruled Rome, or who suffered in the process?

Rufus spent that night gambling, facing loss after loss as he continued to drink and to bet what remained of his dwindling coin supply. The din of voices and clanking cups only increased as the evening wore on, and the acrid smoke of torches filled the room until it was well past stifling. He pushed away the topless, sweating whore who tried to slide herself onto his lap, and she left him alone with a backwards glare.

At last he managed to win back a few of the coins he had so recently lost, and, with some fleeting measure of sense still left, he stood from the table, bracing himself as the room swam around him and his body began to sway. The laughter, the shouting, even the roll of the dice—it was suddenly too much. His head ached; his eyes and throat burned from prolonged exposure to the stuffy, smoke-filled air.

His gambling partners beckoned him back, but Rufus knew he had had enough—and he knew he still had one more destination. The soldier waved off the other men, and they quickly returned to their game, losing interest in the now-unwilling gambler. If he wouldn't put any more money on the table, he was of no use to them.

Rufus stumbled out into the nighttime street to find that it was still busy, despite the moon being at its peak. Beggars crouched in dank alleyways, the stench of piss and decay emanating from them, and muddied street urchins skipped across the road, their keen eyes on the constant lookout for a dropped coin or—better yet—a purse affixed too loosely to its master's belt. Prostitutes stood outside the closest brothel, hoping to lure in tired, drunk men who would be more than willing to part with the remainder of their evening's gambling and drinking money, even if they would find themselves incapable of doing anything that one would expect in a brothel: drink had its curses as well as its blessings.

This was the Rome he knew so well; not the patrician hills, the sprawling residences and fine markets that graced the rose-scented streets of the city's finer areas, those spaces patrolled by the emperor's own soldiers, where well-to-do women and too-plump men strolled about amongst manicured facades, unaware—uncaring—of the poverty, the brutality, and the hunger that still existed around them, not so very far away.

Rufus stumbled further on, intent on his destination. There was another brothel nearby, a smaller one, that catered more specifically to his tastes—and within it was his favorite: Leander.

The guard at the door, a hulking beast of a man even more muscular and solid than Rufus himself, recognized the red-haired soldier as soon as the torchlight flickered across his face. The guard grunted in a wordless greeting and stepped out of the way, allowing Rufus entry.

The eunuch who ran the place sighed as he looked up from his desk, carefully setting down his pen. "Rufus, welcome," he said, voice reedy. "You know how it is here. Money first, services next."

Rufus nodded, fumbling with his coin purse as he approached the desk. He slammed it down, narrowly missing the pen, and braced himself against the surface.

"Will it be Leander again?" the eunuch asked, daintily opening the purse and eyeing its limited contents. "The rest of the night?"

Rufus nodded again. "Yes." His voice was raspy, drink-laden.

"Well enough. He's available." The eunuch counted out a small pile of coins before tying the purse back up and handing it to the soldier, nearly empty now. "On you go."

Rufus didn't bother to issue his thanks, instead stumbling onwards to the inner sanctum of the brothel. He knew where he was headed; he had been here frequently enough, especially of late. It seemed more and more that only Leander had been able to drive away the haunting sound of the sea that Rufus alone could hear, to distract him from the salty scent that seemed to cling to him regardless of how many times he bathed, rubbing at his skin until it was nearly raw. After he had been with Leander, too, he often managed to obtain a dreamless sleep that same night—a respite from Agrippa's haunting face, a respite from what he worried was a lurking madness within himself.

CHAPTER IX

AEMILIA LEPIDA

I shifted my weight from foot to foot as I impatiently waited for Aunt Agrippina in the atrium, my fingers twitching as I wished that I had some small, flat stones to try to skip across the water in the *impluvium* there, just as my uncle Agrippa Postumus had once taught me to do. Amynta, seeing how I fidgeted, was quick to scold me.

"Don't so much as move, *domincella*, or you'll muss your dress and dislodge your hairpins," she said, eyes narrowed as she watched me.

I scowled and was about to utter my best retort when Aunt Agrippina appeared, beaming at me. She was dressed surprisingly simply, her clothing plain and subdued in nature—although I could tell, even from across the courtyard, how fine the fabric was—with a veil drawn over her head. Small, golden earrings that drew little attention were nestled on her lobes, and a lone bangle hung on her wrist.

"Ready, Aemilia?" She smiled as she looked me over, and I realized that my own outfit was a perfect complement to her own, if of slightly lesser quality.

"Yes, Aunt Agrippina, I'm ready," I answered dutifully, although I wasn't particularly looking forward to our little venture together.

Just as we were about to depart, a slave I did not recognize entered the atrium, lingering uncertainly next to the wall. Aunt Agrippina motioned the woman over and listened intently as the newcomer whispered into her ear, the words too hushed for me to make out. Then the woman was gone, and my aunt quickly returned her attention to me with a smile.

"Who was that?" I asked. "I don't recognize her."

"You wouldn't recognize all our slaves," she said dismissively. "We have many."

"What does she do?"

"Really, Aemilia—I told your nursemaid to train you out of asking so many questions. It's an unattractive quality that your future husband, whoever he may be, will surely dislike."

I sighed again, and my aunt raised a brow at me. "Yes, Aunt Agrippina," I said, forcing myself to smile pleasantly before schooling my face into a neutral, bland expression, although I wanted to keep asking questions.

The older I grew—and the more time I spent with my aunt—the more I noticed these strange slaves coming and going, whispering news into her ear or bearing letters on scrolls that seemed to disappear shortly after they arrived, a burned scent lingering in the air. Yet as soon as these strangers were gone, my aunt returned to her normal, cheerful self, always eager to school me, to correct me, molding me into the perfect little Roman lady, and any thought I had that she might be involving herself in the very realms she told me were forbidden to women— politics, namely—quickly disappeared from my mind. My aunt was the prime example of what all well-born women in Rome aspired to— certainly she must be above the suspicion of meddling in anything outside our womanly sphere.

I soon forgot the unknown slave as we left my aunt's home,

Amynta and several other attendants trailing dutifully behind as the door attendant saw us out. We stepped quickly into a waiting litter, its eight men lifting us into the air as Amynta observed with judgmental eyes, ready to scold any man whose arms so much as trembled under the weight of their burden, and soon we were on the move. A handful of my uncle's men escorted us, clearing the roads as we wound through Rome, curious eyes peering into the litter. Aunt Agrippina had kept the curtains open.

"It does good for people to see us," she explained, although she never smiled, never waved to anyone who looked into the passing litter. "We are one of the leading families of Rome. People must remember that, remember who we are."

I only nodded and offered a small smile in response; I knew that I was not counted amongst the leading families of Rome, not any longer—not after my parents' downfalls, separate but equally damning. She meant herself—herself and Germanicus, and their growing brood of children, who would one day have the entirety of the empire at their pale, sandaled feet. But no matter—I didn't like to be looked at, to be noticed. In my limited experience, bad things came to those types of people, at some point or another. The gods were fickle.

It was, in fact, the gods we were going off to see, in a manner of speaking.

"Before Germanicus leaves on his campaign in Germania next year, I have a previous vow to fulfill," Aunt Agrippina had told me several days before our current outing. "I had promised Mars that I would slaughter two dozen bulls for him if my husband returned from Dalmatia not only alive, but victorious. It is now time to follow through on my promise to the god of war—and you shall have the honor of accompanying me."

Now, we approached the Temple of Mars Ultor favored by my aunt. It had been built by Augustus just over a decade ago, and its marble still gleamed as bright as it had upon its completion. Its pediment, held up by massive Corinthian columns, prominently displayed the god of war, flanked by Venus—the supposed ancestress of our family—and Fortuna. Inside, I knew there to be three massive statues: Mars in full military kit; Venus; and Julius Caesar, deified. But our visit today would not take us to the inner sanctum.

We were met as we descended the litter by a priest, who repeatedly bowed to Aunt Agrippina. I was spared barely a glance, and so I turned my attention to the waiting bulls as my aunt and the priest spoke.

Two dozen of the creatures, all of them exceedingly fine specimens—not a single odd marking nor a single scar anywhere on their bodies—were in a pen so small that they could barely move; they seemed to form one hulking, living mass, all of them shifting their weight, snorting, pawing, seeking space that did not exist. The acrid smell of their trampled excrement, tinged with their lathered sweat, stung my nose.

Some acolytes threw a rope around the first bull, one close to the pen's entrance, tightening it around its neck, half-leading and half-dragging the creature out as another young man closed the gate behind, separating it from its brethren. All of them were, for now, clueless as to their imminent fate, and for a brief moment I was reminded of my final night with my mother, ignorant of the fact that she was about to be torn from me.

"Come over here, Aemilia," Aunt Agrippina called, and I obediently went to her, watching as the bull was moved into position and the man employed to slaughter the animals approached.

I had seen countless sacrifices before, of all manner of animals, but I always found that I still flinched every time the blade was drawn across the creature's neck. When I was younger, I had thought that the animals were stupid creatures, unsuspecting even as they were led to their deaths; now, I knew better, if only because I bothered to pay attention.

As the hot red blood spurted out from the first bull's neck, his knees quickly buckling under his heavy body, his brethren began to bellow, the scent of violence reaching their sensitive noses. The next bull to be led out put up slightly more of a struggle—but in the end, it was for naught, as he met the same end as the bull before him.

The sacrifice seemed to take ages, even though the temple had taken measures to ensure its efficiency. As soon as the bulls were slaughtered, expelling their last rasping breath, they were dragged aside and cut up. Select bones, wrapped in some of the animals' fat, would be set aside to be burned, an offering to Mars. The rest of the meat, Aunt Agrippina told me, she had donated to the temple for them to use as they saw fit, eating it themselves or perhaps giving some to the surrounding community; she wasn't much concerned, one way or another, although the amount of meat from that day alone could have fed countless families.

"And now we are done," Aunt Agrippina said brightly, startling me from my silent watch; my eyes were glazed over from having observed the same gory scene over and over again. "My vow has been fulfilled."

I only nodded in response, meekly following her back to the litter, where our attendants stood by. Amynta looked bored and tired; sweat had begun to trickle down her brow as the sun worked its way higher in the sky, and the resultant heat made the coppery scent of the bulls' blood nearly unbearable. I was happy to leave the temple behind.

Aunt Agrippina was in high spirits as we began our return journey home, proudly and possessively surveying the streets of the city, as if her husband already reigned over the empire—as if Rome already belonged to them, to her. She was confident that Germanicus's military successes, and their quickly growing brood, were signs of the gods' favor, a promise that immeasurable power and eternal glory awaited their family.

We were not far from home when my aunt ordered the litter bearers to pause; her green eyes were focused behind me, her faraway gaze of only moments before now sharpened by shrewd intensity.

"Hello, Decimus," she said, smiling. I turned my body around so that I could see in the same direction, and the togate, silver-haired senator filled my gaze. He was on foot, but a canopied litter was not far from him, waiting for his return.

"Agrippina," he responded politely, then turned his attention to me. "Young Aemilia. Where are you off to today?"

"We are returning from sacrificing two dozen bulls to Mars," Agrippina said before I could respond. "As thanks for my husband's victory in Dalmatia last year." Her tone was smug.

Sabinus smiled thinly. "I thought I could smell blood in the air."

"Indeed," my aunt answered happily. "And Aemilia did not even come close to fainting."

I felt heat rise to my face as Decimus chuckled; my aunt had immediately succeeded in infantilizing me in front of the man to whom I had pledged my assistance, as he needed it, to restore my mother and my uncle to Rome. I did not want him to cast me aside, thinking I was still some useless child.

"The sight of blood has never bothered me," I said petulantly, but neither adult paid me any attention.

"Is she betrothed, yet, if I may ask?" Decimus inquired, although he did not so much as glance at me as he spoke.

"Not yet, but soon, I expect," Aunt Agrippina said. "Were you interested, Decimus? I know you are widowed..." She lowered her voice, although there were few people on the road around us to overhear. "This is the second time you have asked after her. I am sure Augustus, given your rank, would be pleased to entertain a suit."

I felt my face flushing again, the thought of being wedded to Decimus, a man at least four decades older than me, making my stomach roil. I looked away from the senator and focused on Amynta, who met my eyes with a reassuring gaze. I tried not to dwell on the fact that my aunt was discussing my future marriage as if I were not right across from her in the litter—as if I were an object to be traded so easily.

"Oh, no, not at all. I am actually recently betrothed myself, to what will be my fourth wife," Decimus explained. "I merely ask because she is such a pretty girl, although her direct family's circumstances at the moment are rather... unfortunate."

"Yes, quite," Aunt Agrippina said, and I detected a steely note to her words. She did not like to be reminded of the exiles of her mother, sister, and brother, instead preferring to act as if they did not exist. "Well, congratulations on your betrothal, but we really must depart now, Decimus." She nodded to him in a polite, if abrupt, farewell and ordered our litter bearers to begin moving once again. I noticed a hint of distaste in her expression before she managed to school her face back into its usual polite mask.

Decimus looked a bit put-out, as if he had intended to say more on the status of my betrothal, but our litter was already being carried away, leaving him standing alone in the road. After a moment, the senator turned to move towards his own litter, and I soon lost sight of him.

"Don't involve yourself with men like Decimus," Aunt Agrippina told me quietly, and she at last drew the litter's curtains, offering us a modicum of privacy.

"Senators?" I asked, playing the fool.

My aunt scowled at me. "You would do well in many ways to marry someone like Decimus, but I get the sense that he is… meddling." Her voice was thoughtful, and I imagined, for a moment, that she might confide in me. "Never mind that now. Just be careful." I sighed, the brief hope of being privy to her inner thoughts fading away as quickly as it had sprung up.

I did not understand exactly what Aunt Agrippina warned me against, but I certainly did not have the desire to tell her that it was too late; I had already involved myself with Decimus. Meddling he might be, but he had spoken to me as if I were already an adult. So, too, had he spoken to me of things that truly mattered: Decimus had promised to help my family, and I believed him. He seemed to be the only one to care what happened to my mother and my uncle, and that alone was enough for me to place my trust in him, no matter what my aunt said.

"You composed yourself quite admirably today, Aemilia," Aunt Agrippina said then, changing the topic. "A proper Roman lady."

I couldn't help but be pleased with her compliment, letting it soothe my irritation with her. Although we had our differences, at times, I looked up to my aunt—admired her. She loved her station in life, the power and influence it brought. I knew, as I had studied her during the sacrifice—her eyes eagerly watching the blood spill from the bulls' necks—that she would stop at nothing to make sure her position, and those of her children, remained secure.

CHAPTER
X

TITUS

Waiting for Aulus to return to Tomis was the easy part. Getting access to the governor was another matter entirely.

After some more poking and prodding in the city, aided by a combination of well-timed questions and well-placed coins, Titus had formed a steadfast suspicion that the slaves in Ovid's household were the family into which Aulus had placed Julia's son, after the infant boy had been dispatched to the governor's care by his grandfather, Lucius.

Titus hoped, but did not know for certain, that Lucius would not have been so foolish as to provide an explicit identification of the babe. But, by all accounts, the governor was far more personally concerned with the slave family's disappearance than anyone in Tomis considered proper. Would such a man stir himself to so much exertion on behalf of a mysterious infant whose identity he did not know? Or did he, in fact, know the child's heritage, and perhaps was seeking to use the boy for some nefarious purpose of his own, when the time was right? Titus clenched his teeth; better not to worry about it, not yet. He would soon find out how much the governor knew, and he would do what needed to be done.

Despite his suspicions, Titus wanted to be certain that the missing slave family truly was in possession of Julia's son; he had to know, without a doubt, before he set off to the west on a wild pursuit into the vast, dangerous mountain ranges of Dacia, a region that even Rome had not yet been able to conquer. The best way to confirm his theory was to make contact with Aulus, to get the governor to—somehow—admit that the infant boy he had taken under his protection almost two years ago came from Lucius, and that he did, in fact, deposit the child into the care of Didas and Galla, then in Ovid's household with a babe of their own, who had subsequently disappeared into thin air with both children. Titus had already paid a visit to the poet himself, who had been of little, if any, assistance.

Now, occasionally shifting his weight from foot to foot, Titus stood near the governor's residence, quietly observing the comings and goings: guards arriving for duty and, those they relieved, exiting, most headed to the bars and brothels of the city; slaves running errands, bearing combinations of letters and covered baskets to and fro; the odd visit from merchants and other well-to-do people of Tomis, all seeking favor with the Roman governor.

It was only a matter of time until Aulus would emerge. When it happened, Titus knew that the governor would be flanked by, at a minimum, a pair of soldiers, hardened veterans who would not shy away from spilling blood. But he had not come to start a fight.

Every flicker of movement near the doors further stoked Titus's anticipation, until at last what he had awaited appeared: Aulus, a wolf-skin draped across his shoulders and a sword on his belt. As Titus expected, he was closely followed by two soldiers.

"Governor!" Titus called out, quickly stepping from the shadowed alley where he had kept his watch. The governor's guards placed their hands on their sword hilts in a silent threat, but the trio kept moving as if they did not hear him. "Governor Aulus!" Titus tried again, falling into step alongside the other men.

"Move along," one of the guards warned him, but still they kept walking, ignoring the man they no doubt believed to be someone of inconsequence, looking for a handout of some sort.

Titus was not deterred, and he kept his pace even with theirs. "Your grandfather Lucius sends his regards."

That, at least, earned him a brief glance from the governor himself, though still the trio continued to move. "Does he, now?" The words sounded skeptical, the hint of a mocking undertone present, and Aulus looked away, disinterested, as soon as he finished speaking.

"He wonders if you might like for him to send you some birds, from the island." Of course, Lucius wondered no such thing, nor had he tasked Titus with such a message—but the soldier hoped that a mention of such details might prove an actual connection to the governor's grandfather.

Titus's small gamble paid off; Aulus took one more wavering step, then stopped entirely, his guards quickly drawing up behind him. "How do you know about his birds?"

"Or where he lives?" Titus supplied brazenly. Aulus did not appear to be amused.

"Speak," the governor barked. His eyes now thoroughly examined Titus, lingering on his military sword and worn-out shoes, both a standard issue that any soldier worth his salt would immediately recognize.

"Privately," Titus countered.

Aulus considered him, tilting his head. "Fine." He raised a hand and waved at his two guards; the pair obediently moved out of earshot, although they remained alert, watching Titus with suspicion. "Now, speak. Are you a deserter, come to beg a pardon?"

"Not quite, though I know I look it," Titus said, the hint of a smile appearing on his lips; it was entirely possible that he had been registered as such back in Rome after failing to report in after his leave period expired. "I will be direct. The infant your grandfather sent to you. Is he with the missing slave family?"

Titus noted a small flash of alarm rush through the governor, visible in the sudden rigidity of his body and the closed-off expression his face immediately took on. But just as quickly as the alarm manifested, it disappeared. "I don't know what you're speaking of." He made to gesture for his guards to return, but Titus spoke again.

"I know he sent him here, in the arms of his slave. Over a year ago, now. He trusted you. I ask you to trust me now." The words came rushing out, earnest in their blunt rapidity. Titus sought the governor's eyes, and the two men stared at one another.

Aulus's hand stilled in the process of summoning his men, and then he indicated for the guards to again retreat. He took a long moment before he spoke again. "Do you know whose babe that boy is?" His eyes were searching, questioning.

"No." The falsehood came easily enough to Titus, and he spoke it unflinchingly.

The corner of Aulus's mouth lifted. "Liar," he breathed out.

Titus began, almost unthinkingly, to reach for his sword: Aulus knew. He had to. And if he knew, then Julia's son was not—would not ever be—truly safe.

"None of that, now," Aulus hissed at him, seeing where the soldier's hand had drifted, even if only incrementally. "I don't know the identity of the boy. I don't care. Everyone thinks it's my bastard. Let them. I trust my grandfather. He showed me more kindness and attention than anyone else ever has, my own parents included. I have nothing but happy memories of him and his island villa—a refuge in my youth, and one I miss dearly. I would do it all again for him, and more, without question."

Titus sensed that the governor was lying—not about his loyalty to his grandfather, as those words rang resoundingly true, but about his ignorance of the boy's identity. It did not take much intelligence to put together the location of Lucius's island residence and that of Julia's exile. Although the banishment of the emperor's granddaughter was still shrouded in some measure of secrecy—those who had known for certain of her illegitimate pregnancy made an exceedingly small circle—rumors were abundant, and knowledge of her affair with Silanus had spread easily enough.

Still, Titus managed to nod, his hand dropping away from his sword. "Do you know where the slave family fled to?"

Aulus shrugged and shook his head. "Into Dacia, I presume. Well beyond my influence. Didas, the patriarch, came from there, sold into slavery as a youth after his tribe raided into Moesia and was defeated. He is a freedman now, but his family remained enslaved. I imagine that's why he absconded with them."

Titus hesitated to ask his next question, but his resources were growing limited. "Is there anything you can offer, in the way of assistance? I must find them." His heart raced more with each word that crossed his lips; trusting Aulus as much as he had already done was a risk, but one he felt he had to take. He hoped that Lucius was not wrong about his own grandson.

"I have a guide, a Dacian who helps with some trading. They have gold, silver, honey, other such niceties that we Romans always want to get our hands on. I will suggest that you travel with him, from settlement to settlement. You won't get far alone."

Aulus extended his hand then, and the two men clasped arms, a truce—even if a slightly uneasy one—struck between them.

Aulus's Dacian guide had proven to be a necessity; with him, Titus was granted access to settlements and fortresses that might otherwise have killed him on sight. Yet at each westward stop, their questions had turned up no answers, despite the guide's best attempts. Either no one knew anything about the missing slave family, or no one wanted *them* to know.

Over a month had passed, the moon growing and receding in each night's starlit sky. By day, the forests grew thicker and less tame, the wildlife more abundant and dangerously less wary of them. Wolves' howling became more commonplace, as did the sighting of intimidatingly large bear scat. The Dacian guide told Titus to give thanks to his gods that no actual bears crossed their path; they were, he assured the soldier, far more vicious than any animal he would have encountered before, especially if they had their young with them.

They pushed on, the guide acting in his capacity as a trader and making all manner of deals for goods that he intended to collect on his eventual return journey to Tomis: honey, skins, and furs were the bulk of it. It was a system that benefitted both the Romans and the Dacians, even if the people weren't at ease with one another—but, for now, it was enough to keep them from any outright, large-scale violence.

Titus began to give up hope. The guide was starting to speak of turning around, noting that their next stop, Sarmizegetusa, would be his last; if Titus wished to push onwards, he would be on his own. If it came to that, Titus knew he would continue—he would not betray his promise to Julia—but he doubted that he would get very far. He did not speak the Dacian language; he did not know the mountain roads that tied their settlements together. He would likely be killed on sight the further into the wilderness he traveled.

Yet it was too early to resign himself; they were nearing their next destination, and he needed to be alert. The settlement of Sarmizegetusa, the guide told him, was the unifying capital of a land segmented by smaller tribal kingdoms; in his mind, Titus had envisioned it to be grand city, something more reminiscent of Rome, or of Byzantium, with cobbled streets, public structures, assorted statuary in honor of notable ancestors and famed Dacian heroes. Instead, it was little more than a very large fort, its walls containing a combination of wooden and stone structures cast about, with little resemblance to the city planning Romans favored.

Nevertheless, as they passed through the gates, Titus scanned the buildings and the people with the same sharp attention he had maintained for the duration of their journey, thankful that his appearance was now not catching quite so much attention, due to the clothing and scythe-like Dacian sword he had acquired along the way. Even his beard had grown out, his once smooth-shaven cheeks covered by a dark growth in the Dacian style. He could not fully pass as one of them, but he did not stand out so much, either.

As he examined the city, his eyes fell upon a woman with a young child on each hip, watching the newcomers' arrival with the usual wariness that greeted them at each settlement. Titus could not explain it, but he knew, at that very moment, that he had at last found Julia's son. He leapt off the horse he rode, not even bothering to fling its reins to his companion, and rushed towards the woman, his eyes fixed on the little boy whose dark, alarmed eyes now stared up at him in perfect mimicry of his exiled mother. Titus nearly wept, falling to his knees.

Suddenly, Titus was shoved roughly back, and he fell to the ground, looking up at a man who hovered over him, shouting angrily in his Dacian dialect.

"I mean no harm," Titus said, raising his hands in what he hoped was a gesture of appeasement. Aulus's guide was already approaching, leading both horses, his face wary.

The man standing over Titus frowned, but he stopped yelling. "Then why approach my woman?" He spoke in Latin, and Titus felt himself relax ever so slightly, even though the words were still accusatory.

"He is my son," Titus blurted out, his eyes fixed on the child. It was a lie he had not had the forethought to plan, but one that he now sensed might be the only way he could stay by the child's side—and one that, even as it crossed his lips, felt oddly right.

The woman and her husband both stared down at Titus in surprise, then spoke a few terse words to one another, reverting to their language.

"Are you Didas and Galla?" Titus asked them, and they stopped speaking, looking at him again, uncertainty writ across their faces.

The man nodded, although his lips were pressed together in a thin, unhappy line. "Come with me," he snapped, turning on his heel and walking away. Titus struggled to his feet and followed.

An uneasy and tentative truce had been quickly brokered between Titus,

Galla, and Didas. The freedman and his wife had bonded with the child, loving him as if he were their own; yet Didas seemed to maintain a strong sense of honor that compelled an apparent obligation to at least consider the issue at hand, namely that of the infant's parentage and rightful caretaker. And so, he had granted Titus permission to stay with them in Sarmizegetusa for a short period of time, while matters regarding the boy could be settled.

Titus's hand now hovered above the ratty scrap of a scroll he had acquired, his mind racing as he thought of all he wanted—needed—to say to Julia: that he missed her; that he still loved her; that he feared for her life, every day; that he constantly dreamed of returning to her; that he plotted different ways to free her, knowing that his plans were all improbable at best and bound to result in a bloody, painful death sentence at worst.

In the end, he wrote only a few words, quickly scrawled by a trembling hand: *He, now found, is safe with me.* He did not sign it; he did not identify the child. Nor did he elaborate on where they were, or what it had taken to come this far. As to a plan for the future: he had none.

The first part of his promise to Julia had been fulfilled: to find her son. Now, he had to fulfill the years-long promise of protecting the boy, a lifetime commitment that he had been quick to make and, now, remained steadfast in his resolution to undertake. He hoped she knew that he would keep his promise; he hoped she would understand why he couldn't write more in his letter, even though his heart screamed at him in anguish for its suppression, his denial of all that it wanted to say. It was the way it had to be, for the safety of them all.

Titus's eyes flicked to the two young children in the corner, being carefully watched by Galla as they played together on the ground. Her eyes met his, still uncertain and suspicious, just as they had been from the moment he had arrived. It would take time for her to believe that he was not the enemy. He could wait.

"Done?" Didas appeared in the open doorway, glancing at the scroll in front of Titus.

The soldier nodded, rolling and then sealing his short letter. He passed it to the freedman, who had quickly, it seemed, become a man of some standing amongst his own people—or perhaps who simply had returned to what his life would have been, had the Romans not altered its course by enslaving him as a youth. "Make certain—" Titus started.

Didas cut him off. "I am no longer a slave, nor even a servant, least of all to you. Do not bother to issue orders. Your scroll will reach Aulus, and he will be asked to send it on to his grandfather, as you said before."

Titus nodded, silent, and Didas slipped away, passing the scroll to a young man lingering just outside the small stone building. Then, it was out of sight, beyond his control. Titus had to hope that he could trust the Dacians into whose community he had so suddenly appeared and, for now, sought to join.

Titus let the recently dispatched scroll slip from his mind. He needed to shift his attention to the boy—to where he might take him, how he might raise him. He felt foolish for not having thought so far ahead, but he had been fixated on simply finding the child, something that had not seemed truly possible until he had actually done it.

He knew that Didas and Galla wondered how it happened that Aulus, a Roman governor, would have bothered to protect the son of the disheveled soldier now in their home; they did not believe his claim to parentage, he knew, not entirely. They were not fools. A sense of unease stirred within him; Aulus's Dacian guide would not remain with him much longer, and he soon would be a lone Roman deep in unknown, hostile territory. He would not be of much use to Julia's son if he found himself dead.

I smoothed my hands over my dress, surprised at the still calmness that had settled throughout my body. Aunt Agrippina and Amynta both bustled about, chattering with excitement, but I barely heard them. Today was my wedding day—a day my aunt had long awaited.

"Jupiter's high priest will attend," Aunt Agrippina was saying for yet another time, pleased that the occasion would be honored thus—and it *was* an honor, a public indication that I was not so completely forgotten, so entirely pushed to the side, that my marriage would pass by wholly uncelebrated within the upper echelons of Roman society.

What Aunt Agrippina did not speak aloud was that Augustus himself wasn't attending my wedding; instead, he had chosen to send a substitute for his role as *pontifex maximus*, chief priest of Rome. The emperor's absence was notable, a silent signal that my family—his family, although he tried to distance himself from those of us whom he felt shamed it—did, in fact, remain in disgrace. But I did not mind; I had no desire to see my great-grandfather, the man who had ripped my mother from me, any more than was absolutely necessary. Thankfully, those occasions were few and far between, despite my direct descendance from him; he had little use for a girl-child who stemmed from a lineage of whores.

I was now in my seventeenth year. Five years had passed since my mother had been exiled. Five years since I had spoken with her, watched her dress for an evening dinner party, listened to her tinkling laugh resound throughout the halls of our old home. And now, instead of my mother knotting the traditional marriage belt around my waist, it was Aunt Agrippina crouching in front of me, fulfilling the custom that had been meant for another.

"Do you still miss her?" I asked softly, watching as my aunt's fingers deftly formed the complicated loops that would, eventually, result in the so-called Herculean knot, to remain in place until untied by my soon-to-be husband that very evening. I did not have to name my mother: there was no one else about whom I would bother to ask such a question.

Aunt Agrippina's fingers stilled for a moment, but then continued on. She glanced to the side, to see if Amynta was present—but she was not, having rushed out of the room to find my misplaced yellow veil, the finishing touch to my ensemble. As my aunt finished the knot, firmly tightening it in place, she stood, eyes nearly level with my own. I now stood a finger length taller than her.

"Yes," she said, as if she was ashamed to admit it. "I write to her, every year. You know that. You could, too, if you wanted." I was perhaps the only person to whom my aunt would admit that she still had some contact with my mother, however limited; with anyone else, Aunt Agrippina acted as if her sister were long dead, forgotten.

I shook my head. It wasn't that I did not want to write to my mother—but Decimus remained steadfast in his recommendation against it. Better, he had told me, that Augustus, Livia, and Tiberius all thought I was angry with her, disconnected, without any remnants of filial loyalty. It was better for my own future, he told me, and better, too, for my mother's and even my uncle's. Yet five years had passed, and Decimus did not seem to be any closer to restoring my family to Rome—to me—despite his promises to the contrary. And I was beginning to lose patience.

Amynta returned then, smiling widely as she brought the yellow veil into the room. Aunt Agrippina took it from her and carefully settled it on my head, arranging the pins herself so that the sheer fabric would drape properly across my hair and, when the time came, over my face.

"There," she said as she stepped back, the single word seeming to cement the reality of my imminent marriage. She smiled at me, as did Amynta, and I forced my lips to curve upwards in an expression that I hoped mirrored their own. But, inside, I felt nothing.

I tried to stand still as the man—my husband, I reminded myself—fumbled with the knotted belt at my waist. The traditional spelt cake from our wedding sat heavy in my stomach, never mind that I had barely managed a single mouthful of it, and my heart thudded over and over again in my chest until it ached. My fingers fumbled uselessly at my sides, meekly grasping the fabric of my dress.

He crouched a bit lower in front of me, and I let my eyes run over the top of his head, which was full haired and, for a Roman, surprisingly blond. Marcus Junius Silanus Torquatus. My husband. But he was more than that, so much more.

Torquatus was, I had quickly learned, a cousin to my mother's former lover—the one who, half a decade ago, had impregnated her. The one who had caused her exile. The one who had, in almost every way that mattered, left me as an orphan. And he had simply been allowed to leave Rome, to live comfortably beyond the city limits—half-heartedly banished, but not truly punished. Not as my mother had been, and was still being, confined to a distant island even years later.

When my match had been announced, and I had learned the name of the man to whom I was to be joined, I did not ask how closely the two cousins had known each other, and no one bothered to enlighten me. I did not ask if they exchanged letters, or if they were on friendly terms. I was not certain I wanted to know; I was not certain if I could bear it. Even now I had to remind myself that Torquatus was not his cousin; he was not at fault for his heritage, or for the shame that had enveloped my family. And I was not my mother; I would not make the same mistakes she had.

Torquatus was at last making some measure of progress with the knot, loosening the belt around my waist. He looked up at me for a brief moment, pausing in his work, and smiled softly. I could not make myself return the expression, but he didn't seem to notice, having already dipped his head back down to return his attention to the knot. My hands clenched my dress more tightly, and I closed my eyes, thankful for the strong wine I had readily gulped down not long before he entered the room. It was, at last, starting to take effect, to provide some measure of blessed numbness—a relief I had not truly been aware, before, that the drink could provide. It was a dangerous revelation to make note of.

He is a good man, I silently told myself then, repeating the very same words my aunt had confidently uttered to me in reassurance about my husband. But I could not know if such words were true or not; at the moment, they seemed unsatisfyingly hollow, an as of yet unfulfilled promise. Nevertheless, those words were all I had.

The belt was undone at last, and it fell away from my waist to hit the floor with a quiet thump. Torquatus stood back to his full height in front of me, and his hands were soon gently pulling at the top of my dress. I stood still, remaining quiet, obedient: the perfect Roman wife.

His lips pressed against mine then, insistent. I parted my mouth, my thoughts racing. His tongue touched mine, warm and wet; where it was active, mine remained passive, limp in my mouth, uncertain how to respond to his movements. His breath, like my own, tasted strongly of wine—although he seemed to be holding his drink better, standing steady and strong while I had begun to wobble.

Torquatus was ten years my senior, an age difference that was not so very great; I had been told I was lucky, fortunate that I would not be yoked to a man in his sixth or even seventh decade as some young women of my age and station were. We were each other's first spouse, too—but whereas he would be the first man I would lie with, I could already tell he must have experienced a woman's touch many times before.

My dress soon joined the belt on the floor, and Torquatus led me to the bed, fingers clasped loosely around my wrist as he guided me onto the mattress. He was not forceful; he was not rough. Yet despite his gentle—even caressing—touch, I knew there was no other choice open to me than what was about to happen. It was my fate, a fate that I thought, at the time, all women must share: submission. It could happen willingly, or with resistance, but it remained inevitable.

I stared at the ceiling, which swam ever so slightly, the wine thudding dully in my head now, and allowed my legs to fall apart as his body found its way on top of mine, pressing down heavily as his breathing quickened. I closed my eyes as he entered me, biting my lip so that I didn't cry out at the sudden jolt of pain that seized my body. The entire thing lasted an indeterminable amount of time; in some ways, I felt that it lasted an eternity, his body rocking back and forth on top of mine as he grunted every so often, yet it also seemed to be over almost as soon as it had begun, his body spasming before he suddenly went very still, then rolled off of me with a sigh. He began to snore even before I opened my eyes, feeling a wetness trickle out from between my legs.

Torquatus was gone the next morning when I woke up, and I was instead greeted by Amynta's smiling face. I could tell she was eager to ask how my wedding night had gone. I would choose to let her remain eager.

"Water," I ordered, and she quickly filled a cup for me. I drained it, and she refilled it, her face expectant as she continued to watch me. This time I drank more slowly. My head ached from the wine the night before.

"How was it, *domincella*?" she finally asked, voice hushed. She could not bear it any longer, even though she knew it was not her place to ask.

I ignored the question, instead asking my own. "Are there pancakes?"

Amynta fought a frustrated sigh, disappointed at my deflection. "Yes. I'll have some made fresh and bring them in." She disappeared from the room, and for the first time I was able to examine my new surroundings—my new home, I reminded myself—in the light of day.

What few personal belongings I had would be brought over that morning, Aunt Agrippina had assured me. She herself was preparing to soon leave Rome—as early as next year—dragging along my little cousins Nero Caesar, Drusus Caesar, and Gaius, her youngest, to join Germanicus in Germania and Gaul, of which he had recently been named proconsul. The physical unity of her family was something she had long desired, and I forced myself to be happy for her—even if it meant that she was leaving me behind in Rome. Abandoned, again.

My hand reached up to grasp the *lunula* around my neck, only to meet with bare skin; my girlhood pendant had been left behind, as was proper. I let my hand fall back to my lap, fingers twitching uncertainly as they grabbed for nothing but air.

Amynta returned with my breakfast, familiarly perching on the edge of the bed as I began to eat. Once again, her face was expectant, eyes searching as she examined me.

"Rufus and I used to meet at night, where the slaves brought in shipments and deliveries at your aunt's house," she confided suddenly, blushing. The hint of an embarrassed smile tugged at her lips.

"How nice," I said dryly. I knew that she was hoping to prompt me to share the details of my first night with Torquatus, but I was not any more obliging than I had been only moments earlier. I took another bite of pancake.

Amynta sighed again. "It can be very… nice."

I did not answer, my eyes fixed on the food in front of me. I did not know how to describe the intimacy that Torquatus and I had shared the night before, and I wondered if intimacy was even the correct word to use. It had obviously been physically intimate—but I had felt nothing throughout it, certainly not the sense of excitement that Amynta seemed to exude when speaking about sex. It had happened, it was over, and I knew it would happen again, and again and again, at least until I produced the expected male heir. I could not know if I would ever consider the act to be pleasurable—for me, anyway. I thanked the gods that I had had the presence of mind to imbibe as much wine as I had beforehand.

"You aren't supposed to let an outsider have access to our

household," I said suddenly. "You shouldn't have met with Rufus where you did." The hint of a smile on Amynta's lips faded entirely, and she averted her eyes. Still I continued to scold her. "You will do no such thing here, in my new household. You will not see Rufus anymore. At all."

Amynta stood from the bed then, head lowered. I saw how her chin quivered, but I ignored it, instead taking another forceful bite of my pancake, unnecessarily grinding the already-soft food between my teeth.

"*Domincella*," she began. The word was barely more than a whisper, but it carried with it a mass of rippling emotion.

"Stop calling me that! I am no longer a child," I hissed at her. "Go away!" I flung the breakfast tray to the floor. Amynta fled, the noise of the crash seeming to chase after her even long after it had faded.

My rage surprised me. It had welled up as if from nowhere, a sudden wave that burst out of me before I had even thought to try to contain it—before I even recognized that it had been there at all. I knew I did not mean the words I had spoken; I had not wanted to hurt Amynta, even if I knew that her relationship with Rufus was based on a lie. I could not bear to tell her the truth of it, instead hoping that, somehow, she might end things herself with the red-haired man whom I had soon come to understand sought her out only to survey me. But if she was content with him, was that happiness—even if built upon dishonesty—truly so bad?

I curled my legs up in front of me, bringing my knees to my chest, only then realizing that I was still naked. My body looked the same after my wedding night, despite my arrival at the destination that was womanhood: nothing had changed, at least outwardly. Resting my chin on a pale kneecap, I closed my eyes, filling my lungs as deeply and slowly as I was able. My heart continued to thud in my chest, so strongly that I could feel it throughout my body, as if it were trying to free itself.

Torquatus is a good man, I repeated to myself. I hoped the words would prove true. I hoped that Torquatus simply being *good* was enough for me, that I could be content with him and with the course in life that the gods had set before me. I refused to think of what might happen if my hopes were unfulfilled. I could not afford to follow my mother's path.

CHAPTER XII

RUFUS

Rufus observed Aemilia's wedding ceremony impassively, stationed obediently behind Decimus in his role as constant shadow: ever present, yet simultaneously near-invisible, ignored; important for his brute, base purpose, yet insignificant—disposable, even—for this very same reason. In front of them, the couple were exchanging their ritual vows, words repeated at all Roman marriages regardless of the betrotheds' class. That much, Rufus knew. Otherwise, the ceremony was far more grandiose than any other he had attended or even passed by.

"Where you are Gaius, I am Gaia," Aemilia said. Her voice was subdued, but she did not waver, the phrase flowing steadily from her mouth. Marcus Junius Silanus Torquatus, her imminent husband, then repeated the words, inverting the gendered names.

Over the past four years, Rufus had watched Aemilia grow from a child into a woman, first from afar and then, after that day in the market, when Decimus had admitted her ever so slightly into his confidence, from much nearer. She never trusted Rufus entirely, despite Decimus's past and continued urging for her to do so—but Rufus did not blame her. As time went on, he found that he didn't *want* her to trust him; it was better that way, both for her and for him. If she told him something—if she feared or desired something—he would be bound to report it to his master, so that Decimus could find some way to use that information to his own advantage. But, somehow, in the past few years, Rufus had started to feel an inclination to shield Aemilia from Decimus, from the plots that the senator incessantly spun and twined throughout the city and its occupants, the bloodshed that always seemed to loom.

Yet despite this, Aemilia and Rufus were not anything close to friends; in fact, they were rarely even particularly pleasant to one another. She did not know of the small, strange place she had taken up inside his mind, and Rufus did not enlighten her—what purpose could it serve? Sharing thoughts, feelings—it was a waste of time and energy and, worse, it was a source of danger. He felt pity for her, if he had to put a word to it, for she was, in many ways, alone—like him. Her family's fate had affected both their lives—though she would never know the extent of his role in all of it—and he could not help but wonder if she, too, carried some measure of madness inside of her, one that constantly struggled to emerge, just as his own did.

Rufus had continued to see Amynta, flirting with her, speaking to her, fucking her. She—the willingly blind, naïve thing that she was—still did not grasp it, but it was all to keep an eye on her mistress, to make sure that, when Decimus needed Aemilia, she would be ready to respond. And so Rufus tread a careful path, somewhere between fully performing the duty his master had tasked him with and simultaneously trying to minimize Aemilia's potential involvement in whatever treachery Decimus had in store. It was not easy, and he was not truly certain why he did it, other than the strange sort of kinship he imagined that he and Aemilia shared.

He sought out Leander that night, as he often did when he felt unsure, conflicted. He had become dependent on him—the only nights he slept soundly were those spent by Leander's side, and so he spent as many evenings as he could at the brothel, the sounds of drink and sex drowning out the noise of the island's waves, Leander's bright face keeping Agrippa's mad gaze from his mind.

When Rufus arrived, the gatekeeping eunuch took his money gladly, waving him through with little more than the usual cursory glance; Rufus was a common entity at the establishment.

"Rufus," Leander greeted him with a slow smile. The younger, blond-haired man was sprawled already half-naked across the bed, his smooth, tanned skin glinting in the lamplight. He rubbed the space next to him, a silent invitation.

Rufus sank onto the bed, fully clothed, and Leander tentatively stroked his clean-shaven cheek. "Difficult day?" he asked softly, blue eyes searching. Rufus only nodded.

A dog barked outside several times, and the men laid together in comfortable silence, the linen bed sheets soft and clean, folded carefully. Rufus could almost imagine that he and Leander were at home together, not in the middle of a brothel.

"I will free you, one day," Rufus announced. He had said it many times before, and he did mean it, no matter how much or how little drink he had in him when he made the pronouncement. But Leander—young, beautiful, and popular in his trade—had a steep price for his manumission.

"I know you will," Leander said. He smiled then, but it was a wistful expression, one that Rufus did not see before Leander leaned over and kissed the soldier, his lips lingering until both their unhappy moods were past.

Decimus was exceptionally jovial that winter, always a sign that one of his many plans was about to come to fruition; he seemed as if he were a young man again, moving with a new rapidity, the heavy folds of his toga, normally so cumbersome, now not appearing to weigh him down at all. He did not always deign to share details of his intrigues with Rufus, but whatever had happened this time was apparently such cause for excitement that he could not restrain himself.

"Your former charge," Decimus confided to Rufus as they strolled the forum, "may soon find himself departing that cursed island."

Rufus slowed his steps for the briefest of moments, surprised. Decimus was referring to Agrippa Postumus. "But—" he started, before catching himself. It was not his place to question; it was not his place to have an opinion.

"But he's absolutely mad?" Decimus asked, completing Rufus's unfinished interjection. Laughter tinged his voice. "No matter. So long as he convinces his grandfather of his soundness of mind in the spring, that is all we need. Augustus is growing old, and he still yearns desperately for a blood descendant to follow in his footsteps, no matter how much he grooms and primps Tiberius and Germanicus. It should not take much for Agrippa to win him back over."

Rufus followed along, hearing the senator's unspoken words within his own mind: it was no matter that Agrippa Postumus was mad, because if he was restored, Decimus would make sure that all else would be taken care of. The youth would only ever be emperor in name, if all went according to plan—but even that would require significant restructuring in Augustus's succession designs. No doubt Decimus had a plan for that, too.

The soldier shook his head, an almost imperceptible gesture that Decimus did not notice, too distracted by the triumph he believed to be forthcoming. But Rufus knew that Agrippa would not be restored, not once Augustus laid eyes on him. He had already been past hope five years ago, declining daily; it would be a wonder if the emperor's grandson could still feed or clothe himself, let alone convince anyone of his sound mental state. If he had been mad before, he would only be more so now.

"Do make mention to Aemilia," Decimus ordered. "Not in too much detail, of course. But she's married now, an adult woman at last. Pity we couldn't secure the match I had in mind for her husband, but no matter… It's time we build her trust further, let her start to become involved now that she has some measure of independence."

"Involved?" Rufus asked.

Decimus paused, examining his foot as distaste colored his face. He had stepped in some sort of muck. "Clean it off," he called to one of his attendants. The slave came hurrying over, immediately falling to his knees to clean his master's shoe.

The senator waited until his shoe was clean, then indicated that the slave should return to his place a short distance away. "Yes," he said to Rufus. "Involved. Give her hope that her uncle may return. By implication, her mother soon to follow, although we have little use for her. And in the meantime, ascertain with the slave woman of hers that you've been carrying on with that young Aemilia is not taking any measures to prevent herself from falling with child. The sooner she produces a son, the sooner I may consider how to use him." The words were spoken casually, as if Aemilia were little more than a broodmare—

and to Decimus, that's likely all she was.

"She will want to know how she may contribute," Rufus said. And it was true; Aemilia was always eager to be given some action, some task that she thought might help her family. Decimus did not often oblige. "She has grown frustrated, of late. Her slave woman sees it too."

Decimus sighed, irritated, and then began to walk again. "I will set a test for her, then. If she desires to be of use to me, instruct her to put a drop of hemlock mixture in her new husband's food or drink. It won't kill him—we needn't be that drastic—but it will make him sick enough that everyone in Rome will hear about it." The senator waved an attending slave over to him, whispered in his ear, and then motioned for him to depart; the man hurried away, quickly disappearing from sight. "That slave will see that he brings a vial to you soonest. Take it to Aemilia today."

Rufus swallowed, nodding. He already regretted that he had spoken; now, he was bound to convey Decimus's instructions to Aemilia, and he feared what she might do. "What will this prove, if she will even do such a thing? You risk both our necks."

Decimus regarded him with narrowed eyes. "I hope you do not suggest that *my* neck is at risk, dear Rufus."

"Of course not, sir," Rufus quickly said. "If she betrays us—betrays me—I will uphold your innocence until death."

Decimus nodded. "Good. As to your question… this will prove that she is with us, and will remain with us, whether she changes her mind or not some months or years from now. Naturally, I will keep evidence of her involvement on hand, should she prove contrary later on."

"But if she will not do it?" Rufus pressed. He was taken aback by his own boldness, but he could not keep himself from speaking. He wanted to believe that the young woman he had come to know—even if distantly—would not be willing to risk her new husband's health—his life, even—for nothing but a mere test of loyalty to his master.

Decimus smiled at him, seemingly unannoyed by the question. "I believe you will find yourself surprised, Rufus. You claim to know Aemilia well… but I do not think you truly understand her, nor the lengths to which she will go for those she loves."

CHAPTER XIII

AEMILIA LEPIDA

I rolled the small glass vial back and forth between my fingers. Only a drop, Rufus had told me, no more than that.

The soldier had been especially cold the last time I'd seen him, even more hulkingly brutish than usual as he stalked up to me and practically growled out the message from Decimus, glancing around to make sure that there were no nearby slaves who might overhear. He had left Amynta behind in whatever storeroom they had commandeered for their most recent tryst; although I had at one point forbidden her from seeing him again, my orders had gone unheeded, and I had neither the energy nor the heart to punish my nursemaid for her disobedience. Instead, I simply looked the other way, trying not to think too deeply about their relationship, built upon a lie that Amynta was only too happy to believe, convinced that she had found love. I shook my head to clear it; my time alone with Rufus was short, as I knew Amynta would not take long to dress and return obediently to my side.

"Why?" I had asked him, eyeing the vial he held in the palm of his outstretched hand, roughened by callouses. "What purpose could this possibly serve?"

Rufus had closed his eyes briefly, his face strained. When he looked at me again, his tone was flat, as if he were simply rehearsing a string of words he had memorized. "Because Decimus commands it. Because he promises that change is coming, that Rome will be different. Come next summer, he says that you may find your uncle and mother restored to you. So, he wants you to prove your... loyalty. He wants to know that you are dependable, before he puts these plans into motion. There is great risk to him—and so you must share in that risk. Consider it a guarantee."

I could tell he didn't believe his own words, but his expression suggested he would speak no more of it. He gestured towards the vial with a jut of his chin, the glass glinting in his palm.

I stared at it. I barely saw my new husband, and what little time we spent together seemed to be mostly focused on planting his seed in my belly. I didn't yet know him well enough to either love or hate him, let alone to harm him. It was a significant risk to me, with the promise of a reward uncertain. But if such an action showed Decimus that I was dedicated to his cause, if it at last contributed, somehow, to the restoration of my family, then there was no question. I would do it. I *must* do it.

I slowly reached out and closed my fingers around the vial, and then Rufus turned on his heel and disappeared. When Amynta appeared a few moments later, her cheeks still red and her hair mussed, I had already closed my fingers around the container and hidden my hand in the folds of my dress. My slave was none the wiser.

My husband had remained in bed, ill, for two full days. At first there had been convulsions, an incessant gasping for air; now, he remained mostly immobile, quiet and still, his breath shallow and rasping. The stench of sweat and piss clung to the air, and I felt suffocated, as if I could not escape it—the smell of death. The slaves averted their eyes from him—from me, too—whispering behind door hangings that he was not long for this world. The doctors were at a loss as to what was wrong with him; no one seemed to suspect poison. But I knew. I had done it with my own hands, quietly and quickly allowing a drop of the vial's liquid to splash into the honey water I brought to him myself. Torquatus had smiled at me, pleasantly surprised by my wifely devotion, laughing that we had slaves for such menial tasks. And then he had taken a sip, and I slipped away, wanting to be far from him when he experienced the first effects of the tainted drink.

"Husband," I whispered to him now. I didn't know why I bothered to keep my voice so low; I doubt he would have noticed even if I had been shouting into his ear. "You must drink some water."

I brought a cup to his chapped lips and helped him drink, one hand placed gently behind his head. The irony of the act was not lost on me: first I had knowingly placed poison-laced water on his tongue, willfully seeking to cause him harm, and now I desperately urged health back into his body by the very same means. After a few sips, he fell back, seemingly returning to his comatose state, and I removed my hand from behind his head. His eyes hadn't opened at all.

I had only used a drop, just as Rufus had said—a single drop, enough to make him mildly sick, I was told, but not to kill him. Not to render him like this. Had I somehow entirely misjudged the dosage, letting more than that lone droplet make its way into his cup? Was he particularly susceptible to whatever mixture that loathsome little vial had contained? Had the noxious concoction been brewed stronger than intended? A quiet whisper in the back of my mind proposed something darker: that Decimus wished my husband dead, and that I had been lied to.

As I stared at my sleeping husband, I brushed a hand across my belly. I wasn't certain, not yet—but I believed I already carried Torquatus's child within me, his seed having quickly taken root. We had certainly lain together enough times since our wedding.

"*Domincella*," Amynta whispered, gently taking my hand. I hadn't even realized she was in the room. She tried to encourage me to stand from the bed, her thumb stroking the back of my hand, her warm skin a stark contrast to my pale, cool flesh. "You must bathe. Eat. Rest."

Amynta's eyes, much like my own, were red-rimmed; her voice was hoarse. She did not speak the fourth suggestion I knew must be hovering on her tongue: that I must stop drinking so much wine. I had turned more and more to the drink, seeking the pleasant numbness it could bestow—after a great enough quantity was imbibed—allowing me to sink into a state of uncaring bliss, my mind far from the ills I had brought upon myself. But Amynta couldn't understand, couldn't truly share in my sadness, let alone my guilt. She did not know what I had done, and she never could know. No one could, or I would be ruined.

It was then that I belatedly understood, in full, Decimus's purpose in requesting this covert violence from me: we were inextricably bound together now, he and I, in our wily, deceptive ways, whether Torquatus lived or died—to Decimus, I am sure it mattered little. Decimus knew what I had done, and I realized far too late that he would have made certain there was some damning evidence of it on hand—or perhaps his word against mine, if needed, would be enough. After all, he was a well-respected senator with means, connections, influence; I was only the mostly forgotten daughter of a disgraced exile and an executed traitor, desperate to restore the tattered remnants of her family, even if it meant destroying her new household in the process.

Simultaneously I felt the crushing burden of my culpability and the strange, exciting promise of what was still to come. I should have been frightened of what Decimus could do to me, now—but, foolishly, I wasn't. Instead, I experienced a surge of anticipation for the future even as I relished the fulfillment that came with action, with accomplishing something, no matter how nefarious, through my own deeds—something I had never felt before. I had always been a bystander, a passive observer even to my own life. And so it wasn't Decimus and his knowledge of the whole foul situation that frightened me—no, it was this newfound sense of satisfaction welling within me, as it had only been reached through harming my own husband. Was that, then, the price of my liberation? The cost of beginning to claim my life for myself? I did not want to dwell on it—such thoughts were dangerous. I had only to look to my mother as a constant reminder that a woman's life was not ever—could not ever be—her own.

I shook my head, as much to clear it of this rush of feelings as to tell Amynta that I did not want to leave Torquatus. My eyes focused on him as he ever so slowly breathed in, then out, but Amynta squeezed my hand again, gently tugging. This time I allowed her to lead me away. I told myself that, whatever happened to my husband, everything would be fine. Decimus would make sure of it; he had to, bound together as we now were. After all, I had done this for him. There was no going back, not now. I had cast my die.

It was on the fifth day that Torquatus managed to open his eyes when I brought water to his lips, an act that had become a ritual to me—penance, perhaps. After he swallowed, he tried to speak, but no words emerged.

"Yes?" I leaned closer, holding my own breath so that I might hear him better.

"You… stayed… with me," Torquatus rasped out; his hand searched for mine, fingers weakly clasping my own. I nodded, squeezing his hand, and then he was asleep again. This time, his breath came evenly, regularly.

I closed my eyes and exhaled a sigh of relief. Torquatus was going to live; I had not killed him after all. Then another thought wormed its way to the surface of my mind: what if he remembered the honey water I had brought him? What if he remembered that his sudden illness came immediately after he consumed the beverage?

The coming days proved that I needn't have worried; Torquatus seemed to have no memory of the day leading up to his collapse. Instead, a new version of my husband surfaced, one who remembered and appeared to value my time by his side during his mysterious and severe illness. I read to him daily as he regained his strength, mostly poetry and his correspondence—so long as it wasn't too political or business-like, things that were improper for a woman to involve herself in—and we talked, getting to know one another. I started to believe that my aunt's words about Torquatus—that he was a good man—might in fact be true, and, in a short time, it was almost as if the poisoning had never happened. Almost.

The next time I saw Rufus, his brown eyes were sad. They sought mine out as he approached me in the hall. "Now you are bound to Decimus," he said without preamble. "You are his creature, just as I am. He's pleased with you." The last words were bitter.

"I'm no one's creature," I snapped at him, "and I'm nothing like you." I did not like the reminder of what I had done; already I had pushed the memory of it far down inside of me, to the recesses of my mind—

and even further than that I had buried that dangerous sense of gratification I had gotten from my decision to act, to claim my life for myself.

Rufus smiled thinly at me before he spoke again. "Your grandfather Augustus will visit your uncle in the spring. Decimus has managed to convince him to consider the restoration of Agrippa Postumus. Perhaps your mother will find that Fortuna may favor her, as well." He did not wait for me to respond before he departed.

Finally Decimus had begun to deliver on what he had promised me, years ago: that he would help return my family to me. I closed my eyes and exhaled.

14 CE

CHAPTER XIV

TITUS

It was only late autumn, but snow already tinged the mountain peaks around them, and, everywhere Titus looked, the Dacians of Sarmizegetusa were busy making their winter preparations: women were putting finishing touches on thick woolen tunics and fur mantles for their families and ensuring that their food stores were organized; the men were bringing in as much game as they could, drying the meat for later consumption and setting aside the pelts. Travel between settlements would soon become more difficult and, eventually, nearly impossible in the depths of the harsh winter snow, a time when most chose to simply remain tucked inside their homes with their families. Winter was the season to share wisdom, to teach the skills of sewing and carving and cooking, to tell stories both historic and fantastical, the latter helped along in their believability by flickering shadows, cast by the flames of warm hearths.

Duras and Scorilo, whispering and giggling together, rounded the corner, the former boy holding a small basket filled with eggs; it was their new daily task to tend to their family's chickens, and they took the assignment seriously. The two were inseparable, brothers through and through, regardless of the fact that there was no lineage shared between them.

Although it had been nearly four years since Titus had found Julia's son, his heart still felt as if it stopped each time he caught sight of Duras—the eyes, the features of his face: everything about the child recalled his mother, a potent, wrenching reminder of the woman Titus had loved and then lost, all within a year.

He still had not told the boy of his heritage. He had only seen six summers, Titus reasoned; he simply could not understand the entirety of it, not yet. But part of Titus—a part that seemed to grow in size each passing day—began to feel that perhaps it was for the best that the boy never learned who his mother was; better that he not be poisoned by the bloodthirsty taint of Rome, even from afar. After all, it was Rome that had cast his mother out, Rome that had wanted the child killed—and still would seek his death, if anyone there ever found out the truth of his identity. The child would be a threat for as long as he lived.

Nor did Titus call the boy by the name Julia had decided upon—Titus, after him, the man she had, in a way, ultimately selected as her son's father, a relationship that was chosen freely, not one that stemmed from blood. No, Duras would have his own identity, one beyond his heritage, beyond the confines of Titus's own background and Julia's fate; the child at least deserved that.

"Are you going to work or sit idle all day?" Didas asked gruffly, snapping the soldier out of his reverie.

"Sorry," Titus answered, employing the Dacian's native tongue. The foreign words still felt strange on his lips, even after years of practice and daily use. In truth, he barely spoke Latin much at all anymore; Didas and Galla would revert to it if the soldier didn't understand something, and he was teaching the language to Duras—and Scorilo, too—but typically he lived and spoke as if he were a true Dacian—not that they would ever regard him as one of them. These days, he was a man without a land of his own. Rome would not take him back, and Dacia would not fully accept him.

Didas only grunted in response to the soldier's apology and resumed gutting the deer carcass strung up in front of him. Titus hefted the axe in his hands and swung, cleanly chopping the small log he had set before being distracted; he quickly set and chopped another, then glanced over at Didas.

Years ago, Titus had been prepared to spin a tale to explain away everything—the boy's placement with the Moesian governor, who had then left him with Ovid; his desperate search for the child; the identity of the boy's mother; why he had not swept Duras away with him to Rome, his homeland, even now. He had been prepared to shed blood for the boy, too, if it had come to that. Yet none of it had been necessary; the freedman and his wife had never asked Titus too many questions after his sudden arrival and abrupt proclamation that he was the father of Duras.

"Galla and I have always loved the boy as if he were our own," Didas had told him, "but we see how your love for him is different, more…" He had trailed off, shrugging. "It is enough, whatever your claim on him is." Didas did not speak aloud the words that Titus knew lurked behind his dark eyes: that he knew the claim was likely not paternal; that not just any bastard boy would bring an elite Roman soldier in search; that the Moesian governor would not have taken such pains for a child of no account.

Nevertheless, those were perhaps the deepest, most meaningful words ever shared between the two men—all the more so because since then they had maintained a distant, superficial relationship, despite the fact that Titus had become something of a boarder with Didas and his wife, contributing to the household as he could and raising the children together as siblings. Each spring he considered leaving with Duras, and each spring he reminded himself that there was nowhere for them to go. Dacia was as good a place as any to spend their lives, safely removed from Rome and its intrigues.

Titus set and swung at a new log, cleanly slicing it in half. As he stooped to grab another, a hurrying messenger caught his eye.

"Didas," the man called out breathlessly as he approached.

Didas continued his work on the deer carcass, not even sparing the messenger a glance. "What is it?" he asked. A bloody organ slipped from the deer's body as Didas's hands moved within.

"News from Rome that King Comosicus will want to hear."

Didas slowly pulled his hands from the deer and wiped them on his chest, eyeing the messenger. Titus stood quietly to the side, the axe clutched firmly in his hands, his attention having been piqued as soon as Rome was mentioned.

"My brother is unwell, as you know," Didas said. "Which is why, I assume, you have come to me." He finished wiping his hands on his chest, leaving streaks of blood; his fingertips, although no longer dripping wet, were still stained a vivid red.

The messenger shifted his weight from foot to foot but did not respond: his silence was an admission of the truth behind Didas's words. Titus had learned soon after his arrival in Sarmizegetusa that Didas was not just a common Dacian man: he was the younger half-brother to a Dacian king who had, in his youth, very nearly unified many of the Dacian tribes, a feat that no one had come close to accomplishing since the infamous Burebista some fifty or so years before. Comosicus's power, though, was dwindling; he had bouts of illness that arose suddenly and lasted an indeterminable amount of time, leaving him unpredictably bedridden. Furthermore, he was childless, without a blood heir. And so Didas, who had been a mere, expendable slave—and later freedman—to the Romans, had risen in influence and esteem amongst his people, at first helping his brother as advisor and then, at the times when Comosicus's strength failed, effectively acting as king. The people whispered that Comosicus would soon adopt his nephew Scorilo as his heir, with Didas to serve as regent, when the time came.

"Come, then," Didas said with a sigh. "Tell me this news from Rome."

"Their emperor—Augustus. He is dead. His stepson Tiberius now reigns."

Titus felt as if he had been kicked in the stomach; he lost his grasp on the axe in his hands and it dropped to the ground with a dull thud. Neither of the Dacians bothered to look his way.

"Good," Didas said, his tone flat and matter of fact. "We should increase our raids into Roman territory to the east and the south. Perhaps this Tiberius will be too distracted, or too weak, to push back."

"Is there no more news?" Titus asked. He heard his own voice as if it came from someone else entirely. His mind was racing; with Tiberius in power, things could change—for the better or for the worse.

Didas and the messenger both looked towards him now. "What do you mean?" the messenger asked, his words laced with annoyance.

"Has he... Tiberius... what sort of changes have there been amongst the emperor's family? Has he..." Titus trailed off. He was uncertain how to express himself, how to inquire after what he truly wanted to know, without exposing too much detail. He could not afford to trust Didas, even after all this time; Didas, responsible now for his brother's tribal kingdom, would have his own agenda, one that would not be favorably influenced by a meddling Roman soldier whose past put him into conflict with the people he now lived amongst.

The men just stared at Titus, then Didas motioned for the messenger to follow him, and they moved away, heads inclined towards one another as they spoke quietly. Titus glanced down at the axe that now lay at his feet, splinters of wood surrounding it. He was, and would remain, an outsider amongst these people.

With Augustus dead, there might be a chance for Julia's restoration; she had committed no particular offense against Tiberius, her one-time stepfather. On the other hand… Tiberius might lose no time putting his household in order, dispatching those who in any way might prove troublesome to his new reign—in particular, those who were blood-relations to Augustus, as he himself was not. He would not appreciate any reminders that he lacked a direct connection to the recently deceased emperor.

The urge to move, to run, to return to Trimerus and to Julia surged within Titus. The boy would be fine in Dacia, he told himself. He had been fine prior to the soldier's arrival; he was more Dacian than Roman, anyway. Perhaps Duras belonged there, amongst the people of Sarmizegetusa, and Titus could return to Julia, where *he* belonged. He would figure out the logistics on his journey; there had to be a way, and he would find it. His mind began to race with plans and possibilities.

Suddenly, Titus viciously kicked the axe at his feet and sent it spinning away across the muddied ground. He was deluding himself; he had promised Julia that he would find and protect her son, no matter the cost. He could not abandon that duty—and he had no idea if Julia, perhaps already restored in Rome and no longer even on that damned island, would be happy to see him. A seed of doubt wormed its way into his mind, and Titus lowered his head, eyes closed, trying to stem the incessant, overwhelming flow of thoughts.

From around the corner of the house, two pairs of eyes watched the soldier, alert and questioning. Scorilo turned his head to Duras and whispered in his ear. "Why is your father angry?"

Duras scrunched up his face, thinking. "He isn't angry. Father's never angry. He's sad."

It was Scorilo's turn to wrinkle his nose. "Sad?" He made a quiet huffing sound. "Sad people don't kick axes."

Duras shrugged, the corners of his mouth turning downwards. "Well, my father does. He's always sad. I don't know why."

CHAPTER XV

AEMILIA LEPIDA

I wanted to scream, but instead I managed to force my lips to curve upwards, revealing my bared teeth in what I hoped was a semblance of a polite, matronly smile. My son, barely a year old, cried out from down the hall, but the noise quickly faded; Amynta was no doubt bringing him to his wet nurse for another feeding. It seemed both only a short time ago, and also a lifetime, since I had been a young, unmarried girl. Much had changed, and I doubted that I would have even recognized my past self.

The men seemed oblivious to anything but each other, sprawled on their couches, drinking and laughing and belching as their wineglasses were continually refilled, barely a drop of water mixed in to help them keep their heads. I kept the smile plastered to my face, pretending to enjoy the dinner—to enjoy the company. Nothing could have been further from the truth. Inwardly, I recoiled from the scene within my own dining room; I swallowed back bile, telling myself it was just my pregnancy. My belly was already swollen once more with another babe of Torquatus's, one which he seemed less concerned with now that he had already secured for himself a male heir; he did not hover in the same way as he had with our first child, when he had frequently sent the kitchen slaves to me bearing all sorts of concoctions that were supposed to ensure that I bore a healthy boy child. I sipped my wine with increasing frequency, motioning for my glass to be refilled at a rate greater even than the men, none of whom seemed to notice.

My husband was positioned in the middle of our guests, Decimus to his right and Lucius Aelius Sejanus, the recently appointed sole Praetorian Prefect, to his left—his new position was the occasion for the celebratory nature of our gathering. Decimus alone made my stomach turn; his failure over a year ago to restore my family from their exiles was still raw to me, although it didn't seem to bother him in the slightest. Instead of recalling Agrippa Postumus from banishment, Augustus had condemned him to continue rotting away on his remote island; not long after, the emperor had died, and his heir Tiberius had killed my uncle anyway, executing him to ensure that his grip on power was secure. My grandmother, too, had suffered a similar—although arguably worse— fate, locked away until she starved to death, as if she were nothing more than some pathetic, powerless animal. I supposed that, to men, that's what most of us women were, to varying degrees.

Decimus, though, enjoyed not so gently reminding me that my mother still lived—he claimed that he, with the assistance of his new and greatest friend Sejanus, had made sure that Tiberius overlooked her in his purge, something for which he felt I continued to owe him. Yet I could not help but wonder if she might have preferred to meet the same end as her own brother, instead of continuing to live locked away.

Nevertheless, I managed to continue to bite my tongue, to smile politely at the senator who had failed me; Decimus did not let me forget what I had done to my husband, nor did he let me forget that it would take little effort for him to reveal evidence of my trespass. Already it seemed as if his attentions had passed to another, and I had been cast aside, the winds of power shifting in Rome since Tiberius's accession. My uncle was dead, and my mother no longer mattered—so I didn't, either. I raised my wine to my lips again, letting the cool glass linger against my mouth as I swallowed once, twice, thrice.

Sejanus was a creature I still could not entirely figure out; superficially, he was charismatic, handsome, charming. Yet underneath this façade, he seemed to be a false, scheming man, one whom I felt was incredibly dangerous, though I was not certain to what extent. He and Decimus together were an even more concerning combination, a partnership into which it appeared my husband was being drawn— although he seemed willing enough, casting off the few, meek protestations I had voiced as womanly imaginations brought on by my most recent pregnancy.

"They're good, powerful men," Torquatus had told me dismissively. "I—we—would do well to cast our lot in with them. They believe I may be able to attain a consulship within the next few years." His tone had been decisive; that, as far as he was concerned, was the end of the matter.

"Are you quite alright, Aemilia?" a voice called out to me.

I scanned the faces around the room—my husband; Sejanus; Decimus and his young wife, a woman I had only recently met—even as I already knew to whom that sickening voice belonged. I steeled myself as my gaze reached the final dinner guest. Silanus, my husband's cousin, smiled softly at me, an attempt at concern writ across his brow. I had not yet had enough to drink to prepare myself to deal with him.

"Perfectly well, Silanus," I responded quietly. I forced my teeth to expose themselves, again presenting a smile that I had no doubt better resembled a pained grimace.

"You truly do look like your mother," he said next, as if he meant it as a compliment.

I noticed, in a disembodied sort of way, that the rest of our guests had ceased their own chattering as Silanus's words reached their ears. Torquatus had warned me, before this dinner, that his cousin had been restored to Rome following Tiberius's rise to power, and that we were to entertain him—he who had impregnated my mother; he who had cast her off as disposable, offering her up in exchange for a lesser sentence for his role in their illicit affair. That resulting sentence had simply entailed him living in the lap of luxury at one of his countryside estates, removed from the city of Rome, while my own mother was a prisoner, seemingly forever forsaken. His betrayal of her was unforgivable.

I could not see what appeal Silanus had ever held for my mother, even years ago, before the lines in his face had deepened, the irrefutable evidence that age was beginning to wear him down. She had thrown away her life for him—she had thrown *me* away for him—but what was he except an appallingly average specimen of a man?

I felt more than saw Torquatus trying to catch my attention, to motion me to respond with the ever-suffering politeness expected of me at all times. He would have me offer a simpering smile, a few gentle words, and then continue on as if this wretch in my own home was guilty of nothing. I refused to meet my husband's no doubt frantic eyes, instead slowly draining my wineglass as I stared at Silanus, the dry burn of the liquid in my throat further bolstering my commitment to utter the words I was already formulating in my mind.

"I look like my mother?" I asked quietly. "Is this what she looked like, Silanus, when you betrayed her to the emperor? Pained? Disgusted?" I kept my grip on the wineglass relaxed, although my hand wanted to clench down upon it, crushing it into a million irreparable shards. I motioned for an attendant to refill my glass, and one quickly obeyed, head bowed.

"Aemilia," Torquatus began, fighting to keep his tone level, "why don't you retire for the evening? I know you're quite tired. Your pregnancy is proving difficult."

Sejanus only chuckled, seemingly entertained by the situation unfolding before him. Decimus watched me, his eyes hawkish, alert. His wife's expression looked pained, though she quickly ducked her chin and averted her eyes, obedient, submissive: the ideal Roman wife, as I once thought I might be able to force myself to become, to remain. But I had begun to chafe under the bars of my gilded cage.

"I'm not tired at all, dear husband," I said coolly, taking another sip of my wine without bothering to water it down first. "At least, not in the way you mean. Rather, I'm tired of pigs pretending to be men. I'm tired of pathetic, dirty rats killing and feasting upon all that once was good, while there no longer seems to be a single cat left in Rome who will do his duty and rid the city of this infestation."

Sejanus had stopped his chuckling, and Torquatus had stood from his dining couch. His body trembled with fury; I had never seen him so angry, let alone had even a portion of that energy directed towards me. "Get out immediately, Aemilia," he hissed, struggling to keep his voice even.

I calmly finished my wine and gently set the glass down, long ago having lost count of how many times I had already drained it; I expected my hand to tremble, to betray me, but it held steady. Decimus's wife glanced at me as I stood, and I saw in her eyes a conflicting mixture of loathing and admiration before she ducked her chin again, returning to her proper role, as if she were a turtle protectively tucking itself into its shell, hoping no one would notice it. Silanus smiled thinly at me and sipped his own wine before I turned and left the room, my mind beginning to go numb—but it was too late to spare me from the brutal range of emotions I had already experienced.

I heard Sejanus speak as my steps began to carry me away. "You need to control her better. You'll never make consul with a wife like that... Perhaps it's time to consider a divorce."

My hands clenched into fists, and I found myself thinking that perhaps it would have been better after all if I had accidentally killed my husband when Decimus had wanted to test my loyalty. It was almost impossible for me to recall the girl I had been, tearful and worried about what I had done; now I felt as if I had not done enough.

I stormed through the house, my steps carrying me to the small shrine for the *Lares*, our household gods, those who oversaw our family's present and future and who sought to ensure our continuing prosperity. There, I sank to my knees; the dull, slightly painful thud as my bones connected with the beautiful, decadently mosaicked ground barely registered with me.

"Gods and ancestors, give me the strength to seek vengeance for my mother," I whispered. "Give me the strength to bite my tongue, to be agreeable, to gain their trust so that I may further my own ends. Give me the strength to make Decimus suffer. Give me the strength to ruin Silanus. I want them dead."

I stared at the shrine, upon which was painted scenes that included coiled and slithering serpents as well as the *Lares* themselves, and I silently vowed to ensure that proper sacrifices were given the following day at all relevant temples, to ensure that the asked-for exchange would occur: copious bloodshed of sheep and bulls and doves to guarantee the strength I had requested. I would take no risks; I would appeal to every deity who might deign to hear me, participate in every ancient rite that might ensure my success.

Perhaps my family truly was cursed by the gods; if so, I would need all their help and more to rectify our fate. If it was too late for my mother, too late even for me, perhaps I could spare my children. My hand rested on my belly, and I closed my eyes, exhaling.

Silanus and Decimus became regular guests of my husband—Sejanus, for the time being, less so, largely because of the great number of obligations he maintained due to his status as Praetorian Prefect. Whether because the gods had granted my request or because I simply had found a new, iron will within me, I managed to bite my tongue, to smile and simper at the men whose destruction I had vowed to work towards, no matter how long it might take.

Decimus's wife, despite her frequent presence, too, at my home, kept me at a distance, and I sensed that she had been warned by her husband not to become too friendly with me. But it was no matter—I had no need of friends.

Eventually, once time and other, more pressing matters had dimmed their recollection of my outburst at the dinner party, lessening their wariness of me, I began to overhear more and more of the men's conversations, exchanges and plans that they spoke of over meals, or in public spaces when we were gathered all together. Unfortunately, none of what I heard proved salacious enough for me to do anything with; while they schemed of ways to further their own power, to expand upon their spheres of influence, they spoke of nothing treasonous, nothing beyond what countless other Roman men might have discussed on a regular basis.

Even had I learned something of particular interest, I had not yet thought about how I might use it. While I exchanged regular letters with Aunt Agrippina—pregnant yet again, as was I, though she remained abroad, on campaign with her husband—I was not sure she would speak on my behalf to my uncle Germanicus without ample, irrefutable evidence of some grievous misdeed, nor would I entrust any suspicions to the easily-intercepted written word, as I would have to do while she remained so far from Rome.

And so, I continued to bide my time, watching, listening, waiting. I found some greater measure of freedom by assigning Amynta an increasing number of tasks with my young son, allowing me to move about more independently, the lack of a babbling infant—and my ever-present slave woman—resulting in my wanderings often going entirely unnoticed. One morning, I was intending to casually walk past the room in which my husband and his two confidantes were ensconced, when I came across Rufus. I began to turn around, hoping he had not yet seen me, but his voice brought me to a sudden halt.

"Have you had much success yet?" he asked, his tone direct. He did not bother with a greeting.

"What do you mean?" I turned towards him, my face expressionless. I didn't trust Rufus, no matter what kind words he periodically threw my way. I suspected that he only sought to use any revelations I might entrust to him against me, relaying them back to Decimus like the loyal mongrel he was. He was little better than his master.

Rufus jerked his head towards the room I had intended to walk past, though the door hanging was drawn closed over it, muffling the low murmur of voices within. "Finding something to destroy them. You might do better if drink didn't addle your mind quite as often as it does."

I opened my mouth to speak, to deny his words, then closed it without uttering anything at all. Had I been so obvious? I resolutely ignored the jibe he had added in; he didn't know what he was speaking of, and it was not his place to talk about it even if he did.

Rufus continued, ignoring the awkward gaping of my mouth as I stood there silently. "I wish to help you." His words were quiet, but they were laced with sincerity—a sincerity I was not certain was genuine.

"Why?" I asked, finding my voice at last. I still did not bother to deny his earlier words, instead intrigued by his claim that he wanted to aid me in my plans to ruin Silanus and Decimus.

The red-haired soldier's face schooled itself into a cold, flat expression, and his tone became vehement. "Because I want to be free of all this, of them. Of *him*." I knew that he spoke of Decimus, though I had not known until now how much he despised his master; I had assumed he served the senator faithfully, if not entirely happily.

I managed to keep my surprise from showing, and I took a few breaths as I thought out how to respond. "I don't trust you." The words were simple—and true. I did not ask why he suddenly had decided to turn upon his master; it did not much matter to me.

"I know," he said, "but you don't have to trust me to use me."

What he said was logical, although not reassuring. I had intended for this to be a personal quest; I had intended to work alone. Involving anyone else was a risk: a risk to my life and to my success, the latter of which I valued more. But perhaps it was a risk that would generate an earlier payoff. Rufus had access where I did not; as Decimus's most frequently attending guard, as his long serving pawn, he had far greater knowledge than I did of his master—and a far greater ability to hurt him.

I nodded and began to walk away, but a new thought caused me to pause, turning back towards Rufus. "Leave Amynta alone," I told him.

"Decimus surely must no longer need you to use her to have access to me—not that I seem to hold much value to him now. He's here frequently anyway, as a guest of my husband." I paused a moment before adding a final thought. "It's cruel to continue to use her so. I know that doesn't matter to you, but it does to me."

Rufus inclined his head slightly in acknowledgment of my words, and then I left him. Amynta would be saddened, heartbroken even, but it was for the best. One fewer person would be involved in the spiraling web of deceit I had begun to weave.

CHAPTER XVI

RUFUS

Although Rufus had remained outwardly stoic as he spoke with young Aemilia, inwardly he was uncertain—anxious, even. For years he had fantasized about fleeing from Decimus, from Rome; sometimes he had even contemplated killing the man and accepting the death sentence that would surely result from his betrayal of the senator. Yet time and time again he had shied away from action, a faint sense of self-preservation always emerging from the remotest depths of his soul. He was not ready to die, nor was he ready to be hunted to the furthest reaches of the empire should he flee. Decimus would never let him escape; he knew too much.

Rufus was not certain he had even made up his mind to speak when he saw Aemilia, but suddenly the words had poured out his mouth like a river overflowing the dam that had kept it too long contained. He knew she didn't trust him, and nor did he trust her, entirely, not to simply cast him out, to betray him for her own gain. But he knew that he would deserve it if she did, and, if sacrificing him would somehow lead to righteous retribution against Decimus, then he would accept it willingly. He only hoped that she would not turn so absolutely to drink that she wasted away before she could contribute on her end of their alliance— but they all had vices to keep in check.

"Where is your mind tonight?" Leander asked him softly, a single finger gently tracing the soldier's stubbled jawline.

"With you," Rufus answered reflexively. Leander laughed, a tinkling sound that always made Rufus feel faintly, happily weak. Perhaps this was why he could not truly contemplate leaving Rome behind.

"No, it's not," Leander scolded, though he smiled as he said it, laughing again. Yet the laughter suddenly turned to coughing, a violent fit that wracked his entire body.

Rufus quickly poured a cup of water, helping the young man to drink, one hand holding the cup to his lips while the other supported his back. Leander's body trembled even after the fit had passed, and he collapsed back onto the bed, dark-ringed eyes closing in exhaustion.

"I'll bring a doctor tomorrow," Rufus said soothingly. "You'll be fine."

Leander didn't answer, seemingly asleep. Rufus gently kissed his brow and stood to leave the room, his gaze lingering on his lover.

Leander had already seen multiple doctors, and none of them could offer a cure for the afflicted youth. His fits of illness came and went, but more often than not of late they tended to linger, decreasing the amount of work Leander could take on at the brothel. He was in danger of losing his place there, of being cast out to a worse fate, and then another and another, each harsher than the last, until he was used up, spent, cast away to breathe his last breath and to die, forgotten and alone on some damp, stinking street corner like a stray dog.

Rufus clenched his fist. He would not let that happen. He cared about very few things at all anymore, but Leander was one of them. Leander had repeatedly staved off what Rufus felt was his imminent madness; had loved him when he had no one else; had embraced him despite his faults, his crimes.

The brothel's gatekeeping eunuch looked up as Rufus left Leander's room, pausing in his task of writing out figures. The pen hovered in his hand, a drop of ink clinging perilously to its tip. "You went over your allotted hour. You owe more." His tone was coldly demanding, and he resumed writing, waiting for Rufus to present the coins he owed.

The soldier cleared his throat, and the eunuch glanced back up at him with a sigh. "I would like to purchase Leander's freedom," Rufus said.

The eunuch scowled at him. "Of course you do. And, as I've told you many times before, you can't afford his freedom. He's still earning his keep here, though barely, and freeing him would set my master back. It doesn't make financial sense."

"He's sick," Rufus growled. "He won't be bringing in any money soon." His clenched fist drew the eunuch's wary eye.

"Yes," the eunuch said quietly, with a rare trace of sympathy, "he is sick. And he's been seen to by all manner of doctors, none of whom seem to be able to do much for him."

"Please," Rufus whispered. It was as close he had ever come to begging. "Please speak to your master. Convince him to let me pay for Leander's freedom. Let him have that, at least, before he…" He could not finish the sentence; he feared that to speak the word would make it come to pass. Rufus looked down at his feet, a sudden roar of crashing waves resounding in his mind, and he fought to breathe.

The eunuch's voice hardened again. "Perhaps my master will consider selling him at a discount if and when his illness renders him entirely unable to work. Wait and see." He resumed writing, and Rufus knew that he would make no more progress—if he had made any at all.

He walked towards the exit, but an insistent, attention seeking cough caused him to stop. When Rufus turned, the eunuch extended a bowl towards him, several *denarii* lying at the bottom, glinting silver in the weak light.

Growling, Rufus dug out a few coins and tossed them into the bowl, storming out of the brothel with heavy, thudding steps.

The doctor Rufus brought to see Leander the next day said the same as all the rest: he wasn't certain he could do much more than attempt to make the young man comfortable. Again Rufus paid the eunuch for the time he had spent with Leander; again he inquired after buying his freedom, to be met with the same response.

"Whatever is the matter with you?" Decimus asked him later, a cheery lilt to his voice. The senator was fresh from a private meeting with Sejanus, and whatever they had discussed had put him in a rather happy mood, a stark contrast to Rufus's brooding.

"Nothing at all, sir," he responded dully. Decimus wouldn't care; his only concern was that Rufus did as he bade, quietly and efficiently. Furthermore, Rufus had no desire to enlighten his master about Leander's existence: at best, his lover would become yet another tool the senator could use against him to guarantee continued compliance, and, at worst, Leander might be considered a liability, suspected of having heard whispers from Rufus of things that were not to be mentioned, things that might implicate Decimus in all manner of wretched doings.

Decimus scoffed. "Go see that slave woman of Aemilia's… Whatever is her name? Amynta, yes?"

Rufus nodded. "Yes, Amynta is her name. But…" He bit off the rest of his sentence, but it was too late.

Decimus raised a brow at the soldier's interjection. "But, Rufus? But what?"

Rufus steeled himself; it always took a greater measure of courage to question Decimus than he liked to admit. "Surely you do not still need me to draw her along? You are quite friendly with Torquatus these days. What possible use is left for Aemilia, or for her slave? They're just women."

Rufus flinched as Decimus laughed at him; it was always a gamble, a risk, asking too much about the senator's plans, but, this time, it seemed he might be enlightened. "Rufus, Rufus," Decimus began. "So shortsighted. No one, not even a woman, outlives their usefulness until they are dead. Aemilia almost killed her husband, to prove her worth, her loyalty. Oh, I know she detests me, now, after her uncle's death and her mother's continued exile, but that doesn't mean I'm finished with her by any means. Never needlessly cast away a piece while the outcome of the game is still uncertain."

Rufus didn't entirely understand, but he knew better than to press his luck by asking what Decimus meant. He simply nodded, pressing his lips together as he tried to quell his simmering hatred of the man whose bidding he no longer wanted to do. If he and Aemilia were successful, he wouldn't have to.

Leander died some weeks later. Rufus wasn't there at the end; in fact, he found out that his lover had passed because two men were carrying

Leander's pale, stiff, naked body out from the brothel when he came to visit. Rufus bore yet another vial of some new concoction in his hands, having been assured that, this time, the mixture would bring relief to his lover. But he was too late.

"Stop!" he cried out, surging forwards and grabbing the arm of one of the men who carelessly bore Leander's body, as if the dead youth were a sack of grain, not the man Rufus had loved. The vial he had held, forgotten, fell to the ground, the glass shattering as its liquid contents spilled out onto the road. "Where are you taking him?"

The man angrily shrugged him off, his grip on Leander never loosening. "Get off me," he snapped. The pair made to move again, and Rufus saw an empty cart nearby, a donkey stamping its foot impatiently as it awaited its burden.

Rufus wanted to stop them, to take Leander, to see to his funerary rites himself. But he found that he was frozen in place, only able to watch as Leander—beautiful, young Leander—was thrown carelessly into the cart, his limbs contorted at awkward angles. One of the men whipped the donkey cruelly, and the cart began to move off. Rufus watched it turn the corner.

The eunuch came out of the brothel and looked at him with something resembling pity. "It was peaceful, at the end," he volunteered to the soldier.

Rufus didn't respond; instead, he was fighting to breathe, the scent of salt-tinged air suddenly seeming to overwhelm his nose, to quash his lungs. One of the only things—no, *the* only thing—he felt as if he had bothered to live for had been taken from him.

CHAPTER XVII

AEMILIA LEPIDA

My husband and I dined alone that night, a simple, quiet affair—just as Torquatus had specifically requested, wanting, as he put it, a bodily cleansing of the rich, heavy foods he frequently found himself consuming when dining with Decimus, Sejanus, and his cousin Silanus. Instead of rock eel with mulberry sauce or marinated and grilled lamb liver, pork shoulder with sweet wine cakes or duck roasted with hazelnut and calamint, tonight we picked at boiled eggs in a pine nut sauce, something that ordinarily would be considered little more than an appetizer. I barely touched my own dish, the smell of it unsettling my pregnant, swollen stomach. Amynta, hovering behind my dining couch, was no doubt already planning to tell the cook to prepare my favorite pancakes for me as a snack for later.

I sipped at my heavily watered-down wine and watched my husband eat, noting that he did indeed look fleshier of late, his cheeks rounder, a slight paunch visible through the relaxed, casual tunic he wore when we were home alone together, in place of his more formal toga. As if sensing my gaze, he paused after swallowing a bite, then looked back at me with a gentle smile, and I found my heart softening, as it always did. Although Torquatus's moments of tenderness with me were fleeting of late—especially after my outburst against his cousin—I felt as if my heart still yearned after my husband, seeking the love and unconditional warmth that always seemed to hover just out of reach. The lingering naiveté of my younger self made me believe that I might possibly one day come to love Torquatus; the sterner voice that seemed to grow stronger each day told me that love and warmth were not ingredients necessary to a good marriage. I was already luckier than most. He is kind, I told myself, mindlessly repeating my aunt's words, and a good man. My husband did not beat me; he did not violently force himself upon me again and again. Our couplings were not infrequent, and not altogether unpleasant, I found, although they always finished before I found myself truly satisfied.

"Decimus said something interesting the other day," Torquatus began, pausing to take another bite of egg. A drop of pine nut sauce slipped off it and landed on his tunic; he didn't seem to notice, but my eyes lingered on the spot.

"Oh?" I asked politely, sipping again from my glass of wine. My foul mood was already on a quick return at the mention of the senator's name. I motioned for our dining attendant to refill my drink; he hastily obeyed before retreating to the corner of the room, perfectly silent and forgettable, just as he was meant to be.

Torquatus emitted a sound of confirmation as he chewed and swallowed, dabbing at his chin with a napkin before speaking again. The spot of pine nut sauce remained unnoticed on his tunic. "Yes, quite interesting. He mentioned that you showed extreme devotion to me during my illness, when I took to my bed for days—when was it?—oh, two years ago now."

My eyes maintained their focus on the sauce stain on my husband's tunic. I made a non-committal noise in response, uncertain what point he was attempting to make.

"It's just that…" Torquatus continued, and he fixed his attention on me with a sudden, intense scrutiny. "I never shared details of that time with anyone. And I had no idea that you knew Decimus, back then."

The unspoken question, laced with a hint of accusation, lingered in the air between us. I wrenched my gaze from the sauce stain and met Torquatus's eyes at last. "Oh, I didn't know him," I lied coolly. "I must have mentioned it to him at one of our dinners more recently. And besides, your illness was fairly well known at the time—you do know how people like to gossip." I sipped my wine, unwilling to volunteer any more information to flesh out the falsehood, lest I find myself caught out by invented details; the drink quickly soothed my suddenly racing heart.

Torquatus nodded, taking another bite of egg, chewing more slowly than the soft food necessitated. "That's not all, though," he said quietly. Again he dabbed at his mouth, once, twice, thrice, pausing and briefly holding the fabric across his lips, almost as if he thought to stifle his next words before he could speak them aloud. "He also said… Decimus said…"

I should have been worried, frantic even. Had Decimus told my husband that I had been responsible for his illness? That I had been the one to lace his drink with poison? I doubted it would lend much to my defense to protest that I had only meant to cause my then-new husband temporary harm, to cause him suffering to prove my loyalty to another man—one who, I had learned, still maintained the upper hand against me as a result, furthering his own agenda while I had gained nothing.

"Whatever did Decimus say?" I asked, my tone surprising even me by its sharpness. "Do tell me, dear husband." I recalled my request of the gods, to lend me the strength to destroy the senator, to destroy Silanus, too—and I wondered if my continued softness towards my husband, my persistent, girlish desperation for love—wretched though it made me—would deny me the vengeance I thirsted after.

Torquatus didn't respond, instead taking another bite of his food. "Never mind it," he eventually said with a small smile. "I'm sure it's nothing."

I smiled back, schooling my face into a blandly reassuring expression before I forced myself to take a bite of my own dinner, washing it down with yet another swallow of wine. My mind was racing, wondering what words Decimus had been whispering into my husband's ear, and why. The senator, I surmised, would not have betrayed me, not yet, while he might still envisage some use for me. No—this was a warning of some sort, a reminder that I was nothing more than what he would allow me to be—a tool, a pawn. I could not help but wonder if Rufus had lied to me about his own desire to destroy Decimus and was instead simply seeking another way for his master to blackmail me. Did Decimus know that I had set out to ruin him, and Silanus, too? Was that the cause of this warning?

I subtly shook my head to clear it, Torquatus watching with distant eyes, and I felt as if I should say something else, something to reassure him.

"The babe is kicking," I said, stilling as the infant inside my belly moved suddenly. It was not a fabrication on my part by any means—but it certainly was fortunate timing.

"Gods willing, it's another son," Torquatus said, smiling widely, as if he had already forgotten whatever Decimus had said to him. I hoped that was indeed the case, and I vowed to be more careful moving forward.

I gave birth later that year to a healthy, screaming, pink-faced girl child. My husband, despite his professed hopes of having a second son, eagerly scooped her into his arms and bestowed upon her the name Junia Calvina.

It appeared that I was more disappointed than my husband to have a daughter—not because I did not immediately feel the love for my own infant blossoming within me, but because I knew that her sex would work against her, as it had her mother, her grandmother, and her great-grandmother before her. I knew that my son would have freedom, success—the opportunity to, one day, make decisions for himself and to forge his own path in life. My daughter would have none of that, nor her own daughters.

As had become the norm for me, I said nothing, keeping my thoughts and feelings locked deep within myself. I could not even trust Amynta, who had been cold and distant with me ever since Rufus had followed through on my demand to leave her alone. Although she did not accuse me directly, I had no doubt she suspected my involvement, as I had been vocal for the duration of their so-called relationship that I did not approve.

Rufus told me that Decimus had not been pleased with the development, but there was little that could be done. "Women are fickle, after all," Rufus had told me, a hint of mockery in his statement. "I told him Amynta would have nothing more to do with me, and he eventually accepted it, though he was angry." The soldier's face tightened as he recalled the senator's reaction, but I did not press him for more details; I could imagine well enough how unpleasant Decimus could be when things did not go as he wished.

At this point, though, Rufus's words had become true; even if he *had* tried to return to my slave woman's embrace, he would have been rebuffed, not just because he had rejected her, wounding her pride, but because something about him had changed: Rufus no longer even attempted to be charming and jovial, to blend in. Now he simply stood by, stoically, looking as if he had aged a decade nearly overnight. I didn't ever ask him what had caused his drastic transformation; it was better not to know, not to care. I could not afford to form an attachment to a man who needed to be nothing more than a tool to me.

Now, Amynta hovered angrily near me at the wedding celebration for Sejanus and his new bride, Apicata. Her eyes were flinging daggers at Rufus from across the room as he stood close, as always, to Decimus, but he did not seem to be aware of Amynta's angry gaze—or, more likely, he was studiously ignoring his spurned lover.

"Amynta," I breathed at her. "You are bristling like a porcupine, and it's unsettling me."

I could feel her body tense even more, if that were possible, and her words were terse when she responded. "Apologies, *domina*."

The term still jolted me; although in the past I had asked her to stop calling me *domincella*, feeling that it was childlike, and demeaning to a married woman who was now, too, a mother, she had still called me the diminutive in private—until Rufus had left her. Now I was only ever *domina*, regardless of time or place, and I found that it saddened me more than I would have expected.

I did not scold her; I could not, for she had done nothing wrong. It had crossed my mind to enlighten her, to reveal that Rufus had only ever used her to be close to me, and that his master had any number of plots ongoing, all of them focused on how to gain and hold the greatest amount of power. But I stayed silent; no good would come from Amynta knowing the truth. She would forgive me, one day; I couldn't bear to think of any other alternative. She was the closest thing I had to a friend.

Sighing, I shifted my attention to Sejanus's young bride, knowing that soon she would join our dinner parties alongside her new husband. I wondered if I had looked that youthful, that pretty and pure, on my own wedding day. I wondered, too, if she knew what scheming her husband was involved in—if she would even care, or if she would be too caught up in her jewels and slaves and producing child after child to concern herself with her husband's affairs. It wouldn't be uncommon; many women of our rank had little to do with their husbands other than periodic copulation, instead diverting themselves with all sorts of small pleasures and vices. I could not judge them: I knew all too well that my own primary pleasure—my not-insignificant vice, as many would be sure to call it—laid in the countless amphorae of wine in our cellars.

As if sensing my gaze, the bride looked at me then, a tentative smile brushing her lips, one which I returned as I began to approach her. Amynta dutifully, if sullenly, trailed behind.

"*Salve*, and congratulations," I began. "I'm Aemilia Lepida, wife of Marcus Junius Silanus Torquatus." I gestured subtly in my husband's direction; as usual, he was ensconced with Decimus, Sejanus, his cousin Silanus, and a few other men, all of them approaching the level of raucous drunkenness that always seemed to accompany any social gathering we attended. It was normal—expected, even—for them to drink to the point of making themselves ill; I tried to save such behavior for when I was alone, lapsing into the worst version of myself as I sought out the ensuing, blessed numbness.

"I know," she said, smiling again. "I am Apicata. You already know my husband, of course." She didn't state her full name—either shyness or arrogance, expecting that I would already know of her family. But of course, I did; it was, after all, her wedding celebration that I now attended. I was not so foolish as to arrive wholly unprepared in my research on her background.

I nodded, and Apicata invited me to sit, patting the space next to her on her couch. I settled myself, and together we surveyed the room.

"What is he like?" Apicata asked me. "My husband, I mean," she added quickly, a blush creeping across her face as she glanced at Sejanus, her eyes admiringly tracing the lines of his togate body.

"Respectable, honorable, promising. He is a good man." I recited off the standard list of qualities that one should ascribe to another's husband without even pausing, never mind that I believed he had not a single grain of any such attributes. Yet what man in Rome did these days?

Perhaps I responded too quickly, or perhaps I was too bland in tone, because Apicata let out a quiet scoff. I shifted towards her slightly, raising an eyebrow.

"I had thought... hoped, that you might answer truthfully," she said quietly. Her tone was sad, although she kept a smile on her face as her eyes scanned the room, aware that people would be watching her. "Don't you remember what it was like to marry a man you barely knew?"

I examined Apicata more closely then, noting that she was younger than I had been when I married Torquatus—perhaps only fifteen years old or so.

"It is our duty," I said simply. I thought that if Aunt Agrippina could have seen and heard me then, she couldn't have been more pleased; I had unthinkingly parroted out the phrase, the admonition, that all young Romans were taught from an early age.

"Yes," Apicata agreed, the single word subdued. She opened her mouth again as if to say more, then closed it, resolve steeling her face. "I apologize for my childish question," she said, and I knew the words were not the ones she had first been planning to say. I had lost what little trust she had, somewhat naively, bestowed upon me, and I found that I regretted it—not because I wanted or needed a friend, but because, belatedly, I realized that she might somehow be of use to me in my own quest to destroy Decimus and Silanus, considering their close relationship to Sejanus, her new husband.

I sighed sharply. "No, I'm sorry," I began, and I allowed a measure of warmth to tinge my apology. "I'm sure you've been told what to expect tonight, but between us, it's a bit different from what your mother has no doubt said…"

Apicata's expression lightened as she turned her attention back to me, and I began to whisper all sorts of bedroom secrets into her ear, watching as her face turned from pink to red and her eyes grew wide.

I had left the wedding celebration only briefly, in search of a place to relieve myself. My steps took me further and further from the gathering until the constant din of the music, the conversations, the clink of glassware all became muffled, a distant event that it seemed I had left ages ago, even though I was sure I had only been gone mere minutes.

Sighing, I glanced around for a slave, for anyone, to direct me to the right place. I had allowed Amynta to remain behind, thinking I would only be gone a few moments, but somehow I had wound up entirely lost—although I had no doubt that the copious amount of wine I had consumed might have had something to do with my current unfortunate situation. The light cast from various oil lamps flickered on the walls, beckoning me in all directions; my head ached, and I paused, rubbing my temples. As I made to return the way I thought I had come, a dark shape moved out from an alcove.

"Oh, hello—" I started, hoping that it was someone who could provide directions, before I abruptly cut myself off. The shape—it was Silanus.

He smiled at me, and I fought the urge to vomit up all the wine that was sloshing in my belly, nearly devoid of food. I made to move past him, lowering my eyes, but he put up an arm, stopping me.

"Excuse me, Silanus," I said, trying to move past him on his other side, but he moved in front of me, again blocking my path. I raised my gaze, a glare fixed on my face as our eyes met.

"You're drunk," Silanus said, laughing, his warm, stale breath making me wrinkle my nose in distaste. He made a half step towards me, and I moved back.

"So are you. Now, please stand out of my way," I said forcefully. My heart was beginning to beat rapidly in my chest, and I felt as if I could hear my own pulse in my ears.

Silanus laughed again and stumbled towards me, his hands reaching out and grabbing me. "So pretty," he said quietly, "like your mother." He reeked of sour wine, and his eyes bored into me with a disturbing intensity.

Then, he pulled me closer and forced his lips on mine; I tried to push him away, wrenching my head away from him, but his hand wound its way into my hair, yanking my face back towards his. His other hand reached down, gathering my dress, pulling it up, starting to expose me.

I managed to pull my face away again, and I saw movement over

Silanus's shoulder. I cried out for help, a noise that sounded like little more than a weak kitten mewling for its mother—and the figure over Silanus's shoulder materialized in full: Decimus.

"Help me, Decimus!" I cried out, all my hatred for the man dissipating in my moment of fear. Silanus stilled then, dropping my dress, although one hand still held tightly to my wrist as he turned to face the senator.

Decimus examined us, and then, to my horror, a cold smile stretched across his face. "Another thing not to tell your husband, Aemilia?" he asked. With a quiet laugh, he turned and left, leaving me alone once more with Silanus.

Silanus wasted no time, again pulling my dress up; I heard the rip of the fabric as he pushed me against the wall, turning me around so that my face slammed into the plaster of the hallway, my head immediately throbbing as sparks crossed my vision and I struggled to remain conscious.

I remember only hints of what happened, vague memories of Silanus's sudden absence from behind me, of my dress half falling back into place. A memory of turning; of seeing Silanus being held at knifepoint; of him issuing a hurried, slurred promise that he would leave Rome; of my attacker hurrying off down the hallway, pulling his toga back into place as he stumbled clumsily over its heavy folds.

"Aemilia," Rufus said quietly, putting his knife away. He averted his eyes from mine, and I managed to smooth my dress down, my trembling fingers catching on a tear. I wiped tears from my face that I had not even known I had shed.

"Thank you," I said quietly.

The soldier only nodded, gesturing down the hallway, back towards the gathering. I shook my head. "I can't go back there," I told him. "Not like this."

"I will tell Amynta to come for you," he said, eyes still avoiding mine, as if he could somehow restore my dignity to me by looking away from my trembling body. "I'll tell her you aren't feeling well, and that you need to go home immediately."

"Thank you," I said again, my voice barely more than a whisper.

Rufus began to leave. "Stop," I said suddenly. "Rufus, I—" I cut myself off, unsure what to say to him—to this man with whom I uneasily shared a common goal. "I trust you," I said. "I trust you now."

Rufus nodded. "You have had my trust." He left then, and I wrapped my arms around myself as I waited for Amynta. I had a true ally, at last—and now, more than ever, I wanted to destroy Decimus and Silanus both.

TITUS

Titus scowled as he kicked his horse into a gallop, chasing after his charges. Duras and Scorilo had surged ahead, ignoring his orders to stay towards the back of the group, close to him—where he could keep an eye on them, protect them.

The boys were on their first raid. Now that they had seen fourteen summers, they were considered Dacian men, and were expected to participate in the troublemaking that the rest of their sex regularly engaged in along the Moesian border. Titus had had to bite his tongue when Didas suggested they join the rest of the men from Sarmizegetusa, who were riding out to join up with other tribes to form a larger, more powerful force; no one argued with Didas, not anymore. As the rumors had predicted even years ago, King Comosicus—who still, somehow, feebly clung to life—had at last named Scorilo as his heir, but it was Didas who, for now, ruled in all but name.

Titus knew that Didas was not a stupid man. The Dacian understood that raiding near and even into Roman territory was like poking a bear with a stick; it was only a matter of time until the bear retaliated, and the retaliation, when it came, would be fast and brutal. But the raids—small though they had been—had been successful so far, bringing in goods and coin and, most importantly, a sense of pride for the Dacian people, a rare unity now sprung from their communal success. Didas was not willing to call off his men, not yet; Titus feared it would be too late by the time he *was* ready.

"Duras! Scorilo!" he barked out, pushing his horse through the Dacian warriors around him. Most of them ignored him; others openly curled their lips. Although he had been living amongst them for over a decade, they still viewed him as an outsider. Even his willingness to shed blood alongside them, against the powerful empire he had once served so loyally, seemed to do nothing but further stoke their distrust and dislike of him. He couldn't blame them: he, too, used to be the type of man who would have been disgusted by a deserter, a traitor. Now he had become what he once so openly despised—and he regretted nothing, because it had all been for Julia. He would have committed even more unspeakable crimes, if only she had asked.

He still thought of the letter Aulus had sent, the first spring after the people of Sarmizegetusa heard the news of Augustus's death. Titus had passed that winter fitfully, the dark, gloomy days leaving too much time for him to dwell on Julia's unknown fate—but that day there had been the vaguest hint of warmth lingering on the breeze, a promise that life would once again emerge from beneath the cold winter snow that still lingered in odd white-brown heaps and mounds. The Moesian governor had not written much, only that she—Julia, though he took care not to name her explicitly—still lived, and that his posting in the region had come to an end; he was returning to Rome, and he bade Titus good luck. And so although Titus had taken great comfort in the short letter, at last knowing that Julia had not been swept away in the quiet but brutal bloodbath following Tiberius's ascension, a small part of him was saddened: Aulus, one of the only other people to have even the faintest understanding of all that had transpired, was leaving, and he would be even more alone in a land that did not welcome him, and which would never be his own. He did not dwell on the fact that the governor's letter confirmed what Titus had long suspected: Aulus had already known the truth of Duras's identity. He hoped that the other man would not now betray it, after all these years.

He caught sight of the boys again—the young men, really—now at the front of the group, their weapons, which had as of yet only seen the blood of hunted animals, affixed to them in preparation for battle. Titus had done what he could to prepare both youths, schooling them in sword skills, spear wielding, wrestling, and horsemanship from a young age. They spoke both their Dacian dialect and Latin fluently, although the soldier had not been able to teach them more than a few words of Greek; he was, after all, by no means a scholar. Duras would likely have little use for what education Titus had imparted to him, but Scorilo, who now was the heir to a tribal king, might find a greater value in it. Titus hoped Didas's son would live to see the benefit.

Titus abruptly pushed his horse between the two boys, who barely seemed to notice his arrival. He wanted to scold them, but he knew his words would have no effect: both boys' gazes were fixed hopefully on the path ahead of them, their eyes shining as they waited for the town that was the group's target to come into sight. One of the scouts had reported back not long ago that the first raid of their venture was imminent.

In contrast to their eager excitement, Titus felt almost queasy. While the people that were going to be attacked were not Roman, they were allies—and they were, for the most part, common people. Killing other soldiers or warriors did not make him think twice; he had killed more men than he could count, and he had killed them without a trace of remorse. But killing women and children and old men who worked in the fields... Titus was not looking forward to what was about to happen.

"Boys," he said quietly; the youths seemed not to hear him. "Boys." This time he was louder, more forceful, and they turned their faces towards him.

"Kill only those who attack you," Titus ordered. "You will not rape any women or girls. You will not kill those who flee from us."

A warrior nearby overheard and snickered. Titus ignored him.

"Yes, Father," Duras said meekly. Scorilo nodded his assent, although he seemed distracted still, only half listening to Titus.

"Stay close to me, too," Titus added. "Overconfidence will get you killed." Both youths again acknowledged his words, and then the town came into sight ahead.

The raiding group's leader began to bark out orders, and Titus steeled himself for the bloodshed they were about to unleash.

It wasn't long after their victorious return to Sarmizegetusa that a Roman envoy arrived, surrounded by what amounted to a small army; he had, he proclaimed, come on behalf of the Moesian governor—Aulus's replacement, a young, brash man who was nothing like his predecessor—and on behalf of Rome itself.

"Why should we stop our raids?" Didas was asking the envoy. Dacian warriors—young Scorilo and Duras included—lingered around their king; the drink was flowing, and they laughed and chatted freely, although each and every one of them bore at least two weapons on his body, prepared to fight if the need arose. The envoy, outfitted in ceremonial armor that did little to hide his paunchy stomach and fleshy limbs, more used to lounging at a banquet than hefting a sword in battle, was ringed by a dozen of his own men, hardened soldiers who kept their faces expressionless as they continually surveyed their surroundings. The rest of their group had set up camp outside Sarmizegetusa, tents pitched in perfectly straight lines behind temporary, wooden fortifications, their presence, for now, peaceful. Titus wondered how long that peace might last, if Didas did not prove agreeable.

"Because, if you do not, Rome will annihilate you," the envoy answered, his tone pleasant and cheerful, as if they were two friends sharing a drink as they tossed some dice around. The room stilled, the soldiers and warriors eyeing one another as they began to listen more closely to the words their leaders exchanged.

Didas scoffed. "If Rome could annihilate us, why would your emperor bother to send an envoy? Why not just do it?" A few of the Dacian warriors nodded their heads.

"Emperor Tiberius does not wish to start an unnecessary war. The divine Augustus brought about a sacred peace in his own reign, one that his heir wishes to continue. Rome is prepared to offer your people a… subsidy, each year. Gold coins, in exchange for stopping your raids. It is to your every advantage to accept." The envoy maintained his pleasant, conversational tone, as if he had no preference whether Didas agreed to peace with Rome or chose to have his people fight to their inevitable deaths. In truth, the envoy probably cared little which outcome arose from the meeting: either way, he knew he would emerge the victor, an accomplishment to add to his list as he advanced in his career.

Titus shifted his weight from one foot to another; he stood behind Didas, in an honored position, one of advisor. Although his beard was long and he had packed away his short sword many moons ago, he still felt out of place, still felt Roman—and he wondered if the soldiers across from him, his former brethren, could see it, if they could sense it. The sooner they were gone, the better.

Didas sighed. He must have known something like this was coming; Rome would only allow so many raids, so many incursions across their borders, before they had to act. Didas was far removed from his former lowly position in Ovid's household; power, Titus thought, suited him, even when the decisions that needed to be made were difficult ones. He wondered, when the time came and King Comosicus at last died, if Didas would truly let his son rule, or if he would cling to control as so many other men before him had done.

The envoy spoke again, taking Didas's lack of opposition to the proposal as mute acceptance. "It is decided, then." He turned slightly, motioning behind him for a chest to be brought forward by two strong-armed men whom Titus had not noticed before: the first subsidy.

Didas only nodded, resigned to the inevitable. Other kings in Dacia, perhaps even Comosicus himself, were he healthy and present, might have chosen differently—and those kings would see their tribes eradicated, their women and children sold into slavery, their settlements burned to the ground. Didas's lack of pride, in that sense, was a boon to his people, even if some of them might later ridicule him for his decision, might accuse him of being bought, of becoming yet another whore to Rome. At least they would be alive to spout their disappointment.

Titus held back a sigh of relief; while he had raided within Rome's territory, that had fallen short of battling his fellow soldiers. Had Didas chosen to reject Rome's embrace, the soldier would have found himself torn between his two peoples, killing his former comrades for the sake of a boy who had no clue who he truly was, who lived amongst people who would reject him if they knew the truth of it.

The envoy was about to leave, but he paused, turning back. A cold smile crossed his face. "One more thing," he said. "Rome demands a son of yours join us. For his education in our ways, so that he may one day bring prosperity back to your people. I assume you do have a son?"

No one was fooled by the envoy's words: what they wanted was not a guest, but a hostage, one that would guarantee the good behavior of Didas and his tribe. Titus was familiar with the practice.

"I do," Didas said quietly; the words came out with difficulty. Titus could see a vein throbbing in his neck.

Scorilo and Duras were not far; they had been listening to the entire exchange, which had occurred in Latin. Scorilo, clearly steeling himself, was about to step forward, to identify himself as Didas's son— to commit himself to being a hostage in Rome, one who was as likely to be executed as he was to be educated in Roman ways. It would all hinge upon his father retaining control over his own people, on keeping Rome satisfied that they were not a threat.

"I am his son," Duras announced loudly, pushing past his friend, his brother in all but blood. "I will go to Rome with you." His Latin was perfect, without even a trace of his Dacian accent, and he raised his chin as he stared proudly at the envoy.

Titus bit the inside of his cheek, forcing himself not to react. Scorilo looked at his friend, confused. Didas, though, breathed a sigh of relief, and his body relaxed. Titus wondered if this was something Didas had put Duras up to, in an effort to shield his own child from a fate that he must have known was a possibility.

"Very well. Come tomorrow to our encampment, and we will depart," the envoy said, brow raised either at the youth's outspokenness or at his clear, correct Latin. He looked the boy up and down, wrinkling his nose as he took in the boy's Dacian clothing, particularly the trousers on his lean legs. "You won't need much. When we reach Rome, you will learn how to dress like a man."

Duras briefly met Titus's eyes, and the soldier knew that the fury he felt within was nearly tangible; the boy quickly looked to the ground, as if he could avoid his anger. Everything Titus had fought for, everything he had sought to accomplish—to keep Julia's son safe, to keep him from Rome, from the heart of danger—had been undone in mere moments.

CHAPTER XIX

AEMILIA LEPIDA

Fourteen years had passed since I had seen my mother, and I was now the same age as she had been, when she left me behind. Twelve years had come and gone since I had stupidly joined myself to Decimus; eight years had sped away since my great-grandfather had died, since my uncle and grandmother had been murdered. In many ways, I felt like none of it mattered anymore—my chance to restore my family was gone, and, at long last, I had started to come to terms with it, although that didn't mean my anger did not still simmer.

"Whatever dreary things are you thinking of?" Apicata asked brightly, looking over at me from the slab she was stretched out on, contentedly receiving her massage from a slave. "Your expression is absolutely tragic. Too much wine last night? Or not quite enough?" She giggled.

I winced as my own attendant pushed on my back, feeling something crack. "I'm not thinking of anything," I said, more sharply than I had intended; I knew she meant no harm.

Despite my plan at her wedding years ago, I had bonded with Apicata more closely than I would have thought possible. What had started as an attempt to simply use Sejanus's new, young wife for my own ends had developed into something I imagined a true friendship might resemble—something different from what I shared with Amynta, who had been bound to me almost since my birth and had no choice in the connection that we shared. No, Apicata and I had willingly intertwined our lives, even if only casually, for reasons that did not include scheming and plotting the downfall of others, no matter my initial intentions for approaching her.

I no longer took pains to eavesdrop on either of our husbands, nor Silanus and Decimus. I was resigned simply to exist, to be a quiet, obedient Roman wife for the remainder of my days—at least in public. Behind the closed doors of my home, I turned to wine more than ever. Perhaps, had it energized me rather than subdued me, dulling my feelings, my actions, my words, Torquatus might have minded—but he simply made sure our supply of wine amphorae never dwindled, never commenting on how much I drank, on how little water I added to Bacchus's glorious red liquid, only sometimes giving me pointed glances at dinner, when we had guests, or out at gatherings, if he felt that I was too conspicuous in my consumption. But he never asked *why* I did it, and I was not certain whether that was because he did not care or because he did not want to know—there was a difference, after all, between those two things.

So far, I had been surprisingly content to have given up my quest for vengeance, although thoughts of that night—of Silanus, pushing against me, his stale, sour mouth forcing itself on mine; of Decimus, mocking my cry for help—still haunted me. Thankfully, Silanus had almost entirely removed himself from Rome; our paths had not crossed since Apicata's wedding. I silently thanked Rufus for that, every day.

Apicata scoffed disbelievingly at my response, turning her head away from me and resting it back on the slab. We maintained a weekly meeting at the baths, enjoying an afternoon of soaks and massages with one another, exchanging news and gossip. It was a nice change from the years I had spent exchanging instructions and insights with Rufus, both of us eager but consistently incapable of destroying those we hated most.

"I was thinking about Aunt Agrippina," I volunteered quietly. It wasn't far from the truth; when one of my more morose moods struck me, my aunt's troubles always seemed to conjoin themselves with my own, as if her ills and misfortunes were mine, too.

"Poor dear," Apicata said, shifting her head back towards me, her eyes sympathetic. "However is she doing?"

"It's been three years since Germanicus died so unexpectedly while abroad, and she still mourns his loss as if it were yesterday." It was true, too—ever since Aunt Agrippina had returned to Rome, personally bearing her husband's ashes, she been weepy, distressed. She had even confided to me that she believed it was no accident that Germanicus had died, although I did not share these suspicions with Apicata—if my aunt was correct, it was a dangerous knowledge to share.

"He would have been a fine emperor one day," Apicata said, stifling a yawn. "So tragic."

Aware of the massage attendants' listening ears, I quickly volunteered my reply. "Drusus will bring glory to Rome," I said confidently. "And to his father, Tiberius, who is the image of health and who shall yet be emperor for many years."

I hoped Apicata wouldn't dispute my comments; she did not share my concern for silent observers. Spies were everywhere these days, eager to report anything spoken against or in doubt of Tiberius; now that he spent an increasing amount of time on the island of Capri, his paranoia that those in Rome worked to undermine him seemed to grow daily. He had even made it illegal to speak against his mother, Livia. It was no wonder that Aunt Agrippina suspected something unnatural about her husband's death: with Germanicus removed, Drusus, the blood son of Tiberius, stood to take over the empire one day, and he would in turn favor his own children over Aunt Agrippina's sons with Germanicus. It was too convenient, everything aligning in favor of Livia and her family at the expense of those connected more directly to Augustus himself— but Augustus was long dead, and his wishes failed to hold as much weight as they once had.

Apicata, thankfully, had already switched topics, and I relaxed again into my massage. "How are your children doing? I fear Sejanus and I won't have anymore... he barely visits my bedroom these days."

She had turned her head away again, and I sensed her unhappiness despite the bright tone she had tried to maintain. Although Apicata and Sejanus had never been particularly close—and were far from sharing much in the way of passionate love for each other—she did truly adore the three children she had borne for him, and she had often spoken to me of wanting more. Her younger son was the same age as my own youngest daughter, and she had once laughingly confided to me about mentioning to Sejanus that they should be betrothed.

I couldn't share my friend's hope of joining our families together: Sejanus was a far cry from what I considered to be an ideal father-in-law for any of my five children. Besides—despite my own husband having held the consulship a few years ago, Sejanus clearly had his eye on families who were closer to power than my children would ever be. While an ambitious mother might consider this to be a fault, I thanked the gods for it: it meant that my children might be safe, might be spared from whatever curse it was that tinged my bloodline.

Apicata hadn't waited for me to answer, instead rambling on to her next topic. It was one of the things I liked about her the most: she filled the silences that I found myself sucked into, and she kept my mind away from my failings. When I was with her, it was easy to forget about Decimus, about Silanus, about my mother. I could forget it all.

"Did you see Livilla's new jewelry at dinner last week?" she was asking. "Absolutely gaudy and ridiculously over the top. I can't believe Drusus would allow his wife to wear something like that."

"Yes, quite gaudy," I agreed quietly, although I had no particular thoughts on the matter, and in fact could barely remember what the offending jewelry had looked like. I was less concerned with Livilla's jewels than with her behavior—behavior that I knew Apicata could not have failed to notice.

"I said as much to Sejanus, but he was quite complimentary of her," Apicata continued on. "I wish..." she trailed off, her voice catching, and I saw her body tremble as she fought back a sudden onslaught of tears.

I silently dismissed the attendants, waving them away. They left the room, and Apicata and I were alone—although I didn't trust that ears weren't still lingering on the other side of the door.

"It means nothing, Apicata," I told her. "She's nothing to him, not really." I did not have to say her husband's name aloud for her to understand.

Apicata's body shook, and she turned a tear-streaked face towards me. "She does mean something to him though," she cried. "He's obsessed with her, Aemilia. I know that's where he is, who he's with. Livilla." She spat out the name. "My parents will never forgive me if he casts me aside."

I cringed; Apicata was getting too loud. "Shh," I hushed her. "You are his wife, the mother of his children. She's married too, to Drusus no less. Nothing will come of this. You'll see that I'm right.

She'll fade away."

Apicata sniffled and nodded. Although I was desperate to believe my own words, a seed of doubt had wormed its way into my mind. Sejanus wasn't one to be lovestruck; he would not throw away his power, his position, simply to bed another man's wife for the sake of it. Something more was going on. After all, Livilla was not just anyone; she was the wife of a future emperor, and sister to Germanicus, whose much-loved memory held sway amongst the people even years after his death.

"I'm going over to speak with Decimus," Torquatus told me, squeezing my arm. I nodded and gave him a tight smile, quickly locating a glass filled to the brim with wine.

We had only just arrived at Sejanus and Apicata's home, and already my husband was off to talk business. We hadn't even seen our host yet, only our hostess; she looked especially sad as I made eye contact with her from across the room. We would speak later, after all the guests had arrived; she was obligated to greet each of them. Sejanus's absence was notable—and rude, although no one would dare verbalize it.

Torquatus and Decimus embraced as they met, and then I saw Decimus introducing a youth who stood awkwardly near him, looking vastly uncomfortable in both his clothing and his surroundings. Rufus and another man, bearded and with long hair, a faint scar running above his left eye, stood behind, both of them surveying the room. Rufus ever so slightly inclined his chin as he saw me, although we had no need to speak—similarly to me, I sensed that he had given up on freeing himself from whatever chains bound him to Decimus. Both of us were resigned to our fates after years of failure.

I turned away, looking over the rest of the guests as I stepped further into the gathering, Amynta trailing behind me. Former consuls, senators, their wives—it was quite an ambitious collection of people that Sejanus had put together, a congregation composed of Rome's elite, all of them eager to simper over the Praetorian Prefect.

"Aemilia, dear," Decimus's wife greeted me. I smiled thinly and returned her greeting, and we both passed on our way; there was no inclination towards friendship between us, but polite, superficial acknowledgements were, of course, expected. That did not mean we had to engage in conversation any longer than necessary.

I encountered other people I knew, exchanging hellos and asking politely after children, commenting on the fashions of the year, the weather—all mundane, typical topics. Still Sejanus did not appear, and I could tell that Apicata was growing increasingly agitated; she had moved away from their home's doors, suggesting that all the guests had arrived. Her husband's prolonged absence was strange, and increasingly noticeable the longer he was missing. The other guests had begun to whisper and glance about, but what caught my attention next was Drusus, who had begun to pace the room.

Apicata approached him. As the highest profile guest that evening, he was due special attention; his distress boded poorly for the success of the gathering. I inched closer, my curiosity to overhear their words getting the better of me.

"...she disappeared shortly after your husband," Drusus was whispering angrily. Spittle flew from his mouth, although he seemed oblivious to it.

Apicata fought not to wring her hands, a nervous habit for which she had once told me her nursemaid used to whip her fingers, when she had been younger. "I—" she began to stammer out, face flushed. Her eyes shone with anxious, unshed tears.

She stopped, suddenly looking behind Drusus with an expression of both relief and anger. Sejanus had returned, slightly red in the face, smoothing his hands through his hair.

"Welcome!" Sejanus shouted out, grinning as he stepped into the room. "Where's my wine?" he asked, even as a slave already rushed to bring him a glass. All his guests looked on as he took a large swallow of his drink.

The host's appearance seemed to restore a sense of normalcy to the gathering, and soon people began to mingle once again, some of them already surging towards their charismatic host, eager to speak with one of Rome's most prominent, powerful men. Only recently had we all heard how Tiberius now quite publicly referred to Sejanus as a 'partner' in his toils—no doubt a painful blow to Drusus, Tiberius's own son. That his wife and Sejanus were involved, in an increasingly public way... it was no surprise that Drusus was so agitated. He was not only losing favor with his own father, but being humiliated, too.

Wineglasses were refilled and appetizers were carried throughout the room, slaves serving dainty tidbits to the guests in advance of the more formal dinner: fresh shrimp glazed with honey; chickpea patties with a safflower dip; bite-sized chunks of roasted hare, coated in a sauce of wine and *garum*; small gourds stuffed with lamb's brain.

As I popped another honey-glazed shrimp into my mouth, movement at the corner of my eye drew my attention: Livilla had returned to the gathering, too, some minutes after Sejanus's own reappearance. Not many seemed to take note of her, or, if they did, they knew better than to be obvious about it, let alone comment upon it. Her hair looked as if she had tried to re-pin it herself, wild tendrils escaping around her ears, and her dress was wrinkled in various places. I could see only a faint, passing resemblance to my uncle Germanicus, and it was one that did not seem to extend to her character.

Drusus approached his wife, knocking into several other guests on his way to her but not pausing to make any apologies. He grabbed Livilla by the arm and yanked her with him towards the door.

"Stop it!" I heard her hiss at him as they passed by me, and she wrenched her arm, trying to pull away from her husband. "You're hurting me!"

Drusus, stony faced, ignored her complaints, tugging her more roughly. "We are leaving." He turned his head to the two slaves who now accompanied them, emerging from hidden alcoves to adjoin themselves to their master. "You, go get our cloaks. And you, go get the litter. Now."

"I don't want to go," Livilla said petulantly. Drusus ignored her, his body tense, mouth pressed into a thin, unhappy line as he seemed to clench his teeth together.

"Whatever is the problem, Drusus? You'll offend me by leaving too soon." Sejanus. Too focused on Drusus and Livilla, I hadn't seen him approach. He sipped his wine, then smiled broadly at the couple about to depart his home. Apicata hovered anxiously behind him, visibly wringing her hands with abandon now, her face drawn and pale. "I have had an exquisite menu drawn up for dinner. Eel is one of the options. I believe that's your favorite, Livilla, is it not?"

"Speak to my wife again, and I'll…" Drusus started, though he cut himself off before finishing his threat. His face was beet red now, a vein bulging on his brow.

The room had grown quiet again, the guests all watching, waiting; I was reminded of vultures circling a dying animal, eager to rip into its bloody flesh even as it drew its last breath. Only now, I wasn't certain which man the vultures were going to go after—the emperor's own son, or his current favorite?

"You'll what, Drusus?" Sejanus asked, a taunt underlying the words. He still continued to smile, although it was now wolfish, predatory. Any trace of friendliness had faded entirely away.

Drusus didn't speak again; instead, he launched himself at Sejanus, a fist smashing squarely into the Praetorian Prefect's face, the blood beginning to flow immediately from his nose. Apicata and Livilla both screamed.

CHAPTER XX

RUFUS

Rufus didn't take much time to gawk at Drusus and Sejanus. The latter's nose was bleeding profusely, and his wife hung on his arm, feverishly speaking into his ear as he stared silently at Drusus's retreating back, his eyes dangerously cold. The single punch had not devolved into a full-on brawl, but it seemed that it was taking a great measure of restraint on Sejanus's part not to attack the emperor's son. If he had, it was unlikely that even being a favorite of Tiberius could save him from ruin.

Rufus, for once thankful that he had retired from the Praetorian Guard and entered Decimus's employ in a full capacity several years ago—and thus no longer had to answer to Sejanus—quickly escorted the senator from the residence. He had already sent orders for the litter bearers to prepare for their departure, knowing that his master would not want to linger at the gathering after such a scene. Decimus, for once, seemed at a loss for words, although Rufus had no doubt that the senator's mind was already hard at work determining whom he would support—his ongoing ally, Sejanus, or the emperor's own flesh and blood—and how the incident might be used to some advantage. After such a public feud, there could be no doubt that sides would have to be taken, although many people's responses would certainly be dictated by

Tiberius's own reaction, once he heard what had happened.

"We'll follow on foot," Rufus told the man who came up beside him. They observed as Decimus stepped into the litter, carefully holding up the folds of his toga with practiced hands.

The other man nodded, watching as his own charge—the noble Dacian youth—entered the litter behind the senator, although he, as if worried he might trip, organized his clothing with far less ease. It would come, with practice; after all, he had only been in Rome less than a year. It must take time, Rufus surmised, to shed one's barbaric ways: to acclimate to the toga, to bathing regularly, to doing things as a proper Roman did.

The litter set off, and Rufus and his companion followed, their steps in synch. Both surveyed their surroundings, alert for any sign of trouble.

"How long have you served your master?" the other man asked Rufus abruptly.

Rufus didn't respond immediately to the halting, choppy Latin his companion spoke. There was something off about him, the Dacian warrior who called himself Brasus. He had been allowed to escort the boy, Duras, as guard and companion for the duration of his education—to use the polite term—in Rome; unlike his charge, he was allowed to retain his Dacian clothes, his beard and hairstyle. Naturally, he was barred from carrying any weapons, though in training sessions he had proven entirely proficient in the Roman arsenal. His Latin, though he took his time to speak and often answered slowly, with pauses between words, was oddly accurate; his knowledge of Rome's streets and alleys, when he thought he was not being observed, was far too thorough for a foreigner who was accustomed to tribal camps and wild forests.

Rufus realized Brasus was still waiting for his answer. "I don't remember. Well over a dozen years, now." The words were cold, not inviting of further questions. Rufus didn't like to dwell on all the years he had spent his life in service to someone like Decimus, nor did he like to share details with a man he barely knew.

Brasus grunted in acknowledgement, eyes scanning the dark road they followed. The senator's torch bearers brought little light to a night unmarked by the moon.

"And you?" Rufus asked. "How long have you been with young Duras?"

The answer came surprisingly quickly. "Since he was a babe." Rufus detected a strong sense of protectiveness in the words, as if Brasus truly did care about the youth—but perhaps that was a normal bond in Dacia, one formed between a warrior and his noble charge as part of a lifetime of service.

"Have you been to Rome before?" Rufus asked next, wondering if he might get an honest answer.

Brasus's response came quickly. "No." The single word was forceful. Rufus didn't believe him—but why would the man lie? There was no crime in having visited the city.

Rufus didn't ask more questions that night; he wasn't sure why the strange warrior stirred his suspicions, but he told himself he didn't need to concern himself with it. Brasus was solely there in relation to young Duras, the son of one of Dacia's tribal kings who had been causing trouble by raiding into Roman territory. He had been placed into Decimus's household as a hostage; the senator was to teach the youth Roman ways and customs, to enlighten him about all that Rome could offer to those who served it loyally. One day, when the boy's father died, he would be returned to his people—with the expectation that he would be a loyal scion of the empire, expanding Rome's reach and securing its influence.

Rufus knew that Decimus was pleased to have been tasked with hosting the youth; it presented him with yet another trail that might, one day, be cultivated into a path to power. But the soldier wondered if Brasus might be an impediment to the boy's indoctrination, a lifeline to customs and to a people that he would do better to forget—not that it was any concern of his, he reminded himself.

Rufus sensed Brasus watching him, and he met the other man's warm brown eyes. Something was lurking there, something that Rufus couldn't yet see. But Brasus only gave a small smile and diverted his gaze, and the two men continued on in silence behind the litter that bore both their masters.

Rufus watched as Brasus schooled Duras in various weaponry, using Decimus's courtyard for the youth's exercise program. The warrior and his charge were quietly discussing something, using their native language—something which Decimus didn't entirely discourage, knowing that Duras would one day need to return to his people, and to engage with them. Besides, the young man already had a surprisingly good grasp of Latin, and had little need to practice it, save for conversing in formal situations. What he had learned before coming to Rome was somewhat provincial, full of slang.

The Dacians glanced at Rufus, but he ignored them. It bothered him more than he liked to admit when he couldn't understand what they were saying, although he dismissed himself as paranoid. No doubt they were simply discussing the next exercise they would run through.

"I'll take a turn with the boy," Rufus said suddenly, tired of sitting and watching. It left him too much time to dwell on things he would rather forget, his thoughts inevitably drifting to Leander, to the island, to Agrippa Postumus. "Short swords." It was his best weapon—rightfully so, for a former Praetorian Guard.

Brasus passed Duras a wooden practice sword, a perfect replica of a real metal blade, and stepped aside, watching his charge as he hefted the weapon in his hand, acclimating himself to its weight. Rufus did the same, and then the pair squared off, legs slightly bent, each of them ready to move in any direction.

Rufus struck first, testing the youth, who quickly and easily deflected his opponent's weapon. Rufus struck again, harder this time; again Duras parried, then attacked, surprising Rufus slightly with his speed and accuracy. The boy was far better with the weapon than he remembered, having sparred with him only a few weeks ago. Perhaps he and Brasus had practiced more—both had claimed the youth primarily trained with the scythe-like sword favored by his own people, and that he had had no exposure to the Roman short sword until their arrival in Rome.

As if sensing Rufus's surprise, Duras forged ahead in an aggressive assault, seeking to capitalize on his brief advantage, but the solider quickly matched his opponent's rhythm, and both were soon drenched in sweat. Rufus found that he was enjoying himself; the boy was proving a worthwhile adversary.

Suddenly, the edge of Duras's wooden practice sword clipped Rufus's hand, and a quick surge of pain flashed through the soldier. It was time, Rufus thought, to finish their little session.

With each clanking strike of their swords, Rufus bore down on the youth, using his greater weight to tire his opponent. He began to take faster, wilder slashes, constantly approaching, attacking without pause, making certain not to betray his next target with his eyes or his body positioning—and then Duras tripped, falling backwards, his wooden sword clattering across the mosaicked floor, out of reach.

Rufus sensed Brasus moving in from the side, a dark shadow in the corner of his vision, but he didn't pause; he flashed his sword forward, stopping it only a finger's length from Duras's neck. The youth's eyes were slightly wider than usual, taken aback by Rufus's aggression.

His eyes... Some faint spark of recognition flared in the back of Rufus's mind. Why did those eyes seem familiar? Why hadn't he noticed them before? They were just like...

"That's enough," Brasus said. "Don't kill the boy." There was a forced levity in his words, and, when Rufus looked at the other man, he saw lines of worry, concern, protectiveness, all of them aging his face.

Rufus laughed, extending a hand to help Duras to his feet. The youth accepted it, brushing himself off as he stood, muttering something in his own tongue, and Rufus examined him again, trying to stir himself to recall whom it was the boy reminded him of.

CHAPTER
XXI

AEMILIA LEPIDA

Drusus and Sejanus; Sejanus and Livilla—it was all anyone in Rome could talk about, although everyone made certain to do so quietly. A few days after the incident, Apicata sent a short note telling me she wouldn't be able to come to our weekly meeting at the baths, and so I took my massage alone, finding that I missed her ceaseless chattering.

I wrote my own note to Apicata later that day, entrusting it to Amynta. "Please see that Apicata gets this directly," I instructed her. "And—"

"And see what's going on in their household?" Amynta interrupted me, a small smile curving her lips. She had long ago forgiven me for Rufus—mostly—although she still studiously ignored him whenever their paths crossed. Unfortunately for her, such encounters were frequent, given the friendly relationship between Decimus and Torquatus. It was a relationship I was unhappy still existed, but I had come to realize there was little I could do to stop it from continuing; if my husband decided that was the company we would keep, then that was all but the end of the matter.

I nodded, returning Amynta's smile, glad that she had already known what I was going to ask of her. Slaves were sometimes able to gain access to places their masters could not; they often glimpsed or overheard things that great pains would be taken to hide from the ears and eyes of people considered more important. And I knew, without a doubt, that Sejanus's household would likely be in a state of uproar after what had happened, although they were attempting to maintain an impenetrable façade of normality.

Amynta hastened off with my note to Apicata, and I wandered through my home to find my children, all five of whom, ranging in age between four and almost nine years, were being occupied by a small army of nursemaids. It had been quite a while since Torquatus and I had lain together, and I suspected, now that I was nearing my third decade, that he had turned his attentions to younger, softer, more tender women at various brothels. I didn't mind; although I loved my children fiercely, my body felt worn and tired, and I was happy for the reprieve from childbearing. No one could say that I had not done my womanly duty.

Torquatus and I had never grown to love another in the same visceral way that Aunt Agrippina and Germanicus seemed to have, for all those years: a passionate longing that might ebb and flow, but nevertheless remained constant in its presence. Nor, now that I was a mother, could I come close to envisioning what my own mother must have felt for Silanus, to have risked her life—to have risked losing *me*— for the sake of being with him. In some ways, since becoming a parent, I felt that I understood my mother even less; in some ways, I found that, over time, I had developed an even deeper resentment of her, for what she had done. I wondered what she would make of it, what she would say, if she knew what Silanus had done to me.

"*Mater!*" A chorus of high-pitched voices cried out almost entirely in unison as my children caught sight of me, and a stampede of small, sandaled feet rushed forwards, trampling over a mosaic of Niobe and her many offspring—one that showed them together, happy, before they were struck down for their mother's transgression. I quickly pulled my eyes from it.

"Children," I greeted them all warmly. Marcus, my eldest, seemed to remember himself first, quickly pulling out of my embrace and doing his best to stand stoically at attention, already a miniature version of his father. The others, at least as of yet, had no such qualms, holding onto my dress as they giggled and talked over one another, their nursemaids silently awaiting my signal to take the children back to the tasks they had been engaged in. The boys would soon have their afternoon tutoring, while the two girls would occupy themselves with different lessons, ones deemed suitable by my husband for the young, noble Roman ladies they were quickly growing into.

I wished that none of my children would ever grow older, that they would never leave me, to become embroiled in the poisons that plagued Rome: politics, plotting, betrayals, an endless, inevitable cycle that ran its bloody course before beginning again with each new generation, a tale that reached even further back than Romulus and Remus. But I knew that to wish for my children to remain as they were was impossible; to ask for them to never age was akin to praying for their deaths, asking for their lives to be ended as had been those of Niobe's children.

Amynta appeared in the doorway, and I could tell from her face that she bore news. A small scroll was furled in her hand, and she lifted it ever so slightly to capture my attention. Apicata had written back to me.

Apicata and I met at one of the local markets, browsing the busy stalls as our slaves and guards trailed after and around us. People openly stared at her, whispering in hushed voices, although it was unclear whether they spoke of Sejanus's brawl with Drusus, her husband's involvement with Livilla, or the fading but still conspicuous bruise across Apicata's left eye.

She shifted the veil she wore, hoping the slight shade it cast might do more to conceal her injury, though her efforts bore minimal result.

"Sejanus?" I asked simply, directly.

She didn't meet my eyes, but she nodded. It wasn't the first time he had beaten her, seized by some anger, some mood, one that often had nothing at all to do with her. Still, it wasn't uncommon for husbands to beat their wives—though most took pains to ensure that at least their property's face wasn't marred by it. Torquatus, perhaps, was a rarity; he had only ever taken his hand to me once, after I had drunkenly complained to him about the company we kept. It had been the closest I had ever come to confessing my hatred of Decimus, of Silanus—and to confessing what I had done to my own husband, poisoning him at the behest of another man, one he now called a friend and ally. But the single slap to my face had brought me to my senses. Torquatus would not, could not, understand.

"Something is going on," Apicata said quietly. Her hands were busy examining jewelry at a stand, picking up and setting down necklaces and rings, hairpins and bracelets, but her eyes darted around the market, and she spoke rapidly, as if worried she might be interrupted before she could tell me of all her news.

"Of course something is going on," I said, more dismissively than I had intended. "Your husband was quite publicly accused of sleeping with Livilla, and then he was attacked by Drusus, in front of dozens of people."

Apicata sighed, a rare anger flashing in her eyes as she looked at me. "Not that," she snapped. Her eyes returned to scanning the market, and she set down the golden, serpentine bracelet she had been clutching in her hands. "Let's move to the next stall."

I followed obediently; although I was curious, I knew better than to rush Apicata to speak. Her hands shook as we walked; instead of pausing to browse the wares presented by the next merchant, she continued on, and soon she began to wring her hands.

"Give us some space," she snapped to her attendants. I, too, motioned for Amynta and my own guards to move away.

"I can't trust them," she said breathlessly. "The guards. They're Praetorians, all of them—all loyal to my husband. More loyal to him than to the emperor." The last sentence was said under her breath; I almost didn't hear it.

I reached out to take her hand in my own; this wasn't the Apicata that I knew, the woman who chattered away happily, who chose to overlook her husband's infidelities, his shortcomings, always maintaining her image as the ideal Roman matron. She waved my hand away; still her eyes darted to and fro around us, never once pausing to meet my eyes as she spoke.

"Something is happening." She had said it before, but she repeated herself, firmer this time. "I... I overheard him. Sejanus... speaking to Decimus, yesterday. I didn't see—I was passing by, and I just paused, but I was too scared they would see me, if I tried... I was going to pay my respects to Decimus—I didn't know he was visiting. No one has, since that night… But then I heard them."

She was wringing her hands more frantically, and, this time, when I reached out to her, she didn't push me away, but instead returned my grip with surprising strength. "I think they're going to kill Drusus."

The words were so quiet that I almost had to read her lips; she spoke them as barely more than a passing breath. I didn't know what to think, what to say.

A moment passed, then several. "Why? Why do you think that?" I asked finally, uncertain. My own gaze began to take note of our surroundings, seeing if anyone watched us, striving to overhear our conversation. A spice merchant at the nearest stall looked bored, calling out loudly to passerby, but he never so much as glanced towards us.

"Sejanus said 'I want him dead,' but he didn't say his name. Although who else could it be, except Drusus? And then Decimus said he knew someone, who had helped a wife poison her own husband, once." Apicata finally met my eyes, and I felt frozen.

Did she know? Had Decimus mentioned my name? I must have been the wife he mentioned. My own fear of my secret being discovered—and not by just anyone, but by the one other woman I considered a friend—paralyzed me.

"What do we do?" Apicata asked, urgently.

I swallowed once, then again, thinking, searching her eyes: frantic; scared. There was no trace of accusation, no hint of knowledge. I did not think she would be capable of hiding it, if she knew what I had done; she was too good, too pure to simply brush it off as something unimportant.

"We have no proof," I said at last. "Was there a letter of some sort, some instructions written down? Was anyone else in the room?"

"I don't know," Apicata said, "I don't know." She was wringing her hands again, eyes downcast, her back hunched, defeated. "I only heard them. I didn't get close enough to see."

I had an idea, suddenly, but it wasn't one I could share with her. Rufus—Rufus might be the key to finding evidence of what they plotted. After all this time, he might be the key to Decimus's downfall—and if it ruined Sejanus, too, then so be it. Any ally of Decimus was an enemy of mine.

"Go home," I told Apicata. "Smile, be agreeable. Be as you normally are. Leave this to me."

"What are you going to do?" she asked. "What *can* you do? I don't want Sejanus to…"

"To what? He won't know you had a part in this," I reassured her, but she shook her head at me, a sad smile flitting across her lips.

"I don't want him to be hurt," she whispered. "He's my husband, after all. What am I, without him?"

I clenched my teeth to stop the retort already forming on my lips. Outwardly, I nodded, a single jerk of my head, but inwardly I knew that, if I could manage to discover evidence of their treason, no one would be spared the impending bloodshed. My old thirst for vengeance had already begun to stir from its long slumber.

CHAPTER
XXII

TITUS

Titus hadn't been prepared to see her—to see Aemilia Lepida, Julia's daughter. It was like seeing Julia herself, from a distance. He didn't get close enough to notice the smaller details he was certain would differentiate her from her mother, those that she would have inherited from her father. Oh, he wanted to—he wanted to see her up close, to touch her, to speak to her about her mother—did she write letters to Julia? Were they in contact? But he knew that all of these things wouldn't—couldn't—ever come to pass.

When Aemilia entered the gathering hosted by Sejanus and Apicata, he felt as if he had been brutally, swiftly punched in the gut, the breath wholly knocked from his body. His eyes followed her, watching as her husband squeezed her arm and approached his own group, wanting to speak to Decimus; he watched as she was served wine, as she moved around the room—oh, how she moved just like her mother, the quiet gracefulness of a body that was surprisingly strong, lithe, athletic for her sex—and he wondered if she, like her mother, had learned how to swim as a girl.

Titus didn't know how long he watched her; it seemed both mere moments and an eternity. Seeing her—recalling Julia, her face, her scent, her laugh, and, worst of all, her ongoing imprisonment—almost made him want to retch, to weep. But, instead, he simply stood there, at attention, lingering behind Duras and Decimus. And it was then that a new thought seized him—Duras, Julia's son. Aemilia's half-brother, who also bore a striking resemblance to his mother—and thus, too, to Aemilia. They mustn't see one another, he thought—they mustn't be seen *next* to one another, where their similarities might be—must be—noticed.

A small sense of panic began to seize Titus; Aemilia was still circulating, but, eventually, her trajectory would align with them. Her own husband had joined their group; it was only natural that the couple would reunite. When that happened, she would come face to face with Duras.

And so, in an odd way, it was with a sense of relief that Titus watched Drusus and Sejanus engage in their patrician cockfight, two roosters strutting around the room as their respective wives watched on—as Aemilia, too, was distracted by the events unfolding at the gathering. When Drusus attacked the Praetorian Prefect, Titus exhaled in a quiet sigh; Duras looked at him questioningly, but Titus was already working alongside Rufus to organize their group's departure. The imminent threat of recognition, of discovery, was gone—Duras remained safe, for the time being.

"You were odd yesterday," Duras said to him the following day, using, as was their practice, the Dacian language, so that no one else in Decimus's household would overhear and understand what exchanges they shared. "Did you see someone you recognized, Father? You seemed…" He trailed off, unable to put into words the expression he had seen on Titus's face.

Titus thought before responding. Over the course of their journey from Dacia to Rome, he had shared a few things with the boy who called him Father—one being that he was, in fact, a Roman, a former soldier who had deserted. That much, at least, was true—so, too, was what he told Duras about his mother: that Titus had loved her, but that the youth would never meet her. Titus didn't think he would ever see her again, either, although he didn't share that particular doubt with the boy.

Duras had assumed his mother was dead; Titus did not enlighten him. It would serve no purpose; it would even be cruel, he told himself, knowing that there was no chance Duras could ever come to know his mother. The boy still believed Titus was his father, but he agreeably upheld the falsehood that Titus was instead Brasus, a Dacian warrior from his tribe, a guardian who had been with him since birth and who now joined him in Rome. To all others, Duras's father was Didas, a Dacian tribal king.

They distanced themselves from one another, to maintain the lie, and only spoke in Latin when they didn't mind others overhearing. Titus even made sure to speak his Latin as if it were his second language, as if he struggled with finding the correct words to use. He kept his beard and hair long, in the Dacian style, and, for the most part, kept to the foreign clothing he had grown used to wearing after all these years, Roman military tunics and armor now things of his distant past.

"Father?" Duras prompted him again.

"No," Titus answered. "It wasn't anyone I knew, just… someone who reminded me of another, who I did know once, quite well…"

Duras shrugged, not noticing the sadness that tinged Titus's words. His youthful excitement about Rome—the sense of adventure, the opportunity to see and to try new things—often managed to overshadow the ever-present knowledge of his own situation, that of hostage, one who would just as readily be killed as be sent back to his homeland, depending on the empire's needs at any given time.

Rufus appeared then, and Titus gave him a small nod of greeting. The soldier—Decimus's shadow, Titus had come to understand—typically joined their training sessions. Decimus had ordered it, seeking to ensure that Duras was educated in what he considered to be superior Roman weaponry and tactics, not knowing that Titus had already covered that part of the boy's schooling. Decimus had also brought in tutors on various subjects, filling much of Duras's days with public speaking, Greek, history, religion, all things that, had Duras been raised in Rome—as the Roman he was by blood and birth—he would have already known backwards and forwards.

While Duras seemed to relish the experiences and privileges that living in a senatorial household conveyed, it made Titus uneasy; it brought forth too many unanswered questions and simmering resentments he thought he had long ago buried within himself. His own mother had once been a slave woman in such a household, until she had fallen pregnant with her master's bastard child; the senator had subsequently freed her, and thus Titus had had the fortune to be born a Roman citizen instead of a slave. But his mother had never identified the senator whose seed had given Titus life, taking his name to her grave. He had thought he had made peace with not knowing—but being in Rome again, living in Decimus's household, a senator who might have known his father, seeing the slaves carrying out tasks his own mother once would have performed, ones *he* might have performed had he been born into servitude… it all reminded him too much of a vastly different life he had once so faintly brushed up against.

"Brasus," Rufus greeted Titus, using the Dacian name everyone believed him to bear, calling him back to the present—a present in which he needed to keep his wits about him. Selecting a pseudonym was one of the first things Titus had known he needed to do; it would do no good to go by his own name, not when he had no doubt that he had been listed as a deserter after disappearing in search of Julia's son.

Rufus and Duras sparred that day, Titus shifting his weight anxiously as the boy did well—too well—with the Roman short sword. Nevertheless, Rufus emerged victorious in their practice bout, helping the youth back to his feet after an unfortunate fall.

Clapping directed their collective attention to the edge of the courtyard where they practiced: Decimus had been watching.

"You've improved, boy," he told Duras warmly, though his tone didn't match his expression. Decimus was like that, Titus had noticed—superficially kind, welcoming; none of it ever reached his eyes, which remained cold and predatory.

"Thank you, Decimus," Duras answered proudly, a genuine smile on his face. Titus worried about him, sometimes—about how often he seemed to forget Dacia, the place that was, in the ways that mattered, his homeland; about how much he seemed to enjoy Rome and all that it offered, the baths and the food and even the women—Titus had seen the boy looking at them more often of late. But, of course, Rome, not Dacia, was his true homeland—all that it encompassed was Duras's birthright as a great-great-grandson of Augustus. It was the same birthright that would get him killed faster than he or Titus could blink.

"Why don't you escort me today? I have some visitors coming throughout the rest of the morning and into the afternoon. You can see how I receive them," Decimus said, his tone at once inviting and arrogant, full of self-importance. He didn't bother to spare a glance at Titus or Rufus; they were, as always, little more than objects in the background, ignored until they were needed.

"I would be honored," Duras said, and the pair left the courtyard.

Not even the boy spared Titus a look as he passed by. Titus told himself it was simply what they had rehearsed, what they practiced daily in this household, in this city, this empire: Duras was a Dacian prince, and Titus—Brasus—merely his guard, and a guard wouldn't be worth a look or a farewell. But Titus could not help the sharp sting that seemed to originate in his chest.

Almost as soon as Decimus and Duras departed the courtyard, another figure appeared: a slave woman, one who scowled fiercely at Rufus even as she handed him a small, rolled up scroll. She turned on her heel and left as soon as it passed into his hands, and he quickly read it, eyes rapidly scanning back and forth before he bunched up the note and shoved it inside his tunic.

"Bad news?" Titus couldn't help but ask.

Rufus started, as if he had forgotten that Titus was there. "No," he answered sharply. He didn't speak again before he hurried out of the courtyard, and Titus was left alone.

Something about Rufus was strange, Titus thought. When the red-haired soldier didn't think anyone was looking, he sometimes stared at Decimus, not with admiration, but with... hatred. Titus knew Rufus didn't trust him; naturally, he didn't place any faith in the other man, either. Neither of them would be worth even half their weight as Roman soldiers if trust came that easily.

With Duras occupied the remainder of the day, Titus had nothing else to do; on a whim, he set out after Rufus, curious what had so unsettled Decimus's righthand man.

CHAPTER XXIII

AEMILIA LEPIDA

Amynta returned without bearing a response from Rufus, although, knowing her feelings about him, I suspected that she hadn't even waited to see if he wished to send a reply with her.

"He'll be there, *domina*," was all she had said, certain that Rufus would have understood my cryptic note to him. I hoped she was correct; if we had any chance of exposing Decimus—if what Apicata had overhead was true—then Rufus would have an integral role to play, being the one with the greatest access to the senator and his household.

I sighed, shifting my weight from foot to foot. I waited for Rufus in my family's tomb on the Via Appia—my father's family tomb, that is. Naturally, his ashes were excluded from inclusion amongst his ancestors; his treason, and his subsequent execution, had made certain of that. No one wanted to memorialize a traitor. Augustus had preemptively forbidden my mother's ashes, too, from ever being interred in his own mausoleum. Even death, when it came for her, would make certain that she would remain an outcast, an exile.

Amynta sniffed behind me as she went again to check the road; it was nearing dark, and we would soon have to return to the city; we could not afford to waste much more time waiting for Rufus to appear.

We had brought no guards with us—I did not trust that they wouldn't relay to my husband where we had gone, with whom we had met—and the roads outside Rome weren't safe at night. Too many desperate people lurked in the shadows of the tombs that lined the Via Appia, some of them hoping to steal the offerings of food and drink left by the living as gifts to their ancestors, others preying upon the wealthy who came to pay their respects to the departed while covered head to toe in expensive jewelry, bulging coin purses affixed to belts stretched tight across well-fed bellies.

Amynta sneezed as she returned to my side, the incense I had set aflame agitating her nose, and I started, the noise more fully recalling me to the present. The urns containing my father's relatives, carefully placed in niches all around me, seemed to loom large, as if the spirits of those whose ashes they contained stood watch. I did not dwell on what they might think of me, their descendant, the offspring of two pariahs who had willingly placed herself on a precarious path.

"He's here," Amynta announced, and I turned to face the tomb's entrance, my hands smoothing my dress down my sides and tightening my cloak around my shoulders. Rufus entered, slightly out of breath.

"Is it true?" he asked immediately, forgoing any greeting. His eyes flashed with rare emotion—excitement, perhaps. "There is proof of Decimus committing treason?"

So, he had understood the hint of my letter; I didn't write out much, worried that, should it be intercepted, it would be my own life at risk. I was glad his mind had been able to piece my words together.

"Perhaps," I said. "But you are the only one who might be able to find it. That poison you brought me, all those years ago... Do you know where—who—it came from?"

Rufus sighed. "No. Decimus did use a slave to fetch it, who

passed it on to me to give to you, but… That slave died years ago. I never accompanied Decimus, or anyone else, to the supplier. There are some things that he doesn't trust even me to witness."

I closed my eyes briefly, drawing in a breath of the incense-filled air. "I believe he intends to use the same person this time. He and Sejanus intend to poison Drusus."

Rufus stilled at my last words; my letter had not conveyed the specific treason Decimus was to be involved in, and he had not guessed.

"How do you know this?" he asked next, a hint of suspicion underlaying his words.

"After all these years, you think I'm plotting an elaborate betrayal of you? I thought you trusted me," I snapped. "Now is our chance to rid ourselves of Decimus—and the evidence of my betrayal of Torquatus in the process."

I felt Amynta stiffen behind us as she processed my words; I had not dismissed her upon Rufus's arrival. Let her know, now, what I had done—how I had coldly poisoned my own husband. I turned to her.

"Amynta, when Torquatus was ill, when everyone thought he might die… It was me. I poisoned him." Her eyes were wide. "I did not intend to kill him… I gave him only a drop, to sicken him." My words were devoid of emotion, simply factual.

"Why, *domina*?" Her words were heavy with judgment, with accusation. "He is your husband—he holds all our fates in his hands." She did not speak the thought I am sure she held in her mind; had Torquatus died then, and if anyone had suspected poison, it would have meant that all the slaves in our household, including Amynta, could be tortured for information, before being executed, down to the last slave child. I had knowingly and willingly endangered not just her, but countless others.

"Because your naïve mistress thought Decimus might restore her family from exile if she proved her loyalty to him," Rufus barked out, his impatience clear. "We don't have time for this—fill in your slave woman later, if you wish."

I glared at him. "Then go. Find out who supplied the poison then—who will supply it now. If he turns on Decimus, if he confesses, Decimus will be finished."

"Sejanus, too," Rufus said. "Decimus will not hesitate to turn on him."

"So be it. Sejanus is of little concern, one way or another." I was surprised at how cold my words were, and Apicata's face flashed through my mind; she had worried about her husband, had wanted him to be left out of whatever retribution would come, even after all he had put her through. But my eagerness to destroy Decimus far outweighed my loyalty to the woman I now considered a friend.

Rufus still stood there in my family's tomb, watching me, expectant. The harsh lines of his face, deepened over the course of time, were accentuated by the rapidly fading light.

"What is it?" I snapped. "As you said, we don't have much time. I don't know when they will make the attempt. It may already be too late—Decimus may already have the poison in hand."

"If the supplier confesses to this, why not confess, too, to the poison he sold before, the one given to you?" Rufus asked.

"He doesn't know that was for me. Only Decimus would. So long as Decimus doesn't suspect me of betraying him, of my involvement in this, he would have no reason to reveal that now. And when both Decimus and the poison supplier are executed, we are free." Rufus and I held each other's gazes, mine full of angry excitement, his dark and unreadable, as it had always been.

"I could just kill them both," Rufus said then. "The supplier and Decimus. We—"

I cut him off. "No. I don't just want them dead. I want Decimus's memory to be destroyed. I want him to be denied funerary rites—I want his own family to cast him out, to curse him for what he has done. He deserves to suffer for an eternity."

A flash of something—agreement? Pride, even?—crossed Rufus's face, and he nodded, a rare, unrestrained smile lifting the edges of his lips. "So be it, Aemilia." He gave a small salute, a soldier to his general, and Amynta huffed as the soldier turned and left, no doubt thinking that he was mocking me—that calling me by my name, without even an honorific, was disrespectful, too familiar.

But I didn't mind; I knew that Rufus had been genuine. That, for the first time in the well over a decade we had known one another, he had viewed me as an equal—despite my sex, despite our difference in station, despite everything that divided us. And it was because, at last, I had let my desire for revenge—brutal, bloody, merciless—dictate my commands. I had become something he could recognize, identify with. I had become like him.

Days passed, and still I had no word from Rufus. I sat with my children and their nursemaids, only half paying attention to them as they played with one another, my thoughts taking me somewhere else entirely. Drusus yet lived, and I began to doubt not only myself, but Apicata and what she claimed to have overheard between Sejanus and Decimus. What if there was no proof to be found, no treasonous, murderous plot to be unearthed? Perhaps the feud between Drusus and Sejanus was just that—a feud, one between two powerful, arrogant men, spurred on by a brutish passion for the same woman, Livilla. I had almost begun to believe these thoughts when news did come. It just wasn't the news I had expected.

Amynta burst into the room, startling both the nursemaids and my children. "Sejanus has divorced Apicata!" she exclaimed.

"Quiet," I hissed at her as my children watched, listening. I quickly left the room, motioning for Amynta to follow me. My mind raced as we headed down the hall, stopping only when I felt we were far enough away so as not to be overheard.

"Sejanus has divorced Apicata," Amynta said again, breathless. "My route to the market takes me past their home. Her belongings are being moved back to her parents' home as we speak."

"Are you certain?" I asked. What would Sejanus gain by the divorce? Apicata came from a respected, wealthy family. He would only divorce if he thought he could do better—but who did he have in mind? Even if Drusus died—whether by misfortune or by murder—Sejanus could not seriously believe that he would be allowed to marry a woman with as much standing as Livilla, could he?

Amynta nodded. "I asked around, to be certain. It is true."

Poor, poor Apicata. I knew she would be devastated—not because of losing Sejanus, but because of the assumption so many would make that *she* was somehow to blame for the divorce. Even worse than that, though, would be losing her children. As property of their father, they would remain with Sejanus, away from their mother with only the exception, if Sejanus allowed it, of occasional visits.

"Bring me my writing tools," I ordered Amynta, and she hurried to obey, returning moments later. I quickly scratched out a note to my friend, impatiently blowing on the glistening ink before rolling the papyrus up. "Make sure Apicata gets this. Take it to her parents' household immediately."

Amynta nodded and departed, and I breathed in deeply, steadying myself. My short letter to Apicata contained nothing scandalous or even particularly noteworthy; it was merely an assurance of my continued friendship and support, with a line added to convey my deepest sympathies. I could do little else at the moment to assist her, but it felt important to send some communication, to reassure her that she was not entirely abandoned—for I knew the feeling all too well.

Thinking that the excitement of the day was over, I was taken aback that afternoon when my husband told me that Decimus and his wife, as well as Sejanus, would be joining us for dinner the very next evening.

"So soon after news of his divorce?" I asked Torquatus, my tone accusatory.

He looked surprised. "How did you hear of that already? Amynta, I suppose…"

"Apicata is my friend," I said firmly. It did not matter how I knew.

Torquatus waved a hand at me dismissively. "Sejanus is our friend," he corrected. "Our interests are aligned with his. You should know this. You cannot maintain a friendship with the woman he has cast off. It would be unseemly."

My lips moved wordlessly, fumbling for something to say, some argument that would convince Torquatus otherwise. But already he was turning away from me, oblivious to the effect his command had had upon me, and I knew that there was no point in arguing. He would not change his mind.

Apicata wrote back to me the following day; I know, because I recognized her slave woman at my door, who was turned brusquely away by the doorman. Torquatus had wasted no time in making sure his decision was relayed to our slaves; Apicata and her people were no longer welcome amongst us, no matter my thoughts or wishes regarding the subject.

I was subdued at dinner that night, listlessly picking at the steaming fish that had just been served, cooked in olive oil and wine mixed with leek and coriander, rubbed in lovage and oregano and pepper. It should have been flavorful; in fact, I knew it was, but so sour was my mood that I found it tasted of nothing. Instead I buried myself in my wineglass, and even that, for once, brought me little relief, no matter how much I drank. Sejanus was laughing loudly, the noise grating my ears.

"I must excuse myself," I said, standing suddenly. The room swam around me. "I feel unwell. Good night."

The dinner guests each uttered a sympathetic word or two before turning back to their conversation; even Torquatus spared me little more than a single questioning glance before looking away, spooning another bite of the soft fish into his mouth.

Just as I was about to leave the *triclinium*, one of our slaves nearly knocked me over as he half-ran into the room. He barely managed to offer me an apologetic bow as Torquatus snapped at him.

"What is the meaning of this?" my husband asked, the anger clear in his voice. He had risen from his dining couch, his body tense with irritation, and our guests all watched with bemused uncertainty.

"*Dominus*, I thought you would want to know immediately," the slave said, the words tumbling out as fast as he could form them with his quivering lips. "Drusus, son of Tiberius, is dead."

A stunned silence followed his words, and my eyes darted to each person in the room: Decimus's wife, mouth agape in shock; her husband, the senator, busying himself by soothing her; Torquatus, still and silent, confused; and Sejanus, the lightest trace of a smirk crossing his face before he schooled his expression into one of polite, concerned neutrality.

CHAPTER XXIV

RUFUS

He had failed. Even as time passed and his doubts grew, he had held out hope that he might find some hint of the poison supplier, of his connection to Decimus. But days had come and gone since he had met with Aemilia at the tomb, the hours stretching one into another with alarming rapidity, and still he had found nothing, not even the faintest promise of something more substantial, despite his best efforts.

He heard the whispers of Drusus's death even as he still searched, his hunt leading him down some of the worst alleyways of Rome, places where the stench was so strong that his eyes ran, that he could barely breathe; places where he openly carried a weapon, ready to strike at anyone who approached him. A sickness, people said; a sudden illness that had seized upon the emperor's son and borne him from the earthly realm to that of the Underworld. No one mentioned poison, or murder. Whatever they had given to Drusus, it had made his death seem natural. No one was asking questions.

Rufus told himself that even with Drusus dead, that didn't mean evidence couldn't still be found to prove that Sejanus and Decimus were behind it. The greater problem now lay with the fact that, with Drusus removed, no one stood between Tiberius and Sejanus; to convince the emperor that his favorite was involved in his son's death might prove difficult, even with proof. At the end of it all, though, Rufus didn't give a damn whether or not Sejanus was held accountable. Decimus was his target, was Aemilia's target—he was the one who needed to suffer, to be killed.

Movement startled Rufus from his thoughts; it was dangerous to be distracted, here of all places. He rested his hand on the short sword belted to his hip, partially obscured by the long cloak he wore, lest it attract attention, and his steps slowed until he came to a halt, listening intently.

He turned, eyes scanning the entrance to the even smaller, danker alley that adjoined the one he found himself in, having heard—after more cups of wine and fistfuls of coins than he could count, all passed into hands more bloodstained than his own—that a poisoner resided somewhere nearby. He could have sworn... No, he thought. Leander was dead, for many years now. Whatever Rufus thought he'd glimpsed, it wasn't him, no matter how much he might wish otherwise. He often tried to visualize his lover's features, bringing him to mind every time he felt that the roar of the ocean's waves might drive him mad, as if an imagined Leander might stave off whatever it was that lurked within him. It didn't always work; sometimes—more and more, of late—the memory of the island, of Agrippa Postumus, won out over the fading beacon of Leander's golden face.

Rufus started to turn away, but a noise—the crush of a foot on something he didn't have the faintest desire to envision—made him turn his attention back once more. He drew his weapon from its hilt as he approached.

With a sudden, silent surge, Rufus threw himself around the corner, prepared to strike down whomever, whatever, he found. But there was nothing there, save for a large rat scurrying away from a pile of muck with a smaller, dead rat laying on top, bloody entrails strung out from its half-eaten body.

Rufus shook his head to clear it. He was getting nowhere with this search, and as more and more time continued to pass since Drusus's murder, he knew that his chance to rid himself—and Aemilia—of Decimus was lost.

Brasus seated himself across from Rufus as they took their meal in the kitchen, grunting a wordless greeting which Rufus answered with a silent nod of his head. He was thankful that the Dacian wasn't overly chatty, either in his native language or in Latin.

The cook, busy behind them, was preparing dinner for Duras, Decimus, and the senator's wife. There were no household guests that evening, but the lack of outsiders did not guarantee a simple meal. The starter—softly boiled eggs that were steeped in a mixture of lovage, pepper, and pine kernels—had just been served; the next course was a combination of lobsters, cuttlefish, and squid in cumin sauce, which was being prepared at that very moment, the cook barking orders at the kitchen slaves who darted to and fro with different ingredients. A cake was to be the dessert, roasted pine nuts crushed up with honey, pepper, milk, and eggs; a slave had already begun to roast the pine kernels in the fire, not far from the table at which Rufus and Brasus sat.

The dessert especially made Rufus's mouth water, but he and Brasus were instead dining on a simple meal of mixed meat stew—the fleshy leftovers that the cook didn't dare serve to Decimus or his guests—alongside bread and cheese, with a small portion each of cheap wine, heavily watered down to mask the faint taste of vinegar. Rufus had met with some measure of fortune when one of the first eggs prepared had come out less than ideal, according to the cook—but the morsel was already a distant memory, eaten long before Brasus had arrived, and the cook would not gift either of them with more castoffs.

"What's the food like in Dacia?" he asked suddenly. He had caught a fresh whiff of the seafood being prepared, and the salty smell forced him to swallow down the bile that rose uneasily in his throat. He would be happy to never eat fish again, after having had it nearly every day on the island.

Brasus glanced up, mid-bite, surprised; Rufus wasn't one to bother with pleasantries and pointless talk at any time, especially during a meal. He finished biting off a chunk of bread, chewing slowly as he thought. "Meat," Brasus said. "Lots."

Rufus grunted. It wasn't a particularly surprising response, and he felt foolish for even asking, although the brief surge of panic that had risen within him was already subsiding, the sudden scent of the salt-laden seafood receding. He took a deep breath, calming himself.

"Where do you go, lately?" Brasus asked.

It was Rufus's turn to chew slowly, to think out his response before he volunteered it. He had not expected the Dacian warrior to notice his recent absences. "What do you mean?"

Brasus waved around the hand that held his bread. "You aren't here as much as you were before. Has Decimus set you some task?"

Rufus looked at the other man sharply. Brasus's Latin was still hesitant, but his eyes and mind were clearly sharp—sharper than Rufus had anticipated. "Yes," he said coldly, "he has. It's a private matter." He hoped that that ended the line of questioning.

Brasus gave him a small smile before pushing a piece of cheese into his mouth, and Rufus fought the urge to leap across the table and punch the Dacian. He had enough issues to contend with without factoring in a meddling foreigner.

Rufus pushed back from the table, standing. The main course was being taken from the kitchen by the servers, and he slipped out with them. He didn't look back at Brasus, but he felt the other man's eyes on him long after he had left the room.

I sank even deeper into myself after Drusus was murdered. It was almost as if he hadn't even existed; people moved on surprisingly quickly, somehow never seeming to suspect that Drusus's death was anything but an unfortunate act of the gods, a sudden and unexpected illness with a tragic end. Sejanus remained in favor; Decimus, his counterpart, grew in power alongside him, gaining in wealth and influence. There were a few whispers at first, of course—no one could forget the night that Drusus punched Sejanus—but whispers, too, fade away in time.

My husband tried his best to remain a part of what he considered their triumvirate, but the other men, to my relief, came less and less frequently to our home, occupied instead by all manner of other obligations, so torn were they in various directions by those who curried their favor. I didn't have the heart to tell my husband that Decimus and Sejanus had never considered him their equal—they had only ever turned to him when they felt he could be of some use to their greater scheming. But I suspected, on some level, that Torquatus already knew as much.

I once again gave up on ruining Decimus. Rufus had tried to pass me messages every so often, suggesting different ways we might attempt to bring the senator down, but even those had dwindled of late. It was as if the leadup to Drusus's murder had been the climax of our attempt at vengeance—and we had failed, the expected apex never arriving, instead subsiding away into a dull nothingness. Decimus did not bother to threaten me now, nor even to look at me when our paths crossed: he saw no use for me anymore, much as he saw little use for my husband.

After the death of his son, Tiberius had quickly adopted my cousins Nero Caesar and Drusus Caesar, the elder sons of Germanicus and Aunt Agrippina. It seemed strange to me that they were now young men, the elder entering his nineteenth year. It wasn't so long ago that they had been screaming, toddling children, all of us living together under Aunt Agrippina's watchful eye. So much was different now—so much had changed.

"Germanicus would have been so proud," Aunt Agrippina told me, smiling sadly. She had agreed to join me for my weekly massage, and now she lay stretched out on the slab that Apicata used to occupy— Apicata, who had quietly removed herself from society, allegedly bedridden much of the time, not from any physical illness, but instead from a malady of the mind.

Against the wishes of my husband, I still secretly wrote to Apicata, Amynta smuggling my letters to her, but I rarely received a response anymore. My friend didn't have the energy, the desire, to maintain contact with me, or with anyone. The only thing that kept her alive, she had once told me, were the rare visits Sejanus granted her with her children. I suspected it was for that reason alone that she didn't speak of the treason she knew her former husband and Decimus had committed: even if she were believed, she feared the reprisal that would be inevitable, which would no doubt culminate in being prevented from ever again seeing her own children.

Aunt Agrippina was still speaking, and I forced my attention to return to the present. "I've sent word to Tiberius, asking permission to remarry," she was saying. She watched me, waiting for a reaction, but before I could answer, she plunged onwards. "I know I'm getting old now, closer to forty than I'd like to admit, and I doubt I have any children left in me... but while I do still love and miss Germanicus, I want some companionship. It is only a matter of time before my children all grow and leave me, so let me marry someone of my choosing—that's what I wrote to him."

I fumbled for something to say, completely taken aback. "I had no idea you wanted to remarry," I said eventually. "Do you have someone in mind?"

Agrippina sighed, rolling her neck as the attendant giving her the massage pressed down on her back. "No, not at all."

I didn't entirely believe her, but I didn't push the matter. She would not have surfaced the idea of marrying again if she did not already have several suitable candidates in mind—no doubt men who might help to guarantee her status, and that of her children. She took my silence as an invitation to continue speaking.

"Speaking of marriages, I also heard that Sejanus has asked Tiberius for permission to marry Drusus's widow, Livilla," Aunt Agrippina said, her tone hushed.

My heart felt as if it might burst out of my chest. So, Sejanus truly had divorced Apicata in search of a better, more connected wife— and killing Drusus had made the woman he wanted available to him, although he had forced himself to wait a few years before trying to claim her for himself. Clearly Sejanus had wanted to put the distance of time between Drusus's murder and marrying the victim's widow.

"What do you think Tiberius will say?" I asked, my tone cautious; I was aware of the ever-present attendants who stood over us, hearing every word. I had no doubt that they earned plenty of coins for relaying overheard information to those who would be more than happy to use the details for their own ends.

Aunt Agrippina's tinkling laughter was her immediate response. "No, of course. Sejanus may be one of his favorites, but his bloodline is nothing. He, at the end of the day, is nothing. Even Decimus agrees— about the marriage, anyway."

I swallowed, my eyes darting to the attendant who massaged my aunt; I could not see the one with whom I was paired, only feeling the continuous, rhythmic pressure of warm, oily hands on my back. Did my aunt have no concern for their listening ears? Whether or not she felt that Sejanus was nothing, as she put it, he remained one of the most powerful men in Rome—especially as Tiberius was spending more time than not at his island villa on Capri. There were those who whispered that Sejanus was now emperor in all but name, unchecked as he was.

"How do you know Decimus thinks that?" I asked, wary of the conversation—but too intrigued to change topics quite yet.

My aunt waved her hand dismissively. "Oh, it doesn't matter. Suffice it to say that I know he conveyed his thoughts on the matter to Tiberius." Her tone suggested she was unwilling to say more, and I wondered if she had finally thought better of discussing such matters where those with unknown loyalties might overhear.

I didn't ask any further questions, but I did make sure to mentally store away the knowledge Aunt Agrippina had just imparted to me. It was interesting that Decimus would speak or act in any way against Sejanus, and I wondered if there might be some discord between them despite the unified front they otherwise presented.

As matters wound up, Tiberius would reject not only Sejanus's suit, but Aunt Agrippina's as well. Both were admonished for overstepping—Sejanus, for reaching above his station in life, and Agrippina for a perceived move against the emperor. For her to remarry would be to elevate another man to a position too high for Tiberius's comfort: the granddaughter of Augustus, who was also the widow of the ever-beloved Germanicus, was a prize he could not afford to bestow upon anyone.

Sejanus, although bitter, didn't seem to let the rejection bother him for long. He held a banquet only a few short weeks later, and Torquatus and I—alongside dozens of other leading families in Rome—had been invited. When we arrived, I was somewhat surprised to see that Livilla was present, acting as hostess, as if, regardless of Tiberius's commands, she and Sejanus were already betrothed, married, even. As usual, everyone noticed, but nobody spoke of it.

Torquatus and I moved through the crowd, exchanging pleasantries, until we reached Decimus and his entourage: his wife; Rufus; the young Dacian prince; and the prince's Dacian warrior, who accompanied him everywhere. I had only ever glimpsed the latter two from a distance before, despite them having been in Rome for several years; it was as if every time I approached them, they moved in the other direction.

"How are you, Decimus?" Torquatus was asking, greeting the senator's wife and the Dacian youth as well. Naturally, Rufus and the Dacian warrior were ignored; they stood behind the group, watching the room alertly. I almost smiled, thinking how absurd their presence was—

we were in the home of the Praetorian Prefect, who had at least a dozen of his men visibly present, and probably more tucked away, out of sight. We were in no danger here—not in the way of brute violence, at least. Politics were another matter.

I quickly exchanged my own pleasantries, through my eyes lingered on the Dacian prince, who had politely introduced himself as Duras. Something about him seemed familiar, but I quickly brushed off the lingering feeling of recognition. I had seen him many times before—just never this close. That was all.

"Tiberius is set on remaining in Capri," Decimus confided quietly to my husband. His tone was neutral, but I could sense the excitement in the way he held himself: back perfectly straight, the fingers wrapped around his drink animatedly tapping the glass, as if he could barely control the coiled energy that had seized hold of his body.

"So Sejanus will run Rome?" I interjected loudly, and everyone's eyes darted to me. My words were bold.

Torquatus made as if to quiet me, but Decimus waved off the beginning of his protestations, smiling at me. "Yes. Our emperor has entrusted him with overseeing the day-to-day affairs of Rome and its territories. He will, naturally, be in close, regular contact with Emperor Tiberius, informing him of all that happens in Rome."

"What of Livia?" I asked tightly. Tiberius's mother had always held tightly to the reins of power, but as she aged, she disappeared more and more from public view; whispers abounded that Tiberius no longer sought her counsel as he once had. I wondered what she might think of Sejanus usurping the control she once wielded over her son, and, indirectly, over the empire.

Decimus laughed, and his grin was wolfish when he answered. "Tiberius sees now that he was mistaken to place so much trust in a woman. He has cast her off."

I forced myself to smile, understanding what Decimus did not say outright: that Tiberius, on an island, surrounded by Praetorian Guards—men who were exceedingly loyal to Sejanus—would hear only what Sejanus wanted him to, and when. Whether or not Sejanus told the emperor the truth or invented tales—well, it would all depend upon what suited his goals. And Livia, one of the last remaining checks on Sejanus's power, had fallen from her son's favor, another line of connection to the emperor removed.

Torquatus, for the first time in recent memory, seemed troubled, as if he had had the same thought as me. "But—" he started.

"But what wonderful news for our dear friend Sejanus," I interrupted, sliding my hand around my husband's arm as I kept a smile fixed to my face.

Torquatus did not seem to realize it yet—or perhaps he trusted Decimus even more than I had thought—but we all were in grave danger. Anyone who might cross Sejanus would stand little chance, not now, with his hold on power greater than it had ever before been. Torquatus opened his mouth as if to speak again, and my hand tightened on his arm in silent, pleading warning: it was not the time to ponder the legality of who ruled Rome and how.

Duras, his eyes fixed on me, suddenly raised his drink. "To Sejanus!" he cried out.

Our group reiterated his cry, and then so did those next to us, and then the people further away, until the entire gathering had saluted the Praetorian Prefect. Torquatus's stuttered questioning of how matters were to be handled was already forgotten, and he now pressed his lips together in a thin line, eyes troubled.

I noticed, as I took a sip of my drink, that Duras continued to watch me, an intense expression of focus on his face. He did not touch his own wine. I felt transfixed by him, again feeling that I knew him, somehow. I felt on the verge of figuring out what my connection to the youth was when Decimus's voice distracted me, and a chill ran through my body.

"Silanus," Decimus said warmly. "I'm so very glad that you've returned to Rome. Great things are on the horizon, for all of us."

I knew that polite manners dictated that I turn to greet Silanus, but my body felt as if it were frozen in place. The hand holding my wineglass trembled, and I looked to Rufus—the one who had saved me from Silanus years ago, who had, somehow, managed to blackmail him into leaving Rome.

Rufus's eyes held mine, a trace of pity—of apology—flickering in them. Whatever he had done to rid me of Silanus had not been enough to keep him gone forever. Sejanus's rise to power seemed to have enticed him to return, whatever reward he might gain from the new power dynamics of Rome clearly far outweighing any perceived risk of encountering me—of encountering Rufus—again.

"Aemilia, you look well," Silanus said, winding around until he was in front of me, so that I would have to see him. He smiled thinly, and I was reminded of a serpent quietly watching its prey, calculating when and where it would strike.

"As do you," I responded. I heard my own words in a disembodied sort of way, as if they came from someone else entirely, not from my own mouth. I could not force myself to smile, instead raising my glass to my lips and draining the remainder of my wine, the dry burn of too much of the liquid at once scratching uncomfortably at my throat. I hoped that no one noticed my trembling hand.

"Aemilia, if I could ask your opinion on a mosaic I saw, over there…" Duras was suddenly beside Silanus, forcing the other man to move aside slightly. Silanus's focus on me was briefly broken, and the youth gestured away from our group.

I quickly nodded and stepped away from Silanus, Duras affixing himself to my side as we moved apart from the others. Slowly, I felt as if I could breathe again, my lungs readily expanding as I briefly closed my eyes in relief.

"Thank you," I whispered quietly. "But why…" I trailed off.

Duras gave me a small smile, kindness in his eyes. And then, it struck me. He had *my* eyes. He had my *mother's* eyes—and not just her eyes, but her brow, her cheekbones, her chin. I was amazed that I hadn't seen it before, because now the resemblance seemed so obvious. But it wasn't possible.

"I—" I started, but I didn't know how to finish whatever sentence I had been about to begin. We stared at each other again intently, Duras now looking nearly as perplexed as I did—and then his warrior, emerging as if from nowhere, whispered something in his ear, the words aggressive and guttural, the sound entirely foreign to me.

The warrior laid a hand on the youth's arm, fingers tightening around his wrist. "I must go," Duras said in Latin, though his tone was agitated. He left with the warrior, the latter glancing back at me once as they crossed the room, his expression uneasy. And then they were gone, mixed into the crowd.

I looked down at the wineglass—now empty—that I still held in my hand. Perhaps I had been mistaken about Duras, about any passing resemblance between us, between him and my mother. I had had a lot to drink, and had little in my stomach. The wine had misled me—never mind that I hadn't seen my mother in well over a decade; her features were no longer crisp and fresh within my mind. Perhaps it had simply been a wine-fueled wish on my part, to see some part of her here, especially in someone who had moved to protect me from Silanus, the man who had started it all, who always brought out a strong surge of emotions from me. After all, it was Silanus who had brought about my mother's banishment; my status as an orphan in all the ways that mattered; my eventual marriage to Torquatus in place of Claudius; even, perhaps, the situation we all now found ourselves in, with Sejanus the leading man in Rome as Tiberius willingly and happily removed himself to an island—the irony of which did not escape me. I felt a flash of anger that the emperor could so easily choose such a voluntary exile, while others were condemned to it.

It was hard to tell if the entire chain of events had been inevitable, if all the things that had come to pass could truly be connected to one another, but one thing was certain: Silanus held responsibility. Silanus had been the one to ruin my life. The rage against him that I thought I had long ago managed to bury came boiling back to the surface, and it took all my restraint not to unleash a feral scream in the middle of Sejanus's party.

Instead, I let the wineglass fall from my hand, the glass shattering on the mosaicked floor under my feet—the mosaic Duras had brought me to, under the guise of asking my opinion of it. I saw now that it was a Greek scene, one depicting two of their gods: Apollo and Artemis, deities of the sun and the moon, two sides of the same coin, siblings.

CHAPTER XXVI

TITUS

Titus fought the rising panic that welled within his body the longer Duras and Aemilia stood close to one another. He silently cursed Duras—cursed Didas, too—for the youth's presence in Rome. None of this had been meant to happen; Duras should have been back in Dacia, where he belonged, far from Rome, far from the politics and intriguing and bloodshed that cursed the city, cursed Duras's entire family.

Neither Aemilia nor Duras seemed to see it yet—to see themselves reflected in a gendered inversion. Aemilia worried Titus more than the boy did—she knew her mother, whom they both resembled, and would have seen herself in mirrors far more often than her half-brother, who, until coming to Rome, had spared little thought for his appearance. He could tell she suspected something, was on the verge of grasping at it…

And then Silanus appeared. Silanus, Julia's lover long ago—the one who had betrayed her to Augustus, who had led to her exile. Silanus—Duras's true father, though neither of them knew it. Titus felt as if the gods were testing him, mocking him—placing all these people, all these problems, at his feet. He wanted to bury himself in the expensive wine that was being served all around the room, wanted to close his eyes and beg the gods to let him awaken from this terrible dream, wanted to make a fist and bash in Silanus's face, making him suffer as he had made Julia suffer, for all these years. He felt, too, a fierce protectiveness of Duras; Titus wanted to shield him from the man who had given him life and nothing else, just as his own father had. Yet more strangely, despite his hatred of Silanus, an odd sense of jealousy stirred within Titus as he watched the two stand side by side, father and son, a blood bond that he would never share with Duras even if he bore the title of *pater* to the youth. But such a title, such an endearment, was built upon a lie.

Aemilia changed, when Silanus arrived, and her new expression shook Titus from his confused thoughts of anger and jealousy, guilt and shame. She must know, Titus thought, that Silanus was the cause of her mother's exile... but there was something more between them. She seemed uncomfortable, frozen—terrified, like a rabbit that hoped it might evade the jaws of the hunting dog looming over it, if only it stayed still enough.

Rufus shifted his weight next to Titus, and he glanced at Decimus's man. Rufus's gaze was locked on Aemilia, and something like concern had worked its way to his face, his body tensing. His hand drifted towards where his sword ordinarily would have been belted—but this was a social gathering, hosted by the Praetorian Prefect, and weapons would have been frowned upon.

Titus knew that there had been something between Rufus and Aemilia—not a relationship between lovers, but some sort of intrigue. He had followed Rufus years ago, when he had met with Aemilia in her family's tomb; he had followed Rufus, too, when he had scoured the depths of Rome in search of something, or someone: Titus had never discovered what. And then, suddenly, their alliance seemed to have ceased, the pair's meetings sporadic and then nearly non-existent ever since they had met in secret at the tomb. Titus hadn't thought about it in some time; he had told himself that it was not his concern, that he already had enough to deal with without becoming involved in whatever troubles Aemilia found herself in. He had promised Julia to look after her son, not her daughter, who was now a grown woman—one who, if she was anything like her mother, would have little need of any help he could provide.

Titus stifled an outburst as Duras suddenly approached Aemilia, positioning himself next to Silanus, and, for a few, brief moments, the trio stood awkwardly, unknowingly together—and then Duras escorted Aemilia away from the group, while Silanus shifted his attention to Decimus and Torquatus, unaware that his own flesh and blood had been standing right beside him only seconds earlier, the son who should have died many years ago.

Titus watched the pair, brother and sister, for a moment. Yes, he had promised Julia, all those years ago, to look after her infant son, not her daughter—but the boy, too, was grown now, nearing his eighteenth year. Duras had little need of him, the man he still thought was his father—and so Titus allowed himself, just for an instant, to imagine leaving. To imagine returning to Julia, to Trimerus, after all this time. Would she recognize him, with his long hair and beard, with his subtle limp, with the lines that creased his face more and more with each year that came and went? In his mind, she looked the same as she always had, if not somehow made even more beautiful by the memories of her that he held tightly onto, frequently reliving them in dreams, in moments of quiet solitude. They brought both comfort and sadness in equal measure, a reminder not only of indescribable love, but of boundless loss.

Titus smiled softly, closing his eyes, envisioning all that he wished the future could hold. And then he forced himself to break the reverie, to advance upon Duras and Aemilia, intent on separating them before they—before anyone—saw what he thought was overwhelmingly obvious. He couldn't leave Duras, not yet—not while the boy still lived in the viper's den that was Rome.

Titus breathed a deep sigh of relief when they departed Sejanus's gathering, and a second sigh when they returned safely to Decimus's home, where Duras quietly retired to bed, not making more than a passing comment on the evening—and saying nothing at all about Aemilia. The more distance Titus was able to put and keep between the two of them, the better. He thanked the gods that no one seemed to have noticed the pair together, to have noticed their uncanny resemblance to one another, and to their mother—although he surmised that the copious amount of free-flowing wine at the party may have had more to do with people's lack of observation than any favor from the gods.

The soldier scratched at his beard, wondering if it would cause any harm to shave it off—surely, having been gone from Rome for so long, no one would remember him. Too much had changed; *he* had changed. Those with whom he had served were likely all retired, happily living with their wives and children on plots of land far from Rome, now trying their hands at farming instead of killing. He wondered, in another life, if that would have been him—married now, a father, working the land. A simple, uncomplicated life, one in which Julia would have been just another faceless imperial to him.

A noise startled him, and Titus turned, glancing around the empty courtyard. He came here often at night, enjoying the still calmness of the *impluvium* in the center of the space, its water level just barely lipping at the edges. He still, years later, felt as if he could hear the constant, rhythmic crash of waves all around him; as if he could smell the tangy, salt-filled air, which circulated in a constant state of breeziness; as if he could hear the cry of the island birds as they flew to and fro, seeking out food and mates and nesting spots as their feathered bodies were borne aloft by gusts of wind that were at once powerful and gentle. If he let it, it could drive him mad.

But no—there was none of that, not here. The surface of the shallow water pool flickered dimly in the faint moonlight that spilled into the open courtyard; every so often, the sound of people moving by, some on foot, some on horseback, drifted towards his ears. The smells were the usual rankness that accompanied large cities, punctuated only here and there by hints of fresh-cooked food or the whiff of a perfumed lady.

A noise, again—and this time, when Titus turned, he saw Rufus.

"You startled me," he said by way of greeting, though his tense body had already begun to relax.

Rufus didn't respond but instead approached Titus, his face thoughtful, and the two gazed at the *impluvium* together in something that was nearly a comfortable, companionable silence.

It was Rufus who spoke first. "It's odd, isn't it, how much Duras and Aemilia Lepida resemble one another?" The words were spoken carelessly, as if he had done little more than comment on the weather, and his gaze shifted to Titus lazily.

Titus froze, the breath leaving his body; his eyes remained fixed on the pool of water before him. His stillness—his lack of response—seemed to be enough for Rufus, who let out a quiet, harsh bark of a laugh, all pretense of carelessness gone.

"I don't know what you mean," Titus managed to say, although his words came too late; his body's response had been enough to betray his knowledge of the relationship between Duras and Aemilia, although it was possible—likely—that Rufus did not yet know the full extent of it. How could he? A passing resemblance was not evidence of anything.

Rufus sighed then. "Who is the boy?"

Titus didn't let himself freeze, this time; nor did he let himself think. Instead, he spun towards Rufus and attacked him. In that moment he thought that to kill him was the only way to stop him, to save Duras, to save Aemilia, too. If it cost Titus his own life in the process, so be it.

CHAPTER XXVII

AEMILIA LEPIDA

Silanus's return to Rome troubled me more than I liked to admit; his face haunted my dreams, and any cloaked man seemed, from a distance, to be my attacker. Amynta noticed—she saw the dark shadows beneath my eyes after yet another sleepless night; she saw how I jumped and twitched when surprised, and overheard me asking to peruse guest lists before deciding to attend events; she watched as I repeatedly drank myself into a blind stupor, draining glass after glass of wine until I vomited it all back up again, the red liquid pouring out of me as if it were blood. She noticed—but she did not know why. No one knew what Silanus had done except for Rufus; I had been too ashamed to tell anyone, even my longest companion, who had been by my side since childhood—let alone my husband, who would, I worried, take his cousin's side over his own wife's. Better to let it all remain buried, hidden—forgotten. But unfortunately I could not forget.

I found myself pacing regularly, sometimes early in the morning, often late at night, my hatred of Silanus resurfacing after years of lying dormant, growing stronger even than my hatred of Decimus, who not only had failed to deliver on all that he had promised me, who had used me and discarded me, prepared to blackmail me whenever it suited his purposes, but who had witnessed Silanus attacking me—and had laughed and walked away, allowing it to continue. Of all the reasons I had to hate Decimus, it was the lattermost that now burned most brightly.

"I need to see Rufus," I announced one morning to Amynta, pushing away my uneaten breakfast. She had asked the cook to prepare my favorite pancakes, hoping to tempt me into eating—but I no longer found them appetizing, no matter how slathered in honey they might be. The sweetness only coated my tongue and made me feel ill.

Amynta didn't attempt to dissuade me, or to ask why. She simply nodded and said, "I'll deliver a note this morning. Where do you want to meet him?"

"My father's family tomb," I answered. "Late this afternoon, before sunset."

The rest of the day seemed to drag on, the sun lazily arcing its way across the sky until at last it was time for me to depart with Amynta, the pair of us stealing away under hooded cloaks. Although my secret wanderings throughout Rome were few and scattered in nature—lest my husband one day realize that I was not, in fact, at home, nor was I busy spinning wool with other reputable women—they were, I found, when I felt most free: simply another nameless, faceless body caught up in the ebb and flow of the city's busy streets. Lost in the crowd, no one cared who my mother was or what she had done; no one knew that I had poisoned my own husband in a naïve show of stupid, pointless loyalty; and no one would guess what I now had my heart set on accomplishing.

The further we went from my home, the more Rome came alive. Corner shops offered places to sit and have a drink, to exchange a few coins for a bite—or more—to eat, from simple, hot sausages to chicken stuffed with pepper, lovage, and ginger; one merchant showed off all manner of olive relishes, ready to be spooned out and sampled. Children played in the streets, laughing and dodging the pots of piss that women threw out of the windows above, scowling as their day's work continued. Travelers bore packs, leading donkeys and ox-drawn carts in different directions; men haggled over the cost of meat as a butcher hacked away at a freshly slaughtered pig's leg. It was vastly different from my usual surroundings, and I found myself wondering if their lives were simpler— easier. But, as we continued on, approaching the Via Appia and its seemingly endless line of tombs, I quickly dispelled such idealistic thoughts, seeing the too thin children who now worked in the streets, the playtime of their better-off peers a wholly unknown pursuit to them; the lean offerings from desperate merchants; the hungry-eyed prostitutes who lingered in doorways, bony arms wrapped around themselves. The border between simplicity and poverty was a thin one.

When we reached my father's family tomb, Rufus already waited outside for us. I gasped when he looked up at our approach: a deep bruise circled his right eye, and a jagged cut ran across the bridge of his now mishappen nose.

Amynta—although she claimed to have forgiven Rufus for using her as he had, years before—let out a happy huff of breath upon seeing his fresh wounds. I scowled at her, but she avoided my gaze, and although she kept her lips pressed together, stymying whatever gleeful comment she wanted to make, I saw a glint of smugness in her eyes.

"Picking fights?" I asked Rufus. It was not like him to be the one who suffered a beating; he had always been the one to dole them out.

He didn't answer, instead looking down at his feet, as if thinking what to say. I felt my heartbeat quicken—something was wrong. "What is it?" I asked, concern now tinging my words.

Before Rufus could answer, another figure stepped out from around the side of the tomb, dropping a hood back from his bearded face:

it was the Dacian warrior, the one who accompanied Duras as if he were the youth's shadow.

I took a step back. "What is this?" Alarm was clear in my words.

"This," Rufus said, finally finding his voice, "is Titus. And I think you should listen to what he has to say."

An uneasy truce had been established between Rufus and the man who called himself Titus—although, until his confrontation with Rufus, he had been known by the Dacian name of Brasus. It also appeared that the supposed Dacian warrior was not actually Dacian at all, but Roman, although he was unwilling to share much of his history beyond a scant few details. As surprising as this revelation was, I was even more perplexed once Titus revealed that his charge, Duras, had a similar false Dacian identity, being fully Roman by birth.

"Who are his parents?" I asked. "In what situation would a Roman-born boy child wind up living in the wilds of Dacia, amongst the worst sort of barbarians?"

Rufus shifted his feet uncomfortably, although he spoke up before Titus, who wordlessly watched our exchange, his expression closed-off. "Duras is your brother."

I laughed then, a harsh noise that escaped me before I could rein it in. "Have you been drinking, Rufus? That is the most absurd thing I've ever heard. I have no siblings."

"No full siblings." It was Titus who spoke now, his voice subdued. "Your mother was carrying a child when she was exiled."

I opened my mouth to argue, to contradict him, but no noise came out. My mind was racing. Aunt Agrippina had told me as much, when I was barely more than a girl—that my mother had gotten pregnant with a bastard child of Silanus's. But she had said that it would not have been allowed to be raised.

"He, or she, is dead," I said at last, the words cold. "Such a child would have been cast out when it was born. What is it you think you will gain by telling me these lies?" I turned, motioning to Amynta, who had been watching the entire exchange with open-mouthed surprise. "We are leaving, Amynta."

I began to walk away, but Titus's voice stopped me. "You saw it, the other night, at Sejanus's gathering. How you seemed to be looking at another version of yourself, and of your mother. You know it to be true."

I turned slowly back around, and Titus spoke again, his voice gaining strength, a new urgency entering his words as if he could will me to understand, to accept it. "Rufus saw it, the resemblance. It would be hard not to—that's the source of his... current disheveled appearance. I did not respond to his discovery kindly. I've spent the past four years trying to make sure that your path doesn't cross with the boy's—at least, not at too close a distance, where your resemblance to one another would be unmistakable. I have to protect him. I swore it."

"Swore it to whom?" I asked sharply. My head was beginning to ache.

Titus didn't answer, and Rufus spoke instead. "Why did you want to speak with me, in person? What couldn't you convey in writing?" A change in topic—but I would let it go, for now.

I rubbed two fingers against my temple, wishing I had some wine to numb the headache I knew was impending. I had nearly forgotten why I had asked Rufus to meet me at the tomb, but it came rushing back now, and the force of my bloody desire managed to almost entirely drown out all the revelations that had just been shared with me. "I want you to kill Silanus. I want him dead."

Rufus didn't seem at all surprised by my request, but Amynta gasped. Titus's eyes widened, although his reaction was nearly imperceptible, his expression returning to its usual stoic neutrality almost immediately.

"How? How do you want him to die?" Rufus asked, a gleeful undertone lacing the words. Titus looked at him sharply, and I knew that he did not know Rufus very well, not yet, not as I did. There was always a vicious undercurrent that came alongside Rufus, a distant, vague scent of blood, a quiet excitement that accompanied the expectation of violence. I didn't like to think of all that he had done at Decimus's behest—but we were allied together now, and I trusted him, in some ways more than I trusted anyone else, even Amynta.

I didn't answer Rufus, my thoughts of vengeance against Silanus instead shifting towards uncertainties I had about Duras—my alleged half-brother, with whom I had come face to face only days ago. I could not focus on Silanus's fate while I still had so many unanswered questions about the youth with whom I supposedly shared a mother. "How did he leave the island?" I asked abruptly. "If I accept that he is my sibling—the son of my mother and of Silanus—how did he go from Trimerus to Dacia? Who else knows who he is?"

I watched as Titus's face began to close off; he was unwilling to share more, to provide the details that would, I was sure, reveal his role in all of this—and, I hoped, some news of my mother.

"The only ones in Rome who know who the boy truly is are the four of us." Titus looked at each of us in turn, from Rufus to me and then to Amynta. "Duras himself doesn't know the truth of any of this. He believes himself to be my son, and knows that I am a deserter from the

Roman army. He believes—and I have not contradicted him—that his mother is Dacian, and that she is dead."

"Tell me how he survived," I said, my words forceful. "Tell me how he left the island, or I will tell him this. All of it. That he is my bastard half-brother, the great-grandson of Emperor Augustus. That his parents are Julia and Silanus. And that you are a liar—that you are not his father."

The last threat seemed to sting Titus the most; he visibly flinched as I spat out the words, flinging them at him like stones. It occurred to me that I had learned something useful from Decimus after all—the utility of threats, of dangling a certain knowledge over someone else's head to force them to submit to your whims, your plots. I did not dwell on how this made me, in some ways, comparable to a man I hated so much, instead relishing the fact that it seemed as if I might soon get the information I desired.

We had not ever entered the tomb; I had not been willing to invite Titus into so intimate a space, not when there was not yet any trust between us. Now, the sky was beginning to darken; a lone vulture circled overhead, scanning for the rotting flesh of some unfortunate creature. I was not bothered by the receding light, the implication that I might soon be missed at home. I would have my answer, I was sure of it.

Titus spoke at last, his voice so quiet that I took another step towards him in order to hear. "I thought the boy was dead," he was saying. "I thought he had been thrown from the cliffs into the sea below, not even a day old. She mourned—days, weeks…"

She. He spoke of my mother, though he did not name her. "You were there," I breathed.

Titus continued as if he hadn't heard me—and perhaps he hadn't. His eyes were looking past me, although they were unseeing—as if he were somewhere else entirely. "Another—" he paused, suddenly hesitant, but then he forged ahead. "Another Praetorian saved him. Sent him away. Smuggled him, to Dacia. I don't know all the details. I can't—won't—name them, any of them. It was treason."

We all hung on every word, but Titus had paused again. I knew that he was still leaving out some details, some specifics—but I felt the truth of the words he did choose to speak, and I was gleaning enough that I didn't begrudge him the names and particular events he withheld.

Titus cleared his throat and resumed speaking, his eyes once more focusing on his surroundings. "I promised Julia, to find her son—to care for him. To teach him. Protect him. And I did; I have done all those things. But then he took the place of the Dacian prince who *should* be here, so now we are the ones in this fucking viper's den." His face darkened.

Amynta gasped, and her cheeks reddened at Titus's foul language—not because she had virgin ears by any means, but because she was offended on my behalf. She had no need to worry herself: I had barely heard the rest of his words after he had said my mother's name aloud. There was something in the way his lips formed the three syllables, how his tongue gently, caressingly brushed the roof of his mouth—how he managed to say her name as if it was a prayer. He had loved her—my mother. And he still did.

I turned away, my arms wrapping around my body as I closed my eyes, a single tear managing to squeeze itself out from under my lids. I believed Titus; every word he had spoken rang true.

"What do we do now?" I asked, my back still to the group. I fought to keep the sudden surge of emotion from my voice.

"We keep the secret," Titus said decisively. "I only tell you now because Rufus managed to piece it together, somewhat, and he demanded, in exchange for his own silence, that you be told. He knew the boy was a relation to you, *domina*." The words were respectful—distant. Nothing at all how he spoke of my mother.

"How is she?" I asked quietly. I was unsure if Titus had heard, he took so long to answer.

When he did at last respond, I was disappointed. "I don't know." The words were filled with a sad regret, one I knew too well.

"Don't you want to know why I so desperately want Silanus to die?" I asked, pushing away all thoughts of my mother, of Duras. My new knowledge did not change my plans; if anything, it allowed me to focus once more on the vengeance I held close to my heart, the distraction of uncertainty about how washed away. Titus watched me, thinking how to answer, but I didn't give him time to respond. "He raped me." The words, when they came out, were surprisingly devoid of emotion. I had never said them aloud before—I had barely even thought them, as if to do so would make me relive the incident all over again. Instead, I had resolutely maintained a façade of denial.

Rufus, the only one already aware of what had transpired, studied his nails; Amynta covered her mouth, eyes filling with tears. But Titus—Titus nodded, holding my gaze as he spoke, his words decisive, final. "Then he will die. But it needs to be when the time is right, for the safety of us all."

CHAPTER
XXVIII

DURAS

Duras shifted his weight as he stood behind Decimus, silently observing as the older senator held his near-daily court in his home, receiving all manner of visitors. Some of them came simply to pay their respects, perhaps bringing an offering or two along; others came to ask a favor, to report some wrong, seeking justice, retribution. And Decimus oversaw it all, a king on a miniature scale—although he called his subjects 'clients' when he spoke to Duras of the event, as if he did not exercise the right of life or death over them. Duras was not so certain.

His thoughts drifted, thinking again of the woman he had spoken with only briefly some time ago—how she had looked like him, almost disconcertingly so. He had said nothing of it to his father; he was worried that Titus might think him a fool, accusing him of enjoying Roman wines too much of late. Perhaps, Duras thought, many Romans looked so, with dark eyes, bronze-colored hair, similar nose and cheek and chin shapes—although he bore almost no resemblance to the soldier who had sired him, and, in the years he had been in Rome, he had yet to come across anyone whose appearance had captured his attention as quickly as Aemilia Lepida's had. But it could be no more than an odd coincidence, a jest of the gods.

"What is your opinion, Duras?" Decimus asked, and Duras was jolted back to the present. He had no idea what the most recent visitor had said, and so could form no opinion whatsoever—but he couldn't admit as much to the senator, his host.

"I defer to your greater experience on the matter," Duras said politely, hoping that his response would prove satisfactory.

Decimus smiled thinly at him and waved a hand dismissively, turning back to the client who stood before him. "I'll invest in your bakery," he said, "but I want a return on my coins within the year."

The balding man—the baker, Duras supposed—seemed about to respond, his face pale as he perhaps doubted the timeframe demanded of him, but thought better of it, bowing as he thanked Decimus and backed away, making room for the next client to approach the senator and ask his favor.

When Duras had first arrived in Rome, he had been surprised that a man of such standing would do something like invest in a bakery—but the longer he had been around Decimus, the more he had come to understand that the senator considered no realm of affairs too lowly or off-limits. "Power can be gleaned from everywhere," he had told Duras.

It was something the youth had taken note of, although not entirely in the way he expected Decimus would have imagined. Rather than fixating on securing power for himself, Duras had turned his attentions to how he might better his people back in Dacia, whether that was observing Roman engineers at work as they repaired the aqueducts outside the city or particular recipes that might work well for preserving the fruits, vegetables, and meats the people of Dacia favored; Roman textile practices, from raw materials to weaving to trading, or how taxation was managed across the empire; and, most importantly, Roman weaponry and warfare tactics. Of all that he studied, Duras was the most dedicated pupil in the lattermost subject.

It was only a matter of time, Duras knew, until Rome turned its sight upon Dacia and its peoples. Divided into tribal kingdoms, they would be easy to turn against one another, one king selling out the next in exchange for some minimal favor with Rome. But in the end, it would lead to all of Dacia being subjugated—and Duras didn't want that to happen, in his lifetime or in that of the next generation. Although Duras knew he was half-Roman, he had seen with his own eyes how even his father—a full-blooded Roman soldier—was more comfortable, more at ease, amongst the Dacian people. How else would he have fallen in love with a Dacian woman, forsaking his brothers in arms, his city, his empire, his entire people for a wild land that still stood strong against Rome's creeping might?

And so, outwardly, Duras was a most agreeable hostage, adopting the Roman language and dress quickly and easily, happily embracing these strangers' customs, sacrificing to their gods, drinking their wine, playing their games—making love to their women.

A flush rose to Duras's cheeks as one of his paramours—a blonde, pale-skinned kitchen slave in Decimus's household by the name of Camilla—passed by, skirting the people waiting to speak with the senator. A basket was slung over her arm—no doubt supplies from the market—and she glanced over her shoulder, her eyes meeting Duras's as she accentuated the roll of her hips, her steps soon taking her out of sight and towards the kitchen.

"What is your opinion on *this* matter, Duras?" Decimus asked, looking pointedly at the youth.

Duras quickly licked his lips, hoping that his face wasn't obviously red, and struggled to come up with a satisfactory reply.

Duras groaned as he climaxed, Camilla giggling as she wrapped her arms and legs around him more tightly, her skin hot and sweaty to the touch. He fought to catch his breath as he rolled off of her, and she turned on her side, smiling as her finger brushed his chin, tracing a line down his neck to his chest, drawing a path through the light hairs that had been there barely a few years.

"I have to go," she said quietly, vivid blue eyes watching him, her finger now lazily moving in circles on his stomach. She was from Gaul, originally—although she had come to Rome at such a young age that she didn't remember her homeland in any detail, let alone her native tongue. Her parents, siblings—they were but a distant memory, all of them killed or similarly enslaved.

Duras shook his head, his hand grabbing hers, and then he quickly rolled himself back on top of her as she squealed and laughed, his kisses soon silencing her.

Duras had had his fair share of women in Rome; apparently, being a Dacian prince was something of a novelty, although he wasn't quite on par with the gladiators, whose bottled sweat, he had learned, commanded a frighteningly high price. Still, as muscle had filled out his youthful leanness, as dark stubble had sprouted on his cheeks, he soon found that he was able to have, for the most part, his pick of women— but it was more often than not that the women came to him.

Although taken aback at first, Duras had soon begun to enjoy himself. He had bedded a girl long before he'd ever come to Rome, rolling around a handful of times on a bed of pine needles in the forest, but this—this was different. His long-suffering father had set some restrictions after discovering Duras in bed with a slightly older, married woman: no more married women, no virgins from the upper classes, no slaves unless they were enthusiastically willing, and so on, all of which drastically reduced his options—but, truth be told, of late he had only been visiting Camilla.

They made love again that night, and when she finally slipped away to return to the room she shared with several other female slaves of the household, Duras dreamed of her, of taking her back to Dacia with him when, one day, he finally left Rome. But he had no idea when that day might come.

CHAPTER XXIX

AEMILIA LEPIDA

"There will come an opportune time," Titus was insisting. "It may take years, but we must have patience. I swear to you that it will be done, but we cannot rush the matter. We cannot force the situation."

Rufus cracked his knuckles, a scowl deepening the lines on his face. A tinge of white was beginning to bleed out into his hair from his temples, lightening the eye-catching red color; I was taken aback that I hadn't noticed before. "It has already been years," Rufus said. "Silanus should die *now*. And Decimus too. I am happy to do it alone, with my own hands, if you're afraid." The final words were followed by a thin, humorless smile, Rufus's jibe intending to cut the other man.

Titus rubbed a hand across his eyes, letting out an exasperated breath, although he did not rise to Rufus's bait. I wondered if he regretted offering to help kill the man who had assaulted me—although I knew, even if we hadn't discussed it, that his hatred of Silanus ran nearly as deep as my own, just for different reasons. He had not mentioned my mother again, had not even come close to speaking her name, but I could not forget how he had said it, just that once—a lover's caress. He could forgive the man who had betrayed her no more easily than I could.

"You will be tortured for it, and you will speak," Titus snapped.

"Don't pretend that even you could withstand what they will do. You will name Aemilia, you will name me, and we will all be killed for your impatience, including Duras. I will not allow it."

Rufus began to utter a retort, but I cut him off. "We will have patience," I said. "I have waited years. I can wait years more. I can wait a lifetime, so long as it comes to pass. We will be rid of both Silanus and Decimus."

My decision, now vocalized, seem to force Rufus to resign himself to waiting for our collective vengeance, although I saw how he clenched and unclenched his hands as he avoided my gaze. Titus nodded, but his usual unreadable expression made it hard to discern whether he was truly pleased with the decided course of action or merely in a neutral state, ever the thinker, the planner, keeping his emotions in check. I did not think he had been eager to include Decimus in our plans for retribution—after all, Duras lived in the senator's household, so anything that affected Decimus would in turn have some impact upon the youth— but he seemed to understand that it was not a topic upon which Rufus or I would change our minds, and so he did not press the matter.

Amynta hovered uncertainly in the background, her expression wary, scared. I regretted that she had become involved. Passing secret letters and helping to arrange meetings was one thing; being involved in a murder plot was something else entirely. She was silent for the duration of our journey back home, not even speaking as we left behind the shadowy tombs of the Via Appia and reentered the livelier streets of the city itself. The scent of dusty, dank buildings and of centuries-old ashes—the scent of lingering death—was replaced by the smells of life: hot, spicy foods and the sweat of men, recently lit torches and fresh animal dung. But none of seemed to register with Amynta, whose face maintained the same expression as it had since she had learned that I actively sought Silanus's death. It was as if he she did not know me any longer.

"I'm sorry, Amynta," I said quietly, when at last we entered the house. The door attendant told us that my husband was still out, and was expected back quite late—and, so, he had not missed my absence, as usual.

Amynta didn't answer, meekly following me as we went to my room, where she silently unpinned my hair and prepared me for bed. I didn't know what else to say to her; I didn't know how to save her from what was happening—to save her from me, from what I felt certain would be my inevitable downfall, and hers, too. And then, the realization popped into my mind, and I felt blind for not having seen it before.

"I will free you, Amynta," I said. "Tomorrow, we will complete the necessary procedures. I'll speak to Torquatus first thing in the morning. You will be a freedwoman. I will give you money, and you can leave. You can go wherever you want, far away from here, and start a new life."

My words gained energy the more I spoke; my sense of excitement would, I hoped, spill over to Amynta and shock her from her current state. But she only looked at me sadly. "Where would I go, *domina*? This is the only home I've ever known. I was born into slavery, for your family." She turned away from me, putting away my hairpins and gathering up my clothes. Her back was still turned to me when she spoke again. "I am older than you, *domina*, and my chance at marriage is long past. So too, are my childbearing years. No one would want me. And I could not survive alone. You know that as well as I."

All the excitement that had coursed through my body only moments before now entirely dissipated. *I* had done this to Amynta, someone I had considered a friend, something of a mother, even, when I was younger. She had spoken to me, years ago, of wanting to find love, of wanting to bear and raise her own children—and even as I experienced these things, sometimes unwillingly or uncertainly, I had not thought that she was missing anything. I had not really thought of her, of her life, at all; she had been there for me, not because of some kindred interests and outlooks that had brought us together, but because she had had no choice in the matter. For the first time, too, I better understood the impact of Rufus upon her, how she must have felt when she thought she had found someone who might one day be her partner in life—and how it must have ripped her apart to find out that it had all been a lie. And seeing him so often, knowing, now, my involvement in it all...

Amynta left the room without speaking again, and I laid awake for hours, mindlessly watching the shadows cast on the ceiling by the sole oil lamp left lit in the room. I realized that I barely knew her at all, the woman who had been beside me longer than anyone, and a burning shame, different from any other that I had ever experienced, wracked my body.

The cyclical nature of the following days and weeks was at once both maddening and reassuring. Waking, breakfasting, reading, bathing, attending gatherings and parties, dining, sleeping; none of it was ever punctuated by the opportunity that Titus was so certain would present itself, the best time to do away with Silanus in a way that casted no suspicion on any of us. But I remained patient, contenting myself, between glasses of wine, with different imaginings of Silanus dying— and Decimus, too: poison making blood seep from their eyes as their breath came haltingly and then not at all; knives protruding from their backs, their necks, their stomachs, their groins; their bodies bloated by drowning; their necks stretched by hanging.

I followed through on my promise to free Amynta, ensuring her that she would remain employed by our household, given a place to live, paid a decent wage that she was free to spend or to save, able to leave whenever she wanted. Torquatus had grumbled about it, not seeing the point in freeing her, especially when she had no marital prospects—someone who ideally might have been able to provide something in return for being wedded to our former slave.

Amynta seemed neither happy nor sad about her new situation, although now that she wasn't obligated to spend as much time with me, I didn't see her as often. I didn't mind, though I missed her company; the more time she spent away from me, the further she was from the plotting I shared with Rufus and, now, Titus, although even that was minimal, each of us having promised to bide our time, to keep our eyes and ears open, and to send messages only when absolutely necessary. I was never worried that Amynta might betray us; even if the distance between us changed over time, growing and receding like the ocean's waves, even if we barely spoke—I knew that she would keep my trust until her dying breath, no matter what happened.

"What are you thinking of?" Torquatus asked softly, rubbing my arm. I hadn't realized he was awake yet.

Last night we had lain together for the first time in well over a year, and once again my husband now looked at me softly, tenderly, as if there still might be the chance for some genuine affection between us, even after all this time. I wasn't sure what had possessed me to agree to his unexpected advances, but I couldn't say that I regretted it. It felt nice to share the intimacy of connection, especially with someone whom I had not drawn into my growing mess of lies. Despite his faults, his ongoing hopes to involve himself with Decimus and Sejanus, Torquatus was not a bad man; he only did what he thought was best for our family. I thought back to his concern at Sejanus's most recent gathering, when it had been revealed that Tiberius would remain on Capri, leaving the prefect in charge of Rome, and I felt a sudden surge of hope that perhaps Torquatus was not as blind to the dangers these men presented as he had once been.

"You," I responded softly. He leaned over and brushed his lips to mine, but when he pulled away I noticed he looked troubled, tired.

Torquatus rolled onto his back, staring up at the ceiling. He was in his fourth decade now—and he looked it, with small patches of gray tinging both his hair and the unshaven stubble on his cheeks, lines creasing the skin around his eyes, more often dull than bright, resigned instead of eager.

"I'm worried," he said, so quietly that I barely heard him, and the words were difficult to register. My husband had never confided his concerns or fears to me, only speaking with assuredness of the great things to come his way, the positions he might be given that would raise up our family, guarantee successful futures for our children. It was, I thought, one of the sources of the distance that had always seemed to linger between us: the secrets we kept, the lies we told one another—and ourselves.

"Why?" I asked, the single word tentative. I did not want to frighten away this new side of the man I still felt as if I barely knew, despite the years we had spent together and the children we shared.

"Decimus has risen alongside Sejanus in wealth, influence, power. Silanus has done well for himself, too, since returning to Rome. But it's as if I've been cast aside, and I don't understand why," he said, the words tumbling out as if he had been holding them back for quite some time.

I bit my lip as I thought how to respond. Torquatus sounded something like a petulant child, more worried about being left out from the group than what the group itself was doing. It was not quite what I had hoped for, but I wondered if there was more lurking beneath his words, something that I might be able to tease out.

"I think…" I started, my hand resting on Torquatus's chest as I took a further moment to consider my words, how best to phrase what I was about to say. "I think that you are above Sejanus. People fear him for the power he wields, but they don't respect him, not really. His family is of little account. Tiberius will not allow him to marry Livilla, as he had requested, because his station is too low. Remember, too, that the eldest sons of Germanicus and my aunt, Agrippina, are set to succeed Tiberius—*not* Sejanus."

Torquatus looked at me then, his expression unreadable. I plunged onwards, committed now to what I had begun. "The scale of power will shift, without question. Tiberius is getting older. It is only a matter of time until Sejanus is no longer needed. Stay your course, husband, apart from these men you once considered friends. It will surely benefit us in the future."

My husband sighed, closing his eyes, and I felt my heart thudding in my chest. I had never before spoken so openly to him of politics, of power—of all the things that were supposedly beyond my sex's realm of influence. I found that I believed my own words of reassurance to him, and I began to hope that, by manipulating Sejanus's claims to power, I had found a way to usurp Decimus's influence, too. Perhaps, if we followed this path, my own goals might be materialized.

"I suppose you're right," he said slowly, looking again at me, a thoughtful expression in his eyes. "Do you think we should perhaps invite Agrippina and her sons to dine with us?"

"I'll go see her personally later today," I said with a smile.

When I arrived at Agrippina's home, things were not at all how I expected them to be. I had seen little of my aunt since Tiberius's withdrawal from the city, and now I knew why.

Aunt Agrippina was sprawled lazily across a couch, barely dressed, hair loose and unkempt; her eyes fluttered in a state that was perpetually halfway between open and closed. A wine jug sat on a small table near her, but what concerned me the most was the small tray of tablets that was situated next to it—opium.

"*Salve*, Aemilia," my aunt said, the words slurred. Her eyes did not meet mine.

Four of her children lingered nearby. Her daughter, also named Agrippina, was lying on her own couch, quietly reading a scroll; the pubescent, curly-haired girl seemed entirely unconcerned by her mother's behavior. Gaius—whom many had affectionately begun to call Caligula, or 'little boots,' after he had followed his father on campaign as a tottering child—played at a game in the corner with his other two sisters, Julia Livilla and Drusilla, the fifteen year old boy instructing his littlest siblings on how to move their stone pieces across the board as they giggled happily, seemingly more interested in stacking the pieces on top of one another than moving them as they were supposed to. Nero Caesar and Drusus Caesar were nowhere to be seen.

"*Salve*, Aunt," I said politely, "and greetings to all my cousins."

218

The children barely glanced my way, and I felt uncomfortable—this was a far cry from the home I had grown up in, one in which everything had been ordered and proper.

Aunt Agrippina lazily waved a hand at me, gesturing me closer, and I obeyed, approaching her couch hesitantly. She patted what little space remained beside her, and I awkwardly sat. The reason for my coming there—to invite her and her eldest sons to my home, to dine with Torquatus and myself as he began to curry favor with the young men who would one day reign over the empire—seemed almost absurd now. I felt as if I barely knew the woman who had raised me from the age of twelve.

Aunt Agrippina's mouth was moving, but as I leaned closer to hear the words she spoke, she stopped. I remained perched there on her couch, trying to think of what to say—what to do. I enjoyed my wine more than was ideal, I knew that—but opium was a different matter entirely.

"Do you think we might speak privately?" I asked at last. "Without the children present?" I thought I spoke quietly enough, but I saw the younger Agrippina's eyes flash towards me defiantly, her fingers tightening on her scroll.

Aunt Agrippina waved a hand again. "No. They must remain here, with me. Where it's safe." Her words were raspy.

I swallowed, preparing to strengthen my voice. "How much opium have you taken? How long have you been mixing it with your wine? What is behind this… this depravity?" My words were accusatory; I felt almost offended that her mind seemed to have left her just when I needed her the most. Aunt Agrippina had always been strong, stronger than anyone else I had known, but that woman seemed to have disappeared.

My aunt seemed to lurch upwards on her couch then, swinging her legs down so that she was seated in a mostly upright position. She glared at me, suddenly much more alert. "They were my family, too," she snapped. "My sister, my little brother, my mother. I was never allowed to mourn them, never allowed to love them because of the offenses they were said to have committed."

I flinched as her words struck me, each of them like a small, physical blow. She spoke of my mother, of my uncle, Agrippa Postumus, and of my grandmother, the elder Julia—all of them, as she so rightly pointed out, her relations just as much as they were mine. I had never dared to share the depth of my feelings on the matter with her; she had always brushed all of it off, barely wanting to speak of them, of what any of them had done, as if she were ashamed. But I realized, now, that her silence, her unwillingness to show her feelings, wasn't because she was ashamed—but because to support them, to speak well of them, to admit to missing them, would have endangered herself, her children, and their futures. She had been forced to choose one family over the other, and she had chosen the one she thought she could still save.

"I'm sorry," I said quietly, meaning the apology with every fiber of my being.

Aunt Agrippina sighed then, the sudden surge of strength, of awareness, seeming to leave her body as she slouched back on the couch, half lying down once more. Her dress slipped, unnoticed, off one pale, slim shoulder, and she seemed much smaller than I had remembered. "Never mind them now," she said quietly. "It cannot be undone."

I knew the truth of her words; I had long ago given up hope that my mother might be restored to me. And there was no return from the Underworld for my grandmother or uncle. Their fates were final.

"I worry for them," my aunt said then, her sleepy eyes fluttering around to each of her children in turn. Caligula and the smallest girls ignored us, but the younger Agrippina had put aside her scroll and was watching us, listening eagerly. "I see how he looks at them. My boys, Nero, Drusus... I barely see them now. They're men. But they're not strong enough."

I felt slightly confused. "Who is 'he,' Aunt?"

"Sejanus," Agrippina breathed out. "He is turning Tiberius against us, against them. I know it. The emperor won't read my letters— I know, because he sends them back, unopened."

"But they are his heirs," I said, even as my mind raced. The letters—Sejanus controlled access to Tiberius now, whether physically or in written form. The emperor might not even be receiving the letters, might not even know that Aunt Agrippina wrote to him.

"Sejanus wants them dead," she said, closing her eyes. Her breathing began to slow.

"I'm sure that's not the case," I told her, but I found it hard to believe the truth of my own words. My hopes to indirectly ruin Decimus by ousting Sejanus from power quickly shifted to concern for the welfare of my aunt and her children, my cousins. "Where are they now? Torquatus and I—we wanted to invite them, and you, to dinner with us."

Aunt Agrippina seemed to barely hear me, and although her lips moved, no sound emerged. She then breathed deeply, evenly: she was asleep, her body still half sitting on the couch, her neck bent at an uncomfortable angle.

"They are with Sejanus more often than not," the young Agrippina volunteered. "He rarely lets them out of his sight. He insists that he is instructing them on how to run the empire." The final sentence came out with a scoff, and the young girl's eyes flashed in anger.

"Is your mother always like this?" I asked my cousin.

221

The young Agrippina shook her head. "Not always, but often, yes, especially of late. She is frightened. She had hoped by remarrying that she would find some security, but…" She trailed off, and I nodded in acknowledgement; Tiberius had rejected her suit, not wanting to elevate any man to the esteemed position that would result from wedding a granddaughter of Augustus, one who was the mother of his own heirs.

I took my leave of my cousins, thinking that I would simply send a letter instead, next time, with our dinner invitation. The young Agrippina had watched me leave, a shrewdness in her eyes that belied her age, and I knew already that her future husband would have his hands full with her. It seemed that the women of our family—both old and young—were smarter than we should have been. I only hoped it wouldn't cost the girl in the same way it had the rest of us.

CHAPTER
XXX

RUFUS

Agrippa Postumus was standing over his bed, watching. Leering. Plotting. A smirk was fixed on his face, and his eyes seemed to glow as he leaned down over Rufus, their faces coming closer and closer together… And then suddenly Rufus was making love, not to Agrippa Postumus, but to Leander—his young, lithe body alive again, writhing in passion as their skin melded together almost seamlessly, just as it had countless times before.

Leander turned his head to look back at Rufus, a smile on his face as happy, carefree laughter spilled out from between his lips—and then it wasn't Leander at all, but Agrippa Postumus again, his laughter growing louder, more shrill, more hysterical, but Rufus didn't pull away from him, their bodies inseparable now, each thrust of his hips binding them closer and closer until it was as if they were no longer two separate people, but a single entity.

Rufus sat up with a start, his heart racing; sweat drenched his body. He fought to catch his breath, to steady his pulse; he fumbled for the water jug he kept near his cot, nearly knocking it over before his trembling fingers wrapped around it. He drank deeply, straight from the container, not bothering to pour the liquid into the small ceramic cup waiting beside it, empty. Arousal still coursed through his body, and he was confused, perplexed. He drank again, his breath at last slowing, his heart no longer trying to beat its way out from his chest.

It was just a dream, he told himself, nothing more. Still, he found it impossible to sleep after that, instead lying awake on his cot until the faintest hint of blue morning light drifted through the tiny, barred square of a window in the corner of the storage space that he called his bedroom. He rose quickly, then, throwing on the first tunic he came across in the dirty mound of clothing on the floor, and he combed his fingers through greasy hair that now grew a red-gray on his head. Too many days had passed since he had last bathed, but such things took too much time, too much effort, he thought. Rufus told himself that he could not afford to be idle, to laze about grooming and primping when the time to act, to kill Silanus and Decimus, might come at a moment's notice. He had to be there for it; he *had* to.

It had occurred to Rufus, many times, to tell Aemilia of his relation to her uncle—that, long ago, he had served as one of his guards on the island of Planasia. The revelation had made its way as far as the tip of his tongue, when he had convinced himself that she would understand; after all, she knew he had served Decimus for many years, had done many things at the senator's behest, things that went beyond distasteful, beyond violent and brutal and thuggish. Perhaps telling her of his past, of his connection to her family, might provide absolution—perhaps it would put a stop to his worsening dreams, or cleanse the air of the salty ocean winds that seemed to follow him with threatening persistence. But he had never been able to tell her, and he wasn't quite sure why—never mind that the more time that passed, the harder it became. She trusted him, now, relied upon him; if he were to tell her that he had known her uncle, she would wonder why he had remained silent for so long. She would suspect something, assume the worst—she might turn on him, abandon him. And he couldn't bear it—the only other person who had accepted him, had known the darkness inside of him and not shied away, was Leander. Leander, who was dead now, forever at a distance—except for when some version of him appeared in dreams, or Rufus thought he glimpsed a vision of him across the room, around a corner, always just out of reach, an unattainable promise.

Rufus understood himself well enough to know that he was not a leader; he never had been. It was why he had become a soldier in the first place, following orders without question; it was how he had fallen into service with Decimus, whose power, whose sheer sense of purpose in life, overrode the quiet listlessness of those around him who simply *lived*, without some end goal always in mind; it was, too, how he had attached himself to Aemilia, seeing something in her—in her anger, her thirst for vengeance—that reminded him of himself, except with a sense of direction, a desire and a plan to channel it. He found leaders, and he made himself their tool, their causes becoming his own. In such a way, he had always managed to find some measure of peace—but even that was now slipping away from him.

Rufus hadn't expected to be summoned by Decimus that day—but now he stood before the senator as the older man lounged on a couch, Duras across from him. Both picked at a collection of fruits, and Decimus, finishing a pomegranate, dabbed at his chin with a linen cloth, the fabric coming away stained a vivid red. Rufus fought off a vision of Leander coughing blood.

"Ah, Rufus," Decimus said, looking up as the soldier came to a halt at a respectful distance from his couch.

"Sir," Rufus said politely.

Decimus popped a grape into his mouth, chewing it slowly as he regarded the man before him. "You left the Praetorian Guard and entered my service quite a few years ago, now, correct?"

"Yes," Rufus said.

The senator picked another grape, roughly ripping it from its stem before gently placing it on his tongue, an act of violence followed by quiet tenderness. The sagging skin on his neck wobbled as he chewed. Duras, as had become usual, looked bored, his eyes scanning the door to the room, tracking any movement, as if he wished to be somewhere, anywhere, else.

Decimus at last spoke again. "Your age is showing, Rufus. You seem slower—weaker."

Rufus did not respond; he did not think that his master wanted nor expected an answer. Better, he knew, to remain silent.

"I no longer require your services, Rufus. I trust that you will remember how well you have been treated here, and that you will keep my confidence." Decimus's eyes bored into Rufus, a silent threat: that to speak of what he had done, of anything he knew about Decimus, would be to sentence himself to death, a dagger in the back on the street, poison in his drink cup as he gambled...

"Sir—" Rufus started.

"I've already selected a replacement for my personal guard." Decimus's gaze shifted to the door. "Marius, enter."

A young man—no, Rufus correct himself, a man in his prime—entered the room, his arms and legs perfectly muscled, his hair short and his chin clean-shaven in the military style. The newcomer looked at

Rufus, then quickly away—dismissing him as harmless. Rufus felt a rush of anger begin to surge within his body, his muscles tensing; he would not be insulted by such a whelp.

"Sejanus has kindly loaned him to me," Decimus said, looking at Marius as if he were an exceptionally well sculpted statue. "He's like you—like you were, I mean, when you were in your prime, when you first came to me."

Rufus struggled to find something to say, some objection to make, trying to quash his pride so that he could reason his way to staying with Decimus. He would be useless to Aemilia if he didn't maintain a place in the senator's household. All thoughts of freedom from Decimus—something he had once desperately longed for, something which now was being given to him so easily—fled his mind. Aemilia— Aemilia's need for vengeance—drove him now, more than his own long-suppressed dreams. In his panic, it did not occur to him that perhaps Decimus's promise of freedom, now so readily granted, was a lie; that even if he kept his head down, his mouth closed, it would not be enough to spare his life.

"Sir," Rufus began at last, hoping that his tone belied a confidence he was far from feeling, "I beg you, let me remain in your household. I can still provide some service, I am sure of it."

Decimus laughed then, some spittle flying from his mouth. Even Duras, paying attention now, regarded Rufus with a look of pity: the old man, in denial about his age, the weakness that no doubt had already begun to worm its way into his muscles, his bones, his mind.

"You can provide no further service, Rufus." Decimus waved a hand dismissively, and Rufus felt his panic begin to overtake him. He could not leave, not now—he had nothing else to drive him through life. His hand began to reach for a sword he did not carry.

"Decimus, if I may," Duras said suddenly, his eyes still appraising Rufus.

Decimus's eyes flicked over to the youth, although his expression was one of interest, not annoyance. "Yes, Duras?" His tone was similar to what masters used with pets, how they indulged a monkey that had learned to dance and performed its routine without command, hoping to please its master and earn a treat.

"I could have use for this man—for Rufus—still," Duras said. Decimus continued watching him, expecting him to elaborate. Duras swallowed, and Rufus realized, then, that the boy was improvising—seeking some way to allow Rufus to remain in the household. He was not certain whether to feel grateful or enraged that this offer—if the youth could carry it off—stemmed not from utility but from pity.

Duras continued speaking. "I've decided to amuse myself by writing up a little history of Roman soldiery. Although Rufus and I haven't spoken much, some of the war stories I've heard him mention sound like just the thing I'm interested in. It would help me considerably to have him close at hand."

Decimus looked unconvinced.

"You yourself said that my written Latin needs much improvement, Decimus," Duras added. "But, I suppose I could simply spend my days at the brothels instead…"

Decimus scowled. "Fine, fine. Rufus may remain, but only for the duration of your project. I expect to see regular progress."

Duras smiled, half raising a finger at Rufus in a silent salute, but Rufus only stared at the youth stonily, wondering if Titus had shared more with the boy than he had been supposed to. Why else would Duras bother to exert himself to ensure that Rufus remained in the household? The possibility that the young man was simply kind—that he had seen

Rufus in turmoil and wanted to help—did not cross his mind. He would not have been able to recognize assistance offered to him without the expectation of reciprocation; such a thing had never happened to him before.

29 - 30 CE

CHAPTER XXXI

AEMILIA LEPIDA

My cousins Nero Caesar and Drusus Caesar were quiet at dinner, listlessly putting bites of baked mackerel in their mouths and chewing as they seemed to only half-listen to my husband, who spoke animatedly, ignoring his own plate of the silphium- and cheese-covered fish. Aunt Agrippina had not bothered to join us, although her sons bore her apologies. I suspected that she had forgotten about the dinner entirely and was likely in the semi-conscious state brought on by her predilection to opium.

"Perhaps one or both of you should visit Capri personally," Torquatus was telling the young men. "Tiberius could not reject his heirs, should they arrive at the very doors of his villa. He would have to see you."

I took a large swallow of my wine, wondering if I was so very different from my aunt. It wasn't opium, but it might as well have been. Already the room was growing hazy around me, a comforting blur at the edge of my vision reminding me of the fact that, if things ever became too much, death was always an option. I knew my aunt thought similarly; I had seen how she eyed her dish of opium tablets, the knowledge that just a little too much of the substance dissolved in her wine would bear her to the Underworld, her troubles left behind.

"Sejanus would never allow us to leave Rome," Nero Caesar told my husband dismissively, his tone flat and disheartened. "He intercepts all our correspondence, to anyone. We are surrounded by his men, at all times. Even now, his guards wait outside your very own door."

His brother added, "The only reason we are allowed to have these dinners is because of our relation to Aemilia. And even then, I worry Sejanus suspects something."

Torquatus sighed, and despite my semi-drunken state, I was able to see how he tried to force a hopeful expression to his face. I had been the one to suggest he cast his lot in with my cousins, thinking that Sejanus—and, by extension, Decimus—would be able to be outmaneuvered. Thus far, I had been wrong. I took another sip, hoping that it might lessen my guilt, even as I knew that it would not. I wondered if I should have said nothing, if I should have simply let matters lie, but I knew I could not have; Sejanus was a friend and ally of Decimus, and for that reason alone his fate mattered. Perhaps I had ignored him for too long.

"We will think of something," Torquatus said brightly, at last taking a bite of his mackerel, which had quickly grown cold. My heart twinged at his optimism, which I had helped to bring about—and which I now feared was doomed.

A distant pounding at the door made us all glance up, freezing in place. Moments passed, and then a breathless, clear-eyed Agrippina entered the *triclinium*. It appeared that she was not, after all, at home with her opium.

"Oh, I'm so very sorry I'm late," she said at last, giving a small smile as we all stared at her.

Torquatus quickly got to his feet, greeting my aunt as if he had expected her, never mind that her sons had told us she was not coming. He quickly ordered a slave to set an extra place at an empty dining couch, and, when Aunt Agrippina was settled, he returned to his own position.

"I have news," Aunt Agrippina said, "and I could not delay in bearing it here, as I fear it will affect us all."

A fresh plate of the baked mackerel arrived and was placed before her, the cheese on top of the fish still sending small currents of steam into the air. Aunt Agrippina didn't spare it a glance.

"I think it's better that there are no additional ears present," my aunt said quietly, and Torquatus hurriedly dismissed the slaves. We all watched my aunt expectantly, waiting for her to speak again. "I've just come from visiting Livia," she said, and I swallowed my surprise. There was little love shared between the two women.

"No one has seen her in months," Torquatus said quietly.

Aunt Agrippina nodded. "The rumors are true. She has been quite unwell, for perhaps even longer than anyone thought—and I have no doubt that is why we now see Sejanus emboldened in his actions. When she was healthier, in more regular contact with Tiberius, she served as a check on the prefect's power. Now…" She trailed off, folding her hands across her lap. "She has not had the strength to regain the favor she lost with her son."

"How did you gain an audience with her?" I asked, wondering how my aunt had managed it, especially when she seemed to have been spending so much time of late in a drugged, semi-conscious state.

"I have those who are loyal to me, in her service," she said. "I hadn't dared risk it before—Sejanus has Livia under constant watch, too—but I felt that I could wait no longer to make my move. Unfortunately, I may have delayed too long. She was barely able to form a coherent sentence."

I leaned back on my couch, silently impressed by my aunt. While I had before seen evidence of her strong, determined nature when it came to securing her position, and that of her family, this most recent revelation was another matter entirely. Her own sons, as well as Torquatus, sat silently for a moment, as if contemplating the fact Aunt Agrippina had managed to place spies in Livia's household—the widow of Augustus, mother of Tiberius. It was no mean feat.

My aunt waved her hand at us, as if sensing that we were dwelling too long on her revelation. "Never mind how. Let's not remain fixated on that. What's more important is what we do next. I fear that Livia is not much longer for the realm of the living, and I worry Sejanus will do something dreadful after her death, once it is truly impossible for her to stand in his way. I'm just not certain what—and I'm not sure how we can prevent it."

"Perhaps Tiberius will return to Rome for her funerary rites," I said. "She is his mother, after all, no matter their closeness or lack thereof, at the end. Nero Caesar and Drusus Caesar must certainly be granted an audience with him then."

Aunt Agrippina digested my words, pursing her lips as she thought. "That may be the best we can hope for, for the time being. Then my sons must do their best to convince him of their loyalty, and their continued suitability as his heirs. It may be entirely too risky to attempt to have Sejanus cast out—his grip on the emperor is quite strong—so we must instead do our best to solidify my sons' positions. We can worry about Sejanus after we take measures to protect ourselves."

My husband and cousins' eyes moved back and forth between my aunt and me, the trio of men watching us—*listening* to us, two women who were supposed to have little knowledge of and even less concern for politics. I pushed my wine away, a sense of excitement

233

catching flame within me, and Aunt Agrippina and I looked at one another, our eyes bright with hope for all our futures.

The year dwindled on, the hottest peak of summer driving Rome's elite to their countryside estates or island villas, if they had not already left while the weather for traveling was milder and far more agreeable. Torquatus and I remained in the city, although we had dispatched our children to a seaside estate belonging to some of his maternal relatives. Amynta had agreed to go along to oversee their summertime retreat, ensuring that the tutors who trailed shortly behind kept to the rigorous schedule we still expected the children to maintain.

Our house was exceedingly quiet without the pattering of their footsteps across the mosaics, their cries and shouts as they fought and played with one another now missing from the hallways. While their absence saddened me, their distance from Rome brought me some measure of reassurance. We all waited for the news that Livia had died, silently praying to the gods that it would prompt Tiberius to return, would force him to keep Sejanus in check. If such a sequence of events did not, in fact, occur, I did not want my children present only to be swept up into the ensuing conflict that I sensed was brewing. Rome was not safe—but it never had been.

It was entirely by chance that I met one summer afternoon with the men I had formed an alliance with two years past, when all of us had agreed to see to it that Silanus and Decimus met their ends. It seemed so long ago—and although I always held my hatred of the senator and my husband's cousin close to my heart, I had spared them little thought lately, at last realizing that Sejanus had become the more immediate threat.

"Lady Aemilia!" I turned, wondering who called my name, and the slave holding the parasol over my head shifted with my movement so that my body remained shaded. The two male slaves accompanying us halted as well, protectively situating themselves on either side of me.

"Ah, young Duras," I said, forcing a smile to my lips as I saw my half-brother approaching, finely dressed in a crisp white toga. Ever since his identity had been revealed to me, and I had understood that our physical similarities were not mere coincidence, I found it incomprehensible that anyone could observe us together and not make some connection as to our familial relationship. As a result, I made every effort to avoid him when I saw that our paths might cross; I had no time to deal with the chaos that would ensue from the discovery of his identity.

Both Rufus and Titus lingered behind the youth, although, as usual, they gave no outward indication that they knew me. "Where is Decimus?" I asked, finding it strange that Rufus would be present when the senator was not, and my eyes quickly scanned the people moving past us on either side, wondering if I had perhaps just not seen him yet. Many of them headed towards the circus to watch the day's races; I, too, was making my way there, intending to meet Torquatus when I arrived.

"Too busy with some pressing matter to step out for the races with us," Duras said.

"Oh?" I hoped he would elaborate.

"A messenger from Sejanus arrived this morning," Duras said dismissively; he had little concern for what the senator or the prefect were up to. "I know no more."

I gave a small smile in response, but my eyes drifted behind him, to Rufus and Titus; neither man moved, but both their faces had new lines of worry. Duras saw my gaze shift, looking over his shoulder at the two men who accompanied him. "Ah, yes, Rufus," he said. "You're used to seeing him with Decimus, I expect. He's my man now."

That was a new development—to me, anyway. "How did that come to pass?" I asked.

Duras laughed. "Decimus wanted him to retire. Rufus wanted to stay. So I convinced the senator that I was compiling a study of sorts, on soldiery, to improve my written Latin, and that Rufus was integral to this project. That was, oh, two years ago now, and naturally my project has barely begun." He grinned, and it was clear that he had no intention of completing, as he called it, his project, if it had not entirely been a fabrication to begin with.

I glanced at Rufus, but he resolutely avoided meeting my eyes, instead looking over my shoulder, as if something there had wholly captured his attention. Two years—and Rufus had said nothing about his new position. Nor had Titus, who, being in the same household, surely would have known of the change in Rufus's station. I wondered if there was anything else they hadn't told me, a seed of suspicion beginning to take root within me—but I quickly quashed it down. After all, I told myself, this changed nothing; Rufus remained in Decimus's household, where he could be of the most use, and that was what was most important. It did not cross my mind at the time that Rufus had had the chance to be free of Decimus—something he had desired for almost as long as I had known him—and yet he had not taken it.

"Shall we go?" Duras asked, and I noticed the crowd was beginning to thin around us. "The first race starts soon—I've become quite a fan of the Blues, and I don't want to miss it!"

I nodded, amused by my half-brother's enthusiasm, and we began to walk towards the circus, in step with one another. I couldn't help but steal glances at Duras as we walked, still mesmerized by the resemblance he, my mother, and I all shared. Rufus, Titus, and my own attendants trailed behind.

"You see it, too," Duras said quietly, although he kept his gaze ahead as we walked, the circus opening up not far away from us now, its massive elliptical shape dominating the landscape.

I quickly averted my eyes from his profile. "What do you mean?"

"How much we look like one another," he said simply, quickly glancing over at me with a small smile.

"Not at all," I said, my words hard, and I scanned the crowd, looking for an escape. "Oh, I think I see my husband. Enjoy the races, Duras."

I had not seen Torquatus at all, but I hurried away before I even finished uttering my small lie, my farewell bordering on rude. My heart was racing. I wondered if Duras knew; I wondered if Titus and Rufus had told him who he was, another secret the two of them had kept from me, for whatever reason. Again, I tried to quash down the seed of suspicion that was fighting to worm its way back into my mind. What purpose would it serve to tell the boy of our relation—of his heritage? It would only further endanger him, and the two of them. I had believed Titus when he said he cared for the boy, wished to protect him. But what if things had changed? What if they sought to use him for their own ends? A strange sense of protectiveness welled within me for the sibling I barely knew.

Torquatus saw me before I saw him, and I jumped when he touched me on the arm, startling me from my thoughts. "Are you alright? You seem so…" he trailed off. "Never mind. The first race is starting any moment now. Let's find our seats."

We quickly wound our way to a reserved pair of stone seats along the finishing length of the circus's racetrack—a prime location reserved for the upper classes of Rome—and situated ourselves just as the first chariots of the day took off, the horses' hooves pounding as already they jockeyed for position on the sand below, the wheels of the vehicles they pulled spinning so fast as to seem almost invisible. The crowd screamed in delight, struggling to shout above each other in support of their favorite horses, their favorite charioteers. Towering wooden structures had been built above the lower stone levels, and they were filled to dangerous capacity with all manner of people, creaking and groaning under the weight they bore as everyone fought to get the best view possible.

The chariots were on their final lap when the accident occurred: two horses, each fixed to the outer sides of opposing chariots, crashed into each other as they entered a turn. Both horses stumbled as they made contact, their legs fighting to keep them up, to keep them running, even as the other horses on their teams tried to surge ahead, wild, seemingly oblivious to their fellow animals' struggle to save them all from what was about to happen. Everything—victory, loss, life, death—hinged upon the lone pair of horses who now frantically scrambled on the sands below.

One of the horses, a dark brown creature with a long black mane and tail, won its battle, its hooves seeming to spray sand as it regained its balance and once more matched its pace to its team, the charioteer cracking his whip as they pulled through the turn and onto the straightaway. But the other horse—a gleaming white stallion—couldn't save itself. In its struggle, one of its legs got trapped under its own body, bending at an awkward, unnatural angle, and then the other horses got caught up, tangling amongst one another as the stallion collapsed, breaking his leg with a snap I could almost hear; they seemed to trample him as the chariot crashed into the wall, wood splintering as the horses groaned, the charioteer disappearing from sight in the carnage.

A deep sense of foreboding seized me then. I did not ordinarily take much note of omens, nor did I subscribe to most superstitions—but something about this was different. I could not explain it, but I knew that something terrible was about to unfold.

CHAPTER XXXII

TITUS

Titus didn't see the chariot crash, although the sudden, deafening roar of the crowd gave him an idea that something shockingly unexpected had happened. Instead of watching the first race, he and Duras were embroiled in an argument, and the sporting event had gone from something eagerly anticipated to something wholly unimportant.

"What aren't you telling me?" Duras asked, anger punctuating every word as he shouted to be heard over the still-quieting crowd. "You treat me like a child—a fool. I deserve to know the truth."

"There is nothing I haven't told you," Titus said, struggling to keep his words even. It still pained him to lie, despite his years of practice, now, but he told himself it was necessary. Duras was not ready.

Duras punched the wall of the stairway they stood in, the wood splintering outwards from his fist. They had never made it to their seats; Titus had sent Rufus on ahead to Decimus's reserved box, one of many set aside for senators and their families and guests that had the best vantage point of the track. But, seeking some measure of privacy away from the prying ears of the powerful men of Rome, Duras and Titus had wound their way further up—rather than along—the circus, half-climbing to one of the upper tiers built of wood. There, with only the occasional, random plebian passing by them, entirely uninterested in their conversation in a way that the upper classes might not be, Titus had intended to warn Duras off of Aemilia, telling the youth that she was troubled, that she and her husband had fallen out of favor with Decimus, that nothing good would come of their association. Duras, he advised, should keep his distance from them both. But the boy had known he was lying—and Titus should have expected that. He had never been good at lying, at hiding the truth. It had become a skill learned by necessity, but never a skill he had mastered.

Titus and Duras stared at one another, and, as Titus examined the young man he had protected, had raised, for almost the entirety of his life, he realized that he had treated him as a child for far longer than he should have. What good would come from driving him away? From treating him as if he were incapable of making his own decisions? Perhaps it was not Duras who wasn't ready—perhaps it was him.

Titus swallowed, closing his eyes as he silently begged Julia for her forgiveness. Then, he began to speak. It was time to tell Duras everything.

In hindsight, Titus envisioned that he might have better explained things—perhaps started out more slowly, led up to each subsequent revelation more gently. But there was no gentle way to tell someone that he had been lied to for the entirety of his life.

Duras had listened silently to every word Titus said. It had been difficult to begin, but as he spoke more and more, it became easier, the words tumbling out of him with increasing rapidity, the only pauses coming when the roar of the circus's crowd grew too loud—the shouts, stamping feet, and clapping hands all drowning him out—or when someone passed by them in the stairwell, their ears too close. It was, Titus found, a relief; with each secret that he shared, he felt as if a weight were lifted from his shoulders, as if years of worry were erased from memory.

But Duras's expression had remained unreadable, closed off. And then, after Titus had laid it all out for him—his true parentage; his bastardized imperial bloodline; Aemilia; his birth on the island of Trimerus and how he had been transported secretly away to Tomis, placed in the care of Didas and Galla in Ovid's household; their subsequent escape into the wilds of Dacia—he told Duras of how Julia remained an exile, how she and Titus had loved one another. How he still did love her. Titus told him, too, that Rufus and Aemilia had known who he was for some time—that they all, now, shared these secrets, secrets that could destroy each of them.

The one thing Titus kept back from Duras was Aemilia's vendetta against Decimus and Silanus—particularly how the latter had attacked her—and how she, alongside Titus and Rufus, plotted to kill both the senator and Duras's father by birth. It was better, Titus reasoned, that Duras remain ignorant of that, at least, lest he somehow be implicated in matters when—if—they ever managed to succeed in their plans.

Duras only asked one question of Titus, at the end, when the soldier had finally ceased speaking, his eyes searching the young man's for some measure of comprehension—of forgiveness. "If you loved my mother—if you still do—why has she remained on Trimerus for so long?" Duras's words were accusatory, his gaze direct.

"Because I promised to look after her child, to protect him—to protect *you*," Titus said, willing Duras—the young man he had loved as a son for all these years—to understand. Still, the words stung him, a reminder that, even though Julia herself had asked it of him, he had had to abandon her in order to fulfill her wishes.

"I am no longer a child," Duras said flatly, "and I have no need of protection." He shook his head, angry disappointment flashing across his face, and began to turn away from the man he had thought of as his father for as long as he could remember.

"I also promised her to love you, and I have. I do. You are my son, no matter what," Titus whispered, but it was too late. Duras had already begun to walk away, and Titus's quiet words met no one's ears but his own. He wondered, then, how he could have ever wasted time worrying about his own father's identity, about the course his life had come close to taking—because none of it mattered, in the end. Blood did not make a family; choice and actions did. He wanted to run after Duras, to tell him that, to remind him that *he* was his father in all the ways that mattered, that despite how Duras's mind must be reeling, everything would be alright. But instead he stood rooted to the ground.

Titus wasn't certain how long he remained in the stairwell, the sounds of the circus a constant cycle of cheers and shouts with brief periods of a more subdued din as the crowd waited for the next race, the number of passerby increasing between events, the odor of their sweat stemming from a mixture of excitement and the oppressive heat that seemed to overwhelm the crowded stands, the sun beating down, merciless, from above.

Rufus ascended the stairs as the races continued on, stalking over to Titus with irritation evident in each step. "What are you doing here? I've been waiting in the viewing box for ages, the sun roasting my skin off," he snapped, his clothing damp from sweat. "Took me at least an hour to find you. Where did the boy go? Taking a piss?"

Titus shook his head. "I told him."

Rufus looked confused. "Told him what?"

"Everything."

"*What*?" Rufus asked. "What god of truth possessed you to make you do such a thing?" His tone shifted from incredulous to angry as he spoke.

"It was time," Titus snapped, slightly defensive. "He's a man now—and I trust him."

"With our lives?" Rufus asked.

"Yes."

Rufus looked skeptical, and another roar from the crowd seemed to shake the stands. "Aemilia won't be pleased," he said at last. "I know her far better than you—I've watched her grow from a girl to a woman, seen how she's changed over the years."

Titus sighed. "She will understand. She has to."

Rufus grunted, shifting the conversation away from Aemilia. "Does Duras know about our plans for Decimus and Silanus?"

Titus shook his head. "I left that out."

"Good," Rufus said. "I'm glad you had the sense to at least refrain from mentioning that. Maybe our lives will yet be spared since he can't betray any knowledge of it. If he babbles out his identity, on the other hand, he's the only one who'll get killed."

Titus studied the other man, noting how old they were both getting—wondering how much of their lives remained to be spared at all. Twenty years had passed since he had left Julia behind on Trimerus, and he had begun to feel an itch, a small voice that nagged at him that not much time was left, for any of them—that he needed to see her, if only one more time, somehow. Duras was right, he thought; the babe he had protected was no longer a child, but a young man—one who now knew the truth of it all. One who no longer needed him or his protection.

"What secrets are *you* keeping, Rufus?" Titus asked suddenly.

Rufus laughed at him. "Many. And they'll go with me to my cinerary urn, the lot of them."

Titus found himself laughing then, too. He and Rufus had shared an uneasy alliance ever since they had first been thrust together; each knew the other kept secrets, bits of knowledge that they did not trust one other with, wary, even after years, that the other might still betray him. Yet somehow they had found themselves to be, in some strange version of the concept, friends.

CHAPTER XXXIII

AEMILIA LEPIDA

It was nearing the end of summer, when the air is becoming just a bit crisper in the evenings and at dawn, when the leaves of the trees seem to begin to shrivel up the very slightest amount—but when there are still days that are dreadfully hot, and people seek comfort in the darkest parts of their abode, sleeping away the afternoon, sipping at drinks cooled with ice brought all the way to Rome from the mountains.

It was one of those latter days, and Aunt Agrippina and I were alone, quietly relaxing on couches; she dozed while I read a scroll, my eyes scanning some old lines of poetry from Ovid, long-since dead of some illness, though his words remained as vivid as ever. He had never been recalled from his own exile—I wondered, in passing, if he had ever figured out the identity of the babe he had unknowingly and indirectly sheltered in his household, all those years ago. Even if he had, nothing had come of it.

I rolled the scroll up with a sigh and set it aside, stretching my arms and back. Slaves were standing nearby, fanning us slowly, and another waited to replenish our drinks. It did not escape my notice that my aunt kept her little dish of opium tablets close at hand, though I had not seen her touch them since I had arrived earlier in the day.

"I do know how to take care of myself, you know," Aunt Agrippina said, and I glanced away from the opium, moving my eyes to her. She didn't look as if she had stirred at all, her lids low and heavy over her eyes.

"I know," I said quietly.

"I'm allowed this small vice," she said, eyes still closed, breathing still even. "I don't always use them, you know. Only sometimes. When I'm most lost…"

I didn't answer this time, and she didn't speak again. I understood the appeal of the opium perfectly—the wonderful numbness it offered, the respite from one's troubles. I found the same relief in my wine, Bacchus's greatest gift—so I was not one to judge.

"*Domina!*" The cry came from within the house, shattering the quiet afternoon. "*Domina*, I have news!" The shout came again, nearer this time, and then a nondescript man came running into the room, his features all perfectly forgettable: mousy brown hair, cut close to his skull, matched the same dull-colored eyes; his nose and chin, brow and cheeks were all unmemorable in their mediocrity. His tunic, too, was not the typical cloth and color of Aunt Agrippina's household slaves, but a dull brown that would catch no one's eye, its cut plain and its quality unremarkable.

He bowed in front of Aunt Agrippina, who was fully awake now, standing in front of the couch where only moment before she had been dozing. "What is it?" Her words remained even, but I saw how her eyes already widened, as if she suspected what news he bore before he even uttered the words.

"Livia has died," he said breathlessly. "I just received word from one of your people in her household—I have been waiting outside for weeks, as you commanded. It was no more than an hour ago."

"It has happened, then," Aunt Agrippina said quietly. She dismissed the informant, and all the other attending slaves, too, leaving us alone. She remained standing.

My hands clenched and unclenched as I sat on my couch; I was uncertain how to feel. I was far from mourning Livia, but her death would now set into motion a series of events which would prove to be either our salvation or our undoing. I wondered if it was worth it, to have moved against Sejanus for the sake of ruining Decimus, and possibly Silanus, too—but then I realized that, even without my personal quest for vengeance, I still would have aided my aunt, my cousins. They were my family, after all. I clenched my hands again, steeling my resolve.

"Should we go see your sons?" I asked her. It was likely we had found out before Nero Caesar and Drusus Caesar—and their part to play was, we hoped, coming soon. "They need to be prepared. They need to gain an audience with Tiberius as soon as he arrives in Rome for his mother's funerary rites."

Aunt Agrippina shook her head. "No. Sejanus has them closely watched, kept under guard—for their protection, ostensibly. He probably knows already that Livia is no more, and he will be keeping my sons even closer to him now. He is no fool. He knows as well as we do that this is a time for change, one way or another—and they stand in his way."

My aunt sat at last, the energy seeming to fade from her body as she hunched her shoulders slightly. She poured a glass of wine, then her fingers selected an opium tablet from her dish, letting it drop with a small splash into her wine as I watched impassively. After giving it a few moments to dissolve, she took her first sip, breathing out a deep sigh after she swallowed.

"What do we do now?" I asked nervously, my aunt's anxious behavior unsettling me. I reached for my own wine, taking a large swallow; after a brief pause, I drained the rest of the liquid and refilled my glass. I did not bother to add water.

"We wait," she said, her voice already sounding far away, the opium beginning to take effect. "And we make all manner of vows to any gods who may listen, asking them to see to it that we emerge from this victorious."

Tiberius did not come for Livia's funerary rites, instead remaining at his villa on Capri. Our hope that his mother's death would mean the emperor's return to Rome—would mean an audience with his heirs, who might somehow turn his ear away from Sejanus and perhaps provide some guarantee of protection for the rest of us—was utterly destroyed.

One of the next signs that something was terribly wrong was that Tiberius did not put forth either of his heirs for Livia's funerary oration, as might be expected, but instead sent orders for Caligula to perform the honors in place of his elder brothers. Both Nero Caesar and Drusus Caesar, ringed by an ever-growing number of soldiers, looked on as their younger sibling spoke shakily, although their gazes were so distant that I wondered if they heard—or saw—much of anything at all; they certainly were not oblivious to their waning favor.

Aunt Agrippina barely held herself together for the funeral, and I could tell that she had taken opium before coming: her eyelids kept fluttering, and her body swayed, as if she could barely stand. No one near her dared to offer assistance, and my own place was too far away to help her myself, so I watched from a distance, a deep sense of loss already forming in the pit of my stomach.

Torquatus had tried to talk me out of visiting my aunt several days after Livia was interred in her husband's mausoleum. "They are damned," he told me. "We can no longer associate with them—it was a mistake to throw our lot in with them to begin with. We must think of ourselves, of our children. Perhaps it is not too late to distance ourselves."

"We had no one else to attach ourselves to," I hissed at him, and my husband stepped back with a look of surprise at my vehemence. "They are my family! What little family I have left! I cannot lose them as I lost my mother."

Torquatus had not tried to stop me again as I fled the house, practically throwing myself into the litter that carried me to my aunt's home. One of my slaves had to knock on her doors repeatedly before anyone came to let us in—the normal door attendant was missing, and the youth who granted us entrance looked unsettled.

I brushed past him, my steps quickly carrying me over mosaics, each telling a different story: Pluto and Proserpina, the god dragging his bride to the Underworld; Aeneas, fleeing a burning, lost Troy—but I had no time to stop to contemplate their meanings, to admire the beauty of the craftsmanship that lay under my feet.

Aunt Agrippina paced her courtyard, several slaves looking on, uncertain what to do, how to help their mistress.

"The end is coming," Aunt Agrippina wailed as she caught sight of me. Her hair hung loose and tangled; she had not bothered to dress in her day clothes—and by her smell, I doubted she had bathed in days. "Sejanus has won. He has turned Tiberius entirely away from us."

When I had decided to come to my aunt, I had not thought of a plan, of what to say or what to do. I simply rushed to her, then, embracing her in my arms as she had done for me when I arrived at her home many years ago, after my mother had been taken from me, and we both wept, fearing for the future.

"You must stay inside," Torquatus told me, an urgent fear in his voice. We were at dinner, but neither of us had touched our food, and it had grown cold. I didn't even have the inclination to drink my wine—I did not think that I could numb any of the feelings that now coursed through my body, an incessant press of emotion that I thought would ruin me.

"What has happened now?" I asked dully, although I was not certain I wanted to know the answer.

"I heard that the senate received a letter, today, from Tiberius," he began, although he seemed to struggle to continue. I waited, staring blindly at my plate of food, until Torquatus at last spoke again. "He has accused Nero Caesar of impropriety of some sort—I did not find out the details of the charge. Your aunt, Agrippina, too—Tiberius has accused her of sexual licentiousness."

"That's outrageous!" I snapped. "I—I—" I did not know how to finish my objection—but I knew it did not matter; what I said in the privacy of my own home, with only my husband for an audience, would change nothing.

Torquatus took a long drink of his wine, as if to fortify himself. "That may be, Aemilia, but… we can do nothing to help them now. We must stay removed from this, and we must hope that our kinship to them, our recent friendship, will be overlooked."

I knew that he was right; I knew that their fates were far past any assistance from us. But it didn't make it easier to accept.

Torquatus was speaking again. "There are people beginning to gather, outside the senate house. They protest on behalf of Nero Caesar and Agrippina. That is why I ask you to stay inside the house—I worry that things may get worse, on the streets. Dangerous. I'm glad we decided that the children should remain outside the city for the time being."

A very small seed of hope took root within me. "The family of Germanicus has always been popular amongst the people," I said excitedly. "Perhaps more will join them. Perhaps there will be riots. Tiberius would have to listen, then, or risk letting the city go to ruin."

Torquatus gave me a small, sad smile, but he shook his head. "I don't think so, Aemilia. Sejanus has many men at his disposal. He will not allow for things to get out of hand."

Torquatus proved to be correct: after a brief delay caused by the protests, in which the senate asked Tiberius what his will specifically was, another imperial letter arrived, firmly reiterating his charges against my aunt and cousin. Tiberius had not, and would not, change his mind: their fate was decided. While I had not truly hated Sejanus before—not as I did Decimus and Silanus—I did so now; *he* had poisoned the emperor against my aunt and her family, and he was now responsible for their ruin.

"Aemilia," Torquatus called my name quietly from the door. I did not roll over in bed to look at him, but he must have known I was awake; it was, after all, early afternoon, although I had not bothered to dress myself. An empty wine jug laid on its side by my bed, and my fingers twitched as I looked at it.

"Aemilia," he said again, and I heard his tentative steps as he approached me, then felt the bed shift as he sat on the edge, close to me, but not touching, as if he feared to make contact. "Nero Caesar has been exiled to the island of Pontia."

The words were like a knife to my stomach, a brutal stab sinking into my flesh. I curled more tightly into a ball. "Aunt Agrippina?" I asked, my voice hoarse.

"She…" Torquatus inhaled deeply, and I felt his weight shift again. "She has been exiled to Pandateria."

I screamed as the words dragged the invisible knife across my stomach, gutting me like little more than a fish plucked mercilessly from the sea. Pandateria, the island my grandmother had first been exiled to. I felt as if it were all happening again, as if I were a girl of only twelve once more: my family, those I loved, all of them being ripped from me, cast into oblivion and condemned to rot away.

Torquatus was speaking again, although I barely heard him. "Caligula and the little girls are going to live with their grandmother. Young Agrippina is safely away in the countryside with her new husband—thank the gods she was married off before this all came to pass. Drusus Caesar remains in Rome, but…" He did not need to finish his sentence. We both knew it was only a matter of time before a similar fate befell him, too.

Torquatus left me, then, and I remained curled into a ball, as if I might be able to hold myself tightly enough to entirely keep out the world around me. I wished, then, that I had my aunt's opium, to numb the pain, to take away the hopelessness I felt; I wished I had the strength to end everything. But instead I simply lay there, a wounded animal, unable to help anyone, even myself.

CHAPTER XXXIV

DURAS

Duras glanced around at Decimus's other dinner guests; all of them were deeply ensconced in conversation, stretched out on their couches, bellies full, glasses of wine in hand. The space closest to him remained empty, its occupant—a rather fat, middle-aged man whose name he had already forgotten—having drunkenly wandered off some time ago, never returning. Perhaps he had found other, more important people to speak with, or had passed out somewhere: he had barely been able to stand when he had left.

Sighing, Duras motioned for an attendant to bring him a second plate of the evening's main course: chicken in the Parthian style, one of his favorites. Pepper, wine, and caraway made up the marinade that first smothered the meat, then asafoetida, a smelly spice he had quickly grown to love, was consistently and laboriously poured over as it cooked, until at last more fresh pepper was dusted on top, just before the chicken was served. His mouth watered even as he waited for his second portion.

The food was one of the things Duras most enjoyed about Rome. The diversity of seasonings, the range of meats, a whole empire's worth of ingredients to draw upon—it was a stark contrast to the simpler offerings of Dacia: hunted deer and hare and boar, most often roasted over the fire and served without sauces or carefully chosen side dishes; rustic breads and cheeses that were flavorful but provincial in comparison to what the cooks of Rome could create. Here, he could travel the world from a dining couch.

He scanned the *triclinium* again as he waited for his chicken: Decimus and Sejanus, embroiled, as usual, in some intense discussion; Silanus, his unwitting father, motioning with his wineglass as he spoke to a senator; other well-to-do men of Rome, their togas carefully positioned around them in heavy, cumbersome folds, chatting of horses and women, wine and food. It was as if nothing had happened over the past few days, as if the city's ever-shifting politics were not once again in turmoil, with one of the heirs to the empire and his mother having been so brutally cast out. It remained to be seen whether they would rot away in their new island prisons, their simple confinement enough to appease the emperor—and Sejanus—or if death would find them artificially early.

Movement caught Duras's eye: Silanus was standing from his couch, draping his heavy toga in place over his body and then raising his wineglass as he looked around at the other men. "To Sejanus," he said, his shouted words quickly quieting the rest of the room, "who has protected Rome from the threat of Nero Caesar and the whore, Agrippina!"

The rest of the men cheered, raising their own glasses and drinking them dry in large swallows; none of them had bothered to question exactly what threat it was that Nero Caesar had supposedly presented, or with whom Agrippina had allegedly committed her own offenses. Duras took the smallest sip of his wine, finding that he could take no joy in the overthrow of his relatives—though he had not known them at all, and now comprehended that he never would. It was the same with his mother, who, though she still lived, was inaccessible to him, forever a stranger despite the intimacy of their shared blood.

Duras understood that, if any of the men with whom he now dined came to know his true identity, they would ensure that he met the same fate as so many of the rest of his family—or, more likely, they would guarantee his outright and immediate murder, unless they happened to think of some use for him first.

His eyes found Silanus again—his father, he reminded himself, though it was odd to use that word for him, as the title had always belonged to another, to Titus. Duras did not physically see anything of himself in the man who had sired him, and what few words they had exchanged had revealed nothing insightful about any shared traits of character or personality. But if what Titus had said about Silanus was true—that he had betrayed Julia and his own unborn son, to save himself—then Duras hoped that he had little in common with the pathetic excuse of a man whose seed had given him life.

A new plate of Parthian chicken at last appeared before him, but he suddenly found that he had lost his appetite. He wanted to go home, to return to Dacia. Although he was Roman by blood, he did not understand these people, did not share their proclivity for intrigues, for betrayal and murder. Duras was angry—angry that he had been lied to for all his life, about who he was and where he came from. But he was also angry, on some level, that Titus, the man he had happily and ignorantly called Father, had even told him the truth at all. He thought he had known who he was and where he belonged, but now... Now he felt lost, misplaced amongst both people. Perhaps it would have been better to remain ignorant, for Titus to have maintained the lie and spared Duras the confusion he now felt.

He stood from his couch, wandering away from the *triclinium* and its occupants and towards the toilets, hoping for a moment of solitude—but when he reached the room, he heard voices from within. He paused, lingering as close to the door as he dared, trying to quiet his breath so that he could hear better.

"The younger Julia still remains in exile on Trimerus," a voice said—Decimus. "There was an attempt to liberate her before, some years ago."

"Yes, I remember hearing of that." Sejanus. Duras had not seen either of them leave the dining room, but he had been too lost in thought to pay much attention. "Why bother killing her now, though? She has been forgotten by Rome. I doubt she is a threat to us."

"But that is precisely why she could quickly and easily be dispatched," Decimus countered. "Nero Caesar and Agrippina are too fresh in the public's mind; we must allow some time to pass before we deal with them further and secure your position. But in the meantime, you cannot entirely discount Julia, no matter how forgotten she may seem to be. Her imperial blood remains a threat."

"I suppose you're right," Sejanus said, and his voice suddenly seemed closer to the door. Duras moved back slightly, straining to hear his next words. "I'll send word to Tiberius, invent some falsehood about her plotting against him, and suggest that he have her executed. My men can do it quietly enough. No one need even know the emperor ordered it."

"Perhaps we should also consider executing..." Decimus was saying, but suddenly Sejanus had emerged from the toilet, fixing his toga back into place, with the older senator just behind, and both of them caught sight of Duras at the same time.

Duras felt his heart thud in his chest, and he struggled to think quickly. "I've got to piss," he blurted out, slurring his words, feigning drunkenness. "Decimus, you have simply the best wine. I don't know how I survived before coming to Rome." He smiled a lopsided grin and swayed slightly on his feet before leaning against the wall, as if he needed help to maintain his balance. Let them think him still the inferior barbarian prince.

Sejanus watched him warily as he finished repositioning his toga, but Decimus waved a hand dismissively at the youth. "Hurry back to the *triclinium*, Duras," the senator said. "Dessert will be served soon."

The two men stepped around him and moved down the hall, their heads bent close together as they resumed speaking. Sejanus glanced back at Duras once, studying him for a long moment, and then they were gone. Duras quickly straightened up, his heart still thudding in his chest. They were going to try to kill Julia—his mother. A woman he had never met, but his mother nonetheless.

Duras found Rufus and Titus in the kitchen. The smell of the Parthian chicken he and Decimus's guests had been served lingered, but the two men were instead hunched over bowls of simple stew, eating in near silence as the cook and his assistants hurriedly prepared the desserts that were to be carried to the *triclinium*. Camilla was in the corner, chopping vegetables—probably for the slaves' own evening meal—and she offered a small smile as he looked her way.

Titus set his spoon down when Duras entered the kitchen, but Rufus continued eating after a wordless grunt of greeting in his direction. Despite their differing reactions, both men looked surprised to see him— he hadn't spoken at all to either of them since the races, when Titus had revealed everything.

"A word with you?" Duras asked, eyes focused on Titus. He spoke in the Dacian language he had been raised with—all the better to avoid the ever-listening ears of Decimus's slaves.

Titus nodded, and Duras gestured across the kitchen, towards a storeroom. He led the way, Titus following behind.

"Decimus and Sejanus plan to have Julia killed," Duras said, without preamble. There was no easy lead up to such a statement. Although he continued speaking in the Dacian tongue, he kept his voice low; the storeroom offered little protection for their conversation, but it was still better than meeting in the hallway, where guests from the dinner might stumble across them.

"What?" Titus looked shocked, his brow furrowed.

"I overheard them, only minutes ago," Duras said. "Decimus suggested it, pointing out that she could still be a threat, saying that now was a good time to act, and Sejanus agreed. He intends to write to Tiberius to convince him to execute her, but they plan to use Sejanus's men and to keep it secret."

Titus seemed to sag, then, his body shrinking as he let out a deep sigh. He did not speak.

"You must go to her," Duras urged. "There is little time. You can get there before Sejanus's men, but you must go now. You'll only be days ahead of them, perhaps a week at most."

Titus appeared to be thinking then, his eyes resting on Duras's face but seemingly focused on something else entirely, as if he were already envisioning the journey to Trimerus. "There are sure to be countless guards with her, even after all this time," he said slowly. "There may be a way... But if I'm wrong, there's no chance I'll make it to her."

"Let's hope you aren't wrong, then," Duras said simply. There was no other option.

Titus nodded at him, and a new sense of urgency laced his words as he began to speak again, marking his commitment to action. "May I take some of your clothes—a simple tunic and cloak? I'll need to shave, too, and cut my hair. I suppose I can manage that on my own. It will be a rough job, but passable."

"Of course, but why?" Duras asked. He had long ago embraced Roman dress and style—it was expected, given his situation as a hostage—but Titus had always chosen to maintain his Dacian appearance, largely in order to hide his identity as a former Roman soldier, as a deserter.

"I'll move faster if I look like a Roman," Titus said simply.

"Oh," Duras said, feeling foolish for not having thought of such a reason. A lone Dacian wouldn't be met with much, if any, goodwill as he traveled across the countryside and sought passage on a ship.

The two men stared at each other then, silent. Titus at last spoke first, breaking the quiet. "I must go." Still, he lingered there in the storeroom, and Duras could read a thousand different unspoken emotions in Titus's eyes. Suddenly, his anger over the past days, which he had held so tightly within himself since he had learned the truth, seemed to dissipate.

"Father…" Duras started, but he didn't know what else to say. Instead, he simply embraced the man who had raised him, protected him, loved him for decades. "Be well. Travel swiftly. Tell my mother…" He wasn't certain how to finish his sentence, wasn't certain what message he wished to convey to the woman who had given him life but whom he had never known, and doubted he ever would.

"I will tell her that you are everything she could have hoped and dreamed of," Titus said, and his eyes shone brightly. "Both you and Aemilia. I love you, my son."

Duras nodded, and then in another breath Titus was gone, leaving him alone in the storeroom, uncertain if he would ever again see the man who was his father in every way that truly mattered. He took a moment to compose himself, to adjust the toga on his body, and then he, too, left, steeling himself to return to the *triclinium*, to take his dessert alongside the men who planned to kill his mother—who would without hesitation kill him, too, if they even thought that he might stand in their way.

CHAPTER XXXV

AEMILIA LEPIDA

I finally emerged from my bed, uncertain how much time had passed. The days had come and gone in a haze, the wine jug beside me seeming to empty and refill itself as vague hints of daylight periodically fought to make their way into the room. A dish of opium tablets, acquired by a trusted slave at my behest, lay by the wine, untouched—although I had not forgotten that they were there, silently beckoning. I was not certain why I had not yet given in to their call; perhaps some part of me knew that if I did, there would be no going back. And I was not yet entirely ready to part with reality, however horrible it had become.

I set my feet down on the cold floor of my bedroom, feeling slightly dizzy as I stood. I grabbed a shawl lying in the corner, wrapping it around my shoulders; I seemed to remember throwing it there, barking at a slave to ignore it, to just bring me more wine instead, and to leave the rest of my room untouched—to leave me untouched, undisturbed. I tried to ignore the stench emanating from my own body, the smell of unwashed skin that had seen night after night of restless, sweaty dreams.

I left my room, my fingers combing my greasy hair back from my face as I half-walked, half-stumbled through the house without direction, without purpose. I found Torquatus silently studying the death masks of his ancestors: the stoic, unsmiling faces of the great men of his line, frozen in time for eternity. He didn't hear my barefoot steps as I approached, and I watched him as he stood still, his eyes moving across the wax visages.

"Trials have begun," Torquatus said quietly, glancing over his shoulder at me. My approach had been heard, after all. "Sejanus—with Decimus in his ear, too, no doubt—has begun to rid himself of anyone he considers troublesome."

I had to clear my throat before speaking, but even then my words were hoarse, my voice having been dormant for days. "Who? Who has he condemned?"

Torquatus was again studying the wax death masks. "Does it matter? Men I considered friends; others I only knew in passing. Some, too, whom I openly disliked. They are being forced into exile, most of them—leaving their homes, their money, all of it passing into the treasury with Tiberius's blessing. They have lost everything. It is not quite a proscription, but it might as well be. The trials are not fair… Many do not even attend, do not try to defend themselves. They know it is pointless."

"Are we at risk?"

My husband did not answer for some time, and I wondered if he had heard my weak, rasping voice. I was about to ask again, but he finally spoke, turning away from the masks to face me. "I'm not sure." He paused for a moment, thinking. "Yes." The final word was uttered with more conviction.

"Because of our association with Nero Caesar? With Aunt Agrippina?"

"That did not help."

"But you have not yet been named," I said, trying to find a sliver of hope. "Why would they delay?"

"They release new names daily. It is only a matter of time."

I could think of no response, and I began to regret rising from my bed at all. The dish of opium, untouched, beckoned in my mind, promising a numb relief from all this, to transform it into a mere dream from which I could escape, temporarily or, if I chose, permanently. I shook my head to clear it.

Torquatus was once again silently studying the death masks, his body fully turned away from me, and I sensed I would get little more from him. But I had an idea, and I hoped that it might save Torquatus— save us.

It felt odd, sending anyone other than Amynta with a message for Rufus—but she remained in the countryside, with my children. It was, I knew, for the best that she wasn't here now, but that did not make me feel any more at ease dispatching my note with one of the kitchen slaves; he was a young man with a kind face, and I hoped that I could rely upon him to be discreet.

I had, as usual, chosen my father's family tomb for our meeting; I did not trust the number of eyes and ears that would surround us in any other place. This was too delicate a matter to convey in Rome's forum or its markets, in its bathhouses or at the circus, and I found that I did not even have faith in the solid walls of my own home. My steps were uneasy as I walked, alone, through the city, not remembering the last time I had been unaccompanied, or if I even ever had been. I had always at least had Amynta, even if we had left behind our guards. Now, every shadow, every shopkeeper crying out his wares, every child darting from an alleyway made me jump, and I tugged my hooded cloak more tightly over my face, more snug around my body. I missed Amynta more and more with every street I traveled down, every corner I turned.

I arrived first, quickly letting myself into the tomb with a small key, breathing a sigh of relief as I closed the door behind me and leaned against it, my eyes struggling to adjust to the lack of light; the dead had no need of windows, and so the tomb had been built without them. I did not bother to fumble for an oil lamp, instead waiting in the dark, sneezing once as the musty air stung my nose, and I wondered where, one day, my own remains would lie. It no doubt depended upon what course my life would take from here, upon what fate lay in store for me.

A knock came from behind me; I moved away, opening the door, blinking into the sudden light at Rufus. Behind him stood another man— not Titus, as I had expected, but Duras.

"What is the meaning of this?" I snapped, eyes fixed on my half-brother as he stood quietly behind Rufus, the uncertain tension in his own body clear.

"He knows everything," Rufus said wearily, wasting neither time nor words as he told me the truth immediately and directly. He knew me well enough to know that I would not appreciate the issue being sidestepped: better to lay it all bare.

"Where is Titus?" I asked next, the anger in my words increasing as I turned my focus from Duras to Rufus. We had agreed not to involve my half-sibling—and now I was betrayed, left out of a decision that Rufus and Titus had clearly made without me, something I had first suspected at the circus. A sudden distrust surfaced in my thoughts, and I wondered what else they might have hidden from me.

"He has gone to save our mother," Duras said, and I snapped my eyes towards him again, still perplexed by how very similar we were. His words unnerved me enough to distract me from my growing anger about his sudden, unplanned knowledge of our relationship.

"What?"

Rufus sighed, shifting his weight impatiently as he looked behind them, clearly worried that they would be seen lingering outside a tomb they had no business visiting. "We have much to discuss."

"Clearly," I said icily, finally backing away from the tomb's entrance to allow them to enter. Rufus made quick work of lighting an oil lamp, the tomb still dim but now slightly improved. Duras closed the door, and we stood together, uncertain who should speak first.

"What is this about our mother?" I said, breaking the silence. It felt odd—not only speaking of her, but using the word 'our,' an acknowledgement that Duras and I shared an open kinship now. I would address that fact later—how and when and why he had been told. For the time being, I simply hoped that we could trust him, though I had little trust left to share.

Duras quickly informed me of the situation, of what he had overheard and how Titus had departed the same night—although what Titus's plan was when he arrived on Trimerus, Duras was not entirely sure. I felt a sense of panicked excitement surge within me at the thought of my mother being freed at last, but then my thoughts raced to all the other, more probable outcomes: Titus's failure; my mother's ongoing imprisonment; her death, if Sejanus and Decimus followed through on their plans. Titus's success was unlikely, but I could not dwell on it, not now. It was out of our hands. In the present, I had to be more concerned with Torquatus, with preventing his—our—downfall. Nothing else would matter if my family lost everything.

"Why did you send for me?" Rufus asked, as if sensing that my thoughts had shifted to another topic.

"The trials," I began. "You are both aware of them?" The question was probably, I knew, pointless: it would be hard *not* to be aware of the ongoing trials. Enough leading men had lost their fortunes and their power that the dynamics of Rome were again shifting; to be unaware of the trials would be inconceivable.

As expected, they both nodded, and Duras spoke. "Decimus has often been meeting with Sejanus—sometimes within the household, but more often he goes to the Praetorian Prefect directly. I know he is involved in these trials, although to what extent I am not certain. He doesn't confide much to me. Although I am his charge, and he seems, for some reason, to favor me, I am not his son, but something more like a pet—and I remain a foreigner, no matter the customs I have adopted." He extended his hands in a gesture of uncertainty, a sad half-smile on his lips.

I realized that I had spared little thought for my half-brother—what his life was like before he came to Rome, how misplaced he must feel, especially now that he knew the truth of his identity. But it was not the time to think of such things; although we shared one of the most intimate of things—a mother—he remained a stranger to me, and I did not now have the luxury of doling out pity on his behalf, nor to exchange stories of our different upbringings.

I quickly spoke of my more immediate concerns. "I worry that my husband will appear in the next list of men that they will subject to these trials," I said. "We were known to favor Nero Caesar and Drusus Caesar, and my aunt, Agrippina. Torquatus used to get along well with Decimus and Sejanus, but... They are no longer the friends they once were, if friendship would even be an appropriate way to describe their past relationship."

Duras looked sympathetic, his dark eyes—a mirror of my own, and of our mother's— watching me; Rufus, as usual, was unreadable. He was not interested in semantics; he wanted action, a task set before him which he could accomplish.

"I have an idea," I continued, looking between them. "I must gain entrance to Decimus's house. He would never invite me, for many reasons, but especially now that I fear my husband is out of favor. But I believe that if I gain an audience with him... I can convince him to spare Torquatus, and he in turn will convince Sejanus."

"How?" Rufus asked sharply. He, more than Duras, knew of Decimus's true nature—knew of his empty promises, his cruelty. To convince the senator to spare a man's future was no easy task: he would prefer to watch a babe drown than to save it, if such a thing suited his interests.

I swallowed, steeling myself before I answered. "It will be a risk. A great one, because I have no proof... And I require Duras's assistance, so I suppose it's just as well that he is here and doesn't need to be indirectly convinced to help me."

Duras offered me a small half-smile again, an indication of his goodwill. "I am happy to be of aid."

"You don't know what I will ask yet," I said, but Duras seemed unconcerned, waving his hand as if to dismiss my warning.

"Spit it out, then," Rufus said, and I glared at him. He had grown far too familiar over the years; anyone else of his station who dared to speak to me in such a way would have been beaten. I lifted my chin and looked away, but I did not admonish him. For all his faults, he had been loyal; he had saved me when no one else could, and I would not forget that.

"I will be invited into Decimus's household by Duras, his

charge," I began, both men listening intently. "I'm not sure Decimus's slaves would let me in, otherwise. After that, Duras, your role is done. If Decimus asks why you invited me in, you can tell him something mundane, such as us running into one another on the way back from the baths, and I had looked unwell so you thought it best that I sit and drink some water before returning home."

"Reasonable enough, even though we are, as far as anyone knows, but passing acquaintances," Duras said, his tone thoughtful. "Go on."

"I will then threaten Decimus by telling him that I know he urged Tiberius not to allow Sejanus's marriage to Livilla—and that if he does not spare Torquatus, I will make sure that Sejanus knows the truth of it. He would never forgive Decimus. It would ruin him."

Rufus looked perplexed, as did Duras.

"How would you know something like that? Is it even true?" Rufus asked.

"My aunt Agrippina said something, once... She said that Decimus agreed with her, that Sejanus didn't have the bloodline to marry someone like Livilla. And that she *knew* Decimus had said as much to Tiberius." I tried to make my voice sound more confident than I felt; it was the first time I had spoken my plan aloud, and I worried it sounded unlikely to succeed. But I had no other plan in mind—I had to try.

"How do you think *that* will convince him to spare your husband? He's all the more likely to kill both of you," Rufus said, scowling.

"I'm not finished," I snapped at him, my temper flaring.

"How did your aunt—*our* aunt, I suppose—know that?" Duras asked, and I could tell that his mind was working through the possibilities.

"Aunt Agrippina had a spy or spies in Livia's household," I said.

"If she could accomplish that, then I have no doubt that she had someone in Decimus's household, too. Perhaps someone who is still there. My aunt knew the value of keeping an eye on those who can exert influence on all our lives... though that did not spare her from exile."

Rufus scoffed. "If there was a spy in Decimus's household, I would have sniffed out such a rat long before now."

I scowled at him again, but it was Duras who spoke. "If that person is still there... It's a staff of dozens. Finding them would be impossible—and we have little time. Without them, there is no evidence."

"That is why this is a risk," I said. "I will proceed with the plan anyway. Decimus is likely to threaten my life, and that of my husband. I will simply lie and say that I already have a letter with my accusation, and enough proof, prepared to be sent to Sejanus, should something happen to anyone in my family."

"Decimus will not fall for that," Rufus said, but his tone had changed; he was no longer making a mockery of my plan now that he knew I meant to follow through with it. Now, he was worried. "If Torquatus loses everything, then let him. That does not mean you must be disgraced, too, Aemilia. You should distance yourself from him. Save yourself."

I shook my head, smiling sadly. "I cannot."

Rufus sighed and muttered something under his breath, annoyed at my resistance. "I will be there, then, watching, when it happens. I will protect you, if Decimus should try to destroy you after your plan fails. But tell me this—why endanger yourself for Torquatus? A man you did not choose?"

"Torquatus and I may not be passionate lovers fated for one another by the gods, but he is my husband, and the father of my children.

And he is a good man." It was the first time I had said the words and meant them—the first time I had truly believed them.

Rufus stared at me as I spoke, and for once I could clearly read the emotions that flitted across his face: a red flush of anger, followed by pale fear, then a resolved, steady determination. I was not prepared for the words he then uttered. "I was on the island with your uncle," he blurted out suddenly. "I was a guard for Agrippa Postumus. And a spy, for Decimus." He hung his head then, avoiding my eyes, and seemed to shrivel up, a man far older than his years.

Duras stood still, confused. My mind raced, and a rush of emotions coursed through me as I absorbed Rufus's confession. "Why tell me this? Why now?" I asked. I had not yet seized upon any singular feeling, and instead tried to remain numb; I worried how I might react if I did not.

"Because I am not a good man," he said, the words tumbling out of him. "I never have been. But I want to…" He trailed off, and still he refused to meet my eyes. "I want to change." His final words were defiant, and he raised his gaze at last, his eyes wet as he looked at me, his expression pleading, begging for forgiveness, for absolution, for approval.

But I could not give him any of those things—not so immediately, not so soon after discovering that, once again, I had been misled. Lied to. I shook my head and began to turn away, already moving towards the tomb's door. "The plan is set," I said, refusing to think more of Rufus and his connection to my uncle. And then I left.

CHAPTER
XXXVI

RUFUS

Rufus had little faith that Aemilia's plan to save her husband would succeed, but neither she nor Duras had been inclined to listen to him. He found himself, rather unexpectedly, missing Titus; he was certain that the other soldier would have agreed with him, and perhaps the two of them together might have been able to convince the siblings of the folly of it—but Titus was gone, and Rufus was left on his own.

Wine fogged his mind as his steps carried him down the street, the smell of piss and smoke and food all mixing together in a scent that defined his own Rome, one that he wondered if Aemilia and Duras even knew existed, far from their clean, well-guarded houses, their many-course meals spiced with exotic ingredients, slaves to attend to their every need, their every whim. Men lingered in groups, some playing games of dice and others arguing, brawls brewing; half-naked women eyed him from dark doorways; the sounds of drinking and shouting, gambling and dancing drifted out from taverns. None of it coaxed him nearer.

Rufus had regularly visited different brothels ever since Leander's death—he did not think he had gone back to the same one twice in a year, instead waiting until enough time had passed that they were sure to have new faces amongst their young men. He was searching, always searching—he knew there would not be another Leander, could not be. Yet still he hoped, hunting for even just the slightest, briefest moment of familiarity, a jolt of whatever it was that he had had with Leander. He had not yet found it, and he doubted that he would—but something pulled him perpetually onwards, as if some relief from his quest might just be around the next corner.

The blueish light of dawn had begun to tinge the skyline. He dreaded Aemilia's arrival at Decimus's household, her attempt to threaten the senator into submission, an ill-fated venture—he was sure of it. He hadn't meant to drink so much wine, hadn't meant to leave the night before. He had intended—promised—to be there, watching, just in case the worst should happen, if Decimus reacted violently, if Aemilia needed to flee for her life. But he still had time, he told himself. It wasn't dawn, not quite yet; he would return soon, to be there when Aemilia confronted Decimus. But a small, taunting voice in his mind wondered if she would truly want him there—if she would accept his help. She had been cold when he had finally confessed to her how he had known her uncle; she had not forgiven him, as he had hoped. As he had needed.

Rufus shook his head and stumbled into another brothel, one he hadn't visited before, feeling as if he were on the verge of finding what he sought. Something here was different—promising.

A guard eyed Rufus warily; he swayed on his feet. "I'm looking for a…" Rufus began, but the guard only scowled at him.

"Wrong person to ask," the man snapped. He gestured further inside. "Go there. You'll be seen to."

Rufus wandered in the direction he had been pointed, the thick, suffocating scent of incense nearly overpowering him as he ran his fingers along the grainy wall, half to catch himself if he stumbled and half to simply *feel*, to remind himself that he was not in a dream.

He reached the end of the hall, the narrow space opening up into a larger room, another guard standing in the corner, as young men and women of every possible appearance, every origin, sprawled on different surfaces—and there, on a pillowed couch, half dozing, was Leander, his golden skin seeming to glow, beckoning Rufus closer, hinting at the promise of comfort, of relief, of a blessed dreamless sleep for the first time in years.

Rufus surged towards the young man, a cry spilling out from his lips, and then he tripped, falling, his arms flailing in a hopeless effort to catch himself. The guard was already moving towards him, yelling out an angry exclamation. Rufus's head struck a table as he fell, hitting the ground with a thud. Looking up through the blood that stung his eyes, he saw that it wasn't Leander at all—the youth looked almost nothing like Leander, not up close. Rufus sighed, closing his eyes as he sank into oblivion, the roaring of crashing waves drowning out the alarmed, confused murmuring around him.

Rufus woke, shivering, in a dark, dirty alleyway. The feeling of something moving on his leg drew his eyes, and he saw a rat leap off his shin and scurry away. He groaned, closing his eyes again; his head ached, and the faint, coppery taste of blood lingered in his mouth. It wasn't long before he was again unconscious, the black nothingness a welcome relief.

The next time Rufus woke, it was even darker than before. The day, and its light, were long gone. He struggled to sit up, noting that his cloak, his sandals, and his money pouch were all missing. He had been robbed, and he had been dumped in an alley, left for dead—although he wasn't certain in what order the events had occurred. The last thing he remembered was looking up into a cold, questioning face that wasn't Leander, as he had so desperately hoped.

He tried to stand, his fingers clawing at the dirty wall next to him, his head swimming as he left his prone position on the ground, trying not to look at the heaps of refuse he had been mixed in with—rotten food, human shit, a dead dog, its body bloated. His bare feet squelched sickeningly as he began to move, gasping for breath, partly from exhaustion and partly from the claustrophobic odor of the alley.

He emerged into the larger street, which seemed nearly abandoned. He did not recognize where he was, nor did he know the hour—but he feared he had missed Aemilia's confrontation with Decimus. He wondered if she had found the protection for her husband she had so desperately sought; he wondered if, instead, she now lay dead somewhere, her dark eyes fixed in an unending stare, just as Leander's were, in the end.

Rufus sank back onto the ground then, in the middle of the road. A shadowy figure skirted around him quickly, uneasily—he knew he was a strange, bloodied hulk, worthy of nothing but fear, of disgust. No one would help him; no one would even look at him. A tear ran down his cheek, fighting a small path through the dried blood and grime on his face, and then another.

He forced himself back to his feet, stumbling in the first direction his gaze had drawn him to. He needed to orient himself, to find some landmark he recognized. And then he would find his way back to Decimus's household. He had no more fear of death—and he had no more reason to live. He would kill Decimus, and he would, at last, be free—free from the haunting dreams of Agrippa Postumus; free from whatever madness seemed to chase him without relent, the near-constant drone of crashing waves, the ever-present scent of ocean air. He would be free from it all, and Aemilia, his final mistress, would be safe at last. He would have her trust again, and earn her forgiveness; his final act would make him a good man. He did not care what such a thing might cost him.

CHAPTER XXXVII

AEMILIA LEPIDA

I stood uneasily in the atrium of Decimus's house, periodically walking in anxious circles around the *impluvium*; I stared mindlessly into the shallow water as my steps bore me around it, again and again. Duras had performed his role well and easily enough, inviting me in as we had planned, depositing me on a couch to rest and dispatching a slave—a blonde-haired girl with the look of a Gaul about her—with honey-water, to help me recover from my feigned illness; he, as we had decided, did not reappear. I had taken a sip of the water but was too nervous to remain seated, instead preferring to pace as I waited for the senator to return home. His path would have to cross mine, sooner or later. I forced myself to be patient.

The only thing missing was Rufus, although I told myself he was there somewhere, just too well hidden for me to see. He had insisted on being present, worried that Decimus might try to kill me with his own hands after I revealed my knowledge. I had thought Rufus was being foolish—Decimus was far too cunning to murder me in his own home—but the thought of his presence had reassured me, despite my residual anger at how he had hidden his connection to my uncle for so many years. Still, I was already thawing towards him; having slept on the matter, and given all the other, more pressing issues at hand, I knew that I could forgive both his involvement—certainly it was only under Decimus's vile command—and his delay in telling me. I regretted, too, my violent rejection of his silent plea for forgiveness, and vowed to make things right with him as soon as I finished with Decimus. After all, despite our strange relationship, Rufus had become one of the most constant, reliable figures in my life, although I doubted that I would ever dare admit as much to him. He knew things about me that no one else did, not even Torquatus.

"*Domina*, can I get you anything else?"

I started; I had not realized the slave girl had returned. "No, no, I'm fine," I said breathlessly. Her blue eyes watched me curiously, although she quickly lowered her gaze when I returned her stare, a faint blush creeping across her pale cheeks.

"Why do you stare at me so, girl?" I asked, more harshly than I had intended.

"My apologies, *domina*," she said, seeming to shrink into herself. I could tell she fought to keep from backing away from me, the sudden flare of my temper alarming her, frightening her.

I sighed. "What is your name?" I softened my voice.

"Camilla, *domina*," she said, eyes still on her feet, her hands clasped tightly in front of her in a gesture that seemed to be defensive.

"Camilla, why do you stare at me?" I asked. In truth, I didn't much care why she stared at me, but I was in desperate need of some way to soothe myself, to calm my nerves as I waited for Decimus to return.

"You remind me of someone, *domina*," she answered, her eyes quickly darting back up to me before fixing themselves again on the floor, a still-deepening blush reddening her cheeks.

I laughed, a somewhat shrill, shrieking noise that I quickly stifled, and Camilla seemed concerned now, taking a visible step back from me after my hysteric outburst. I had no doubt who it was I reminded her of—Duras, whom she saw and likely served on a regular if not daily basis.

"Bring me some wine," I ordered, no longer tempering my tone, and I began to pace again, my steps taking me urgently in circle after circle until I felt dizzy. I had sat on the couch by the time Camilla returned with two jugs—one of wine, and one of water—and began to serve me. "No water," I ordered, and, despite a questioning glance, she obeyed.

I drank deeply from the glass of red liquid, draining it within seconds, closing my eyes as I waited for my heart to slow its incessant beating of alarm. When I opened them, Camilla was again staring at me, and, before she lowered her gaze, I caught the surprised expression of sudden realization on her face.

I motioned for her to refill my glass, and I drank again, although only a single, large swallow this time. "Who do I remind you of, Camilla?"

She pressed her lips into a line before she lied. "There is a particular merchant our cook likes to buy his spices from, *domina*. You remind me of his wife, who helps at his shop."

I laughed again, taking another sip of wine; it was already going to my head. I hadn't eaten in over a day, or more; I couldn't remember now. A sudden recklessness seized me. "Why are you lying?"

"I—" she started, but then a noise behind me drew her attention. She quickly assumed the posture of an attending slave, awaiting orders, and I fought to keep from trembling, my sudden reckless boldness dissipating as quickly as it had arisen. Decimus had returned.

"Hello, Aemilia," Decimus said, his voice friendly, welcoming, even, as if he were not at all surprised to see me sitting in his home, drinking his wine, talking to his slave. "Camilla, you may go."

The slave girl quickly departed, the soft thud of her steps receding until the only noise was our breath, Decimus's and mine. I did not turn, did not face him, instead taking another sip of wine, finding that it suddenly tasted bitter, wrong—polluted by his arrival. The brief sensation of lightheadedness, the first hint of numbness it had brought me only moments before—they were gone now, and I was more on edge than ever.

I felt more than heard Decimus moving around, entering my view, and then he settled himself on a couch, carefully positioning his toga as he reclined. His eyes appraised me, a faint, cruel amusement in them. "Dare I ask why I have the pleasure of your unexpected company this afternoon? The door slave mentioned that Duras brought you in, having found you ill outside. Such a kind young man. Yet here you are, seemingly quite well."

"I won't waste time with pleasantries," I began, and even I heard how my voice trembled. I cleared my throat, willing myself to find some measure of courage. "I know that you opposed Sejanus's proposal of marriage with Livilla. That you made certain Tiberius heard your thoughts on the matter."

Decimus's eyes narrowed, but he said nothing—neither an acknowledgment nor a denial of my accusation. I continued, my voice growing stronger. "Sejanus would never forgive you if he learned the truth of it—if he even suspected you may have been involved in preventing his marriage. You have too much to lose, now, to risk him finding out. It would ruin you."

Decimus spoke at last, and his eyes, which had been amused

earlier, were now dark. "I assume you have proof, and that you want something, or else you wouldn't dare threaten me."

I nodded. "Make certain that Sejanus does not have my husband brought to trial as he seeks to consolidate his power and strengthen the treasury. Leave my family out of this."

Decimus seemed to think for only a moment before he nodded. "I agree."

I nodded in return and stood, feeling vaguely faint. It had been almost too easy, too according to plan. I was about to walk away, to leave, but I hesitated. "Write a letter to Sejanus now, while I am here, telling him that Torquatus should not be brought to trial. If he is, I will make certain that Sejanus knows what you did. And if I am harmed in any way, I have a prepared letter, hidden with a trusted friend, who will ensure that Sejanus receives it." I spoke my final lie with ease.

Decimus sighed heavily and bellowed out for his scribe; within minutes, the man had appeared. The senator quickly dictated a note, allowed me to look it over, and then ordered it to be delivered to Sejanus immediately. The scribe nodded and left us alone once more.

"Are you content?" Decimus asked, studying me. I nodded, and then I turned my back on him and left, feeling as if I were in a trance.

I wasn't certain that I could believe it, or that I could trust Decimus. I kept the litter curtains tightly drawn on the way home, half expecting to be stopped, to be dragged out and brutally killed in the streets. I spent that night, too, sleepless, tossing and turning as I envisioned the countless ways Decimus could have Torquatus and me killed. Yet the morning light arrived as surely as it always did, and I began to hope that I had succeeded, and that everything had gone just as smoothly as it had appeared to.

Duras arrived in the morning, unannounced, looking as if he had come almost straight from his bed; his clothing was haphazardly pulled on and his hair was uncombed and out of place. Dark stubble covered his face, and his frantic eyes were ringed by smudges of sleeplessness.

I was so taken aback by his arrival that I admitted him immediately to the house, my past caution about our association forgotten in such a moment. Torquatus had not yet risen, so we kept our voices low; I hoped he would not awaken. Duras and I quickly moved into the atrium, and the door attendant resumed his post.

"Decimus is dead," Duras said as soon as we were alone, his words coming out in an urgent stream.

"What?" I was confused. "I left him alive and well yesterday afternoon. Everything had gone as we planned."

Duras shook his head. "He was going to have Torquatus tried and executed. He was to be killed, not just ruined."

"But…" I didn't know what else to say. It made no sense.

"Camilla followed the scribe. The letter he showed you was never sent. Another was about to be dispatched in its place."

Camilla—the slave girl. "How is she involved?" I asked, but Duras's blush was answer enough. "I hope you can trust her," I said, my words a warning. I worried that our circle of confidantes was growing too large.

"I do," Duras said, his voice quiet but filled with conviction. "She came to me, after she saw you. She figured it out quickly, that we are related."

I felt that I should have been more panicked to have had our secret exposed, but I did not have the energy. "Does she want money, to keep her silence?"

Duras shook his head. "She told me last night that she is—was—your aunt's spy in Decimus's household. She has more loyalty to you than to him, based on that kinship alone. Your aunt was always kind to her. She had even promised Camilla her freedom—to help her escape from Decimus, to forge her freedwoman's documents, to give her money to start a new life, far from Rome."

I blinked, surprised at this turn of events, and my thoughts returned to the deceased senator. "How did Decimus die? Surely Camilla didn't..."

"No. She did intercept the letter Decimus had intended to send to Sejanus, so your husband is, for now, safe on that front, unless Sejanus decides to try him on his own accord. It was..." Duras hesitated, watching me closely, a sadness in his eyes. "It was Rufus. He came back last night, covered in blood and dirt and who knows what else. And he simply grabbed a sword and ran Decimus through before anyone could stop him. He was shouting about someone named Leander, and how he wouldn't let you, Aemilia, be taken too. He didn't even know that our plan had failed; he couldn't have. But he acted anyway."

I wasn't aware of my knees hitting the floor, but suddenly I was looking up at Duras, blinking in confusion. "And what happened to Rufus?" I asked, although I already knew what Duras would say.

"He killed himself right after he finished gutting Decimus, once he watched him take his final breath. I saw it happen. I am witness to the fact that it was no slave of Decimus's at fault, so the household will, at least, be spared." I knew he thought of Camilla.

I nodded, feeling numb. "You must go," I said, "before Torquatus awakens. I don't want him to find you here, to start asking all manner of questions. He doesn't know…" I trailed off. My husband did not know any of this, and I feared his reaction should he find out the multitude of secrets I had hidden away from him. It would not be enough that some of those secrets had helped to save his life.

Duras watched me, lingering, and then he crouched, embracing me for the briefest of moments. "Goodbye, sister." The words were barely more than a breath, and then he was gone, disappearing as the light strengthened and the smell of breakfast drifted to my nose from the kitchen, a familiarity at odds with the events that had just occurred.

I remained on my knees for some time, alone. I missed them—my mother, my grandmother, my uncle. I missed my aunt, too, and Amynta. And now Rufus, whose loss cut me more deeply than I could ever have imagined. He had done it for me, I realized. He could have been free of Decimus years ago, when he had been released from the senator's service, yet he had remained in the bonds he despised so that he might protect me from further suffering. Tears ran down my face as I remembered how I had turned my back on him, when he had told me how he had known my uncle—in the role of a prison guard, a tormentor. He had wanted forgiveness, understanding. I had not given it to him when I should have, and now it was too late. But despite how I had failed him, he had remained true to the end; he had achieved a portion of the vengeance we both had longed for and worked towards for years. Now, only Silanus remained—but given all that had happened, I wondered if the cost of destroying him might be greater than I could bear.

CHAPTER XXXVIII

DURAS

Duras's feet hurried over the worn stones of the road as he made his way back Decimus's house, which now found itself in unexpected mourning. A heavy stillness hung over the household, and a small crowd had already gathered outside, people lingering on the street as they stared at the doors with wide eyes and whispered in hushed tones about what might have happened inside. No one seemed to notice Duras's arrival.

Rufus's body had already been dragged out of the house without ceremony; it was now tossed haphazardly on top of a small cart, about to be borne away to an uncertain place. Duras forced himself to look at the man's corpse, noting that his gray-tinged red hair seemed bright once more, now that it was compared to his pale, lifeless body. A jagged wound had ripped open the old soldier's stomach, and his moist entrails still hung half out in a dark, red-brown clump, threatening to spill onto the ground. Duras tried not to gag, closing his eyes as he hoped that whatever it was that Rufus had sought—peace, absolution, vengeance— he had found it at last.

When he entered the house, slaves were already at work cleaning the blood from the floor. Buckets of water and sullied rags were everywhere, and Duras thought that they seemed to be doing little more than spreading the gory mess across the mosaic underneath. Decimus's body was nowhere to be seen, but the sound of his wailing widow from down the hall suggested that he already had been moved, the preparations for his funerary rites already begun, though his body could barely have gone cold.

Duras quietly went to his room and sat down on the bed with a thud, feeling desperately alone in a world that was beginning to overwhelm him. All he wanted was to return home, to Dacia—and such a possibility was now nearer than he had dared hope before. He had not mentioned it to Aemilia—it wasn't the appropriate time, given all that happened—but King Comosicus had at last died, losing the battle with his final illness. Didas, whom Rome had recognized as a tribal king in all but name while he reigned on behalf of his brother, had sent word of his passing. Duras was certain that Scorilo had already taken up the reins of power, though Didas did not dare to convey such news; after all, Rome thought that it was Duras, not Scorilo, who was the son of Didas, and Comosicus's chosen heir.

Duras rested his face in his hands, wondering if anyone knew that the wrong boy had been sent to Rome, all those years ago. It would only take one missive from the Moesian governor naming Scorilo as the new king to ruin the tenuous position of privilege Duras currently held—and to endanger his life. The powers of Rome would not appreciate that they had sunk years of education and training and resources into a youth who would not, in the end, serve them as a client king. But with any luck, he would soon be sent back to Dacia, supposedly to assume the power they believed was his by right, and no one would realize before it was too late, when he was long gone from a city he had no desire to see again.

"What troubles you?" Duras glanced up: Camilla, her worried blue eyes looking him over. "Decimus is gone now," she said, voice hushed. "Aemilia and her husband are safe. You should be pleased. I don't understand what possessed Rufus, at the end. He was like a madman... But it was for the best, whatever the cost."

"I am pleased," Duras said quietly, although his tone was nearly expressionless. He was tired, and he wanted little more than to lie down and close his eyes. "Relieved, anyway."

Camilla came towards him, sitting softly on the bed, and rested her head on his shoulder. "I used to think that we might run away together, before Agrippina was sent into exile. I used to imagine that, when she helped to free me, we would leave Rome and start a new life somewhere." Her words were tentative, filled with hope, and with love.

Duras shifted his head, looking down at her, but she kept her chin tucked, and he could see little more than her blonde head nestled tightly against him. "King Comosicus has died. I'm going back to Dacia. To rule." There was no preamble to the words he knew would surprise her— would upset her. Although he did not know the timeline of his departure, he did know that it was now inevitable, barring the discovery of his false claim to kingship. His return to Dacia had always been the plan—his, and Rome's. He had not factored in how love might make him feel so conflicted.

Camilla pulled away from him. "What? When?" He had not hidden the truth from her, but he knew that she had hoped his departure from Rome would be a far-off event, one that neither of them had ever dwelled upon, thinking that if they ignored it then it would not trouble them.

"I'm not sure yet. It may be quite some time. I need to be officially released from my... position here. I only just found out before Decimus..." He trailed off, and when he spoke again his words were quiet. "I don't know where I belong anymore."

"Rome is no place for you," Camilla said, and she began to rise from the bed. "You are too good for a place like this. Too good for *people* like this." She stood over him now, her face set, as if she truly believed that he was better off away from Rome, away from her.

"Camilla," Duras began, reaching for her hand. But she pulled away from him, taking a step back towards the door, her body coiled in emotion that threatened to overwhelm her.

"I love you," she breathed, tears welling in her eyes. She spoke the words as if they were a farewell.

Duras surged to his feet then, moving towards her and embracing her in almost one motion. They stepped together back towards the bed, falling onto it even as they wound around one another, their hands and lips exploring the other's body with frantic desperation. Camilla's tears tasted salty on his tongue, and he kissed them away.

Duras joined Decimus's funerary procession, walking along silently not far from the professional mourners whose wailing more than made up for his lack of emotion. They ripped at their hair, shredding their clothes and beating their breasts as they honored the murdered senator with their shrieks and cries. Little was said of Rufus; Duras only learned that the murderer, as he was now referred to, had been denied cremation, his body thrown out beyond the city's edges for the wolves and vultures to rip apart, scattering his remains and denying his soul any peace. Duras did not dwell on the image, hoping that Rufus's spirit might somehow evade its sentence.

Aemilia and Torquatus were there, too, but he had no time to speak to his half-sister. She seemed to move as if in a trance, as if she were physically there but her mind was somewhere else entirely. He did note that Torquatus managed to approach Sejanus, exchanging a few words with the Praetorian Prefect, and that they parted as if on friendly terms. Surely Aemilia's husband would be safe, now, from Sejanus's trials, just as she had wanted.

There had been no word from Titus. Enough time had passed that, if he were going to be successful in reaching Julia, he would have made it by then. Either he had failed, and perhaps was dead, or he had succeeded—and by necessity had had to disappear. Duras tried not to dwell on it, knowing that the uncertainty would drive him mad.

"Duras!" A voice called to him, and Duras looked around, unsure if he had heard his name or merely imagined it; the high-pitched wails of the mourners were disorienting. "Duras!" He saw him then—Silanus, his father. The man pushed his way towards him through the crowd, offering a half-smile when he arrived. The two clasped arms politely as they continued walking in the procession.

"Silanus," Duras greeted him, surprised that the man would bother to seek him out. "*Salve.*"

"I've heard you're on your way back to Dacia soon," Silanus said, examining Duras with eager eyes.

"Yes," Duras said warily. News of Comosicus's death had spread, but, so far, no one had discovered that it was Scorilo, not Duras, who would now be king. He wondered what Silanus wanted from him.

"I was wondering," Silanus began, "if we might come to an understanding with some sort of trade... Not on the books, if possible." He flashed a wink at Duras, as if they shared some measure of friendship; in reality, as far as Silanus knew, they were but passing acquaintances. Duras did not respond in kind to the gesture.

"Trade of what? Our honey?" It was one of Dacia's most sought-after goods, and Duras wondered if Silanus had some scheme in mind. He found it hard to focus on their conversation while the ongoing wails of the mourners had begun to stir an ache in his temples.

"I've heard Dacian honey is some of the best, yes," Silanus said. "But I've heard even better things about Dacian slaves, the women especially. I was hoping to import some, with your help. If you could get me a good price, we would both stand to make a significant profit."

Duras stopped walking, and those in the procession behind him complained, bumping into him and then pushing around, muttering under their breath. Silanus, caught off guard, had kept walking, and now had to push his way back against the crowd, earning them both more curses and angry looks.

"What do you say, young Duras?" Silanus asked, grasping onto Duras's arm to steady himself in the crowd. He smiled again, as if oblivious to the fact that they were in the midst of a funerary procession, far from the ideal place to talk business.

Duras felt a rage rising within him. He had spent little time with the man whose seed had given him life, but what few interactions they had had, combined with what he knew of Silanus's betrayal of his mother, had left little room for tolerance, a tolerance he now felt stretched precariously thin. "No," he snapped. "I'm not interested."

"But—"

Duras pushed Silanus violently, turning away as the man stumbled, and he quickly lost himself in the crowd, trying to fight back the anger that had begun to cloud his senses. What he wanted to do was beat Silanus until his nose broke, his jaw shattered, his teeth fell out—this pig of a man with whom his mother had once formed an attachment he could not come remotely close to understanding. To ask Duras to sell his own people into slavery... To think that he might betray them to make an easy profit.

He walked blindly, allowing himself to become lost in the sea of people, most of whom he was certain barely knew Decimus, barely mourned him; for if they knew him at all, how could they truly lament the loss of such a monster? He could not wait to leave Rome, a viper's den, as Titus had often—and rightly, he knew now—called it. He would not miss it.

CHAPTER XXXIX

AEMILIA LEPIDA

Torquatus did not know any of what had transpired between Decimus and me, from the time I had been a mere child up to the present; he did not know that Rufus, a man whom I knew and cared for much more deeply than just in passing, had, in the end, been the one to spare us—to spare him—from Sejanus's trials. For my husband, Decimus's death was simply a gruesome, unpredictable murder that happened to benefit him by its timing; with the senator out of the way, he managed to find a path back to Sejanus, to reassure him of our friendship. As far as Torquatus knew, it was Fortuna who had saved him.

I hoped that the rekindled friendship between Sejanus and my husband would not grow too close again; whatever power Torquatus might seek was not worth risking his life should he one day cross the prefect with a slight, whether it was an actual offense or merely one that was perceived. Better to maintain a safe, neutral distance between us and Rome's ruler—for that is what Sejanus had become, although he still lacked the title of *imperator*. There was no longer any hope that Tiberius would depart his island retreat, that he would return to Rome and oust the prefect from his position of power. The city and its people were resigned to the new order.

After Decimus's funeral, and when enough time had passed that Torquatus and I were certain that our friendship with my aunt Agrippina and her sons would be overlooked by Sejanus, my children finally returned from the countryside. It felt as if I had not seen them for more years than I could count. To the last one, each of them was taller; they were all growing almost faster than their clothing could keep up. My oldest of three sons had seen sixteen years now—a young man. Even the younger of my two daughters was on the cusp of womanhood, nearing her thirteenth summer, and I knew that I would lose them all soon—my daughters first, both likely to marry in the next few years, but the boys, too, not much later. I hoped that they would be overlooked by Sejanus as they neared adulthood and entered the political realm; I hoped that my husband's resumed friendship with the prefect would guarantee that, at least. If I had my way, I would have kept them in the countryside, idle and carefree forever, and perhaps I would have joined them there, too. But it was not up to me.

My husband came to me that night, both of us made giddy by the return of our children, the reunification of our family. Our kisses were fonder than they had ever been. We lay together afterwards, the flickering light of oil lamps casting shadows around the room, the quiet sounds of a city constantly in motion drifting towards us through the walls—the rolling wheels of carts passing by, quiet footsteps of people intent on their destination, the bark of stray dogs on the prowl. It was a stark contrast to our wedding night, in many ways; I was no virginal bride, uncertain how to behave, what to expect. But Torquatus was just as gentle as he had ever been, just as kind, his eyes warm as he looked at me; I smiled back softly, enjoying the feel of our naked skin pressed together. Yet, even as I rested my head on his chest, I could not help but wonder what it would be like to bear a deep passion for someone, to be driven nearly mad by one's lover, to want a man so badly that you felt as if you needed him or else you might fade away into nothingness—and then I quickly drove away such thoughts, a feeling of guilt rising in their stead. Even after all these years, I held tightly to the remembrance of my mother, of her passion and of all the misfortune that it had caused; it was a deterrence to wondering too much, for too long, about love. Such feelings had no good outcome.

"Drusus Caesar was formally imprisoned today," Torquatus said, stroking my arm, bringing me back to the present without preamble. I lifted my head from his chest.

"I'm not surprised," I said—and I wasn't. At the same time that his elder brother and mother had been exiled, he was put under guard; his now formalized imprisonment did nothing to alter his already existing confinement. "But what prompted it? Why the official change in status?"

Torquatus stopped touching me, rolling onto his back with a sigh. "You will hear soon enough, once word spreads. I heard from some other men at the baths today... Nero Caesar has been executed on Pontia. His brother is now kept under closer guard as a result... I wouldn't be surprised if he meets the same fate, sooner or later."

My breath caught. "Aunt Agrippina?"

Torquatus quickly shook his head, the simple motion reassuring me at once. "Still alive. Still imprisoned on Pandateria."

I managed to take a breath, feeling a small sense of relief; there was yet hope for my aunt, then. I barely dared ask the next question, my voice so quiet that I barely heard it with my own ears. "Has there been any word of my mother lately?" I wondered if Titus had reached her; I wondered if Sejanus had, in the end, suggested to Tiberius that she be quietly executed—and if Tiberius had issued such an order.

Torquatus went still then, and I could tell that he was thinking—and so I knew already, before he had even begun to speak, that something bad had happened. He was simply trying to decide how to phrase what terrible news he was about to reveal to me. "She passed away, from an illness that had been plaguing her for quite some time," he said softly. "I'm sorry, Aemilia."

He made to roll over to touch me, to offer comfort, but I moved away from him, sitting up in the bed and wrapping a shawl around my naked chest, suddenly self-conscious, defensive. He had never understood the depths of my struggle with what had happened to my mother, how it haunted me, even years later. Now, he had shared my bed before even deigning to tell me that she had died.

"Are you sure it was an illness?" I asked, my back to him. I managed to keep my tone even, despite visions of my mother being executed, of being locked away in a dark, windowless room to starve to death, flashing through my mind.

"That is what I heard." His words were gentle, tentative. "I only learned of it today. I'm sorry I did not tell you earlier…"

I tightened my arms around myself, unsure of how to feel. It was hard to mourn a woman I had already said goodbye to long ago; it was almost as if she had died when I was a young girl, the very same night she was taken away from me. I had wept; I had refused to believe. And then I had been angry—at her, at Silanus, at Augustus. At myself, for not being enough for her to love; she had felt the need to throw herself entirely into her lover, a choice which had ultimately left me alone, an orphan. Although I had at one time thought I might be able to restore her to Rome—to me—my efforts had amounted to nothing, except to increasingly endanger myself and my family.

Perhaps I should have written to her—but at first I had been too full of rage at her abandonment, and then Decimus, when I had still believed that he might truly be able to restore her to me, had advised against it. After that... after that I had had no restraints upon me except that I always found myself too busy—with my children, with entertaining, with my own scheming, my own problems. In truth I knew that I had had the time to write to her, but I had never done it, never found a way to capture my emotions on a feeble scroll, ink a poor substitute for warm breathy words and wet salty tears. And now it was too late. Over two decades had passed, and I had not sent my mother a single letter, a single word. Just as I had delayed in forgiving Rufus, so too had I delayed in forgiving my mother, and now it felt as if peace would forever be out of my grasp. And for that, I had no one to blame but myself.

I turned around to face Torquatus, at last ready to seek comfort in his embrace, in whatever words he might offer—only to find that he had slipped away, unnoticed, as I had begun to process my thoughts. I was alone, and I began to weep, feeling once again like a little girl, abandoned in the dark of night.

Shortly after Saturnalia, I wrote a note to Apicata inviting her to the baths, hoping that the lure of a massage and some hot steam—a stark contrast to the cold winter we were experiencing—might tempt her from her hiding place, just as I hoped that it might stir me from my lingering dark mood. I had not been able to pull myself from my guilt over both Rufus and my mother; sadness clung to me, and I wondered if I deserved it, retribution for my failure to forgive them when I had still had the opportunity to do so. My desire to reconnect with Apicata was not a coincidence; selfishly, I thought that, if I could rekindle our friendship, I might find some relief from my own suffering.

Apicata was still barely seen in public, and it seemed her parents had long ago given up on her remarrying. No one wanted to be associated with the woman Sejanus had cast off, and so Apicata was treated as if she were a bad omen personified: ignored, shunned, only whispered about in the shadows—and even then only in passing, for to speak of such a thing in too much detail might draw ill fortune to the gossipers. Society had abandoned her.

Amynta pursed her lips as I passed her the letter. "You know that your husband still does not approve of any friendship with her," she said.

"I know, but I miss her," I said. "We were friends, once, and I have few enough of those left..." In truth, I had none. Amynta nodded, turning to leave. "Amynta, wait."

She turned back expectantly, looking tired, as she usually did in the winter—but something about her was different, and had been so ever since she had returned with the children from the countryside. "Yes, *domina*?" She still spoke to me with deference, though I was no longer her mistress, and had not been so in a long while.

"When you came back from the villa in the country, you seemed... different. Happier." My words were questioning, but I did not want her to feel interrogated. We did not share our confidences in the same easy way we used to, and, as a freedwoman, she no longer owed me the same degree of loyalty that had once been expected.

Amynta hesitated, seeming to think before she responded—perhaps wondering how much to admit me back into her personal thoughts and feelings, if at all. "Yes. I... I met someone. A freedman, who is a butcher now. He is widowed, and his children are near grown. He's very kind..." She stopped speaking, a blush rising to her cheeks as she looked at her feet.

"I am happy for you," I said quietly, smiling. "Does he want to marry you?"

"He does, but... even though I am free, now, I am not sure I can leave you. I'm not sure you're ready." Her eyes sought mine, assessing, worrying.

I laughed. "Amynta, I am now almost thirty-five years old. I think I am ready for my nursemaid to leave me. Although I will miss you always." I sobered as I spoke the final words.

She blushed again, smiling, and at last I began to truly feel that things between us were righting themselves after years of unease. "I suppose you're right, *domincella*."

We both laughed then, her old diminutive address for me sounding silly now, a reference to a time long past, to the naïve girl I used to be. "Perhaps in the summer, Torquatus and I might come to your wedding?" My words were tentative, but hopeful.

Amynta nodded, her eyes beginning to shine with tears. "I would like that." She quickly excused herself, then, bearing my letter off to Apicata, and I felt my eyes, too, begin to moisten. I was happy for Amynta, but it still stung that another person would be leaving me after all this time. My circle of confidantes, never extensive to begin with, was rapidly dwindling. Soon I truly would be alone.

Despite my quiet hopes otherwise, it came as no particular surprise that Apicata rejected my invitation to the baths; what did surprise me was her suggestion to meet elsewhere, at the Temple of Jupiter Optimus

Maximus on the Capitoline Hill. I was taken aback not only by her agreement to see me but by the strange location she had selected; it was not a place typically chosen for casual socialization.

Amynta and I arrived at the specified time, just as the sun was beginning to set. I pulled my cloak more tightly around myself, stamping my feet to keep them warm as well as to stave off the sense of unease that had begun to take hold of me; the dark silhouettes cast by the many shrines and statues of the precinct made me feel as if we were being watched. A few people still moved about, but all were too cold to stand around chatting to one another for long; the promise of warm hearths and hot meals beckoned them home. No one looked twice at us, and I realized that Apicata had chosen the late hour so that we would not be seen together.

"Aemilia," a quiet voice greeted me, and I started. The woman it belonged to, lurking in the shadows cast by the temple's massive columns, looked little like the Apicata I remembered; pale skin was stretched tight across her thin, hooded face, and deep wrinkles made her eyes appear recessed. She looked older than me by far, despite being my junior by a handful of years, and I swallowed back a gasp.

"Apicata?" I asked tentatively; it had been years since I had seen her. She nodded, and I approached, Amynta following a step behind. Once I was closer, I could tell for certain that it truly was her, and I embraced her thin body with tears in my eyes. "My dear," I said, "I have missed you so."

Apicata nodded, but she did not smile, and her return of my embrace was half-hearted at best. "Sejanus will be consul next year," she said, her voice urgent. "He will announce his betrothal, too, any day now."

"Betrothal?" I asked, withdrawing from our hug. I stamped my feet again, my breath making small clouds in the air. Amynta coughed behind me, muttering something inaudible. "Apicata, why are we meeting here? I am happy to see you, but…"

"Livilla," Apicata spat, her eyes flashing. "He will marry that whore at last. She will have my children. My children! I knew years ago that nothing good would come of it, that she was no mere distraction for him."

I wasn't certain what to say in response. "I'm sorry," I said at last, but it was as if Apicata did not hear me.

"I want her dead," she was saying, and her gaze focused on me with a desperate intensity. "And *you* can help us."

I was truly confused, then. This was no meeting between friends; this was some effort to draw me into things I no longer had any desire to be involved with, not after my aunt and cousins had been ruined; not after Torquatus had nearly been tried and executed; not after Rufus had killed Decimus but destroyed himself in the process. "I'm afraid I can be of no help, Apicata. I'm so sorry…" I began to pull further away, disturbed at what Apicata had become, and I realized with a start that she reminded me of my worst self, not so very long ago, when I had been obsessed with punishing Decimus and Silanus, with murdering them and ruining their reputations into eternity. Yet after the death of my mother and Rufus's bloody suicide, I had at last come to understand that there was no peace to be found on such a path, only more loss.

"Cousin." A new voice, light and airy, greeted me as if we had encountered one another at the baths or in the market, not in the dark recesses of a looming temple on a cold, wintry night. I turned, and behind me had appeared my little cousin, the younger Agrippina. Pure white furs were draped carefully around her shoulders, their color a nearly perfect match to the young woman's pale face, and for a fleeting moment I felt as if a wolf had appeared—but as she took a step closer, the vision disappeared, and once again it was simply my cousin before me.

"Little Agrippina," I said, the confusion evident in my voice.

"Just Agrippina is fine," she said, with a small, cold smile. "I have been married for two years now. I am no longer a little girl."

I nodded, wary of what was happening. "Are you and Apicata acquainted?" The words sounded foolish even as I said them; it could be no coincidence that my cousin had appeared at the meeting place Apicata had chosen, our paths crossing at the same time.

Agrippina let out a tinkling laugh. "Yes. But she has done her part now. Apicata, you may go. Let me speak with my cousin." The words were spoken lightly, but the order in them, the expectation of deference, was clear. Apicata disappeared, withdrawing into the shadows, and I watched my cousin expectantly—cautiously. "Dismiss your woman," she said, eyes darting to Amynta. "I wish to speak with you and you alone." Her words were harder now.

Amynta opened her mouth as if to protest, but when she met my gaze she simply nodded and moved away, muttering to herself again.

"What is this, cousin?" I asked. "Why have Apicata arrange this meeting and then dismiss her? Why not write to me directly, if you wanted to see me? I thought you lived outside the city now, far away from all this." She knew I did not mean our surroundings, but the never-ending intrigues that seemed to plague Rome and all its people.

Agrippina laughed again, but it was a cold sound this time. "My eldest brother is dead, the next imprisoned. My mother rots on an island like her mother before her—like your own mother once did. I am sure you can understand why I do not trust letters, and why I come in person to see to my interests. I barely trust my own slaves, even those who are mute or deaf. Any meeting between us would be viewed with suspicion.

And so we must have our secrets."

She was not wrong; I nodded, though I was still wary. "I understand."

"I developed a… friendship with Apicata because we have mutual interests, in a manner of speaking. Although she does not want to hurt Sejanus—worrying that any ill that befalls him may spread to and envelop their children—she has been, and will still be, useful to me."

"And what do you want from me? I am tired. My days of intrigue are over. I want to live a quiet life, with my children. I want for them to be spared what has happened to so many in our cursed family." Until recently, I could not have imagined saying such words, but they were now resoundingly true; I wanted nothing more than to leave this way of life behind me, hoping that in doing so I might protect my family.

"Then, for that, you would forsake your aunt? My mother, who raised you?" The words were sharp, and I felt slightly chagrined. "We are your family, too."

"I—" I began, but my cousin cut me off.

"Caligula will depart for Capri, come spring," she said. "Tiberius has summoned him. I am not certain why. Perhaps to keep an eye on him, although he could easily throw him into prison alongside our brother Drusus Caesar here in Rome."

"How do you know this?" I asked.

"I learned a few things from my mother," she said, flashing me a small, cold smile that again reminded me more of a wolf than of the little girl I had known not so long ago. Little Agrippina had taken to the viper's den well, it seemed.

"You have spies?" I asked. Her lack of response was confirmation enough.

"Caligula will do his best to sway Tiberius back towards our family. I am sure it will be difficult, but I believe it can be done."

I sighed, impatient. The cold was beginning to numb my lips. "Why involve me in this, cousin? I know you do not tell me these things for no reason. You expect something from me."

"Of course," Agrippina said simply. "You and I share blood. We share the same anger, the same need for vengeance."

"No," I said. "I no longer have the same anger I once did. It brought nothing but more trouble and more death."

My cousin continued, and her tone became beseeching. "Help me to restore my mother as yours never was, cousin Aemilia. Please."

I studied her, this wolf of a young woman, and in truth I could not tell whether she was genuine in her words, her desires, or if something darker and more dangerous lurked beneath, some motives that had not yet become clear. "No, little Agrippina," I said. "I'm sorry, but I cannot. I've grown too old, too tired. Rome belongs to you now, its intrigues and politicking. I am happy to be done with it, and I wish you luck. You will need it."

A range of emotions flashed across my young cousin's face: indignation, anger, and, at last, acceptance. She sighed. "Fine. I hope you find happiness in your... quiet life, Aemilia." She spoke the final words with distaste, as if she could not envision ever pining after something so simple.

She began to turn, ready to move off into the cold darkness, but I called out at the last moment, a sudden idea seizing hold of me. "Wait a moment."

Agrippina turned, looking at me coldly. "Have you changed your mind?"

I shook my head. "No, but I have a favor to ask of you." For all that I had told myself I was ready to leave behind my need for vengeance, a small part of me seemed to disagree, and it fought to be heard; the opportunity before me was too ripe to pass by.

"You expect favors from me when you have not offered your aid? Some might consider that rude."

I ignored her jibe. "I assume, if… when… you are successful in ruining Sejanus, that other men, too, will fall. Please make sure that Silanus in on that list." I spoke quickly, silently vowing that, if Agrippina failed and Silanus did not meet his end, then that would truly be the end of it; I would find peace, even if he still lived.

My cousin studied me thoughtfully, and, after a moment, she gave another one of her cold, predatory smiles. "Gladly. I've always despised that odious lech of a man." She did not ask why I named Silanus, and I breathed a sigh of relief, not wanting to share the story of my hatred even one more time. Agrippina hurried off then, leaving me shivering in the cold, and I knew that if anyone could bring about Sejanus's fall, it would be her—and gods help anyone who stood in her way.

31 - 32 CE

CHAPTER XL

DURAS

Duras tilted his head back, swallowing deeply as he drained another glass of wine. It took a great measure of restraint not to throw the empty glass against the wall, to watch with satisfaction as it shattered into hundreds of sharp little pieces. Against his will, he still lingered in Rome—Sejanus had not yet approved his departure for Dacia, although he gave no reason why—and no one dared question the prefect's decisions, or lack thereof. Duras had tried, once, and had been met with a look of scorn, Sejanus not even answering him before turning away, as if he had not spoken at all. Duras knew that Sejanus had not yet discovered his false claim to kingship—he would already have been killed if that had been the case— but he was not certain how much longer the secret could be kept. Each day that Scorilo reigned in Sarmizegetusa was a threat to Duras's life; he needed to be far from Rome before the lie he had perpetuated was discovered.

Yet instead of preparing to depart on his longed-for journey, Duras was at a dinner party, celebrating Sejanus's birthday, as had become public custom in Rome. He was wasting away his life at revelries and circuses and games while he instead longed for the brisk mountain air of the only place he had ever thought of as home. He wondered if he would still recognize it, would still remember the land, or his people, and Scorilo—and if any of them would recognize or remember him. He wondered, too, if Titus—if he still lived—might have returned there.

Torquatus and Aemilia were at the gathering, his half-sister's husband happily dining on marinated and roasted lamb as he smiled and chatted easily with the other guests. Aemilia was more quiet, reserved—as was normal, for her. Ever since Duras had gone to tell her how Rufus had killed Decimus, they had had little interaction, but he knew that it was for the best. Discovery of their kinship would be just as damning as the discovery that he was not now a Dacian king. Their eyes met then, briefly, and Aemilia offered him a small, passing smile, which he returned with a subtle nod.

The last time they had spoken, Aemilia had informed him of their mother's death. She had summoned him to her father's family tomb—for the final time, she had vowed—and told him that Julia had apparently passed away after suffering from a prolonged illness; there had been no execution, as Decimus had once planned. She had died before such a thing could happen. Duras had felt a deep sense of loss, although it was hard to truly mourn. After all, he had spent most of his life believing his mother was already dead; even when her identity, and her ongoing imprisonment, had at last been revealed to him, he knew that there was little chance he would ever meet the woman who had given him life, and so he had kept her at a distance from his heart. He and Aemilia both knew that Titus had known their mother better than they ever would—had loved her, too, more than they ever possibly could. He was the one who would mourn the greatest, and the longest.

Duras got up from his couch to piss, the effects of the wine forcing him to stumble down the hall, his vision slightly bleary. Decimus's widow had allowed him to stay in the household, taking pity on her husband's charge whom it now seemed Rome had forgotten. He would have been happy enough on the streets, he thought, but this way he at least remained close to Camilla.

Silanus was already relieving his bladder when Duras arrived at the toilets, and he struggled to greet the man politely. "*Salve*, Silanus." To think that, in some other life, he might have called the man Father to his face.

Silanus ignored him, still angry, despite the passage of time, over how Duras had responded to his business proposition at Decimus's funeral. He finished and stalked off, roughly wiping his hands on his toga, and Duras breathed a sigh of relief, enjoying the brief solitude he had been granted. Eventually, another dinner guest arrived, drunkenly lurching and almost falling as he struggled to lift the folds of his toga before relieving himself. Duras quickly left the toilets then, but he turned down the hall towards the kitchen. He was not quite ready to return to the gathering, and he hoped that seeing Camilla, even if only for a moment, might bring him some peace, inspiring him to remain calm and polite for the remainder of the evening.

A crash from within a storeroom near the kitchen caught his attention, the sounds of a struggle drifting out. Without thinking, Duras changed his path, and when he pushed open the door he found Silanus pinning Camilla against the wall, his hips thrusting into her as one hand help up her dress and the other yanked her head back by the hair. Tears streamed from her eyes.

"Silanus!" Duras roared, and he began to charge the man, but Camilla cried out.

"No!" The word was like a slap; he did not understand why she would reject his help, but he came to a halt, his body shaking.

Silanus looked up at Duras then, barely pausing before he

thrusted into Camilla again, and she winced, although her eyes remained locked with Duras's. "Do you want a turn next?" Silanus asked, grunting as he yanked Camilla's head back further, her neck bending at an almost impossible angle. "I see why you favor this one. I've noticed how you look at her. Pretty little thing." Silanus laughed, taking pleasure not only in Camilla's pain, but in Duras's discomfort, his fury.

As Duras stood there helplessly, he understood abruptly why Camilla had told him to stop: she was a slave, and she did not belong to him. He had no right to stop Silanus from doing with her what he wanted; he doubted that even Decimus's widow would much care, if she found out. It was more likely that Camilla would be the one to be punished, in the end. The best thing he could do for her, right now, was to leave—to trust that Silanus would not permanently damage that which belonged to another. She was, to them, nothing more than property.

"Go," Camilla said, biting out the word, and then she closed her eyes, not wanting to look at Duras anymore. Silanus, confident that Duras could—would—do nothing, already ignored him, turning his head away, satisfied that he had offended Duras just as he felt the youth had offended him by rejecting his business proposition.

Duras's hands curled into fists, and he knew that he should listen to Camilla. But he couldn't force himself to turn his back on her. He threw himself on Silanus, and he hoped that he would have the restraint to stop himself short of killing his father.

Duras arrived at Aemilia's door later that night, a cloaked and hooded Camilla held protectively under his arm. He wondered how long it would be before Silanus awoke in the storeroom, finding himself bruised and bloody. Still, the man was alive, which was more than Duras had thought he would be able to allow; he barely remembered Camilla pulling him off of Silanus, perhaps saving her attacker's life. He was not certain what punishment might now await him for attacking Silanus, but it was too late to avoid it; he had done what he felt was right, and he had no regrets. Camilla was safe.

"You're fortunate that Torquatus is still out," Aemilia hissed at him once she had told the door attendant to allow them entrance. She had left the gathering much earlier in the evening, no doubt hoping to retire early; she already had her bedclothes on. Now, her plans disrupted, she looked Camilla over coldly. "I want nothing to do with whatever this is."

"I came to ask your help," Duras began, still holding Camilla tightly to his side. She kept her eyes lowered. "I need you to hide Camilla. She cannot stay in her household."

Aemilia sighed, but her expression seemed to soften slightly as she looked at the pair of them again. Still, her tone was hard. "Why?"

"Silanus raped Camilla," Duras said directly; there was no point in hiding the truth. "In Rome she may be a slave, merely property to be used as people wish, but that doesn't matter to me. I love her." He sounded defensive, as if daring Aemilia to argue with him, to defend what had happened to Camilla or to protest that he could not love a mere slave.

Aemilia briefly closed her eyes, her body tensing as if she struggled with some internal battle. When she opened them and spoke again, her tone was surprisingly gentle. "You do realize that there might have been an easier way to help her? I could have tried to purchase her freedom, had you asked, before all this happened. I did not know how deeply you cared for her. But I suppose this is the path the gods have chosen now… I will hide Camilla for as long as I can, but not here. I will not tell you where, but trust me that she will be safe." She sighed again, seeming to think, and then her words spilled out with a quiet ferocity that surprised Duras. "I will not repeat this, and I will not answer any questions on how or why. But when the time comes, if Sejanus falls… Silanus will die as well. Come to me, in the ensuing chaos, and I will help you both to get far from Rome. Now, you must leave, before Torquatus returns."

Duras had a thousand questions he wanted to ask, but he bit his tongue and nodded. He and Camilla embraced, exchanging a few whispers, and then he left, trusting that Aemilia would do as she had promised—and hoping that she was correct about Sejanus's fate. For Sejanus to fall seemed impossible; the prefect was at the peak of his power, reigning over Rome in every way that mattered. Only the title of *imperator* was missing. He wondered what it was Aemilia knew that he did not. But so long as Silanus died—so long as he and Camilla might leave this terrible place—he found that he did not care how it all happened.

CHAPTER XLI

AEMILIA LEPIDA

I breathed a sigh of relief as Duras left my home. I had come close to telling him how it was not only Camilla whom Silanus had raped, but me as well—a secret that only Titus, Rufus and Amynta had known. But when I saw his anger, and his love for Camilla, I could not do it; I could not add to the burden he already bore, could not cripple him with an even deeper desire for vengeance that I knew would ruin him—just as it had come close to ruining me. He was nothing like the man whose seed had given him life, but everything like Titus, the man who had raised him. I hoped that he would hold onto the traits that made him who he was.

Camilla, though, was a keen observer. "You understand," she said simply, when we were alone. I was bustling her through the house, to where I could hide her from my husband until she could be sent to the countryside—to Amynta and her new husband. She would be safe there, until Duras could come for her.

"Understand what?" I asked, distracted as I thought through my plans, hoping that I was not wrong, that Sejanus and thus Silanus would both truly fall.

"You have been raped," she said, matter of fact. "I could tell, when Duras told you what had happened to me. You changed: your voice, your eyes, how you held your body. The same has happened to you, too."

"It has happened to many of us women," I responded, anger lacing my words. "But we will each have our vengeance, gods willing."

Camilla only nodded sadly. We did not speak again, and the next morning she raised a hand in silent farewell as a donkey cart bore her away.

The potential trouble that might have arisen from Duras attacking Silanus never materialized; the latter was far too humiliated to make a fuss about a Dacian, a foreign barbarian, getting the better of him in a storeroom, and it seemed that he never breathed a word of it to anyone, hiding away from public view until his bruised face was once again presentable. There was not even a hint of gossip about the matter. Decimus's widow half-heartedly put out notices about her missing slave, but her fortune was too great and her concern too little for much of a search for Camilla to be put on, not when another slave could simply be purchased to take her place.

What was far more intriguing that summer was the copious number of letters that began to arrive from Capri, filled with all sorts of conflicting thoughts from Tiberius; in one the emperor would praise Sejanus and in the next he would question him. Some, too, were ordinary conveyances of his commands, while others suggested his imminent return to the city. No one knew what to make of it, with many wondering if Tiberius had finally, truly gone mad—but there was enough uncertainty that most of Sejanus's followers distanced themselves from him, waiting to see how events would unfold, if they should shift their loyalties in case the emperor might at last return to Rome and upend everything. Tiberius's nomination of Caligula to an honorary priesthood further confused matters, and people once again began to look to the disgraced house of Germanicus as a potential seat of power. Little Agrippina's plan seemed to be succeeding—and I was relieved not to be a part of it, but to simply watch from the side as an observer rather than an actor, a passive role I had once despised but now embraced.

The air was beginning to turn crisp when it happened; a pounding on the door startled me awake from an early afternoon doze. I stumbled down the hallway, and the door attendant turned to me questioningly. We expected no visitors.

"It is a young man—the Dacian, *domina*," he said.

"Let him in," I said, and my heart began to race. Something must have happened—something substantial. Duras would not have come otherwise.

He stumbled through the door, a panicked excitement energizing his movements. He was dressed simply, in comfortable, basic clothes that attracted little attention; a travel pack was slung over one shoulder. "Sejanus has fallen," Duras said, the words rushing out of him.

I felt as if I might lose my balance, and I placed a hand on the wall to steady myself, dismissing the door attendant with a wave of my hand before I spoke. "How?"

"He was summoned to the senate house by a letter from Tiberius. He—everyone—seemed to expect some great honor to be conferred. But a man seized him—Macro—and he has taken over the Praetorian Guard at Tiberius's command."

"When did this happen?"

"This morning, but I waited, to be… There are riots now. Sejanus was just executed, strangled and thrown down the Gemonian stairs. The crowd tore him to pieces, and now they tear down his statues, too. Unrest is growing. I thought, given what you said, that now was the time to come, to go to Camilla. No one will think to wonder where I am for quite some time."

I nodded, thinking. "You will journey to the countryside, to my freedwoman Amynta and her husband. Camilla has been with them, waiting for you." I hurried down the hall, Duras following, and searched for a scroll to write on. I found one and scratched out a handful of words, passing it into my brother's waiting hands. "These directions will help you to find them. I will send money, too, to help cover your passage to wherever it is you and Camilla wish to go. Amynta will help to arrange it all. A horse will be readied for you within the hour."

"Silanus?" Duras asked.

"It is only a matter of time. Others will fall in the coming days and weeks. He will, too." I smiled coldly.

"I regret that I will not see it," Duras said, his eyes flashing as he lifted his chin.

"I know," I said quietly, "but be assured that it will happen."

Duras enveloped me in a hug, then, brushing the top of my head with a kiss. "Thank you, sister," he whispered into my ear, "for everything." And then he was gone, the door slamming shut behind him as he fled Rome and the chaos that had begun to rain down upon the city.

The next to fall was the oldest son of Sejanus and Apicata; he was arrested and executed all within the same day, just as his father had been.

It seemed that my old friend's fears—that her children would suffer if their father fell—came true, and my heart broke for her.

Two days after her eldest child's death, Apicata committed suicide. Torquatus told me, although he did little to measure his words as he relayed the news; for all he knew, our friendship had ended long ago and we had had no contact since. I bit the inside of my cheek as he detailed it all, hoping that the pain would distract me from the tears I fought not to shed.

"She left a letter, before she slit her wrists," Torquatus said, sounding mesmerized. "She accuses Sejanus—and Livilla, too—of poisoning Drusus. Livilla's slaves were tortured, of course, and they confessed to the truth of it."

I winced as I thought of Apicata taking a blade to her slender wrists, her body already weakened by years of unhappy rage at the course her life had followed. It had taken her child's death to at last convince her to accuse Sejanus and his lover of the murder they had committed nearly a decade ago—although I was certain that the young Agrippina, too, must have pressed my friend to finally reveal what she had known. I doubted my cousin would much mourn Apicata's loss; she had been a tool, and she had served her purpose.

"What will happen to Livilla?" I asked.

Torquatus winced. "She has reportedly been locked in her room by her mother," he said, "where she will be left to starve."

The same fate my grandmother had suffered. Although I had no love for Livilla, I did not envy her the sentence to which she would now be subjected. The men always seemed to have the easy way of it: outright execution, a quick, brutal end. Women were made to suffer even as they died.

"Sejanus's other children are to be executed as well," Torquatus said quietly. "Tiberius wants no trace of the man to remain, no drop of his blood to live on."

I forced myself to attend those next executions, feeling that I, in some strange way, owed it to Apicata to see her remaining children depart into the realm that came after ours. There was a crowd at the Gemonian stairs, common people lingering at the bottom, waiting for the soon-to-be corpses to be flung down into their waiting hands; Torquatus and I stood at the top, not far from the two scared youths awaiting their fate.

Apicata's daughter went first. Her sentence had caused some initial uncertainty, for it was technically illegal to execute a virgin, as the unmarried girl was assumed to be, having barely seen eleven summers. The brutal, efficient solution had been to rape her before she was escorted from her prison cell, the state of being that might have saved her from her fate summarily torn from her. Now, seeing her face muddied save for the clear tracks where tears had run down her face, her dress disheveled and torn, I was relieved beyond measure that Apicata was already dead—that she did not know what had just happened to her daughter, and what was so soon about to occur. I closed my eyes as the girl was strangled, only a single, soft cry managing to escape her lips, and I felt tears spill from my eyes as the executioner quickly moved onto the boy, hearing his heavy steps thud towards Apicata's next child, who stood motionless, unresisting, as the life was choked from his thin, pale neck.

When I opened my eyes, their bodies were being heaved unceremoniously down the steps, rolling with a sick, dull thudding noise, their limbs moving at awkward angles. The crowd below watched silently; there was no great roar, no cheering, no surge to seize the bodies and tear them to shreds. They might be the children of Sejanus, now the most despised man in Rome's recent memory—but they were still children.

Torquatus and I went home, and he held me as I sobbed—for all I could think about was our own children, and how such fates might still await them, one day. After all, it was only a matter of time until the next viper moved into the den of Rome.

More trials and executions began the following spring, led by Naevius Sutorius Macro, the new man of Rome, a loyal servant to Tiberius—for now. I had seen too much corruption to entirely trust that his power would not go to his head, as it had so many others. It seemed almost inevitable.

Silanus, at last, was disposed of, his trial and execution swift and without delay. I did not honor him with my presence at his death; he did not deserve it. Instead, Torquatus and I made love, relieved at being alive, at being together.

I did wonder if Agrippina had had much to do with it, in the end, or if Silanus would have been caught up in the bloodshed anyway, having had some connection to Sejanus. Regardless, I felt a sense of relief, of freedom—one that I hoped would reach to Camilla, now beside Duras, and to my mother, wherever her spirit had taken up residence. My family was far from me, and I knew I would not see them again until death reunited us all—but I had a family in Rome, too, one that was present and accessible to me, filled with people who were just as important as those who were absent.

"What are you thinking of?" Torquatus asked me quietly,

stroking my arm as he so often did after we had made love.

"You. Our family. Our future," I said, and I turned and smiled at him. We embraced, hugging one another for a long moment until our lips met, a gentle kiss that grounded me, reminding me that I was not alone. I felt a small spark inside of me at his touch—passion, even love, perhaps—and instead of pushing it away, I allowed it to grow.

29 CE

CHAPTER XLII

TITUS

Titus felt uncertainty begin to overwhelm him as the small ship neared the dock; armed men were waiting, the unexpected arrival of the vessel on their horizon a cause for alarm, especially given the lateness of the season. It was no time for easy travel. His eyes searched the small group, hoping that the face he had counted on seeing—the man who was integral to his entire plan—would be there.

At the back of the group, watching, a short sword at his tunic-clad hip: Aulus Caecina Severus, former governor of Moesia. Titus raised an arm in greeting, hoping that the man he had met once, so many years ago, would remember him. Aulus either did not see him or did not recognize him, his face remaining blank, his body stationary—but the ship drew ever closer, and Titus could not, would not, turn back.

They disembarked under the close supervision of Aulus's men, although the crew had no intent of staying for long; the delivery of Titus had been their primary purpose. Whether or not he returned with them was of little concern.

"Aulus!" Titus called out, and the old governor approached, eyeing him uncertainly.

"What purpose do you have here?" Aulus asked.

"Do I look so different? I'm old, I know, but…" Titus trailed off, thinking of what he could say to jog the man's memory of him. "Did you decide to take up bird keeping, then, at your grandfather's villa? It's a nice change from Dacia, I'm sure."

A sudden recognition flooded Aulus's face. "Come with me," he said, gesturing for Titus to join him. They began to walk up to the villa together, Aulus's men trailing behind, still wary of the newcomers.

"It's been a long project, restoring this place," Aulus said, gesturing to his home. "After my grandfather died, no one bothered with it. It fell into disrepair, and all the slaves absconded. I was in Rome for a few years, after retiring from Moesia, but I eventually decided to settle out here, now that my wife has died, and my children are all grown and married…" He trailed off, watching Titus, waiting for the other man to share his own part of the story; Aulus knew Titus's arrival was no mere coincidence.

"I'm glad of your choice of residence, because I need your help," Titus said. "Is…" It was hard for him to speak it aloud, to say her name to a man he had never fully trusted, despite his role in saving an infant Duras. "Is Julia still on the island across?"

Aulus nodded. "I have dined with her, a few times, since I settled here. But we have never spoken of my grandfather's role in saving her child—for I *do* know that's whose babe it was, though I assure you that I have kept my silence all these years. Unfortunately, there are too many prying eyes and ears to discuss much of substance when we see one another."

"I—" Titus started, but something in Aulus's eyes stopped him: a sad expression, one that almost seemed to mourn for him.

"She is not well," Aulus said, and he turned away from Titus, entering his villa. The sound of birds chirping and singing greeted the men, and Titus saw countless cages filled with the creatures. "She has been ill for quite some time. A doctor came from the mainland, some months ago, requested by her guards. His prognosis was poor. She does not have much time left, I fear."

"Better than the prognosis from Rome," Titus said, his thoughts racing, and he shared with Aulus the news: Livia's passing; the exiles of the elder Agrippina and her son, Nero Caesar; the threat to Julia's life.

Aulus sighed, opening a cage to feed a bird a few seeds from the palm of his hand. "How may I help?"

One of Julia's current guards was the son of a man who had once served on campaign with Aulus, a connection the former governor drew upon heavily as he issued an invitation to Julia for dinner. A second note implored her guard to bring only himself; there was no need to ruin a quiet dinner with an abundance of armed men hulking about, Aulus wrote.

When Julia and the guard arrived, a modest rowboat slowly bearing them across the channel that separated their small islands, Titus felt his heart begin to race. He peered at them through a window, but they were too far—and his vision had become too poor—for him to see Julia in any significant detail as she was assisted out of the boat. She moved slowly, hunched slightly, and seemed to stop frequently, as if catching her breath. He withdrew from his perch, retreating into the villa as they neared, Aulus guiding them along the path. She would arrive at any moment.

Aulus, Julia, and the guard stepped into the villa, the chirping of birds greeting them. Aulus quickly sent the guard off to the kitchen to have his own meal, and Titus, waiting only until the man had disappeared from sight, approached. Julia's back was to him as she spoke with Aulus, but the governor smiled at her softly and excused himself, moving off in the same direction as the guard. Julia stepped towards a caged sparrow, peering at it intently.

"Julia," Titus said, her name barely a whisper. He felt as if he was dreaming.

She seemed to freeze, her breath halting for a long moment, and then she spun around, disbelief in her dark eyes as she saw him only a few feet away.

Titus felt a tear slide down his cheek as he gazed at her, noting the gray in her hair that now dimmed the bronze; the wrinkles that lined her face, years of worry, of imprisonment, making their effect known. And then they embraced one another, the distance between them closing as if it had never existed, and they both sobbed, clutching at each other in happy desperation.

Julia's coughing fit was what separated them at last, and she pushed a small cloth to her mouth as she bent over, fighting to breathe. When she finally pulled the cloth away from her lips, it was tinged red with blood.

Titus helped her move to a couch, half carrying her as she still struggled to breathe. He settled her on the cushions, sitting close, his still-trembling fingers touching her dress, her skin, her hair, her face with an adoration that he felt could never be satisfied.

"I almost didn't come," Julia rasped out, a shaking hand again touching the blood-stained cloth to her lips. "But something..." She coughed once more, closing her eyes. "Something urged me to."

Titus leaned forward and kissed her on the forehead, his lips lingering on her too-hot skin, skin that he had thought he would never again feel.

"Are you here to organize my escape?" Julia asked, smiling through the exhaustion that had quickly taken over her body.

"Of course, my love," Titus said softly, and he laid down next to her on the couch, their faces close together as he wrapped himself around her body, everything that had happened—the years they had been apart, the deaths they had both witnessed, the intrigues and scheming—seeming to fade away. "I'm going to take you far, far away from here."

AUTHOR'S NOTE

While I have generally tried to stay fairly true to known dates, events, and relationships between people in *Daughter of Exile*, I would like to note that the character of Duras—while a real historical figure—was not actually the illegitimate child of Julia the Younger, and his role in this novel as her son (and as Aemilia's half-brother) is imagined. As mentioned in the author's note in *The Longest Exile*, Julia's child with her lover, Silanus, likely died on its own or would have been killed after birth.

Historically, Duras became a Dacian king, ruling c. 69 – 87 CE, succeeding Scorilo (who, in this duology, is the adoptive brother of Duras). The real Duras and Scorilo probably *were* related, but the exact nature of their connection is unknown—Duras may actually have been Scorilo's son, or they were, perhaps, brothers by blood. We also know that Scorilo did have a brother who was sent to Rome as a hostage at some point, which is a storyline I adopted for this novel.

Julia the Younger never left the island of Trimerus, dying in 28/29 CE around the age of 47—her exile having been the longest of any of the Julio-Claudians who were subjected to such a fate (the others either were executed in a matter of years, or eventually recalled to Rome). This is where the title *The Longest Exile* originates.

AUTHOR'S NOTE

I opted to have Julia die of an illness, allowing her to briefly reunite with Titus before she passes away—the happiest ending I could come up with while remaining true to history in terms of her death while still in exile on the island. However, from an academic standpoint, I think the close timing of Julia's death to that of Livia (in 29 CE) is worth further study, especially as I believe there is an argument to be made that the common dating of Julia's death to 28 CE may not be fully accurate. Did Livia, in the end, actually become something of a protector to Julia the Younger during her exile, and her own death opened the door to Julia's execution by Tiberius, perhaps influenced by Sejanus? After all, once a Roman woman survived into young adulthood and then made it through childbirth, it wouldn't have been abnormal by any means to live to an elderly age—which 47 was not. Given the predisposition of the Julio-Claudians for murdering those they considered a threat—including their own relatives—and the thin historical record when it comes to Julia the Younger, I wouldn't say it's outside the realm of possibility that she may have at last been killed off, versus dying of natural causes—but we will never know for certain. I did include a mention of the plot/idea to have her killed, to cover all bases!

The end of Sejanus and his family/circle in 31 CE is a historically gruesome one, which I have tried to recount accurately, inclusive of Apicata's suicide (before which she did write a letter accusing her ex-husband and Livilla of poisoning Drusus some years before), the forced starvation of Livlla, and Sejanus's execution and those of his children, including, quite tragically, the rape-before-execution of Sejanus's young daughter.

Silanus—the lover of Julia the Younger—did in fact return to Rome during the reign of Tiberius, but his involvement with Sejanus is imagined, as is his related downfall.

Similarly, there is nothing to indicate that Aemilia herself encountered Silanus or Sejanus, or how close or frequently any contact may have been between her family and such men—although given their high rank, it's entirely possible that her husband may have had an association with them. Regardless, the backdrop of Sejanus's long-term insurrection provided an interesting canvas for Aemilia's story, and I took many liberties with it as I tried to envision how such a young woman may have felt—the daughter left behind in Rome.

After the execution of Sejanus (when this book concludes), the exile of Agrippina the Elder and the imprisonment of her son, Drusus Caesar, did not end, as perhaps one might expect with the removal of Sejanus. In fact, in 33 CE, both were killed, surely on the orders of Tiberius, who may have seen the benefit of removing two threats to his power: the elder Agrippina never left the island of Pandateria (likely she was locked up and starved to death as other banished Julio-Claudian women were) and Drusus Caesar never left his prison cell in Rome, likely being executed outright.

Tiberius died in 37 CE, and Caligula (Agrippina the Elder's son, and one of the more infamous Roman emperors) succeeded. He personally set sail to retrieve the ashes of his brother Nero Caesar and his mother Agrippina from their islands, installing them (along with those of Drusus Caesar) in the Mausoleum of Augustus in Rome. Yet a mere two years later, in 39 CE, he was exiling his own family members—Agrippina the Younger was most likely sent to Pontia, while his other sister, Julia Livilla, was most likely exiled to Pandateria (there is some uncertainty about the specific islands the sisters were sent to). The reasons for their exiles are uncertain, but, as usual, it was likely related to political plotting, masked by charges of sexual misconduct.

It wasn't until Caligula was killed in 41 CE and Claudius (to

327

whom Aemilia Lepida was once betrothed) came to power that the sisters were restored to Rome—although Julia Livilla was sent back to Pandateria that very same year and killed shortly thereafter (likely in another incident of forced starvation). Agrippina the Younger, meanwhile, continued to machinate her way into further power (which I will briefly touch on below).

Aemilia Lepida and her husband (who truly was some relation of her mother's lover, although how close of a relation is uncertain) had five children in total, and almost all of them suffered in some way due to their connection to the imperial family. Junia Lepida appears to have been the only one of their offspring to have lived a relatively peaceful life—at least by comparison to her siblings.

Their son Lucius (who was briefly engaged to Claudius's daughter, Claudia Octavia) was ordered to commit suicide in 49 CE after Agrippina the Younger spread a rumor that he had committed incest with his sister, causing him to lose his office and be expelled from the Senate. Agrippina the Younger then proceeded to marry Claudius (her uncle) and have him instead betroth his daughter to her son, Nero.

Junia Calvina, the sister with whom Lucius was rumored to have had an incestuous relationship, was exiled by Claudius. She spent ten years in banishment before being recalled to Rome by Nero.

Unfortunately, Nero's generosity did not extend to Aemilia's surviving sons. Marcus, the eldest, was killed in 54 CE when Nero succeeded, to ensure that he would not attempt to seize power himself (although this may have been the result of machinations by Agrippina the Younger, rather than on orders by Nero himself). Another son, Decimus, was forced to commit suicide by Nero in 64 CE after allegedly bragging about his descent from Augustus. Both young men were considered threats to the emperor due to their lineage: an inescapable theme in this duology, and throughout Roman imperial history.

It is unclear when and how Aemilia died.

Agrippina the Younger, despite her rise to power, eventually met a grisly end, killed by her own son, Nero, in 59 CE in what was supposed to be an elaborate manner that originally involved the planned capsizing of her ship. This initial plan failed, and Nero had his mother killed by the sword after she failed to drown. If you arc interested in reading more historical fiction that involves Agrippina the Younger and Nero, I highly recommend Margaret George's duology on the emperor.

Decimus, Camilla, Rufus, Leander, Amynta, and Titus are all invented characters.

The Roman world was a brutal one—yet it is a world that continues to fascinate us. I have always found the Julio-Claudians to be particularly captivating—there are more plots, betrayals, exiles, murders, and scandals than can be captured in this duology, and I encourage you to read more about all the figures involved.

ACKNOWLEDGEMENTS

As always, thank you to my husband, Gabriel, for your support and encouragement.

To all our animals, whether they are furred, scaled, feathered, or haired—you're all so loved, and your place in our hearts and lives is immeasurable.

Jacques de Spoelberch, this duology would not be what it is without your feedback and guidance.

To you, the reader—thank you for joining me on this journey. I hope you enjoyed the stories of Julia the Younger and Aemilia Lepida, and I hope you are inspired to read and learn about other women throughout history.

ABOUT THE AUTHOR

Tana Rebellis is a pen name of Kasey Morris, who also writes romantic comedies. She studied Classics at Princeton University and then Classical Archaeology at Oxford. When not reading, writing, or working, she's spending time with her animals and her husband on their farm in Virginia.

www.TanaRebellis.com
Instagram: @TanaRebellis
Twitter (X): @ExploreClassics

Printed in Great Britain
by Amazon

48781018R00199